Books by Heather Grothaus

THE WARRIOR
THE CHAMPION
THE HIGHLANDER
TAMING THE BEAST
NEVER KISS A STRANGER
NEVER SEDUCE A SCOUNDREL
NEVER LOVE A LORD
VALENTINE
ADRIAN
ROMAN
CONSTANTINE
THE LAIRD'S VOW
THE HIGHLANDER'S PROMISE
THE SCOT'S OATH
THE KNIGHT'S PLEDGE
HIGHLAND BEAST
(with Hannah Howell and Victoria Dahl)

Published by Kensington Publishing Corp.

The Knight's Pledge

Sons of Scotland

Heather Grothaus

LYRICAL PRESS
Kensington Publishing Corp.
www.kensingtonbooks.com

LYRICAL PRESS BOOKS are published by

Kensington Publishing Corp.
119 West 40th Street
New York, NY 10018

First Electronic Edition: March 2022
ISBN: 978-1-5161-0710-0 (ebook)

First Print Edition: March 2022
ISBN: 978-1-5161-0714-8

Printed in the United States of America

For Jackson, for Lillian, and for Emmelia.
You each make me a better person.

Prologue

February 1442
Castle Dare
Northumberland, England

Euphemia was yet a mile away from the castle when she saw the glow against the inky night sky. There could be no mistake that the Montague hold burned.

She struggled through the winter-brittle underbrush, grateful for her thick woolen cloak as the thorns sought their way beneath the hem, ripping at her thin gown and lashing the flesh of her legs. They would soon discover her gone from the chamber that was her prison at Darlyrede, and so she must hurry—run, when the terrain allowed. Whether the rumors were true, and she found Thomas Annesley at Castle Dare or not, Euphemia now understood that she could never return to Darlyrede House if she wished to live.

She knew too much.

She must warn the Montagues at once of her suspicions—surely they would take her into their protection until the king could be told.

She at last came to the fringe of the wood and looked upon the chaos surrounding the once elegant stone keep. Smoke lay thick around the motte, the red glow of the forge revealing the survivors milling there as if lost. The creaking and popping of timbers being devoured only emphasized the significance of the charred shell. There was nothing left to save.

Euphemia made her way among the refugees without fear of being discovered—she already knew that in the plain cloak with the old, pale blue gown beneath, her hair flowing and tangled and littered with the detritus of her flight, no one would take her for the Hargraves' supposedly pampered niece.

"The poor children. To lose both parents at once."

Euphemia stopped and looked around with wild eyes, but could not discern from where the snippet of conversation had come.

Lord and Lady Montague were dead?

No. No, no, no...

The sound of a young child sobbing wafted through Euphemia's shock, and she turned slowly to discover a little girl—not likely older than four—shivering in a heap on the frozen turf, her threadbare nursery gown stretched ineffectively over her knees.

"You're just a baby," Euphemia breathed to herself, and her fingers went at once to the clasp at her throat, forgetting for a moment the blow dealt to her plans. "Here," she whispered as she crouched down near the girl and piled the warm wool about her. "Here you are. Why are you alone?"

"Mama?" the girl whimpered, and as she looked up, Euphemia beheld milky, sightless eyes surrounded by thick, sooty lashes in the perfect face. "Mama?"

Euphemia rushed to her feet and stumbled backward, staggering away from the child while trying to muffle her hysterical sob. This was a horrid dream, surely.

But until she woke, she couldn't pause. She must find the Montague children. She must find them before Vaughn Hargrave did, for if he felt at liberty to commit such vile atrocities in the waking world, what would he do in a nightmare?

At last she saw them, there on the fringe of the inner circle, watching the last of the hold be consumed while their elderly nurse knelt in prayer nearby. Lucan, older than Euphemia's ten and five by perhaps only a year, with little Iris clinging to his leg, still in her nightdress. Handsome, young Lucan still in his tunic and trousers, his eyes wild and red-rimmed, his narrow face pale beneath the fall of his dark hair. He held what appeared to be an orphaned slipper in his right hand.

Orphaned, perhaps like the blind girl child; orphaned like Euphemia. The Montague children were now orphans, too, and just as endangered as she was, even if they didn't yet know it.

"Master Montague," she rasped as she neared him with her arm out. "Lucan."

He whirled around, giving her only the briefest glance. "I have nothing for you," he barked. "Go with the others until the morn."

"Lucan," she pressed, glancing around nervously at the crowd. Vaughn Hargrave could be anywhere. "You must come away with me at once. You and your sister. We must go to the king. The Crown will aid us." She reached him at last and took hold of his arm. "We must—"

He whirled around and struck Euphemia with the slipper in his hand, so unexpectedly and so soundly that she twisted and fell to the ground, her frozen cheek now burning from the blow. "I said, I have nothing for you, wretch," he shouted. "I am lord here, now. You are not worthy to serve the house of Montague, let alone hold the king's name in your filthy mouth." He took a step toward her.

Iris still clung to his leg and she let out a fresh wail. "Lucan, stop!"

The elderly nurse had risen and was now coming toward them, her wrinkled face tear-streaked. Euphemia met the woman's eyes until the young master of ruined Castle Dare recalled her attention.

"Go," he growled at her. "I don't ever want to see your face again, or I'll cut you down myself." He turned away from her, gathering his sister up from the cold, smoky ground, and half carrying little Iris further along the burning ruin.

"Are you alright, girl?" a man's voice called out.

Euphemia looked up and saw a servant approaching near the Montague children's nurse—a groom or the like, from his dress. Neither servant recognized her, she was sure. Behind them both though, Euphemia caught sight of steel gray hair…

She scrambled to her feet and turned back toward the wood, running, stumbling; tears leaving hot, wet tracks on her cold cheeks.

She would die in the forest rather than subject herself to the supposed mercy of any nobility ever again. From hell, all of them. She would freeze, or starve, or be devoured by wild animals—she didn't care anymore.

Yes, Euphemia Hargrave would die that very night—she must. But she vowed she would never, for all eternity, forget the pain Lucan Montague had caused her.

Chapter 1

January 1459
Steadport Hall
Northumberland, England

Lucan Montague stared at the rich draperies gathered into an intricate swirl over his head, the hills and valleys of the canopy touched by the eternal sunset of the blazing hearth fire to his left. The hues predicted nighttime, and indeed the sun had set over Northumberland hours and hours ago, yet Lucan's throbbing foot and the memory of bright blue eyes would not allow his furrowed brow to smooth into slumber. The smell of smoke still burned in his nostrils despite several irrigations, and he wondered if his hands would ever be free from the black soot stains. He wondered if he'd ever *been* free of them, really. Hadn't they been lurking just beneath the thinnest layer of his skin? Lurking like a phantom miasma, the demons from his past now returned…

It had been two days since Darlyrede House had burned; two days since his sister Iris had married Padraig Boyd before the shell of the ruined estate; two days since they'd come to sturdy Steadport Hall as guests of Lord and Lady Hood to recover and make their plans.

Two days since Lucan had slept.

Padraig and Iris were already gone off to London now, and Lucan should have accompanied them. Tavish and Lachlan would be arriving there for the meeting he had summoned them to long ago, and Lucan's presence would be demanded. But Lucan was unwell. Perhaps more unwell than he dared even admit to himself.

His head pounded, and his foot throbbed where Euphemia Hargrave's arrow had pierced his boot, pinning him to the forest floor that day what seemed years ago now.

Nay, not Euphemia Hargrave, he reminded himself. She calls herself Effie now—Effie Annesley.

Lucan called her a criminal. A criminal whom he would report to the king when he made his disastrous testimony about the debacle of Darlyrede. Not only had Lucan lost the man he was charged with finding, one of England's richest estates was now smoldering rubble and the nobles overseeing it—Vaughn and Caris Hargrave—were dead.

And Thomas Annesley, the man who'd been on the run from the Crown these past thirty years after being accused of killing his fiancée on the eve of their wedding, had a daughter. A daughter with eyes the color of the cornflowers that had carpeted the rolling hills between Castle Dare and Darlyrede House.

A daughter who had lived in the wood with a band of criminals for fifteen years.

A daughter who had shot Lucan through the foot.

Lucan would return to the king a failure. A disgrace to his station as a knight of the Royal Order of the Garter. He had no idea where Thomas Annesley was. Lucan had cost England a fortune and been laid up by a *woman*.

Lucan told himself he was only taking advantage of Lord Edwin Hood's hospitality in order to recuperate and rest, but in reality, Lucan knew that he was hiding like the cowardly failure that he was. Thus, his being unable to sleep was perhaps justified.

He was thinking that perhaps he should simply own up to his new pusillanimous existence by retreating to France with his tail firmly between his legs when he heard the door to his borrowed chamber creak open in the dim light of the fire.

Lucan frowned and lifted his head from the cushions to peer down the length of his body, past the thick bedpost toward the door. It must be halfway to dawn—who could be creeping about the chambers at this hour?

A dark head poked into the room, the shielding door awash with reflected firelight at first shadowing the coloring and features of the face of his visitor with the blackest shadow. Then a thick-set body emerged to carefully close the door behind the intruder, and Lucan recognized the sturdy tunic, the dark red hair like sheep's wool lying on the broad shoulders.

Lucan's heretofore furrowed brow raised in surprise. "Rolf?"

Darlyrede's steward flinched and turned immediately to face the bed. His already pale face was made the more so by the gloomy shadows beneath his hound-eyes, his dark red beard framing the man's apparent distress.

"Sir Lucan," Rolf said. "My apologies for disturbing you at such a late hour, but I fear it is most urgent."

Lucan pushed himself to his elbows, his melancholy and self-pity vanishing. This was a very welcome distraction. "Is it Iris? Padraig?"

"Nay, lord," Rolf said as he crossed the floor and began to gather Lucan's discarded clothing.

Lucan threw back the bedclothes at once and grasped his left calf to lift his injured foot and swing it over the bedside, where it's throbbing increased.

Many thanks, Effie Annesley. You hag.

"Ulric?" He reached out his arms to slide them into the sleeves of his partially laced gambeson and then pulled away to shimmy into the quilted piece. "He's to already be arrived in London."

"Nay, lord." Rolf dropped to his knees to assist with fitting the trousers over Lucan's bandaged foot and then fit his left boot—regrettably split up the shank to accommodate his swollen, crippled appendage.

Blasted Effie Annesley...

Lucan rose, drawing up his breeches and lacing them while Rolf assisted with the boots. The chamber seemed wont to tilt and wobble for a moment while the pounding in his head increased, but it passed almost as soon as it had begun.

Then Lucan took his belt and wrapped it around his waist, pulling the buckle tight against his flank. He glanced up as Rolf held forth Lucan's sword.

"Where are we going?"

"I don't wish to tell you, lord."

"You don't wish to—?" Lucan took the sword and slid it into his sheath. "You're not the sort to play coy, Rolf, and your loyalty is stalwart, so I have no doubt of the sincerity of your plight. But I would know what we are about at this late hour, when you have come taking such pains to be unobserved."

Rolf's throat convulsed as if he forced himself to swallow, and his eyes were dark, wild. And yet he remained composed. "There is no time to waste. I will tell you to where we hie once there is no chance that we might be overheard." He paused. "Please."

A secret? A desperate secret. Lucan's eyes narrowed for in instant, but then he shrugged. "Very well."

It's not as if he'd anything else better to do besides disparage himself, his foot, and blasted Effie Annesley.

It took only moments to be through the compact hold of Steadport Hall and into the stables to retrieve Agrios, who stood saddled and at the ready. Rolf's mount, too, was waiting at the wide opening, loosely tethered with his muzzle in a bucket of oats, munching loudly in the darkness. It was clear even in the gloom that Darlyrede's steward's horse had been hurriedly wiped down after a hard ride, and the stable floor was dark with water near the trough while a sleepy stable boy dozed with his head in his hands on a nearby stool.

"I've got it," Lucan muttered with gruff embarrassment when Rolf made motions of assisting him in mounting. The steward stepped away without argument to coax his reluctant mount from its treat. It took Lucan three awkward starts, but he at last sat astride as Rolf led his horse through the stable doorway and held the door while Lucan ducked beneath the lintel, his head pounding so that starbursts seemed to be exploding on the periphery of his vision.

Effie Annesley had turned him into a cripple, at the mercy of others' aid, just as surely as if Lucan were an old widow woman.

Effie Annesley, risen from the dead.

A moment's superstitious hesitation overcame Lucan as he followed the steward into the cold, black Northumberland night, Agrios's hooves crunching into the snow. "Rolf," he called out. "Tell me true: do we return to Darlyrede?"

Any other would perhaps have missed the man's hesitation in answering, but Lucan had known Rolf Littlebrook since Lucan himself had been a boy, and so he saw the blink of a pause, heard the awkward guile in his lie. "Nay, lord."

"Rolf…"

"I swear it, lord," Rolf insisted. "We will pass by the place and, aye, 'tis true that tonight's misfortune is tied to Darlyrede House, but it is not our destination. Someone needs help, and by my word, you will know what can be done."

Lucan blinked. "Who needs help?"

"Effie Annesley, lord."

Lucan pulled up hard on Agrios's reins, causing the destrier to balk at the uncharacteristically rough treatment. He turned the horse back toward the stable.

"No," Lucan said.

"Lord—"

"No," he called loudly into the frigid air, the refusal manifesting like a crystal cloud in the January night. He heard the steward's approach but did not turn toward him.

"Please, lord," Rolf pleaded as they entered the barn again. The weary stable boy was just turning about once more, disappointment clear on his face. "You're the only one who—"

"The only one who's been crippled by Effie Annesley?"

Rolf looked decidedly uncomfortable. "I'm not certain that's true."

Lucan snorted. "I'd wager it's not." He only just managed to keep from crying out as he swung his leg over the saddle. "Wait," he barked at the sleepy stable boy, who would have pulled Agrios away. A wave of dizziness washed over Lucan so that he was forced to grip the saddle with both hands and rest his forehead against the fragrant leather. Beads of sweat burst out along his hairline and raced down the sides of his face; nausea swirled in his stomach.

He heard Rolf bring his mount to a halt beside him, but Lucan could not raise his head to glance at the man derisively as he wished to.

"Leave us," Rolf said, presumably to the attending boy. A moment later, he said in a low voice, "Lord, you're not well."

"All the more reason to once more seek my bed," Lucan acknowledged. "I'd not waste what little strength I have to get Effie Annesley out of a snare she's most likely made herself."

"It's not her in the snare, lord."

"But you said—"

"It's her boy."

Lucan's racing heart had slowed somewhat and so now he did turn his head to regard the steward, who seemed to have paled another two shades. Lucan remembered the red-haired lad from his sister's wedding to Padraig Boyd.

I'm George Thomas Annesley, how do you do...

"What's wrong with the boy?"

"He's...missing." Rolf seemed in greater pain that Lucan, although Lucan didn't know how that was possible. "Please come," he whispered.

Sweat seemed to be pouring down Lucan's back now. "Why should I care what happens to a bandit's brat? In fact, why should *you*?"

"Lord?" Rolf's brows knit together. "Perhaps you should—"

"It's not as though she can further your status now that Darlyrede is burnt and she is wanted by the Crown," Lucan explained. "In fact, if I should see her, I would only arrest her, which I do doubt would be of any assistance in whatever plight she now finds herself in. Most deservedly,

I should think, as well." Lucan paused. "You seem to be quite far away just now, Rolf."

* * * *

Rolf Littlebrook caught the knight just before he could slide to the stable floor, his noble battle steed having done his duty in just holding his master aright these past several moments. Agrios didn't so much as flinch as Lucan crumpled.

Rolf lowered the knight to the hay-strewn ground, seeing clearly his gray, greasy pallor beneath the lock of black hair. He was more unwell than Rolf has guessed, and now he was unconscious—dead weight. Rolf didn't relish the idea of the trip back through the hold to return Lucan to his bed, nor the calling of the surgeon and the questions that would arise. He'd already wasted precious time in traveling to Steadport Hall. Apparently, neither the surgeon nor the priest from Darlyrede had done Lucan any good thus far. For such a young man to lose his foot would be a tragedy. If Winnie were here, she would know how to treat him.

He stilled, thinking. Dare he?

In the next moment, Rolf haltingly folded the tall knight into an awkward embrace and then staggered to his feet. Agrios stood as still as any stone wall as Rolf draped his master across the saddle. He fastened the stirrup high up around one of Lucan's upper thighs to keep him from sliding to the ground. It wouldn't be a comfortable ride, but hopefully he would stay good and unconscious until they were deep in the wood.

By then, it would be too late to return.

Rolf pulled Agrios's reins over the horse's head and regained his own saddle, leading the fine, inky horse into the equally inky night. The well-trained animal followed obediently, seemingly knowing that the cargo he carried depended upon it.

It would take much longer to arrive at the Warren this way, but it was likely better to arrive late with Lucan Montague than not at all.

Perhaps for Lucan Montague most of all.

Chapter 2

"He's here."

The words were whispered into Effie's ear, but they roused her like a blast from Vaughn Hargrave's arquebus. She opened her swollen eyes and looked up into Gorman's face. His eyes, too, were red, dark-hollowed, above his thick beard. She made no reply, only held up her hand so that he could help her from George Thomas's little bed. She followed him from the carved-out chamber in the rear of the warren of rooms and into the tall, twisting stone corridor toward the cathedral, still gripping the blasted parchment they'd found early yestermorning.

After fifteen years, Effie no longer noticed the mineral smell of the caves. Her eyes were exquisitely adjusted to the way the torches played off the chiseled-sharp, glittering planes of the walls and she knew them all as well as she knew the curves of George's small face. There was no daylight in the caves, save for just inside the entrance, and in one chamber where a tiny sink hole in the forest floor far above sometimes allowed a beam of light to fall in the center of a tall, conical cell Gilboe had claimed as his oratory.

The lower portions and pathways of the corridors were worn smooth and rippled, perhaps by ancient, long evaporated rivers, but the upper portions of the caverns bore the marks of chisel and driven stone, the Warren having been stretched and widened by human hand for years to suit the hidden village it now contained. In addition to the common storage and stable areas, the Warren currently boasted seven private cells, as well as two large dormitory chambers where unpartnered adults slept. The echoey sound of the shallow, subterranean river grew louder, and beyond the next curve of stone wall the ceiling soared away into invisible darkness as Effie and Gorman entered the cathedral.

The cavern was filled with many of the residents of the Warren, and all were in a grim fluster as Effie drew nearer. She braced herself for the argument she knew was inevitable. Effie certainly hadn't wanted to call for him, but Rolf and Gorman had convinced her that Lucan Montage could help them. And so help them, he would.

He must.

Gorman stopped suddenly in front of her, nearly causing her to run into his back.

"Rolf?" he queried in a strange tone.

Effie stepped around in time to see the man who had served as Darlyrede's steward for decades place a dark, limp bundle on the floor. Rolf rose, and his usually placid face was troubled.

"Where is he?" Effie demanded.

To her dismay, Rolf Littlebrook glanced down at the motionless pile of rags on the stone.

"Did you need to render him unconscious in order to bring him?" The others moved aside deferentially as she stepped forward and then knelt at the side of Lucan Montague.

"That was a fortuitous coincidence, I fear," Rolf sighed. "He'd outright refused before he fainted. He's unwell, Effie. I thought perhaps Winnie…"

"He was fine two days ago," she said curtly. His lashes were dark against his pale, chiseled cheekbone, like a crag from the Warren itself. His lips were bloodless and gray. Although the January cold still rolled off his clothes, Effie felt Lucan Montague's forehead with her palm and found it fiery, and greasy with sweat. "He's burning up with fever."

Behind her, Gorman sounded incredulous. "You brought a sick man into the Warren, Rolf?"

"I don't think 'tis an illness, son," Rolf corrected. "I believe his injury festers."

Effie looked up quickly at Gorman's father. "His foot?"

Rolf nodded.

"Dammit," Effie muttered. And then, louder, "Dammit!" She rose to her feet, confronting Rolf. "He's useless to us in this condition."

"Perhaps Winnie—" Rolf began again.

"I don't have *time* for this, Rolf!" Effie shouted, hearing her voice growing dangerously shrill, but panic was rising within her again, panic she had only just been holding at bay with the hope that Lucan Montague might aid them in some way. Now, she could not seem to hold back the floodtide of terror that was crashing and climbing against the banks of her mind as the one supposed to be George's savior lay feeble at her feet.

"They have *my son*! They have *George*!" she shrieked. "How am I to ever think of—"

Her words were interrupted by thin, cool bands encircling and squeezing her upper arm. Effie whipped her head around to find the serene, wizened face of Winnie, her white, white hair frizzed around her head like dandelion fluff. Her pale gray eyes bored into Effie's as she pulled Effie away from the form of Lucan Montague and knelt in her place.

The old woman tugged up her draping sleeves, revealing spotted, skeletal arms. Her long fingers with their short, round, shiny nails skimmed over Lucan Montague's form, pressing his body here and there, laying her ear atop first his chest then his abdomen. She moved toward his feet on her knees and waggled squeezed-together fingers at his left boot, which had been obviously altered to accommodate his foot. Effie knew she should have felt some shame for being the cause of the injury, but she could not muster any sympathy for the man, lying here in the Warren's safe cathedral while George Thomas was missing.

His arrival had done nothing more than delay them further. He should just hurry up and die if he was wont.

As if the old woman had read her thoughts, Winnie looked up at her sharply.

Effie stared back. She didn't care what Winnie thought of her, either.

That's not true, her conscience warned, seeming to be of one mind with older woman.

Thankfully, Winnie sent her expressive gaze to Gorman, who flew to her side at once as the boot was painstakingly removed. Effie watched as Winnie's withered hands motioned in the air, the fingers of her right hand tapping those on her left, then drawing a pair of circles on her palm. She brought her two fists together and then swiped her hand over her left forearm.

"Only one?" he queried.

The frizzy white head shook and Winnie held up two fingers. Then she patted her lips briefly and wrung her clasped hands in opposite directions.

Gorman gained his feet and disappeared into the rippling shadows along the perimeter of the cathedral, and Winnie seemed to forget him immediately as she withdrew her long, slender blade from the belt around her tiny midsection. She inserted the tip of the knife carefully into the top of the stained bandages wrapped past Lucan Montague's ankle and painstakingly cut down toward his heel.

Winnie peeled back the sections of rough-woven flax cloth to reveal Montague's swollen foot, crusted with dried blood and seepage from the black, ragged slit of a wound caused by Effie's own arrow. The cut wept and was malodorous, even from where she stood. She recognized again that she should feel some remorse, but her heart felt frozen in her chest and all she could do was stare at the man on the ground.

Gorman returned then with one of the youths and, kneeling at Winnie's side, they deposited the items she'd silently requested. The old woman took a rag and dipped it into the wooden bowl of steaming water and placed it, sopping, on top of Montague's foot.

The man started with a harsh cry, causing all in the group who watched to flinch, but Lucan Montague did not rouse again, even as Winnie began to wipe at the injury. Effie noticed a painful lump forming in her throat and, when the old woman brought forth her slender blade again and carried it toward the swollen appendage, Effie felt the bile rising. She turned away from the scene and walked quickly from the cathedral, tucking the parchment into her belt and then breaking into a run as she reached the upward slanting corridor that led to the entrance.

The steep grade forced her strides to long lunges, and she at last reached the top with her hands on her knees, her head hanging down, her shuddering breaths not delivering enough air to her lungs as saliva pooled in the recesses of her jaws. She went down on her knees in the moonlight, already growing pale with the approaching dawn.

She looked through the bare branches of the forest, their rolling, winter-prickly canopy stretching away to the North West. This time last year—and the fourteen winters before—Effie could have stood in this spot and occasionally caught a glimmer of light from far away Darlyrede House. How many times she'd looked across this expanse with both hatred and hope in her heart, longing for the day when she would be avenged, when her mother and father would be avenged, and all the wrongs done to them and the people of Northumberland were righted. She slid her legs to the side to sit on one hip, cocking her right leg to wrap her arms about her knee.

Now that horizon was dark; Darlyrede House was a ruin. And there was no hope left. No matter that her half-brother, Padraig Boyd, had returned to England—there was nothing for him to claim now. And the one thing Effie loved most in the world had been taken from her.

George Thomas. George…

"Effie?" Rolf's gentle, low voice sounded behind her, amidst the shuffling of his footfalls on the grade.

She sniffed and wiped her face on her trousers leg. She hadn't wept since that night long ago, the night another grand manor had burned, and now the night had turned into a pale sunrise.

"Aye, Rolf."

He squatted at her side. "He's sleeping now. Gorman's watching over him lest he wakes. I believe Winnie has done much for him."

"Perhaps she has, and he will live," she allowed. "But you said yourself that he already refused you."

"He doesn't know the whole of it."

"And you think he will have pity for us once he does?"

"He's a good man, Effie."

"He's the king's man, Rolf," she reminded him. "And even *if* Winnie can heal him, and even *if* he agrees to help us, it will be too late. We should have set out yesterday."

Effie took the steward's silence as agreement with her assessment of the situation, but after a long moment the gentle man began to speak.

"It's not too late. I never gave up hope that Gorman would be found. Five years, Effie. Five long years of not knowing whether he was dead or alive. And not only was my son returned, but now I have you, and George. I had nothing—now I have a family."

"Gorman was older than George," Effie pointed out past her constricted throat. "He escaped, and the man responsible for his abduction is dead. I cannot be optimistic about this, Rolf. My slight grip on sanity will not allow it."

"I'll not ask you for optimism," Rolf said quietly. "But let us dwell on the predicament immediate to us: Lucan Montague is here, now. I feel that if he can help us, he will."

Effie turned to look up at the man who had become like a father to her. She wanted to tell him that his trust in Lucan Montague was misplaced. That the high and mighty knight of the Royal Order of the Garter was selfish, spoiled, and greedy. Once a pampered, adolescent brat who had been swaddled and swept away to be reared in luxury in France, now he was a pompous coward who thought only of saving his own skin and furthering his reputation among the nobility. She'd seen it herself, hadn't she? One didn't easily forget such a lesson.

But footsteps on the path saved her from making a response. Effie looked over her shoulder and saw Gorman approaching the mouth of the cave entrance, his long strides effortless, his face wearied and yet made more handsome by his trials. She could see just there as the sunrise lightened the shadows under Gorman's eyes from where George Thomas had gotten the wideness of his cheekbones and his sturdy forehead.

Her son was made partly from this man approaching, and unlike Lucan Montague, Gorman Littlebrook *was* good, through and through.

Rolf gained his feet to face his son. "What news?"

"He's stirring," Gorman allowed as he reached them. He looked down at Effie. "You're exhausted. Give me the message—I'll speak to him."

She shook her head. "We'll do it together."

Gorman helped her to her feet. "Perhaps it would be best if you were not the first person Sir Lucan sees when he awakes."

"What do you mean?"

Rolf took the opportunity to disappear into the mouth of the cave without further comment.

"I mean," Gorman said gently, "that 'twas you who shot him. He holds you a grudge for it, and if we are to enlist his help, perhaps—"

"I *apologized* to him," Effie insisted. "At Darlyrede before more than a hundred people! It's not my fault an incompetent priest rubbed shite in his wound."

"I don't think he'll see it that way."

Effie felt her ire rising, and it was a welcome change from the despair and terror that had haunted her since that sunset in the wood two days ago when she had seen George's footsteps disappear in the snow beside a set of hoof prints.

But she knew that, for George's sake, she could not drown herself in one emotion in order to numb another. It could be potentially deadly to her son. And Rolf was right—Lucan Montague was here. Rolf trusted him. Effie trusted Rolf.

"I'll make amends. Again," she vowed, looking up into Gorman's eyes. For a brief moment, it was like the old days, the spark she felt when Gorman Littlebrook turned his deep brown gaze upon her, the look on his face a combination of admiration and desire.

He dropped his head and kissed her lightly on the cheek. "It'll be alright, Effie," he said against her skin. "We'll get him back."

* * * *

"I don't think he's stirring. I think he's dead."

Lucan considered the words spoken by the watery-sounding voice beyond his eyelids. He had died and gone to hell, or he was having the worst nightmare humanly possible.

He lay upon some sort of slab, he supposed, feeling the rock-hard surface biting into his shoulder blades and skull. His foot felt as though it were actively on fire, the flames penetrating to his very bones, charring them within his blazing flesh. He was so nauseated that he fancied he could feel the tip of his stomach tickling his Adam's apple, the noxious contents within sloshing up his esophagus with each careful, shallow breath that failed to deliver enough air. He felt sticky and soaked with his own malodorous stench, a combination of sulphur and rotting meat.

He dared crack open his eyelids. The ceiling above him was black, rippled with the wild light of flames. And then there was a shadowed face blocking out the light—elfin, pale, with a blonde plait hanging down toward him.

Effie Annesley.

Not a nightmare, then. Definitely hell.

"You," he rasped.

Then her detestable visage was gone, replaced with the concerned countenance of Gorman, the bandit he remembered from the fire at Darlyrede House—the man who had risked his own life, and his freedom, to help Padraig Boyd free the trapped occupants from the flaming hall.

"Sir Lucan," Gorman said. "How fare thee?"

"Where am I?" Lucan demanded, his voice sounding weak and raspy, to his great dismay. Although he did suppose one wouldn't sound exactly gay having been plunged into the bowels of hell. "What of my horse? Where is Agrios?"

"Your gallant mount is well and enjoying a hearty meal after performing such a fine service for his master," the bandit assured him. "Rolf saw to it himself, after he was certain you were being looked after."

Lucan felt the little knot of worry in his chest loosen. "Where am I?" Lucan repeated.

Then *she* was back. "The Warren," she said. "Rolf brought you here after you fainted. You owe him a debt for it—you could have lost your foot, letting those butchers have at you."

"Yes, let's do blame those who tried to help me rather than *the woman who shot me*," he said through gritted teeth.

Gorman eased back into Lucan's line of sight. "Your foot should heal now. Winnie has drained it and covered it with a poultice to draw out the fever."

"It burns like the devil," Lucan sighed and let his eyes drift closed again. He was so tired. Too tired even to argue at finding himself in the very den of the thieves whom he should have already placed under arrest. He didn't even care at this point if he died. He was tired of chasing criminals, tired of chasing ghosts, tired of chasing an elusive future—he just wanted to rest.

"Wake up," *she* demanded.

Lucan opened his eyes to glare at her with all the anger he could muster. "Do you mind? As much as I resent admitting it, it appears as though I am quite unwell. And I've obviously been kidnapped. I should like to recover somewhat before you attempt to harangue me to death."

"Trust me, it won't be your foot next time," Effie promised.

"Enough," Gorman interrupted. "Sir Lucan, I am sorry to bother you when you are indeed in need of rest. But I fear that we have no time to waste. We would tell you what has happened now, so that you might formulate a plan to aid us. If you are willing, of course."

Lucan frowned. He remembered now—Rolf coming to his chamber...the boy.

George Thomas Annesley, how do you do?

He looked to the woman, whose expression was as unmovable and enigmatic as the stones around them.

"Your son," Lucan said.

"Our son," Gorman corrected.

Lucan tried to conceal his surprise as the bearded man continued.

"He sneaked out of the Warren late in the day of the wedding to follow Effie when she went to survey the damage to Darlyrede. He was taken before she realized he'd followed her. We didn't know by whom until yesterday."

"Ransom?" Lucan ventured.

"Not quite." Gorman turned and held out his hand towards the woman, still watching him with what appeared to be barely concealed disgust. She withdrew a crumpled sheet of parchment from her belt and handed it to Gorman, who unfurled it, but then paused, glancing at Lucan.

"Shall I? Or would you rather?"

Lucan raised his hand and motioned with his fingers. Gorman placed the page in his hand while Effie Annesley approached with both her hands now gripping a rather ornate silk cushion she'd procured from the shadows. Lucan glanced at her warily.

"Don't worry," she grumbled as she stuffed it behind his head. "I'll not smother you before you've read it."

Lucan shook out the page and turned it toward the light of the torch anchored somewhere behind his cot. The sheet was marred by a ragged hole in the center and Gorman obviously knew the question on Lucan's tongue before he could ask it.

"We found it nailed to a tree yesterday, near where George's footprints disappeared."

We have the boy. He will be delivered to the king. Have mercy on yourself.
VP

"VP?" Lucan asked as he looked up from the page. "Vivienne Paget? She is the only one I know of with those initials living in the vicinity of Darlyrede."

Gorman's face was grim. "I'd wager my life on it. But she wasn't alone, and she was not the mastermind behind this plan."

"Because it says 'we?'" Lucan was unconvinced. "Perhaps it means we, my servants and I. Or the royal we."

"Oh, for God's sake, it's Caris Hargrave," Effie Annesley snapped. Lucan turned his head to regard the woman as she explained herself. "Vivienne Paget doesn't have the physical strength to lift more than a kerchief to her disgusting mouth. She'd retreated to Elsmire Castle after her scum of a husband was killed."

"Caris Hargrave is dead." As much as Lucan despised Effie Annesley, he would not allow her to hold such morbid fantasies, especially if the welfare of a child hung in the balance. "Padraig Boyd left her, dead of an attack of asthma, in the dungeon of Darlyrede House when he rescued my sister. The manor collapsed in flames around her."

But Effie was already shaking her blonde head. "She's not dead." Her words were little more than a strangled whisper. She rushed forward and jerked the page from Lucan's grip, pointing at the last line. "*Have mercy on yourself.*" She tossed the page back to him. "She must have said those exact words to me a thousand times. I can *feel* her. Crawling like a leech under my skin, still. She's not dead. And she has George."

Lucan was prevented from perhaps saying something foolish by the entrance of a pair of figures, each bearing a tray. One was the berobed friar from the hunt, the dubious patron of the supposed children's charity, and the other was tall, broad shouldered in the woolen kirtle and lace trimmed underdress. Golden curls peeked out from the hood of a short cape, hiding the visitor's visage even as they and the friar jostled each other to reach Lucan's bedside first.

"Why, good day to you, Sir Lucan," the friar said, the fiery light of triumph in his eyes as he elbowed his statuesque partner aside. The man was still sans eyebrows, his oddly cropped dark hair swishing across his forehead. He gave a shallow bow. "I thank God that we have met again, this time in more pleasant circumstances."

"I don't know that I share your gratitude for the situation," Lucan muttered.

"As we had no time for formalities when last we met, I am Gilboe," the friar went on, ignoring Lucan's sarcasm. "And I have brought you a repast from God's bounty, prepared with my own hands." He bowed again as he offered forth his tray, laden with what indeed looked to be a delightful selection of delicacies, had Lucan possessed any appetite whatsoever.

But the monk was shunted aside rather forcefully as the blonde pushed forward. "What good Sir Lucan better wants," a sultry, lisping voice scolded, "is a good, hot, satisfying drink." The face hidden in the golden curls turned toward him, and Lucan almost yelped at what was possibly the shadow of beard beneath the pale, soft-looking skin.

"A stiff one," the tray bearer added with a wink. "Dana, at your *complete* service, lord. Mead?"

"Will you go or not?" Effie Annesley's demanding query dragged Lucan's already fuzzled attention from the peculiar attendants.

"Go where?" He was confused, a feeling foreign to him, and it was causing an even more unfamiliar sensation of panic in his chest.

"Didn't you read the—argh!" Effie growled and grasped at the sides of her head, turning away from him.

Lucan's muddled brains chose just that inopportune moment to note that she was once more wearing trousers, of all things.

Gorman swept into his line of sight, blocking out the unsettling view of the hint of the curve of Effie Annesley's backside beneath the flared hem of her tunic.

"We believe George has been taken to London," he said calmly, clearly. "As you have been employed by the king for some time, and are rumored to now have evidence to the Hargraves's crimes, we need your help."

"The king will most likely have me arrested as a failure," Lucan said. "And"—he waved his hand about, encompassing all present with the motion—"he should certainly have the lot of you done, as well."

Dana drew back with a gasp. "I beg your pardon."

Gilboe raised his face to the shadowed ceiling with his eyes closed. "Forgive him, Lord."

Lucan ignored the melodramatics. "It's likely nothing more than a trap to lure you to London to give yourselves up. Caris Hargrave is dead, I tell you."

Effie spun around and charged toward the cot, but Gorman held a warding arm to his side, protecting Lucan from her wrath.

"Even if she is dead," Gorman allowed, "and even if this is only a snare to apprehend us, the fact remains that *someone* has taken our son. Our George," he added and the pain on his face was just as palpable to Lucan as the pain in his own foot.

"No matter the cost, we must make sure that he is safe. Sir Lucan, you are the only one of us with any hope of getting near the palace outside of shackles. Will you help us?" The man's brown eyes were intense, sincere, and Lucan couldn't help but feel a recognition there. "Please," Gorman said softly.

"I need time…" Lucan began.

Effie pushed Gorman's arm out of the way. "We don't have time!"

"I have to think."

"You can think on the way there," she challenged.

"I doubt I could sit a horse."

Dana piped up brightly. "We have the corpse wagon!"

"Oh, *right*," Gilboe responded with dawning enthusiasm. "He could lie in the back!"

"That's actually quite good," Gorman admitted.

Lucan found he was frowning. "I don't think I like the sound of a corpse wagon. My horse—"

"I'll ride your horse," Effie volunteered.

"The hell you will."

Gorman shook his head. "No, we'll tether him to the back; he'll be more likely to follow willingly if he can see his master."

"You can rest along the way," Dana cooed.

"And ask God's guidance for what you might do," Gilboe suggested.

"Or," Effie's eyes were neither sympathetic nor enthusiastic, "you can say no. In which case, we shall blindfold you and leave you in the deepest part of the forest. So you shan't be able to lead others to the Warren."

"I do doubt I would find it so difficult," Lucan jeered.

"It's eluded you for fifteen years."

He felt his ears burn, but tried to hide his consternation. "You realize you've kidnapped a knight of the realm."

"How dare you accuse Rolf of such a thing," Dana huffed. Lucan thought for a moment that he glimpsed an Adam's apple, but then it disappeared beneath a rather square jaw dropped in disappointment. "Hasn't our Winnie healed you?"

"That remains to be seen."

"You'll be a hero," Gilboe encouraged. "A warrior for the Lord."

"You're certainly free to crawl back to Steadport Hall and wrap yourself in your wounded pride and rot beneath the weight of your ego. Until the king sends for you himself," Effie added pointedly. "We leave within the hour, with or without you."

Lucan felt all four pairs of eyes watching him. He knew he wasn't yet thinking clearly, but he was being pressed into making a choice. If he refused to accompany the party of bandits, they would leave him in the woods to find his way back to Steadport Hall. His condition may worsen unaided.

If he agreed to go with them…well, it was only hastening the inevitable, was it not? And if he improved en route and changed his mind, he could always abandon the mission.

"Alright," Lucan said at last.

"Huzzah!" Dana squealed and gave a short burst of applause.

Gilboe turned with a swirl of brown robes, one of his stubby fingers pointing heavenward. "I'll ready the corpse wagon."

"Gilboe, alert my father as well," Gorman called after the friar.

"Oh, Rolf is already with the horses," Dana advised and then glanced at Lucan with a proud smirk. "So conscientious. Like father, like son, no?"

Lucan felt his eyes widen. So that's where he recognized Gorman's gaze. "Rolf is your father? Why didn't he tell me?"

Gorman turned back to look at Lucan, a nonplussed expression on his face, but it was Effie Annesley who replied.

"Poor, naïve Sir Lucan," she sneered. "Believe me, that's the very least of what you don't know."

Chapter 3

They indeed set out within the hour, the morning sun turning to steam the icy crust that had encased the light blanket of snow overnight. The bright yellow rays burst through the tree trunks like silent weapons, causing squinting eyes, shielding forearms, ducking faces. Breath rose over the small party like a cloud of heavenly witnesses, but they, too, were silent as horses and riders, and, at the very rear, the narrow corpse wagon with the dignified Agrios tethered to the board, rolled and rocked up the hill toward the more defined road at least a mile away from the Warren.

Lucan Montague had already been fast asleep when Effie returned to the chamber to help bring him out of the Warren and load him into the cart. He'd been dazed and startled upon his awakening, disoriented to the point that he'd forgotten to scowl and snap at her, and Effie had noticed the fatigue around his eyes. Eyes that had aged a great deal since either she or Lucan had been the noble children of Northumberland. Lines had crept from the corners of both their eyes, like roots crawling across the surface of rocky ground seeking vain purchase, creases bracketed their mouths as if the years of smiles, frowns—tears, perhaps—were nothing more than asides to the lives they'd led. He was older and ill, and confused as to why the party of strangers was moving him so quickly through a dank cave and into the bed of a rough cart in the shattering light of dawn.

She glanced over her shoulder yet again at the cart as they crested the top of a hill. He was weak now, and she was the strong one.

Effie shook herself and faced forward as they began the descent down the other side of the peak, putting him from her mind and warning herself not to let Lucan Montague's enfeebled state soften her disgust of him.

"Alright?" Gorman asked at her side.

Effie nodded. She wasn't alright, and Gorman knew it. But she was going on. They all were, because they must. Wasn't that what each one of the band had learned to do?

Only a small party of the family were making the long journey to London. Effie and Gorman; Rolf, to give his lordship someone familiar to journey with; Winnie, to care for the invalid. Also Gilboe, whose friar's robes almost always proved useful on a prolonged expedition. And—

A racket from the rear caused Effie and Gorman to slow their mounts and look behind them again. The procession was stopped, and a lanky figure was tethering another horse to the board of the corpse wagon and then climbing inside the bed with the unawares knight.

Chumley.

Effie huffed a quiet laugh before starting forward again. He had been much put out with them for rousing him so soon after dawn, having drank himself to sleep in the smallest of hours, as usual. The day was too new for Chumley to sit a horse, and so noble Sir Lucan would have a companion to keep him warm on this first part of the journey and not even know it. At least he'd tried. Chumley knew better than most that they'd be unlikely to encounter any brigands on the road at this hour and wouldn't need him until his prime of early evening. Just as well that he rest now.

Seven misfits, on their way to London. Any one of them liable never to return. And all for George.

Hang on, my babe, Effie sent up in silent prayer. *Your family is coming for you.*

* * * *

Lucan smelled strong wine before he even opened his eyes. Strong, sour wine, but only in short, warm bursts interspersed with cold, fresh air. And there was brightness beyond his eyelids that seemed unwarranted.

The chambermaid must have pulled back the drapes of his bed. Hag. But right away he noticed the absence of the sick throbbing of his foot, and he felt the muscles of his face relax for an instant.

Good lord, what *was* that rancid wine smell?

He opened his eyes to the bright blue sky above him, the wispy white clouds rocking with the motion of his bed.

The corpse wagon. The Warren. *Effie Annesley.*

At the sound of a drawn-out grunt, Lucan turned his head to the left and gave a startled cry.

A gaunt, bewhiskered face lay on Lucan's shoulder, his cheek hollowed with each breath from his gaping mouth, emitting the foul grape smell that had stirred Lucan from his rest. The man—whoever he was—was asleep, and snuggled up to Lucan's side like a lamb.

A drunk lamb that had been pickled in a wine tun to the point that he'd grown a beard before he'd starved to death.

Lucan squirmed away with a shrug, allowing the man's skull to slide to the floor of the wagon with a thud. His bed companion did not stir as a shadow fell over his face. Lucan looked up.

"How fare thee, lord?" Rolf inquired solicitously.

"Who the hell is that?"

"Chumley, lord."

"Why is he in the cart with me?"

"He was rather under the weather when we departed."

"Get him out."

"I'd not risk my life, lord."

"He doesn't appear to be quite as dangerous as that," Lucan said with a frown. "If you won't do it, then get *me* out."

"We'll be stopping to rest the horses soon," was his only answer.

Movement of another rider slowing to the opposite side of the wagon drew Lucan's attention—it was a white-haired old woman dressed in light gray that matched her unsettling clear gaze. She motioned down the length of Lucan's body.

"Winnie wishes to know how you feel, lord. It was she who tended your foot."

The frown did not leave Lucan's face. "Better, I think."

The woman nodded without a word and urged her horse forward once more.

"How long have I been asleep?"

Rolf looked up at the sky. "Four hours, perhaps?"

The old woman's place was filled by Effie, and Lucan felt absurdly self-conscious at the woman seeing him so enfeebled. He pushed with his elbows to sit up just as the oblivious Chumley gave another rousing snort.

"Ah, the princess awakes," Effie goaded him. "Alas, it seems that your prince has been laid low by love's gentle kiss."

Lucan struggled to sit against the front board of the wagon, observing the high sides and reinforced metal bracings inside the conveyance that bit into his back and shoulders, and he noticed as his right pinky became painfully wedged that the planks of the bed beneath him were so gapped that he could see the dirt and rocks as the cart rolled over them. He yanked his hand free.

"Necessary evil, I'm afraid," she said. "It's for the liquids to drain."

Lucan must have pulled a horrified face, for Effie Annesley chuckled before she said, "The good knight is unusually squeamish. Quarter mile to the Break, Rolf." Then she disappeared past the front of the wagon.

Lucan turned his head to glare up at Rolf, who, much to Lucan's irritation, appeared to be holding back his own smile. "Not to worry, lord," he said. "The corpse wagon hasn't held an actual corpse in years."

"It seems in good repair," Lucan grumbled. "Reinforced even, for a conveyance that's not in use."

"Oh, it's in use. Just not for corpses. Quite handy."

Lucan felt his eyes narrow.

"For this and that," Rolf elaborated. "It was acquired from a rather disingenuous vicar who"—Rolf paused. "You know, it doesn't really matter, does it?"

"Probably best that I don't know," Lucan said slowly, eyeing the steward warily.

Rolf nodded. "Quite right."

Believe me, that's the very least of what you don't know.

Lucan didn't trust himself in the moment to say anything civilized to the man he'd known for years to be a trusted servant and friend, and so he held his tongue as the corpse wagon bounced him and his drunken companion over the rough road.

It slowed to a stop after several moments and Lucan craned his neck to peer over the front board and see beyond the wide rump of the chestnut mare that pulled the wagon.

The party was stopped in the road as, one by one, riders on horseback departed by way of the berm and disappeared over a sudden drop. Raising himself up higher on his hands, Lucan saw that the road disappeared in a ragged chasm, taken up again on the far side of a dark gulf that he recognized.

They'd reached the Break—a part of the Dillonshire road where a bridge had once spanned the breach but had crumbled away long ago. It was a favorite haunt of bandits, and famous for travelers being waylaid and robbed as they crossed the wide but shallow, rocky river of the gulf. Lucan reached down instinctively to check for the hilt of his sword as Rolf untied Agrios, and was surprised to find his weapon still in its sheath.

The cart lurched forward again, and Lucan wedged himself into the corner as the cart horse carefully maneuvered the steep descent toward the river. At his side, Chumley's bent legs slid in increments along the floor of the cart until the man was curled in the fetal position, but it didn't seem to trouble him at all as there was not even a stutter in his rhythmic snores. Several tense moments later, the cart horse pranced along the flat bank beside the trilling winter river.

Rolf turned Agrios loose at the water's edge and then swung down from his own mount. He approached the cart, where Lucan was already sliding toward the edge.

"A moment, I pray, lord," he said as he loosened the other horse tied to the cart.

"I can manage, Rolf," Lucan muttered.

Lucan held his injured left foot aloft as he slid to the ground onto his right—

And promptly collapsed to the rocky bank.

"Dammit!" Lucan could feel all eyes in the party turn to him as he lay sprawled on his side. Rolf and Gorman were soon grasping him beneath his arms and lifting him while his pride writhed.

"You're yet very ill, lord," Rolf chastised quietly. He and his son helped Lucan to a nearby sycamore and lowered him down against its painted and balding trunk.

"Isn't this a rather dangerous place to rest?" Lucan asked gruffly to cover his embarrassment. "There could be a robbery."

"Only if we're lucky, lord."

Once Lucan was seated, the white-haired Winnie and Gilboe approached, the friar hefting a shallow, square basket against his thigh. The old woman knelt near Lucan's foot and pressed gently about the bandages, carefully scrutinizing each of Lucan's exposed toes, while Gilboe opened the lid of the basket to reveal a variety of small bottles and pouches inside.

Winnie smiled gently and made a series of gestures with her hands, and Gilboe immediately closed and fastened the basket once more while the old woman looked up at Lucan. She held her palms toward him pointedly and then caressed her throat with one hand. Then she rose to her feet and left them.

"She wants you to rest," Gilboe said and handed him a corked skin. "And drink."

Lucan took the skin gratefully, trying to recover from his pride-damaging fall, although no one else in the party appeared to be paying any attention to him at all as they opened satchels and uncorked their own skins some distance away.

He was anathema, after all. A necessary evil to their mission.

Lucan supported the skin in both hands and turned it up, filling his mouth with the wine. It was bitter and burning, searing the insides of his cheeks and throat as he swallowed and then gasped a breath of air.

"It's fortified," Gilboe confided too late.

"Fortified with what?" Lucan demanded in a raspy voice. "Sulphur?"

Gilboe looked thoughtful for a moment. "Hmm. Perhaps," he allowed optimistically.

The sound of hoof beats wafted down from the road above and everyone in the party seemed to freeze for an instant, all in like postures.

"Two horses," Effie called out in a low voice, and then paused again, listening. "Both carrying riders. Travelling light."

And then the party burst into action, each going about a specific task as if being directed, although no one said anything.

Gilboe climbed up to stand in the bed of the corpse cart over the still-sleeping form of Chumley.

Rolf disappeared with Winnie into the trees.

Effie Annesley pulled dark, cloth-like objects from the saddlebag and tossed some to Gorman, who walked toward Lucan. Effie shook out one of the objects and slipped it over her head as Gorman did the same, his pace not slowing as he neared the sycamore, a hood still in his hand.

Lucan realized what the bearded man was about. "No," he said, holding up a hand.

Gorman paused. "You wish to be recognized?"

"Recognized by whom?"

Gorman shrugged. "Could be anyone." Gorman didn't give him any more time to think before he'd jammed the hood over Lucan's head. "Just lie there and be injured."

"I'll do my best," Lucan said wryly as he adjusted the hood to see out of the eye slash.

Effie Annesley had taken up a stance about ten feet from the cart bed, her bow in her hands, an arrow knocked and pointing at the ground. Gorman came to her side, similarly posed. Effie nodded toward the friar.

Still standing in the bed of the corpse cart, Gilboe took the signal and withdrew a cross from the folds of his robes and held it aloft, yelling as the rumble of hooves drew nearer.

"Turn back!" the friar wailed.

Effie and Gorman, their faces concealed, raised their weapons and pointed them at the monk as a pair of riders began to descend the Break.

Gilboe continued. "In the name of God!"

"What's going on here?" one of the riders called down.

"Turn back, friends," Gilboe shouted. "Turn back, lest you be set upon by the devil's minions!"

"Stay right where you are," Gorman advised, his and Effie's bows turning together in one fluid movement toward the interlopers to the Break.

The riders, two young men, well-dressed and, as Effie had guessed, travelling without cargo, held up their hands and looked at the pair of hooded bandits warily.

"Oh, Lord, have mercy!" Gilboe wailed. "Have mercy on these innocents!"

"Come on, then," Effie advised, her voice noticeably lowered in timbre, and Lucan was reminded of her speaking in the wood the day of the hunt before she'd shot him. How had he not been able to tell she was a woman? One look at those trousers…

He glared at her from inside his hood.

Effie and Gorman divided and bracketed the riders as they approached.

"I've done what I can to serve thee, Lord," Gilboe continued to rail at the sky. He gestured toward the sleeping Chumley. "I've tried to deliver the body of our dear brother!" He flung an arm toward Lucan. "I've laid one of the brigands low through your power with mine own hand!"

Lucan huffed. As if the fat friar could best him even if Lucan *was* a corpse.

"I can do no more, O Lord!" Gilboe wailed.

Gorman spoke up. "Hand over your purses."

"We'll not," one of the men replied indignantly.

"Hand them over," Effie warned, "or the priest gets it." She turned her weapon back toward Gilboe.

"You wouldn't dare," the other rider scoffed.

Effie let her arrow fly and Gilboe dropped to the cart bed with a scream. Lucan's breath seized in his chest.

"You're next," Gorman advised, as Effie pulled another arrow from her quiver and set it to her string. "Hand them over and you may pass. Or we kill you and take them any matter. The first option allows you to leave with your lives."

"I told you we should have taken the other road," the first rider grumbled to the other as her jerked at the strings of his purse."

In the cart bed, Gilboe hadn't so much as twitched.

Two purses flew through the air to land in the dirt. Gorman stepped back, widening the path for the riders to pass.

"Ride hard until the bend," he said. "We'll be watching. If we see you slow, you're dead. If we see your faces again—also dead."

"Go," Effie commanded.

The two young men kicked at their horses and were soon splashing through the river and up the far side of the bank. In a moment, they were gone, the dust from their hooves floating over the break in a weak, dry cloud.

Gilboe raised his head. "Are they gone?"

"Aye," Gorman replied. He bent to gather the purses as Effie walked into the shallow water to retrieve her spent arrow.

She raised up and pulled the hood from her head, prompting Lucan to also unmask.

"You're unbelievable," he said to her as she neared him, but she acted as though he wasn't there at all.

Winnie appeared on Rolf's arm from the wood behind them and the steward asked, "No trouble?"

"None," Gorman replied, tossing the purses to Gilboe.

The band sat on the ground near where Lucan watched them incredulously. Effie obviously felt the weight of his scrutiny, for she looked up at him with a clear lack of patience in her sigh.

"What is it, Sir Lucan?"

"You just robbed two innocent men," he accused. "And made them believe you'd killed a monk, for God's sake!"

"Innocent, I don't know," Gorman said. "Two pampered noblemen on their way to the brothel at Dillon for the holiday, if the coin and the saint medallions against the clap in their bags are any indicator. Getting a bit of tail through the graces of their daddies' coffers."

"That's no crime," Lucan insisted.

Everyone in the group stared at him soberly.

"This is the way it's to be all the way to London, then," he said, growing more and more irritated with the idea that he'd been dropped into a world he knew nothing about; where what seemed simple and obvious was neither.

"Yea," Effie replied. "Yea, it is. We can leave you here if you wish."

Winnie made a series of hand motions toward Effie.

"What did she say?" Lucan demanded.

"She said you're very innocent for a knight. I have to agree with her. Your sensitive sensibilities would likely lay you low ere we reach the king, and even if you survive, you might die of guilt before you can spill your guts to Henry."

Lucan frowned in confusion while Effie continued to stare at him. "So? Do you continue on or nay?" she taunted, and Lucan clearly heard the challenge behind her words.

He didn't know why, but he said, "I continue."

"There you are then," Gorman said, and he tossed several coins in Lucan's direction.

He caught some of them before they hit the dirt. "What's this for?"

"Wear the hood, share the good," Gilboe said with an enthusiastic smile. "And may God bless you, Sir Lucan."

Lucan looked back to Effie Annesley, who watched him still. Her lips were parted, desperation and challenge in her pale eyes. Lucan felt as though she were trying to peer into his soul.

In the dappled light of the Break, Lucan had to admit that she was beautiful—like a haloed figure in a religious portrait.

Or perhaps an adder camouflaged against the underbrush, ready to strike. Yes, that was more accurate.

Blasted Effie Annesley. It was going to be a very long journey.

Chapter 4

They came in on the North Road, or so Lucan Montague said. Effie had never been to London before, although she'd heard enough of it to recognize the hazy black cloud that heralded the city hours before they came in distant view of it. Now, after nearly a fortnight on the road, Effie paused at a rise to take in the scene from atop her horse, bracketed by Lucan Montague to her right and Gorman on her left.

Her heart skipped a beat and her stomach fluttered at the sight of the crowded spires and haphazard multilevel buildings, their floors seeming stacked atop each other like children's blocks. The entire place looked gray-black, even though it was only a pair of hours past noon and the winter sunshine was bright around them. The sky was like a clean, new parchment whose center had been held too close to a candle flame, causing a black, ragged char mark in the center: London.

Somewhere in that dark conglomeration was George Thomas.

She knew that beyond the snaggle-toothed horizon of the city snaked the gray Thames, crowded with vessels of every length and mast. Ships that brought people from all over the world to this crowded chaos, and could also take them absolutely anywhere, never to be seen again, if they so wished.

She tried not to think of that.

"Where is he?" she asked aloud. "Where is George? There?" She gestured to the tall, square structure near the river on the left side of the city.

Lucan shook his head. "I highly doubt Henry would place a boy of six in the Tower, although with any luck, that is where his abductors will end up. There." He pointed in the opposite direction, far across the city to Effie's right, where a walled complex of buildings crowned by the arched dome of a cathedral could just be glimpsed beyond the metropolis. "Westminster."

Effie urged her horse forward once more without further comment. Gorman and Montague matched her pace.

They entered the city proper at Bishopsgate. Effie's heart pounded in her chest at the press of people, animal, and conveyance, at the noise and the smell. She had never imagined any place could be like this, and she wondered how frightened George must be.

They wound their way through the crowd, through people from all levels of society, it appeared. There were old women wearing little more than rags, bent nearly double with bound parcels strapped to their backs; the nearer they came to the center of the city, fine ladies and gentlemen in long, rich robes, their servants surrounding them and clearing the way. Merchants at stalls strung with carcasses or dried foodstuffs, cloth and rugs and pottery. It was colder here between the buildings, as if the hulking city shunned the very ideas of light and warmth. Everywhere was noise and the smell of rot and old soot. They seemed to be heading directly toward the river.

"Where are we going?" she asked at last, not liking the hesitant sound of her voice, but feeling uncharacteristically unsure of herself in this foreign environment.

"The Strand, first," he said easily. "I've a friend with a house there at my disposal."

"But we must see the king right away," Effie protested to his back, and it was not lost on her that Lucan Montague was in his element here, and it showed in his demeanor.

"Not looking like this, we mustn't," he said over his shoulder. "We've been traveling for a fortnight and smell it, I'm sure. Look it, I know. We'd not make it as far as the courtyard in this condition, I'm afraid."

"Lucan, they have my son," Effie argued. "They must let me in."

"You don't yet know whether they have your son or not," he replied smoothly. "Besides, we must have a place for Chumley to safely sleep it off and Winnie and Gilboe to stay. Unless the good friar has a desire to visit the Bishop?" He craned his head further to look pointedly at the man, whose face was now hidden by his deep hood.

Gilboe cleared his throat within the shadow. "Ah, I think not."

Effie hated the knight's smug expression as he turned back around. He thought himself so smart.

"I do doubt any of you wish to spend the coin required to put yourselves up in a reputable inn. A cheap one would see you departing in your own corpse wagon. Unless it was first stolen and sold before they killed you. Which is actually quite likely."

"Lucan—" she began again.

But Gorman reached across with his open hand. Effie took it. He squeezed her fingers.

"He's right." Gorman released her as he was forced to maneuver his horse around to let a tall, top-heavy merchant cart bumble through the crowd. The horses sidestepped and tossed their heads. A moment later, he looked at her as they continued on. "Sir Lucan knows London. Isn't that why he's with us? We have to trust him."

Effie pressed her lips together but raised no further arguments.

They turned right at last, onto a street that held nothing of the crowds they'd just accomplished—no merchants lined this thoroughfare, only the figures of servants and soldiers and horses. Children played here—both the well-dressed and those of obviously lesser means. Between the shoulders of the stately dwellings, so unlike the timbered structures they'd passed through, Effie caught glimpses of boats and could smell the river. The road was no better though, marked with so many pits and ditches that Effie had to keep alert. They stopped before a white stone, three-story dwelling, and a servant appeared at once from the arches of a gate house.

"Sir Lucan," the man said, snapping his fingers to the side. A pair of boys came running from around the edge of the arch, their caps askew, their bare feet bluish through the grime. "It is a pleasure to see you again."

"Stephen." Montague swung down from his horse. "I've just come from Darlyrede House, which has suffered a great tragedy. Her steward and some of the other servants accompany me. We hope to see the king on the morrow. Lady Margaret hasn't returned yet, has she?" He handed Agrios's reins to the older boy. "He's tired lad."

"Aye, Sir Lucan," the stable boy acknowledged.

"No, lord, she is yet in Greece, as you likely suspected. She will be disappointed to have missed you. I'll see that the servants are shown appropriate quarters, with your steward's assistance."

Lucan and the well-dressed servant looked to Rolf expectantly, and Effie felt her teeth grit together.

"Rolf?"

"Of course, lord."

The knight nodded. "Very good. I shall call for you in the morning, when I am ready to depart. Good night."

Then Lucan Montague turned and limped up the walkway to the painted wooden door, where a footman waited. He threw the door wide well before the man's actual arrival on the threshold, and Lucan disappeared inside the house, leaving the rest of them in the street.

Effie felt like her heart would burn out of her chest as she swung down from her horse. How dare he abandon them all like rubbish?

Gorman hefted Chumley from the wagon and carried him over his shoulder as the six of them followed the prissy steward along the down-sloping pathway beneath the arch. By the time they reached the rear, more young boys were leading their horses and one was driving the cart up the wharf alley and into a damp stable yard. They ducked into an open doorway in the house's stone foundation.

It was a kitchen, low-ceilinged and furnished smartly with workbenches and shelves along one long wall. The opposite of the room was comprised of a large, open hearth; a small fire was banked, the spits and pot-arms empty. Stephen led them through this room and into a narrow passage where the stones were whitewashed. He stopped beside a planked door, painted with the same finish as the stones.

"The majority of the house servants are abroad with my lady. You may have use of their chambers." He nodded toward Effie. "This one shall be yours. There is warm water in the cistern in the kitchen. The servants' privvy is across the alley. Cook will fetch you to help prepare the meal."

Effie's gaze found Gorman's as the snooty man dismissed her by turning and heading further down the corridor. His steady gaze said *patience*, as usual. Effie bit her tongue and shoved at the door with her shoulder. It stuttered roughly across the packed dirt floor and opened to pitch darkness.

The meager ambient light filtering in from the doorway was enough for Effie to locate the candle. She had to carry it out to the kitchen to catch a flame and then make yet another trip to fill a pitcher for washing and hunt down a cake of soap and rag. Once back inside the room, she closed the door and surveyed her cell.

Her arms nearly spanned the breadth of it. The bed was little more than a wide rail against the wall, and the single small table was hardly large enough to hold the pitcher and bowl next to the candle. The only other appointments to the room were a row of hooks. It smelled stale and damp, and the chill seemed to seep up through Effie's boots, not unlike the dampness of the caves in the Warren, but the stench of the city pervaded everything, and Effie couldn't seem to blow it from her nostrils.

She prepared to wash, loosening her plait and then the ties of her vest. She had nothing else to put on, and she couldn't bring herself to strip down entirely in the depressing cell which had no bolt on the door. She washed inside her billowing shirt, her face and neck, and then soaked and soaped her hair, scrubbing at her scalp until it tingled. She squeezed the water from her hair and replaited it, then brushed at her vest and trousers with the spent rag. She was chilled to her bones by the time she was completely dressed again.

She looked at the narrow cot against the wall. Exhaustion suddenly seized her, and she thought she might burrow down under the thin blanket and—

Her door scraped open, causing her to spin around and reach for the blade on her belt. A short ogre of a woman with a massively bloated underchin more than filled the narrow rectangle, framing a gigantic floor length white apron and a matching kerchief topping a seemingly tiny head.

"On yer feet, slut," the woman growled. "The meat shan't make itself." A ham-sized forearm squeezed past the swollen abdomen to toss a long white cloth through.

Effie let the apron land on the ground and her exhaustion disappeared as her ire was sparked. She tried to keep hold of her temper—the cook was only doing her job. "There's been a mistake—I'm no kitchen maid."

"Oh," the woman gasped dramatically. "I beg your pardon, my fine lady!" Then her thick brows lowered. "In case you've not noticed, this isn't a country house, nor is it a charity. You don't work, you don't eat, and I've no cock for you to suck." She glanced down at the white swath on the damp, black floor. "And you'll be washing that as well, now. Be quick about it."

Any empathy for the crude woman's responsibilities vanished; what must it be like to work beneath this woman's oversight day after day? Effie was in such shock at being spoken to in such a manner that she could only stand and stare while the cart of a woman squeezed off down the corridor to the kitchens. She hadn't been spoken to so crudely since…

Since the night Castle Dare burned and she'd been mistaken for a servant.

The tears and fury in his young, blue eyes, the feel of the leather on her cheek.

I don't ever want to see your face again!

Effie purposefully trod across the apron as she quit the chamber, but instead of turning left toward the kitchen, she entered the corridor to the right, her hand on the hilt of her blade lest anyone thought to stop her.

She'd already had quite enough of the hospitality of London's nobility.

* * * *

The manservant left the toilette accessories on Lady Margaret's vanity table and Stephen himself brought Lucan a suit of clothes.

"From your last stay with us, lord," he said.

Lucan stared for a moment at the red velvet tunic laid out carefully on the bed. He'd forgotten the costume he'd been wearing the day Thomas Annesley had been sentenced to the gallows.

"Will there be anything else?" Stephen asked.

Lucan started. "Actually, Stephen, my boots need to be replaced. Is it possible...?"

"I am certain I can find you something suitable. Anything else, sir?"

"No, Stephen, thank you."

"Very good, sir. I shall call you for dinner."

Lucan began jerking his ties free as the chamber door shut. He couldn't wait to be quit of the filthy clothes, which felt melted to him after a fortnight of rough travel. They'd only taken shelter at roadside inns a handful of times, and Lucan feared his black gambeson was hopelessly stained with road dust. He sat on the bed to remove his ruined boots, then his trousers and hose. He looked down at his left foot which bore a terrible purple and red scar, and flexed it appreciatively. He was all but healed.

All but healed, and back in London.

He had just finished washing when he heard the door open and close quietly behind him—that Stephen. He was naught if efficient.

"Just set them inside," he groaned mid-stretch—his lower back was in knots. "I'll fetch them after I've dressed."

The lack of response caused him to turn partly around.

Effie Annesley leaned against the closed door, staring at him as he stood naked before her.

"What the hell are you doing in here?" he demanded.

"You told them I was a *servant*," she said. "And now the cook thinks me to brown your gravy."

"I couldn't very well tell them that you were a wanted fugitive now, could I?" Lucan rejoined, acutely aware of his manhood in the cool chamber.

Effie shrugged and then looked around the well-appointed room appreciatively, her demeanor so calm that one might suppose happening upon naked men was common for her.

"My, my," she said. "I can see why you were in such a rush to leave the peasantry behind."

Lucan felt justifiably exposed in naught but his skin, but as Effie Annesley didn't seem at all disturbed by his lack of clothing, he was loathe to scurry to cover himself like some nervous adolescent.

He ignored the idea that he was disappointed that Effie wasn't interested in looking at his body.

She pushed away from the door to leisurely stroll about the perimeter of the room, taking in the rich hangings and ornate woodwork. Lucan reached for his trousers and sat on the bed to quickly slip them on. By the time he stood again to fasten them around his hips, Effie had reached his end of the chamber and turned at last to face him.

"Finish dressing. You're taking me to Westminster."

Lucan couldn't stop the huff of incredulous laughter. "I beg your pardon?"

"Get. Dressed," she repeated calmly, with a slight inclination of her head. Lucan noticed her plait was dark—wet—and was leaving a damp patch on her vest. "You wished to bathe and change; you've done so. I'll not play housemaid in your little charade. I've come here to retrieve my son."

Lucan sighed and turned to face the bed while he picked up his shirt. "The king won't be seeing anyone this late in the day. Better that we arrive first thi—" His words stopped, his arms in both sleeves, the material stretched between his elbows as he felt the point of a blade to the left of his spine.

"Put your goddam shirt on and take me to the king. Now."

Lucan turned slowly, deliberately, the point of the blade dragging across his shoulder blade, his biceps, until it was positioned over his heart, and he was looking slightly down into Effie Annesley's sparkling eyes.

"Upon my honor," Lucan said gravely. "You don't want me to do that, Effie."

"*Now*, Lucan."

He moved quickly, twisting the shirt around the hilt of the short sword and yanking, pulling his arms free and sending the linen-wrapped weapon flying across the room. He reached out and grabbed her arm when she went after it, and she immediately ducked and twisted, bringing up a knee toward his groin. Lucan dodged the blow and spun Effie by her arm so that her own fingertips reached up between her shoulder blades. She gave a little cry of pain and so he relented a bit but did not release her.

"Hmm," he mused near her ear. "Interesting position I find myself in. Would you agree that one is deserved of revenge upon the woman who nearly cost him his foot?"

There was a rap upon the door then, and Stephen entered the chamber with the promised boots in hand.

"Forgive me, sir," he said, raising his right hand to shield his eyes while he trotted at a crouch to place the tall footwear on the edge of the carpet. He turned at once and fled, closing the door behind him.

Lucan leaned down toward Effie's ear again, ignoring the warm smell of her skin that seemed to envelop his head like a cloud. "Don't ever point a weapon at me again unless you mean to kill me straight away."

"Let go—"

"*If you do*, I will leave you and your son to rot." He pushed her away from him and then went to retrieve his shirt, tossing the blade to the floor at Effie's feet. He snapped the folds from the linen and slipped it on. "I've enough complications of my own to contend with in London without you mucking things up further for me than you already have."

"Oh, mucked things up for you, have I?"

Lucan ignored her goad as he slid his arms into the red velvet and attended to the hammered clasps. "I will take you to Westminster—yes, right now—if only to be rid of you. But know this: if Vivienne Paget and—however unlikely I find it—Caris Hargrave have indeed taken your son to Henry with their claims, should you show up there tonight demanding audience at dinner, he will absolutely have you arrested and imprisoned until he is ready to deal with you. And once he knows where you are, he will be in no hurry. On this you can depend." He walked past her toward his boots and could feel her gaze burning holes in the velvet. When he had retrieved them and turned, he found she was indeed glaring at him.

He sat in a carved chair to don the boots.

"You don't understand," she said quietly. "You don't have a son…"

Lucan finished the lacings and looked at her from across the rug. He sighed. "You'll do George far less good locked in a cell there than getting a much-needed night's rest here. I've already sent word to the king of my arrival in London. He'll be ready for us. Well, me, anyway."

He could tell the moment when his reasoning reached her by the ever-so-slight fall of her shoulders. Perhaps no one else would have noticed, but to Lucan it was a raised flag of surrender. The light of combativeness behind her eyes went out, like a candle flame snuffed behind a milky pane of glass, and a ridiculous urge to comfort her rose in Lucan.

"Whose house is this?" she asked suddenly.

"Margaret Stanhope, Lady Towsey."

"Is she your lover?"

"At one time, yes," he answered honestly. "How did you know?"

"The servants are well familiar with you," Effie said. "And those are obviously your own clothes, by the way they fit you."

"Keen observation, Euphemia," Lucan said. "You'd make a fine investigator should you ever choose to give up your criminal ways."

"Don't call me that," Effie snapped, but there was little bite in the bark. "I haven't managed to survive this long by ignoring details."

"No, I don't imagine you have," Lucan mused.

"And I'll have you know that I shan't be passing the night in that scullery hole in the cellar. Whether you want to admit it or not, we are still of equal station, you and I."

"I see," Lucan mused. "So you're petitioning me to place you in a chamber above floors? I believe the one next to this is prepared." He wondered at the little thrill of anticipation that ran through him at the idea of Effie sleeping next to him in the house. It was absurd—she'd slept closer to him during their fortnight on the road, and he hadn't cared one whit.

Perhaps he was only interested because she'd threatened to kill him. Again.

Effie shook her head. "That won't be necessary—I'll share Gorman's room."

"Of course," Lucan said quickly, feeling the fool. "In any case, I do insist on employing Stephen to locate something else for you to wear for our audience on the morrow. While I don't personally disapprove of your"—he paused—"*garments*, I do expect the king to be less likely swayed by the maternal pleadings of a woman entering his court in trousers."

Lucan thought she might have blushed, but he didn't know if it was embarrassment for not thinking of her clothing, or the fact that his statement was alluding to the sight of her shapely rear-end.

"And while I didn't personally disapprove of your own… *display*," Effie said, "you might have wished to don your hose before putting on your trousers and boots. I've found them to be terribly chafing without."

Lucan looked down instinctively, realizing just then that his feet were bare in the stiff leather.

He looked up at the sudden sound of the door closing.

She *had* noticed he was naked.

Chapter 5

Effie left the house on the Strand with Lucan Montague after an early, silent breakfast, although she hadn't been able to eat a bite. The cobbles in the wharf alley were damp with fog, and indeed the morning mist still blanketed the river valley, washing everything in soft light and filling the lanes with hush.

Lucan Montague had seemed loathe to converse since announcing to the family that morning that a message had arrived from the king, granting them audience. His continued silence suited her—she didn't think her nerves could withstand trying to carry on a conversation, even if it would inevitably deteriorate into yet another argument which was likely to take her mind off their destination.

Effie was so nervous, so anxious, she felt she might jump out of the borrowed gown she wore. It was bulky and cumbersome, too long at the hem, an unpleasing color, and rather than increase her confidence at being appropriately attired, the wearing of the gown only added to her unease. This was not who she was, London was not her home; the people she would meet and speak with today were not her friends. But she would do whatever was necessary to regain her son. She held the image of George's little face in her mind as she gripped the reins with white-knuckled fingers and rode through the already busy street at Lucan's side.

He wore the red velvet tunic again, and used as she was to seeing him in nothing but black, it was as if a stranger accompanied her. Just as well. He had given her little insight beyond the few cautions of manners and expectations for speaking to Henry, as if she were some rough commoner. Although, to be fair, she suspected neither of them had any real idea what they would encounter once they arrived.

She took a deep, slow, silent breath as the full vista of the Westminster complex rose before her. It was more than magnificent, and although Effie thought she would look upon the myriad of royal structures with dread, she marveled at its beauty as they passed through the opening.

The crunch of hoof on gravel echoed within the low stone walls and then rolled up the tall facing of the massive building. The courtyard was immaculate if stark in its winter landscape, more like an illustration with its dull tones of masonry and gravel and bare branches to welcome them. The pools were all but empty, no fountain bubbled, no flowers bloomed, and yet every crisp line, every bare bed emphasized the royalty of the place.

A pair of footmen or guards—Effie wasn't certain, as every man she saw appeared to be armed—came to take charge of their mounts once they reached the pointed stone archway framing the doors, and Effie was annoyed at having to wait for assistance to dismount in her awkward attire. She and Lucan were admitted into the dark hush of the hall.

She tried to steel herself against the grandeur of the interior, but it was of no use. The ceiling soared up from tall stone walls, swirling into carved oaken beams that met in the peak what must have been nearly a hundred feet above Effie's head. The floor, too, was massive, with its wide, square slabs of stone. But even as she gasped at the hall, her hand went to her mouth. For there at the far end of the cavernous chamber, on those great slabs of stone before the steps and the king's dais, a trio of children played. The door behind Effie shut with a thud and a gust of hooting wind, and one of the little faces raised, staring down the wide center aisle.

"Mama?" The single, quiet word was like a chorus within the stone walls and floor, echoing, spinning joyfully in the air.

"George Thomas," Effie breathed, and was running at once, nearly tripping on her skirts before she remembered to hold them aloft. "George!"

He got to his feet and met her, Effie going to her knees as her son flew into her arms.

"Mama, what took you so long?" George demanded. "Is it because you are wearing a gown?"

"I came as fast as I could, my love." Effie squeezed him and then held him away from her to scrutinize him. "Are you well? Have you been treated well?"

"Oh, yes, Mama," George said. "I have my own chamber and a nursie who is ever so good. I have lots of playmates and there are lessons. And Grandmamma visits me nearly every day."

Effie felt as if someone wrapped a hand around her throat. "Grandmamma?"

George nodded, his rosy cheeks and his red hair just as vibrant as they had been in the wood, perhaps even more so, Effie thought, as his skin seemed to have paled. "Grandmamma Hargrave. She and Lady Paget brought me to see the king. That's him, right there." George half turned and pointed behind him at the man Effie only now noticed was sitting on the dais behind the center of a long table.

Sitting on a throne.

Footsteps sounded near her, and Effie looked up as Lucan Montague reached her and George. His blue eyes were icy, his thoughts unreadable. But his attention was for George alone.

"Good day, George. Do you remember me at all?"

"Good day. Yes, I do, sir. You are Lucan Montague. Mama shot you in your foot. Is it all better?"

The man's thin lips quirked. "It is. Thank you for asking."

"You are quite welcome. I am ever so glad that you have brought my mama to me. Have you met the king? His name is Henry, but I am to call him 'my lord' whenever anyone else is about."

"I have met the king," Lucan said. "In fact, I am here to see him myself."

"That is very good, Sir Lucan," George said sincerely. "It's ever so nice that you can be here with Mama and Grandmamma Hargrave and Uncle Padraig."

Effie shook George's hand to draw his attention to her. "Uncle Padraig is here?"

"Oh, yes, Mama. And not only him, but Auntie Iris, and Tavish and Lohock...Lock—" the boy struggled. "It's quite hard to say it the way he does."

"Do you mean Lachlan, George?" Lucan offered. His face seemed rather more pale than usual, and Effie wondered if something was amiss she was as yet unaware of, or if the interior of Westminster naturally sapped the life from its inhabitants.

"Yes, sir." George looked back to Effie. "Did Father come, too?"

"Shh," Effie said, drawing her son into another embrace. "He is not far away, my love. On that you can depend. And you shall see him very soon."

"Effie," Lucan said quietly. And then he turned and walked toward the dais alone.

The other two children George had been playing with upon Effie's arrival had vanished sometime during her reunion with her son, leaving the hall empty save for the king and a single servant.

"Oh, yes," George Thomas piped enthusiastically. "Let's do go with him, Mama. I just know you and my lord will be great friends."

Effie swallowed and tried to force a smile while George pulled her to her feet with both hands. Perhaps she would have succeeded, her relief was so great at finally getting to look into his sweet face again. But just as they started forward toward where Lucan had gone to one knee, the single, round-topped door to the left of the table opened, and a ghost entered the hall.

* * * *

"Your Grace." Lucan knelt and bowed his head before King Henry.

"Ah, Sir Lucan. So glad you at last decided to attend me—Ulric arrived what must be three weeks ago now," he chastised, but his tone was not unkind.

"Forgive me, lord," Lucan replied. "I was yet recovering at Steadport Hall, and"—his words were cut off as he rose and the door to the left of where Henry sat opened. An old woman shuffled into the hall.

Her face was deeply lined now, the skin around her eyes drooped. Her lips were colorless and drawn like the neck of a purse, and her gown sagged around her shoulders as she leaned heavily on the arm of her tall, skeletal companion. Bright streaks of white gleamed where before none had lived in her once glossy-brown hair. Lucan felt a sizzle of disbelief race up his spine, and it paralyzed him for an instant.

By God—it *was* Caris Hargrave, returned from a fiery grave.

Or hell.

Behind Lucan, George Thomas's voice called out, "Grandmamma! You were right—look who has come!" The boy then dashed past toward where Caris Hargrave had swayed to a halt next to Vivienne Paget.

"George, no!" Effie shouted sharply.

The boy stopped as if pulled up short on a leash and he turned around with a bewildered look on his face.

"Come to me at once," Effie demanded, the command breathy.

"But, Mama—"

"At once, George Thomas!"

Lucan did not turn as the boy walked obediently back in the direction from which he'd come—he couldn't seem to drag his gaze from the terrible sight of what Caris Hargrave had become.

"It's alright, George," the wraith rasped, and it reminded Lucan of fine gravel sliding over sandstone. Her smile was small, as if the bones of her face were frozen. She looked past Lucan with those frightening, wilting eyes. “Hello, Euphemia.”

Effie stepped to Lucan’s right and sank into a deep curtsey, her face nearly touching the stones. “My king.” She stayed there and the moments dragged past. No one in the hall moved, save George Thomas, who shifted slightly from foot to foot, as Henry took his time to welcome the newcomer to his court.

“Euphemia Hargrave, I presume,” he said at last.

Effie rose, graceful in a way Lucan couldn’t imagine after being folded in half in such a fashion for so long.

But it was her son who replied, “This is my mama, Hen—*my lord*.”

“I took the name Effie Annesley many years ago, Your Grace,” she said.

“A rather questionable decision, wouldn’t you now say?” the monarch queried.

Effie lifted her chin. “Forgive me for disagreeing with you so soon upon our first meeting, lord, but no. I’m proud to bear the name Annesley.”

“Is that so?” Henry seemed surprised. “There may be something to hear, after all. We shall soon see.”

A servant had come in after the old women and placed two chairs on the floor before the left side of the dais. Vivienne Paget helped Caris to sit and then took the other seat herself.

Another servant appeared with a chair that he placed on the opposite side of the aisle as the king looked back to Lucan. “I’ll get to you in a moment, Sir Lucan.”

Lucan bowed and went to the chair, leaving Effie and George Thomas standing alone, juxtaposed between the other inhabitants of the room. The servants left quietly through the door behind the table.

“Why have you come to my court, *Euphemia Hargrave*?” Henry asked, and Lucan couldn’t help but wonder if the king was purposefully goading Effie with the hated moniker.

“My son was abducted from the wood beyond our home. I found a letter penned by Lady Paget that informed me that George Thomas had been brought to London. I’ve come to retrieve him.”

“You don’t seem surprised to see Lady Caris,” he led. “You must have believed her dead, if the accounts I received of the fire at Darlyrede House are to be believed.”

“Evil is difficult to kill, my lord. The devil himself likely ejected her.”

Henry raised his eyebrows, and the corners of his mouth drew down. “Hmm. Harsh words from a woman who was herself raised in luxury at

Darlyrede." His gaze went suddenly to the boy, holding on to his mother's hand. "George."

"Yes, my lord?"

"Where did you tell me you lived again?"

"The Warren, lord."

"Ah, yes." Henry nodded, as if just then recalling the detail. "And what exactly is the Warren?"

"It's a *giant* cave, lord."

"I see. Have you always lived at the Warren?"

"Yes, lord."

Now Henry looked to Caris Hargrave, who was pressing a kerchief to mouth. "Lady Caris, did you abduct this child from a cave?"

The kerchief came down and a reedy breath of air whistled in through the stingy lips. "No, Your Grace. I assure you I was in no condition to abduct anyone. I had just crawled from the rubble of Darlyrede. Dazed. Bleeding. My hands burnt from the heat of the stones—look, the wounds yet heal. Darlyrede was deserted. I thought I would die at any moment." She gasped a pair of breaths. "One of the horses had been overlooked. Not saddled, but with a bridle." Another gasp. "I managed to hold to it. It took me into the woods where George Thomas, my angel, found *me*."

"He had sneaked away from his dinner to follow me, Your Grace," Effie interjected. "He's always—"

Henry held up a palm, silencing Effie. He looked back to Caris. "You did not force him to go with you."

"He could have easily run away," Caris whispered. "Instead, he led the horse to a place where he could help me mount. I wasn't very steady. I did however ask him to come with me to Elsmire Tower, where lived my only friend in the world, lest I fainted along the way. I promised him a goodly coin if he would help me."

"Is this true, George?" Effie asked.

"Yes, Mama. You and Father always told me that is our duty to help people who need help. She was ever so ill."

"I intended to send him home right away," Caris continued. "I'd no idea who he was. It wasn't until I asked him where his parents were that I realized that I was holding"—she broke off, pressed the kerchief to her lips again briefly—"I was holding my own flesh and blood, abandoned in that dangerous, snowy wood."

"He wasn't abandoned," Effie shot back.

"When I understood he was Euphemia's child, and then heard of the animal den in which he was being forced to live, I knew that I had no choice but to bring him to you, lord. To throw us all upon your mercy." She looked back to Effie and, perhaps to an outsider, Caris Hargrave's expression could have been construed as pleading sorrow, but Lucan saw the cunning there, hiding in the wrinkles, shimmering in the white streaks of hair, like a malevolent phantasm.

"It's time we told the truth, Euphemia. To the king and to each other."

"What are you talking about?" Effie demanded. "Nothing resembling the truth has ever passed your lips."

The king pulled a rope on the wall behind him, and the door opened at once, admitting a servant.

"Bring in the others," Henry commanded.

The servant stepped aside, and Iris Montague appeared, looking serious and wary. Lucan's sister was followed by her husband, Padraig Boyd, who, while not at all as decrepit as Caris Hargrave, seemed also to have aged a decade since last Lucan had seen him. Then Tavish Cameron and Lachlan Blair appeared followed by two women—a blonde and a redhead—both of whom Lucan recognized.

Each of them met Lucan's eyes.

Once they were all standing nearby, the king looked to the old woman again. "Proceed, Lady Caris."

"Thank you, Your Grace." She gasped a pair of breaths and then swung her gaze to Effie. "Euphemia. Your suspicions all those years ago were correct. You are in fact my granddaughter, the child of Cordelia Hargrave and Thomas Annesley." No one in the room seemed surprised by this confession, and Lucan wondered at the information that had already been passed before his arrival.

"I tried to protect you from it, but I can see now how wrong of me it was to do so."

"Did you cut me from my mother's womb?" Effie demanded.

The atmosphere in the hall tingled with anticipation.

"I did," Caris allowed crisply.

* * * *

Effie felt the room tilt ever so slightly at this admission. The hall was as silent as a tomb.

At last. *At last.*

"I did it to save your life," Caris continued in her raspy whisper. "Had I not done, you would have died along with your poor mother, who was dead even as you emerged."

Effie was glad she hadn't eaten anything that morning, else it would have ended up on the stone floor in that moment.

"You killed her," she managed to choke out. "Your own daughter."

The king interjected. "You make a very serious allegation for one who was not cognizant of the goings-on at the time, Euphemia. Thomas Annesley has been well known as the perpetrator of your mother's murder. He's been convicted of it."

Effie's gaze flicked to the right of Henry, where her brother Padraig had moved to stay his wife. His face was grim and the warning for Iris on his face was clear: *Hold your tongue.*

Why?

"Lady Caris seems to wish nothing more than to rescue your son from certain poverty," Henry continued. "Poverty, and perhaps a future filled with lawlessness that could only end in his destruction."

"My lord," Effie began.

"Have you been in contact with Thomas Annesley?"

"No, Your Grace," Effie managed to answer. "To my knowledge, I've never met him."

"That sounds very much like a half-truth to me, Euphemia," the king chastised, but went on. "Is it true that it was you and your band of thieves who started the fire at Darlyrede House, which resulted in the deaths of Lord Vaughn Hargrave as well as several servants?"

Effie's breath caught in her throat. "No, my lord! We had no intention of—"

"Did you shoot and kill Lord Adolphus Paget in the wood the day prior to the fire?"

Effie's blood turned to ice—was this a trial? "I…I cannot say, my lord."

"You cannot say? Was it you who shot Lucan Montague, my own knight, on that same occasion?"

Effie's eyes reflexively flicked to Lucan. His normally serious expression was grave, and it gave her no comfort. She looked back to the king.

"It was, my lord."

"Hmm. So we have a confession, at last. Good."

The situation was spiraling out of all semblance of reason or control and Effie felt unable to draw sufficient breath.

"We shall deal with those charges at a future time," the king continued calmly. "I assume Sir Lucan will be more than happy to cooperate with your prosecution. But the matter at hand is more pressing, and that is the apprehension of the fugitive, Thomas Annesley." He looked to Lucan. "I would now address you both."

The knight rose and came to stand next to George Thomas. "My lord."

"I assume you are not hiding the previously recognized Baron Annesley in your gambeson?"

"No, Your Grace."

"Can you remind me, Montague, of your charge when you last left my court?"

"To gather evidence against Thomas Annesley and locate any heirs."

"The latter part of your duty you seemed to have taken quite seriously, if the Scottish mob infesting my court is any indication."

Lucan held his tongue.

"However, even when you were alerted that Thomas Annesley had escaped the Crown's custody, you did not apprehend him."

"He couldn't be located, lord."

"You couldn't find him."

"No, lord."

"I surmise you did not exert yourself in that task. But where is the evidence you compiled in the stead of his presence?"

There was a slight pause and this time it was Iris who frowned a clear signal to her brother. Effie wondered what other secrets floated just above her head in the grand hall.

"All that I had gathered was consumed in the fire at Darlyrede House, my lord." Lucan cleared his throat. "But if I may, lord, I would state that it is my personal belief that Thomas Annesley is not guilty of any of the crimes of which he is accused."

Henry did not seem surprised. "Well, that is a problem," he mused. "I am not accustomed to looking like a fool, nor do I wish to have any further accusations of madness cast upon my rule. Therefore, before we can continue in untangling this convoluted mess casting knots from here to the farthest reaches of that vile country to the north, we must put end to the beginning."

A sense of dread swept over Effie like a wash of fire, her skin flushed and tingled, her stomach turned.

"Sir Lucan Montague, you will take custody of Euphemia Hargrave at once, and together you will locate Thomas Annesley and return him to court to at last receive his punishment."

"What?" Effie breathed.

"Should she escape you, I will not hold it against you—after all, she has already tried to kill you once. If you must act in self-defense, well, so be it. It will mean that much less for me to decide upon your return."

Effie realized her mouth was agape as the king turned his attention to her and she pressed her lips together, trying to stay their sudden tremble.

"As for you, Euphemia, I shall not punish the son—or daughter, in this case—for the sins of the father. There is little doubt in my mind that Thomas Annesley killed Cordelia Hargrave. Whether or not you are complicit in his later crimes is another thing, entirely. If you return with Thomas Annesley, dead or alive, you shall face the charges against you and be tried fairly. If you are as guilty as I suspect, you shall have no qualms about escaping Sir Lucan's chaperone and abandoning your own child at my court, and the Crown shall have adequate reimbursement for its aggravation."

"Please, I'll not leave him here, my lord. I cannot."

"You can and you shall. He is happy enough here, are you not, George? Would you be happy to wait here for your mother to return from her duty to me?"

George's little face scrunched in a confused frown. He looked up at Effie. "You would come back for me, wouldn't you, Mama?"

Effie crouched down and grasped her son's thin shoulders, looking into his eyes through her shocked tears.

"I will always come for you, George Thomas. Nothing could keep me from you. Nothing, do you understand?"

George nodded and some of the anxiousness fell from his face. He turned back to the king.

"I would rather go with her, if it should please you, my lord."

"I'm afraid that isn't possible, son."

"I see." George looked up at Effie, and this time, it was he who gave her hand a shake. "Don't worry for me, Mama."

"If either of you—Euphemia Hargrave or Lucan Montague—fail to return with Thomas Annesley, the child heretofore known as George Thomas Annesley shall become a ward of the Crown, to be raised as I see fit. And both Darlyrede House and Castle Dare lands will be forfeit.

"Do not, under any circumstances," the king warned, looking down his nose at them, "return without him."

"But, my lord," Lucan began.

"Are my instructions unclear, Montague?" Henry snapped.

Lucan paused only a moment. "No, lord."

"Good. I will have this business resolved one way or the other. It has been too long, and I tire of it. Padraig Boyd," he called out suddenly. "As Thomas Annesley's only legitimate heir, and the one in most recent acquaintance with him, it only makes sense that I place you in custody so as to preclude any misguided ideas of aid for your errant sire. As your loyalty remains in question, your petition to enlist yourself in my army is denied. Believe me when I tell you that it is for your own good. A charge of treason is difficult to overcome. You are to remain within the apartment I have provided you, under guard. You shall not emerge lest you wish to take up residence in one of the cells."

Henry looked to the other men, bristling at the word of the forced captivity of their brother. "As for you, Lachlan Blair and Tavish Cameron, although you have no relationship with the accused, you are hereby officially warned against interfering. Do not misunderstand—I recognize you as Scots who have thus far committed no crime against me. Yet I feel I must avail of yours and your lovely wives' patience as my royal guests until Sir Lucan returns. I'm certain you shall continue to be quite comfortable in the same apartment, although, as you are guests, I will of course extend you the courtesy of freedom of Westminster grounds after Sir Lucan departs."

Effie didn't hear the last of the king's placating niceties as her face turned slowly toward the smirking, shriveled old hag still sitting before the dais. A murderous rage bubbled up from her guts, her breaths came in pants, and she felt her muscles gathering, readying…

But hands were on her biceps gripping her in the instant before she lunged, and Lucan Montague held her easily in place. The momentary madness left her with an icy rush.

What would have become of George Thomas had she acted so rashly?

"Are you well, Euphemia?" the king inquired sharply.

"Yes, lord," she choked out. "Quite well. Forgive me."

"Then kiss your son, and be gone from my hall at once."

It was too soon. Too sudden. These few moments with George Thomas were not enough to sustain her on this fool's journey.

She must be strong.

Effie crouched down once more and enveloped her son, her eyes squeezing back the tears. "Be a good boy, George Thomas," she whispered with a squeak. "Mind your lessons."

"Oh, I will, Mama," he promised. "But do come back soon."

"I will hurry back so quickly, you won't even know I've been gone." Her voice was reedy, like wind over the moors. "Do as the king says and give me a kiss now."

George pecked her cheek noisily and then went to the other side of her face to repeat the gesture. "That one's for Father," he whispered in her ear before he drew away.

"Come along, George," Caris Hargrave cooed in her haggish voice.

"No," Effie said, rising to her feet, her hand still on George's shoulder. "Not with her. I won't allow it."

"*You allow nothing in my court*!" the king shouted, the sudden volume and fury at odds with his heretofore composure. "I will do with the boy what I see fit, until you have fulfilled my commands!" He looked at Effie's son. "George Thomas, come to my side until your mother has gone, lest she lose her very mind and make a mistake that prohibits any chance of your profitable future."

"Yes, lord." George looked up at her and gave a little smile. "Don't worry, Mama. He is ever so kind. Truly."

Effie's heart cracked as she felt his small warmth withdraw. She caught sight of Iris Montague staring her down, and the woman who had married her brother gave her a single, solemn nod.

Lucan Montague bowed deeply. "Thank you, Your Grace." He glanced at Effie.

Effie curtsied stiffly, but could not bring herself to speak.

"You are dismissed," the king said.

Lucan took firm hold of her arm—perhaps too firm, Effie would later decide at the bruises that formed thereafter. But she also knew that it was only his guidance that allowed her to leave the hall on her own feet.

They came out into the crisp, cold, midmorning sunshine of the austere yard, and Effie's knees buckled as the huge doors closed with a thud of finality. Lucan Montague caught her up against him as the first wail came, and he held her on the threshold of Westminster Hall as she sobbed.

Chapter 6

Everyone in the motley band of criminals besides Chumley was waiting for them in the wharf yard when Lucan and Effie returned to the house on the Strand.

Gorman started toward Effie's horse before they had reached the sandy, damp plot, and Lucan could see the desperate concern on the burly man's face. "Where is George? Was he there?"

Effie nodded, her pale face startlingly blotched, her lips and eyes swollen. "He is with the king."

They were the first words Effie had spoken since they'd left court.

Winnie came forward to tug on Effie's skirt. She made a quick pair of hand motions, her high brow knit over her clear eyes as she looked up.

Effie reached down and took hold of the old woman's hand. "He is very well."

"What happened?" Gorman pressed as he caught the bridle, but Rolf brushed him aside and so Gorman went to place his hands at once on Effie's waist, swinging her down from the horse and holding her to his side in a familiar manner. "You've been weeping, so it can't be good news. What—?"

"Let's go inside," Lucan suggested, dismounting and turning Agrios over to Stephen. "Have Cook send some strong ale to the solar, if you would."

The man didn't so much as glance at the others gathered in the yard. "Right away, lord. Will you come through the front?"

"No, this way will be fine, Stephen. Thank you." Lucan turned and led the group through the low door into the kitchen and then through the twisting maze of arched passages that made up the cellar.

Another Warren, he thought darkly.

Up the narrow, dark staircase to the main floor he led them, to where the tall front room sat off to the right of the entrance hall. Lucan breezed through, his step hesitating only briefly when he saw the lanky Chumley slouching in one of the ornate, cushioned chairs. His eyes were open—even from across the room Lucan could detect their bright red color. His long, thin fingers held up his head at his temple, his elbow braced against the edge of a carved table top, which had been decorated for the winter season with a bowl of nuts.

Lucan didn't think he'd seen the man semi-conscious before noon more than twice.

A young kitchen maid appeared at the doorway, bearing a large tray supporting a wooden pitcher and a pair of matching cups. She slid the tray onto the table, glancing nervously at the lethargic Chumley. His lizard-red eyes caught hers.

"We'll be needing a brace o' cups, love," he said in his low, smooth voice. "P'haps a bit larger ones than the thimbles was sent, if you've a mind. Another pitcher, as well."

The maid's eyes grew wide, and she looked at once to Lucan, who nodded at her as he leaned his shoulder against the mantle of the fireplace, crossing his arms over his chest. No one else in the room was paying him the least attention—they were all gathered in an anxious semi-circle around Effie as she sat in the matching chair on the far side of the small table from Chumley. And so Lucan took the opportunity to observe, and to gather his own thoughts.

Rolf poured a tall draught of the ale into a cup and pressed it into Effie's hand.

She took a long drink and then lowered the cup to her lap, with her fingers wrapped about it securely. "George Thomas is at Westminster. I saw him and spoke to him. He is well. Very well, actually," she allowed in a quiet voice. "Caris Hargrave and Vivienne Paget were also there."

Lucan expected the group to gasp or exclaim or show some type of shock at this news, but it was as if Effie had reported nothing more than a casual observation of the weather. Rolf approached him with the other cup, and Lucan gratefully took it as the maid entered with the requested dishware.

She skittered out again quickly when Chumley gave her a wink and a "you're splendid, love."

"Why didn't you bring George back with you?" Gorman asked.

Effie swallowed visibly before she spoke, and yet her voice still sounded strangled. "I couldn't."

"These are surely made for children," Chumley growled, holding up one of the cups. It was even smaller than the ones the maid had initially delivered.

Gilboe snatched it from his hand and proceeded to pour.

Gorman insisted, "Why? Why couldn't you bring him?"

Effie raised her face at last, but it was to look across the room at Lucan—she couldn't bring herself to say it, he realized. Everyone turned to give him their attention, even as the rattling rush of nuts clattered onto the rug and rolled about the wood planks as Chumley then proceeded to fill the deep bowl with ale.

Lucan stated the facts of the situation as put to them by the king as concisely as possible.

Again, there was no cry of outrage from the group. It was almost as if they'd expected the worst, and this was not it.

Winnie sank down to her knees beside Effie's chair and stroked her hair, pulled her head onto her bony shoulder and cradled her cheek.

"Very well," Rolf said with a matter-of-fact nod at Lucan before looking to Effie. "We shall leave at once, of course. Where do we begin the search?"

Lucan felt his eyebrows rise. "Ah, well. I don't think that will be necessary. It has very little to do with you all. Perhaps it would be best if you returned to your home."

Everyone stared at him as if he had grown another head.

"Really, I mean we would attract unwanted attention if we were to attempt to gain Scotland together. Easy prey for..." Lucan broke off, awkwardly.

"Bandits?" Chumley offered helpfully.

"Well," Lucan stammered. "Yes. Bandits, I suppose."

"He isn't wrong," Gorman offered. "With seven of us..."

Gilboe nodded. "Yes, just so. We'll return to the Warren, right away."

Lucan was a bit surprised at this easy surrender, but only for a moment.

"Dana?" Gorman suggested. "And Bob."

"Bob?" Lucan repeated.

"Bob the Butcher's Boy," Gilboe offered with a gentle smile, as if that somehow clarified things. He then looked to Gorman. "James."

"We must have James Rose," Chumley murmured. He saluted with the bowl before bringing it to his lips again.

Winnie made quick motions with her hands.

Gorman nodded. "Kit Katey; yes, of course."

"Wait," Lucan interjected. "Who are all these people? They are people, are they not?"

Chumley belched. "They're not horses, love."

"You were unconscious most of the time in the Warren," Rolf offered. "There are many more of the family whom you didn't meet."

"You're suggesting we add *more* members to our party?" Lucan closed his eyes, held up a hand, and shook his head. "That's simply not possible. Time is of the essence, and we must travel quickly."

"We travel quickly," Gorman insisted.

Lucan tried to hold back his exasperation. "We'll attract attention."

"Isn't that what we want, though?" Gilboe asked, a confused expression on his face.

"What?" Lucan stuttered. "No!"

At Effie's side, Winnie's hands and fingers danced in the air, little slippery, sandpapery, smooth sounds.

"Yes," Rolf said with a nod. "I agree."

Gilboe smiled in satisfaction. "Precisely."

"Splendid." Chumley reached for the pitcher.

Lucan offered his palms, looking from face to face. "What?"

Effie spoke at last. "It can only be to our benefit for Thomas Annesley to know that his daughter is alive. Perhaps *he* will find *us*, which should save a good deal of time."

"I'll start at the taverns this night," Chumley offered. "There are six in the immediate vicinity of the Strand. By the time we leave on the morrow, word will already be spreading."

Lucan stilled and his eyes met Effie's once more. Did she know what she was doing? Did she realize that she was warranting Thomas Annesley's execution?

Of course she did, Lucan told himself. She would do anything for her son, even if it meant causing the unjust death of the father she'd never met. An innocent man who'd had his very life stolen from him. How could she?

Lucan reminded himself that Effie was a Hargrave, after all. Perhaps this was the portion of blood that was willing to allow a blameless old man to suffer so that she could have what she wanted.

But wasn't that what Lucan would do, as well? Surrender Thomas Annesley, a man he now felt he knew better than either of his own parents, a man wronged, in order to have a stretch of grass where Castle Dare had once stood?

"I don't agree that this is the best course of action," he said at last, hearing the strain in his own voice.

Effie stood from her chair. "Then don't come with us."

Lucan felt his head draw back as if she'd struck him. The air in the solar should have been thick with awkwardness, but the other observers only looked back at him plainly.

"This is my operation," Lucan announced calmly. "By order of the king himself, Effie Annesley is in my custody, and it shall be I who decides the manner in which we proceed." He looked to the bearded man at Effie's side, hoping to enlist support. "Perhaps Gorman will agree to be my advisor, if that better pleases you all."

"Ah, you've got it all wrong, love," Chumley murmured in dark delight. "Effie's our leader. She has been since she was a score. Old Robin left her charge of the Warren."

"Who is Old Robin?" Lucan looked back at the woman, and it was as if the tender scenes at Westminster of Effie with her son, Effie weeping in Lucan's arms, had been nothing more than a dream. She was, again, the woman who had shot him in the wood.

She ignored his question. "I don't care what the king has said. You'll not be my jailer and you certainly don't own me. I'll allow *you* to go with *us*, in thanks for finding us shelter in London. But don't undermine me, Lucan. I'll have you turned out, your precious reputation and worthless inheritance be damned." She drained her cup, set it down on the tray and swished from the room in her skirts just as confidently as if she had been in her woodland garb.

All the others followed her without another word for Lucan, although Rolf did give him a somewhat apologetic bow and a departing, "Lord."

All save Chumley, who still slouched in the chair, the deep bowl resting on his thigh. His chin was nearly on his chest as he openly regarded Lucan with something akin to amused curiosity in those bloodshot eyes.

"So that's the way she thinks it's going to be," Lucan stated.

Chumley chuckled. "Oh, no, love—that's the way it's going to be. And it's the way it should be. You want no other leading this charge, on that you can depend."

Lucan felt red to the tips of his ears—his neck throbbed as though it were on fire. "And what would an old drunk know of the ways of a charge handed down from the king? I daresay there's more to it than what you might hear around the piss pot in a whorehouse." Even as he spoke them, the atypically vulgar words left a distasteful feel on his tongue.

Chumley's eyebrows went up. "Hoo. Well, you might be surprised, Sir Lucan. I daresay, you just might yet be." He drained the bowl, tipping it up with both hands, and then set it on the table where it wobbled to a rattling standstill. "Let this old drunk give you a piece of advice that may or may not have been gleaned from around the piss pot in a whorehouse: Don't cross Effie. If you do, know there's not one of the family who won't cut you down. Cut you down dead. You're worth less than the shit on her shoes to any of us."

He winked at Lucan. "Including me, love."

Lucan's blood boiled. He was angry and humiliated, and had just been warned by a fellow who couldn't even stand during the day without first having imbibed of an entire pitcher of ale. He ought to seize up the man and toss him onto the Strand.

A corner of Chumley's mouth quirked up, as if he could read Lucan's thoughts. He waited.

Lucan also waited, his intuition clanging like a bell.

"Perhaps later?" Chumley said at last, and used the arms of the chair to push himself to his feet. He began walking across the rug, his gait now steady and sure. He quit the room, leaving Lucan alone at last.

* * * *

Lucan ate dinner alone that evening, all the band having deserted the house on the Strand for nearby taverns.

Lucan had not been invited.

He wasn't yet certain how he would proceed come the morning, when they were to once more depart for the northern reaches of England. He was mulling over his options when Stephen entered the dining hall and walked briskly to the side of Lucan's chair.

"A visitor for you, lord. He's come to the kitchen door."

"Who is it?"

"A soldier, lord. From Westminster, I believe."

"What does he want?"

"I don't know, lord. He wasn't forthcoming when asked. Shall I send him away?"

Lucan considered it with a frown. "No. No, of course not. Bring him through."

A moment later, Lucan's concern evaporated, and he gave a silent sigh of relief as the familiar form appeared. "Ulric, what are you doing here? Not been sent to arrest me, I hope."

"Nay, lord," Ulric said with a grin, coming near to Lucan's chair as he rose and clasping hands. "The king doesn't know I've come, and I suspect it'd be myself arrested if he should find out. I've leave for the evening, thanks to your return—on my way to find a bit of sport. But I have been first charged with delivering to you a parcel."

Lucan recognized the satchel right away as Ulric ducked from beneath the strap—old and faded and patched. He'd first seen it on the island of Caedmaray, and then for the last time at Steadport hall.

It was Padraig's.

Lucan took the bag from Ulric. "You can't know how glad I am to see this. Will you have a drink?"

"Nay, lord—I'm out the way I came, as quickly as I can manage it. The fewer them who see me, the better for us both."

"Quite, I'm sure," Lucan said, barely able to restrain himself from tearing open the flap and checking the bag's contents in that moment. "But do tell me, how are the sons of Scotland?"

Ulric grinned. "They aren't as impressed with His Majesty's hospitality as is young George Thomas."

"The old woman? Lady Hargrave—what's the word?"

Ulric shook his head. "I wouldn't know, lord."

"I understand," Lucan said gruffly. "I won't keep you, then. Thank you, Ulric."

The captain bowed and then turned and left the chamber.

Lucan slid the satchel onto the table, shoving aside the platter containing his forgotten meal. He loosened the flap and peeked inside the bag. A thickness of dark cloth greeted him, and Lucan pushed the doubled garment aside.

Iris's portfolio!

He noticed a folded piece of parchment slid behind the tie. Lucan freed it and opened the note, written in French.

Our apartments have been turned out twice since our arrival. Do not, under any circumstances, carry it with you. Trust no one.

All my love.

A feeling of disquiet washed over Lucan. They were searching the rooms at Westminster. Padraig was being watched by guards. Tavish and Lachlan were being politely detained in the palace.

It was obvious Henry was not taking any chances. And so where once Lucan thought the king had been an unbiased ally, it was clear that Henry must for now be considered an enemy of the mission. He'd made it very plain that he'd felt Thomas Annesley—and, perhaps to a lesser extent, Lucan—had made a fool of him and his judgement. He had two noblewomen crying murder of their husbands in his court, the child of an accused criminal in his care, and a guest wing full of England's acrimonious Scot neighbors. The lands of Darlyrede House and Castle Dare were on the line. Lands that could fall back to the Crown, to be doled out as favors to more agreeable, less troublesome nobles. And a forest full of robbers who had tormented Northumberland for more than a decade were running the streets of London, beneath his very nose.

Lucan refolded the note and set it aside. He reached into the satchel for the thick leather portfolio, but paused even as his fingers gripped the smooth, worn covering, his intuition once more ringing.

"Everything well, lord?" Lucan hadn't even noticed Stephen's return.

Trust no one.

Lucan nonchalantly withdrew his hand from inside the satchel, dragging out a bit of the dark cloth onto the tabletop.

"Yes, very well, actually," he said. "My captain has just returned some clothing of mine that I'd left behind in the barracks when last I was in London. I suppose he thought I would have need of them."

"Ah," the steward said. "Fortuitous, indeed. Now you will have something else to wear on your journey then, lord."

"Mmm," Lucan murmured noncommittally as he pushed the cloth back into the satchel along with Iris's note and fastened the tie. He hadn't told Stephen about the journey, and he was quite sure none of Effie's troupe had, either. Perhaps Stephen had never truly left any of them alone—only waited outside the chambers, listening to them all the while.

The steward stepped forward. "Shall I see it laundered?"

"No, I don't think that will be necessary. It will only get soiled at once, any matter." Lucan pushed back from the table and took hold of the strap. "I think I shall retire early tonight, Stephen. See that I'm not disturbed, if you would."

"Certainly, lord," Stephen said with a bow as Lucan walked around the man. He called after him, "Leaving on the morrow then, are you, lord?"

Lucan kept walking. "I've not yet decided."

"Very well. Good evening, Sir Lucan." The farewell faded as Lucan mounted the stairs in the entry hall and took them two at a time to Lady Margaret's bedchamber. Once inside, he bolted the door behind him and listened at the seam for footsteps on the stairwell, but all was silent.

He looked down at the satchel dangling from its strap, still gripped tightly in his fist.

Iris had said to trust no one, and in truth, there was no one he could trust. Not even Stephen, for God's sake!

Perhaps no one he *wanted* to trust, he corrected himself darkly. But there was one who had perhaps even more to lose than did Lucan were this information to fall into the wrong hands.

Blasted Effie Annesley.

Chapter 7

Effie was on her way back across the wharf alley from the privy house when she heard the stealthy footsteps on the damp, sandy gravel behind her. She whirled around with her blade at the ready.

Lucan Montague held up his palms in the dim, ambient light of the near-full moon. He was in his typical black garb once more, his slender, pale face and the strap of a satchel across his chest the only discernable features in the night.

"Easy," he said.

Effie slid her blade back in its sheath. "You're lucky I didn't gut you. What are you doing sneaking about in the middle of the night, accosting women in dark alleys?"

"Unless I wished to alert the staff, I had no other way to ensure I did not miss your return. I'd like a word. In private."

"Come to apologize, have you?"

"I've nothing to apologize for."

"Well, what do you want, then?" she demanded, crossing her arms over her bosom. The cider she'd drank that night and the lively company of the taverns had relaxed her, and she was feeling just kindly enough to indulge the pompous prat.

He gave the house a brief glance. "Walk with me a short distance if you would."

Effie sighed but fell into step an arm's length from the knight as they headed down the sloping alley toward the wharf.

He didn't make her wait. "I had a visitor from Westminster this evening."

Effie's heart stuttered in her chest. "About George?"

"No. My own captain, delivering to me this satchel from Iris, containing all of the intelligence about the Hargraves she was able to compile while posing as Lady Caris's maid."

"Ah, yes—the faithful Beryl. I wonder, does the king know that your family is so full of liars, Sir Lucan?"

"Of all people, I would think a woman born of the line of Vaughn and Caris Hargrave as well as the man who is most certainly now the most wanted criminal in all of England would be the last to cast disparagement upon another's lineage."

"Touché, I suppose. Any matter, I thought all the information had been lost in the fire?"

"Mine had," Lucan allowed. "The soldiers' quarters at Darlyrede House was the first structure to burn—all of my personal papers were inside."

"Iris was assisting you in your investigation, all the while?"

"I suppose she was, although I was unaware of it. I'd left her in France, and didn't know she'd absconded until she'd been in residence at Darlyrede for six months."

"It's surprising she would choose to leave the plush French accommodations in which Vaughn Hargrave installed the pair of you after Castle Dare burned."

"I wouldn't describe the abbey as plush," Lucan said with a frown. "Iris was supposed to remain there until I had secured a safe place for her to come home to. If something had happened to me, she would have a home at the abbey."

Effie hadn't been aware Iris Montague had been interred at an abbey, but the cider hadn't afforded her enough charity to admit to the man that she'd been mistaken. "Well, while I'm sure it was tempting to live the rest of her life as a nun, she obviously didn't have much faith in you to return. One might say it was a good thing she chose to take matters into her own hands. Padraig might not be alive otherwise. And you wouldn't have whatever information is contained in that satchel."

"Yes, true," he said mildly, surprising Effie. "Iris's portfolio contains scores of details about the Hargraves' lives that I could never have been privy to. Maps, timelines, accounts of guests, villagers. It's priceless, to both you and me." He paused. "Do you wish to examine it?"

"No," Effie said at once, trying to subdue the shudder that wanted to overtake her. "I've enough firsthand knowledge of the goings-on at Darlyrede. But why didn't Iris give the satchel to Henry?"

"The message she included told of the guest chambers at the palace being repeatedly searched. Perhaps she has reason to believe Henry is also not on our side."

Effie frowned. "Of course he's not on our side. If that satchel fell into the wrong hands, all the information could very well disappear before it could be presented in front of witnesses at court."

"Just so," Lucan agreed. "Which must be why she sent it to me for safekeeping until we can do just that. But she must also suspect I shall be followed—Iris warned not to travel with the satchel."

"So it couldn't be left at the palace, and we shouldn't take it with us." Effie thought for a moment and took a chance. "We might hide it in the Strand house until we return."

Lucan shook his head. "I don't trust the staff. Stephen, especially."

"Neither do I," Effie murmured, relieved.

Lucan appeared surprised. "What reason would *you* have not to trust them?"

"Primarily, I haven't been sleeping with their mistress. And also, one of the stable boys followed us about tonight," she admitted. "He wasn't very clever, but he was persistent. He stayed with us until we turned into the alley. Reporting to the steward, perhaps?"

"He must be," Lucan Montague replied. "Stephen is like God Almighty on the Strand. He runs the world along this stretch of the Thames when Lady Margaret is away."

"Who is *he* reporting to, though? His mistress is in Greece."

"It can only be someone at Westminster—who else would care? There are few in London of rank between Lady Margaret and the king, since her husband's death."

That gave Effie pause. "An important woman, your lover."

"Ex-lover," Lucan reminded her. "It was her husband who was powerful. A noble diplomat to the Mediterranean states. English by birth, but wealthy in his own right from his family roots in Greece. Lady Margaret still visits there often. The estate is marvelous."

"A more pleasant place to spend the winters, I suppose. On the Mediterranean," Effie allowed, clearly hearing the bite in her words.

But Lucan was oblivious to her bitterness. "It is."

Effie bristled at her envious and resentful feelings. Lucan Montague had been free to gad about the world with his mistress to warm, rich estates while his own sister had been locked away in a nunnery, and Effie and the family ran the Warren, trying to keep the countryside of Northumberland from starving, or worse. But she held her tongue as they walked a bit further along the wharf.

"I thought I might ask if you had any suggestions where to place the portfolio for safe keeping," he said.

"You want *my* advice?" she reiterated with a sideways glance.

"And Gorman's, of course."

"You know he isn't my husband, don't you?"

"I suspected as much. If you are the daughter of Thomas Annesley and Cordelia Hargrave, you're noble. No matter that Gorman comes from well-respected parentage, you could never have married him and hoped to claim so much as a splinter of Darlyrede House."

"That sounds rather mercenary," Effie said. "Perhaps I don't care one whit for Darlyrede and its holdings."

"First of all, I don't think that's true, if only for the benefit of your son. Secondly, if it is true, why *didn't* you marry him?"

He had managed to do her up in a trap of her own laying.

"My point is," she said, ignoring his question, "you didn't come to Gorman. You waited for me. In a dark alley. So that I nearly stabbed you."

"I've been recently and thoroughly informed of your sovereignty within the group, so one might say I chose to start at the top with my inquiry. You've already shot me, a second injury would be painfully redundant."

Effie chuckled. "Dear Chumley."

"I thought the old blighter was going to try me on after you left the solar."

"Be glad he didn't," Effie said.

This time it was Lucan who laughed. "You must have a very low opinion of the skills by which I secured my rank as a knight."

"Not at all," Effie said. "It's only that you would have been as a babe wielding a daisy on a long stem against Chumley."

"Oh, now I *am* offended."

She stopped, prompting Lucan to do the same. They faced each other on a little slope of cobbles going down to the gentle rush of the Thames. The moonlight rippled on the rounded stones and the air was crisp and taut and held back the smells of the day suspended in the sheer clouds wafting across the inky sky.

"Do you trust me, Lucan?"

"Not at all," he said at once.

"I don't trust you either," Effie replied, strangely pleased with his insulting answer. "And it's no secret that I don't happen to like you. But if we are to work together toward a common goal, we shall be placed in a predicament that would seem to force a certain level of dependence. A state of which I am in complete abhorrence."

"I find I must agree. Begrudgingly, of course."

"Of course. Very well. If we are in agreement, then I must advise you, if only for your own safety, that the drunkard you are so condescending toward is none other than Roger Cholmeley, Lord of Millsbury."

Lucan's expression did not change. In fact, he seemed to be carved from moon-washed stone. "You're joking. Roger Cholmeley was killed by the king's men after—"

"After he flew into a drunken rage and beat his wife and young daughter to death?" Effie finished.

"Worse than that. It was said that he—"

Effie cut him off again. "I know all too well what the rumors were, and still are."

"And I well know the reputation of Roger Cholmeley as one of the king's men. Lord Roger Cholmeley fought his way out of the midst of thirty Scottish soldiers at the Battle of Sark. He carried his own captain across his shoulders for twelve miles to safety and rescued his entire company. It's still talked about among the soldiers. *That* Lord Roger Cholmeley?"

"Yes."

"He can split a reed with a dagger at twenty yards?"

"Twenty-five, actually."

"He can kill a man with his bare hands and not leave a mark."

"Quite true."

"The same Roger Cholmeley who also drinks ale from a nut bowl and is hungover until sunset every day?"

"That Roger Cholmeley." Effie gave the man a moment. "He was away on business for the hold when his daughter went missing. His wife was found dead in their home. Roger was sought for the crime, but our man was already tracking his daughter. He found her, but was ambushed by the villains while trying to free her. They killed her in front of him and then left him there to die. But he was found by—"

"By the king's men," Lucan finished. "I know the horrible story well. Roger Cholmeley killed every man but one that day, and it was that last officer who ended the man's life, going over the side of a bridge with him into the Tees. Roger Cholmeley drowned as the current carried him and Archimbault away."

Effie shook her head. "No."

"Archimbault broke both of his legs in the fall. He's still considered a hero—a monster killer. He's made his life's labor from it."

"Archimbault's a coward and a liar. He jumped over the side of the bridge willingly, that's true, but it was to escape Chumley."

Lucan Montague turned and looked over the rolling, moon-sparkled water, obviously deep in thought. "It's very hard to believe, you must understand."

"Whether you believe it or not is your own choice," Effie said mildly. "But I thought you should know, in preparation for the day your mouth runs away with your big head again, leaving your arse behind. He'd surely kill you, and then I'd have to find somewhere to bury your body and that's more than I have time for, currently."

He turned his head to look at her with his lips parted in disbelief. And then he laughed.

Effie tried to suppress her answering smile. "I say we leave the satchel at the Warren."

"In the protection of wanted criminals?" Lucan's mouth quirked. "Perhaps not the best idea for ensuring the posterity of the information."

Effie sighed. "Then what say you?"

"I hesitate to put forth an opinion at the risk of undermining your authority, and then forcing you to procure a surreptitious gravesite."

"Lucan..."

Lucan held up a palm. "Alright. Regardless of Iris's caution, I think we have no recourse but to take it with us."

He had surprised her again. "I agree. There will be more careful eyes on it."

"Many more, if the conversation in the solar is any indication."

Effie ignored the comment. "I would trust any one of the family with George's life. If they know that the bag is to be guarded, guarded it shall be."

Lucan nodded. "I've no choice but to take you at your word. Very well. We shall depart at first light then. I bid you good night."

"Lucan, wait," she called out.

He stopped and turned halfway toward her, waiting.

"You've met my father."

He paused. "I have."

Effie swallowed. "What's he like?"

"He is very much like Padraig," Lucan said mildly. "Or Padraig is very much like him, I suppose."

"He's old now."

Lucan nodded. "Perhaps not in years, but in spirit. Yes."

"Do you think he killed my mother? I feel in my heart he couldn't have. Perhaps that's foolish." She didn't know why she was telling him this. He didn't care.

"No. I don't believe he killed Cordelia Hargrave. I don't believe he did any of the horrible things he's been accused of."

Effie nodded toward the bag across Lucan's chest, the faded leather bright in the moonlight against the knight's black, quilted gambeson.

"Because of what's in there?"

He almost smiled. "No. Good night, Effie." He walked into the mist of the alley yard and disappeared around the front of the house, leaving Effie alone outside the servant's entrance.

* * * *

The cook was nowhere to be seen when Effie passed through the kitchen. Lucky for her, Effie thought to herself; Lucan Montague's dismissal of her to the servants' quarters had soured her mood, although she wasn't sure why. She had intended on entering the house through that same door before Lucan had waylaid her. She had been in—well, if not a fine mood—a more optimistic frame of mind upon the family's return from the Strand Vicinity Tavern Tour. Lucan Montague had not insulted her, accosted her—he'd not even really argued with her. He'd left her in the same location in which he'd found her, and Effie had walked in the house on her own two legs through the very portal she'd intended.

She was certain her sour mood was still somehow Lucan Montague's fault.

She came to the door of the small chamber she was sharing with Gorman and pushed it open. He was already lying in bed, one arm behind his head, his eyes closed as the candle light played over his face and beard, deepening the shadows of his mouth and the folds in his loose shirt showing above the coverlet.

He opened his eyes at the door scraping closed. "Alright?"

Effie nodded. "Montague stopped me in the alley." She crossed the room, untying the laces at her sides. She couldn't wait to get out of those blasted skirts. "He's decided to go with us in the morning."

Gorman tapped his ear and then pointed at the door. His hands spoke: *Steward in the next room. He waited for you to return.* Aloud, he said, "I'm not really surprised."

Effie quickly signed out the basics of satchel's contents using the motions Winnie had taught them.

When she was down to her long chemise and hose at last, Effie crawled into the space Gorman created for her, where he lifted the corner of the blanket. This bed was twice as wide as the pathetic excuse for a cot in the scullery's cell, but it still meant that she had to curl into Gorman's side with her head on his chest in order to not roll out on the floor. She found she didn't mind.

"It's been nice sleeping together again," he murmured against her hair as if he'd read her thoughts, and then kissed her head.

"It has," she agreed with a smile. He was warm and solid and smelled like… like Gorman. She turned her face up to his.

He kissed her and Effie kissed him back.

"I still love you," she whispered against his mouth.

"I know," he said before he kissed her again.

It was like being home in the Warren again, and Effie could pretend that they were in the chamber they used to share; that George Thomas was asleep in his cot in the alcove. That it was the family against the world, good against evil, and they were winning.

They made love, and it was comfortable and good. And for a little while, Effie could forget that they were in London. She could forget that George Thomas slept under the same roof as Caris Hargrave. She could forget that, in the morning, she would begin the search to bring Thomas Annesley before the king.

He is very much like Padraig… I don't believe he did any of the horrible things he's been accused of.

She could forget about Lucan Montague.

Chapter 8

It was a more difficult journey to return to the Warren than it had been to reach London, thanks in part to cold, heavy, late February rains that fell like slushy nectar and turned the roads to deep, frigid bogs that threatened the very lives of the horses and their riders. Every day of travel left the caravan members soaked to the skin, shivering, and with numbed extremities that took painful hours to revive around a struggling fire. They abandoned the corpse wagon on only the third day.

Lucan kept a vigilant eye to the rear of the party as they traversed saturated fields carpeted with broken stalks—some still stiff and sharp enough to pierce a boot when walking the horses around the wallows, while thunder rumbled above the low clouds. He'd seen no sign of them being followed so far but, thanks to the rain, the days were all dark, foggy, and prevented a crisp line of sight.

Every shadow could be the hem of a cape, every crack of water falling through the trees a twig snapped by a trailing spy. It made Lucan unusually jumpy.

Streams and rivers had burst their banks, and the party were stranded in camps between villages on several occasions, waiting for water to recede from a bridge or crossing before they could carry on. The water usually lessened enough by morning, but the halfhearted sunrise often revealed that the bridge itself had followed the flood, and they had no choice but to travel upriver several more miles to find a crossing, the unspoken realization that entire days of travel were being wasted darkening the days even more so than the boiling storm clouds.

It had made the band rather irritable and sharp tongued, especially Effie Annesley. So when the dark, watery outline of an inn emerged from the misty rooflines of a village that night, a collective, relieved sigh rose up with the horses' foggy breaths.

Lucan shook water from his cape as he ducked through the doorway into the common room at the end of the party. The low murmur of conversation among the patrons ceased for a pair of heartbeats as they regarded the newcomers, but resumed in earnest a moment later. Effie Annesley caught his eye and gave him a curt nod, her blue eyes like wet slate in the flickering glow of the cozy room.

Lucan turned at the signal to seek the proprietor of the establishment—he was permitted to speak now, apparently. At many of the inns they'd passed through, Effie had forbidden Lucan to secure the lodgings, saying that once the owners heard his "prim language, he'll take us all for princes and rob us blind." This inn seemed more respectable, and so it was Effie's policy in such cases to appeal to the owner's sense of pride at the privilege of sheltering such a dignified guest and his entourage, as Lucan had been instructed to imply.

A short, plump old man with a shining pate in the center of a thick ring of white hair was driving the two handles of an enormous serving tray, as a strapping young man carried the front edge. They came to the end of one of the long trestle tables positioned on the stone slab floor and set the tray on its hidden legs. The old man began passing leather tankards down the line of seated patrons. Lucan crossed the floor toward him, weaving through the maze of tables.

"Excuse me, I'm looking for the innskeep."

The old man glanced at Lucan briefly, a smile affixed beneath his bushy gray mustache. "That would be me, lord. But a moment, I beg. There you are," he said with a groan as he stretched a bit further with a tankard to reach the last patron at the table.

He twisted his hands in a white length of cloth tucked into his apron, scrubbing at them as he turned to face Lucan fully at last. "Looking for a bed, are you, lord?"

The old man never lost his friendly expression even as his eyes took in Lucan's full measure in a blink, and Lucan would have wagered that the proprietor could have then given an accurate accounting of his person down to the cost of his boots.

"Yes. As well as accommodations for my household. The rain has grown tiresome."

The old man glanced over toward the bar where the band clustered. Chumley had already procured a tankard from a passing maid and the bottom was turned up. Said serving maid was currently pressing against

Gorman in a friendly manner. Effie and Rolf appeared engrossed in conversation, Winnie's hand tucked into the crook of Rolf's arm; only Gilboe watched Lucan openly, a broad smile on his face. He nodded at the proprietor encouragingly.

The innskeep looked back to Lucan. "Certainly. I've a chamber left. Board for your animals. Includes supper victuals for your servants. The men can bed down in the stable. Ale is extra."

"How much?" Lucan pressed.

The old man's grin widened before he answered.

Lucan thought it a rather polite robbery, but he handed over the requested amount of coin while managing not to roll his eyes, realizing that Effie only instructed Lucan to secure lodgings in establishments in which the rent was likely to be steep regardless of his "prim language."

The old man tucked the coins into a pouch hidden beneath the side of his apron opposite the towel. "I thank you. Top of the back stair, lord. Come to table when you are ready."

Lucan turned and nodded Gilboe toward the stairs along the rear wall of the common room as he started back across the stone floor. Gorman slid from beneath the serving maid's attention, plucking at Rolf's cape before following Gilboe toward the steps. Lucan took his place at the bar at Effie's side, opposite Chumley. Winnie tucked her hand beneath Lucan's arm, and he found he didn't mind.

"I'll eventually run out of money, you know," he advised Effie gruffly.

"Getting out of that rain tonight is priceless," she answered.

"Then *you* should have paid him."

Chumley lowered his tankard and Lucan's gaze followed Effie's in going to the man at once.

He reached for another from a passing tray, speaking in his low, smooth tone without looking at any of the trio directly. "Nine in the tavern. Three fine mounts with tack in the stable, although I cannot say whether they are travelling in company. Also four jacks, but only two with tack. Loft over the stalls with two bedrolls."

"Merchants," Lucan guessed. "With their wares. That leaves some well-to do travelers and perhaps some of the local villagers to make up the rest of the crowd."

Gorman inserted himself smoothly between Lucan and Effie.

"The chamber is safe. Only one other above the kitchens, reached by an outside stair. Occupied."

"They got the warm room," Effie lamented, and Lucan realized the chamber they'd rented likely overhung the exterior walkway between the stable and the tavern. It would be noisy and cold, but hopefully dry.

Gilboe shrugged. "No matter—good Sir Lucan's paid for it, hasn't he? The Lord has willed that we should eat without getting pissed on all night; let us proceed."

Lucan pressed his lips together and waited a moment before Winnie tugged him along to join the rest of the party at an empty table.

The food was bland, but warm and filling, the stew thick and congealing in the stale bread trencher. The ale was crisp and dry and so, like Chumley, Lucan availed himself of the generous serving maid each time she passed. He watched Effie Annesley more closely as the tankards emptied, as a blazing fire to Lucan's back lit up her features like a summer sunset. Her hair was drying, the little tendrils that had come loose from her customary plait curled up like honeysuckle petals around her jaw. She smiled often, laughed, leaned into Gorman with her palm on his chest.

Lucan then turned his attention surreptitiously to Gorman Littlebrook. He supposed the man would be considered handsome, with his wide, burly form, his thick, masculine beard and penetrating gaze softened by the deep crow's feet at the corners of his eyes. He was older than Lucan, but by how many years, Lucan could only guess. Rolf's only son—only child. It was said that Darlyrede's steward's boy had likely died years ago after being caught stealing and then disappearing during the ensuing chase. It had all occurred before Lucan had been to France, and so besides a week or two of gossip amongst the servants at Castle Dare, he'd heard nothing more said of it. The only thing Lucan could definitively recall was that Gorman Littlebrook was presumed to have died, bringing both shame and grief—not to mention a debt—to his father. But yet, here Gorman was, alive, sitting next to Rolf Littlebrook, who had yet to offer any explanation to Lucan.

Lucan found he was suddenly a bit offended, and so to prevent his thoughts turning maudlin, he let his fuzzy gaze wander around the table further.

Gilboe... what sort of religious house would foster such a strange man? And where *were* his eyebrows?

Chumley... the deadliest man in England? Surely not.

Winnie... was she a witch? Her mannerisms seemed too polished. Perhaps she'd killed someone she was trying to heal.

Or someone she'd meant to curse.

Either everyone at Lucan's table was stark raving mad, or Lucan was.

He gave a soft snort and took another tankard. They weren't talking to him, any matter. The conversation went on about people and places with nonsensical names, events that Lucan knew nothing about, and no one cared to explain them to him. Likely this was much the same stuff as they discussed around the fire at camp, but Lucan wasn't forced to be in such proximity to them at those times. No matter; he didn't want to hear them now, either.

"Nunch of bonsense," he muttered under his breath. "Bollocks." He'd just go to bed.

Lucan stood up and was pleased at the lightness in head. He shuffled out from the chute of the bench and began walking toward the narrow, tilted staircase along the back of the tavern.

"Ho, now—leaving us?" Chumley's voice called out and then a moment later a hand clapped on Lucan's shoulder, effectively turning him about and walking him back toward the table. "We'll have none of that, love. Making merry yet, we are."

Lucan halted. "I don't wish to make merry. I wish to go to bed."

Chumley laughed and then leaned his head closer to Lucan's. "We don't go off alone in places like this, you see."

"Places like this?" Lucan challenged, looking around broadly. "You mean respectable places? Are you afraid one of you might catch morals if left alone too long?"

Chumley threw back his head and laughed as if he'd never heard anything funnier in the entirety of his life. "By God, he's got it!" he shouted toward the table gaily, but his fingertips dug into Lucan's shoulder, as he murmured. "You're being watched, love."

Lucan glanced at the drunkard's eyes and saw the flash of sincerity there, and it did much to sober him.

"Where?" Lucan asked as he sat down in the space made for him between Effie and Gorman.

Chumley pushed a fresh tankard across the table toward him. "In the corner near the hearth. Do you recognize him?"

Lucan half rose as if adjusting his seat and looked in the direction that had lay behind him where he'd previously sat. He saw the man Chumley meant, and he was indeed staring Lucan down in a very obvious manner.

Lucan spoke into the tankard as he raised it. "I've not seen him before." He feigned a sip. He'd have to keep his wits about him now.

"Hired," Gorman muttered.

Rolf nodded. "We can't let that satchel out of our sight tonight."

"And we must be rid of that questionable guest." Effie looked at Gilboe, who had been smiling and nodding all the while in agreement. "Bannockburn Protocol?"

"Hmm." The monk looked thoughtful for a moment, gazing about the room casually. "It's possible," he said at last.

"Wait," Lucan asked, shaking his head a bit in an effort to clear it further. "What's a Bannockburn Protocol?"

"If we tell you what it is, it won't work," Gorman replied.

"If you don't tell me what it is, I won't participate," Lucan warned.

"That's the beauty of it, lord," Gilboe insisted with hushed excitement.

Lucan waited. "What…?"

Gilboe raised his nonexistent brows. "What?"

"What's the beauty of it?"

Effie buffeted him with her shoulder. "Just drink your drink, Lucan."

"I really don't think I shou—"

Effie took hold of the tankard before him and placed it into Lucan's hand, pressing his fingers around it. Her skin was cool and smooth and sent a little fissure of unexpected lightning coursing into his abdomen.

"Shut up and drink."

Lucan clenched his teeth together for a moment, his head cocked. He wasn't used to taking orders from anyone, let alone a woman who had already done him lasting harm, and one whose touch elicited an unwanted physical reaction from him. But he raised the tankard to his lips and took a reluctant sip, while surreptitiously glancing at the man in the corner again. The conversation among the band members started up once more as if they'd never been interrupted.

Madness.

The man looked away just as Lucan's gaze fell on him. Dark hair beneath his hood; likely dark eyes to match what might be olive coloring, although it was difficult to tell for certain with the shadows of the corner wrestling with the flickering light of the hearth. His clothing was nondescript; Lucan couldn't tell the quality of the man's footwear from where he sat.

Now Lucan's bladder was insisting he excuse himself. As he had just recently thought he was preparing for bed, he'd planned on stepping through the rear door of the tavern before heading up the stairs to his chamber. The delay and the added drink had increased the urgency he felt, but he didn't wish to incur the inquiries as to his intended destination by the woman sitting at his side, although he wasn't at all sure why he cared that Effie Annesley knew he needed a piss.

The mere thought irritated him so that he stood immediately and stepped over the bench. "Excuse me," he murmured, and remembered the phrase used by the soldiers. "Checking the horses."

He expected someone to follow him, but only Chumley glanced at him before breaking into a hearty guffaw, apparently in response to something Rolf had said. The whole band broke out in loud laughter, causing the other patrons to glance over at their table.

So much for getting away inconspicuously, Lucan thought. At least none of them had offered to accompany him to the weeds.

Lucan pushed into the dark drizzle behind the inn, fat droplets of rain cascading from the thatch at the corner of the dwelling and splattering noisily into a run-off ditch. He reached beneath his gambeson and adjusted his trousers to accomplish the task he'd come out for. After finally becoming mostly dry and comfortable while inside the inn, the cold night air was refreshing and did much to clear his head from the fuzzled, cozy atmosphere of the tavern, and he took a deep breath as relief began to wash over him.

He was just finishing his sigh when a muffled "oof" behind him in the darkness made him start, but occupied as he was, he could do little more than glance over his shoulder.

"Who's there?" he demanded.

There was a loud crack; a moan. Splashing sounds, like boots in puddles accompanied various thuds and hollow blows. A sound like fabric ripping.

"*Son of a whore*," a man's voice lamented, closely followed by a panicked whoop.

"No, no, no!" someone argued shrilly.

Lucan strove to finish his business and redress. "Who goes there?" he asked again, whirling around and laying hand to the hilt of his sword, stepping toward the darkness.

He was nearly run over by a charging horse, a bare foot or some such solid appendage catching him near the collar bone as it was, and sending him staggering back through the mud. Lucan watched the departing animal as it raced around the far side of the tavern and disappeared, something bulky and pale laid across the saddle.

Two dark, hooded figures appeared out of the inky drizzle and Lucan raised his sword. "Stop where you are," he warned.

One of the men pulled off his hood: Gorman.

"No cause for alarm, Sir Lucan. Our spy has been asked to take accommodations elsewhere." He tossed an object at Lucan.

Lucan caught it with a jingle—it was obviously a purse heavy with coin.

"That should take care of tonight's lodgings," Chumley said as he removed his own hood and tucked it into his belt. His left arm carried a dark bundle of some sort. "I'm keeping the clothes though—not had a new suit in a year or more."

Gorman clapped Lucan's shoulder as the two men from the Warren passed back toward the tavern. "Good work."

Lucan stood in the quiet drizzle for another pair of moments, his sword in one hand and a purse of stolen coin in the other, while his ale-slowed mind attempted to catch up to the events.

"I was bait," he realized aloud to no one at all.

Chapter 9

By the third day, after leaving the tavern where the suspected spy had been routed, the earth was at last wicking away the standing water from the roads, but the torrential rains had been replaced with bone-chilling winds. All the land was encased in fairy-light ice and even though the sun seemed to shine down ferociously, sending out fiery arrows of blinding refractions through the crystal-laden boughs, every breath seared Effie's lungs and her mount's mane tinkled as they drew nearer and nearer the Warren.

Leaving London—leaving George Thomas—had been one of the hardest things she'd ever done. The pull of him was like water over a falls: nearly insurmountable. The days on the road had distracted her, allowing her to concentrate on nothing more than their intermediate destination, but now that they were within a mile of home, slowly traveling single-file under the weight of ice in the south of Northumberland, George haunted her again.

This is where we found the berry patch last fall...

There is the lake overrun with frogs and slippery, green logs...

The path to the left leads to the spring...

Effie's head hung lower as her horse instinctively followed Gorman's on the right hand trail, almost as if she couldn't face seeing anymore of the landmarks that punctuated the life of her little boy. Her eyes filled with tears—hot in the frigid wind.

"Are you unwell?" Lucan Montague's voice called out from behind her.

Resentment kindled in her breast. Unwell? What would he know of it? He didn't care about her, or about George, or about any of them.

But she only shook her head and put him off with a wave.

They arrived at the mouth of the Warren at last. The lookouts must have heralded their return, for the sloping entrance to the cave was filled with family expressing relief at their return, and the despair that had briefly overtaken Effie sank below again as she donned the mantle of her role.

Dana was at her side helping to pry her from the saddle, sheets of ice sliding from her cloak like a shedding of skin. Effie found herself in a crushing embrace.

"Thanks be to God," Dana's raspy voice praised. "Where is George Thomas?"

"He is safe," Effie assured them all in a voice raised to reach the entirety of the group. "But he is being held by the king against my return with Thomas Annesley." She tried to keep her voice from breaking.

There were no gasps, no cries of outrage. These were a people who could no longer be shocked at the evil and unfairness in the world.

"Let's go inside and get you warm," Dana murmured. "And you will surely tell us what we must do."

The Warren gave her power. Sitting in the Cathedral around the roaring fire, eating good food in the midst of the people who were her family, Effie quickly regained her strength and her resolve.

She could almost even forget the knight sitting on the periphery of the group, watching her closely with his cool stare while Gorman gave those gathered an outline of the situation and Effie filled in the details.

Bob the Butcher's Boy offered the first question, his round, pale face splotched with freckles beneath his startlingly orange hair giving him the appearance of one much younger. "Do we know where Thomas Annesley is?"

Chumley answered. "We've set the word among the taverns. The rumors so far have been only what we'd expect—he's been seen here, there; he's dead; he's absconded to France. None of which we suspect are true."

"He's likely returned to Scotland," Lucan Montague offered, and all eyes turned to him. "It's where he's made his home the last thirty years—longer than he ever resided in England. If not on Caedmaray, then perhaps in the area around the mainland village of Thurso."

"That will take weeks to reach in this weather." Bob frowned.

"It can't be helped, I'm afraid," Gorman said, and the authority and diplomacy in his voice made Effie proud. "We'll take roughly the route Thomas himself traveled when he left Darlyrede House, pausing at Effie's brothers' homes to leave explanations of their delay with their houses. Effie's identity as Thomas Annesley's first-born child has been revealed, but whether Tommy will take it for a hoax or not is unknown. We've been careful on our journey from London, but by the time we cross over the

Borderlands into Scotland, word will have spread. Rolf will stay behind in the Warren, both to preserve his reputation and position, as well as continue on the work here. Winnie, also, will remain."

Effie glanced at Lucan Montague and saw the furrow between his eyebrows. Her attention was drawn back to the group as Winnie stood, her hand motions compact and brief.

I'm going.

"We don't know how long we will be away," Effie warned the woman. "And it's been a difficult journey for you already."

Winne inclined her head graciously, even as her hands flew. *I understand. But what if someone gets shot through the foot?*

Every gaze in the hall turned to regard the knight.

"What?" he demanded.

Gorman leaned closer to Effie's shoulder. "She's right, you know. It won't look well on you if he should die next time."

"I demand to know what you're saying about me," Lucan insisted.

Effie sighed—Gorman was right, of course. "Not everything is about you, Sir Lucan. Very well, Winnie."

"If I may preclude further argument," Gilboe interjected with a humble bow before addressing the family. "We have already considered members of our little pilgrimage, as it were."

"As always, anyone called upon can refuse," Chumley interjected. "This promises to be a dangerous expedition."

A sullen looking young man leaning against the rear stone wall called out. "Might we get on with it? Or must Chumley mother us all night?"

"You, James Rose, are one," Gilboe informed the young man.

The youth looked neither surprised nor flattered. "Well, I should think so."

"Dana," Gilboe went on.

Dana gave a little bounce and clapped enthusiastically. "Oh! How wonderful!"

"Kit Katey?"

The woman raised her slender arm from her seat beyond the fire. Her shiny, straight black hair flowed like water over her shoulder and her almond shaped eyes were clear and sparkling. "Yes, Effie. I will go with you."

"And Bob," Gilboe finished, prompting the red headed butcher's boy to clench his fist in triumph. "With Chumley, Effie, Gorman, Sir Lucan and myself, that makes our party ten. Small enough to travel quickly—"

"And large enough to cause problems," James Rose interjected with a smirk.

Effie had to smile at him.

"We leave with the sunrise," Gorman informed everyone. "I suggest you all pack carefully and sleep warm tonight—it shall likely be the most comfort you'll have for several weeks. Those leaders remaining behind, please see me and Rolf in the gallery."

Dana left Effie with a bone-crunching, one-armed embrace before departing at Gilboe's side, their arms linked and their heads leaned together. Chumley sauntered away at once for the barrel. Winnie became enveloped in the group of young women of the Warren that included Kit Katey.

Which left Effie standing alone, her gaze going unbidden to Lucan Montague. He was already watching her, of course. Sitting on his low stool, his bowl suspended between his knees by long, limp fingers, the food within largely forgotten.

Where was that weeping boy she had witnessed those many years ago? Had his connection with the Hargraves killed him? Or was he still there, somewhere inside the cool, selfish man staring at Effie? Could he still feel pain? Loss?

Effie didn't think so.

"Was there something you wanted, Sir Lucan?"

He paused a little too long. "No."

Effie walked toward him. "That's not true. You're near to bursting with questions."

Lucan shrugged and scraped at the remnants of his meal with the wooden spoon. "One does wonder how this myriad collection of criminals would come to take up residence in a cave with a secret Lady of Northumberland."

She was rather surprised that these were the thoughts that had occupied him. "You think we're all criminals?"

"Aren't you?"

It was Effie's turn to shrug. "I suppose we are now. It wasn't that way for most of them, though."

"How?"

Effie chuckled. "I'll just tell you everything about them, shall I? So you can report it to the king and earn your rewards."

"Forgive me," he said suddenly, and Effie had to purposefully press her lips together to keep her mouth from falling open. "I wasn't interrogating you; I've done nothing but collect information for several years now. It's a habit I may well be stuck with for the rest of my life. I was only curious as to what crimes they'd been charged with."

"So you know what blow to expect?"

"No," Lucan replied easily. "Because I think I recognize some of the names from Iris's portfolio. Persons gone missing from Northumberland."

Effie's stomach clenched. "I doubt that."

"James Montrose."

"We've no one here by that name."

"No, but you have a James Rose, who would fit the age and description of a boy gone missing from his well-to-do merchant family."

Effie's eyebrows rose reflexively. "His parents reported him to be missing?"

"His grandfather did," Lucan clarified, watching her too closely for Effie's liking. "Years ago."

She must be more careful. "Well, even if it was him, what crime could he have committed? A boy running away. It happens."

"Like you did, you mean?" That piercing stare never left her. "You sound like Vaughn Hargrave's defenders."

"How dare you?"

"Why would young James Montrose have run away from a family that had just opened a very successful business in York? His future was promising beyond the vast majority of untitled youth. Why would he forsake all that to live in a cave?" His gaze swept around the hall, one long-fingered hand opened toward her in appeal. "If he'd only been lost, wandered away, he would have eventually come upon *someone* and solicited help to be reunited with them. Unless perhaps someone prevented his return. Someone from here, perhaps?"

"You've no idea what you're talking about. We in the Warren are a family," Effie said evenly. "Not that you would know anything about what that means."

"Very little, you're right," Lucan allowed. "My parents were killed in the fire that destroyed Castle Dare."

"I know that," Effie snapped, unable to keep the image from her mind of a young Lucan, his sooty cheeks streaked by tears, when it had always been his hatefulness of that night she'd remembered. "You seemed to have managed quite well under my grandfather's wing."

Lucan stared at her again, saying nothing, but Effie could tell that his mind was working, and it gave her a foreign feeling of wariness.

"Don't threaten anyone in my care with your ridiculous theories, Lucan," she warned. "George Thomas's safe return is my priority now, true. But only just behind him are any one of the people who live in the Warren."

"I'm not threatening anyone, Effie," he replied quietly. "I simply don't think you've been hiding away in this cave waiting for Thomas Annesley to return."

She waited a pair of heartbeats. "See to your horse." She turned and walked toward the arched passage that would lead to her and Gorman's chamber, realizing she had begun to shake.

Effie Annesley had not been known to exist since the night that Euphemia Hargrave had disappeared. She had been a legend, a ghost, in the Northumberland forests. She'd never been born—her parents had never held her. No one could discover her, because no one had known of her presence.

Tommy had fled Darlyrede House barely more than a boy more than thirty years ago. He'd gone into Scotland and eventually made his way to a remote fishing island where he'd lived in anonymity for most of his adult life. And yet, thirty years later, Lucan Montague had managed to find him.

And now that same investigating knight had managed to stumble into the midst of the deepest, darkest pit of evil that had all but consumed Northumberland—and it wasn't the Warren. One he'd never even cared look hard enough to see and even now had no idea it surrounded him. From what Effie knew of Lucan Montague thus far, he would not rest until he had found what he was looking for.

Effie could only hope that he was looking for the truth.

* * * *

Lucan set the wooden bowl on the stone floor and rose from the stool, walking across the cavernous hall toward the upward sloping entrance passage. His footfalls were swallowed up by the echoes of commotion the inhabitants made while conversing and preparing for departure. No one paid him any heed as he left the cathedral.

He slowed halfway up the entrance passage, just as the walls curved to the left. Gorman's voice carried to him.

"—until we are well past. Tomorrow night."

"Who is there that we should warn?" a voice unfamiliar to Lucan asked.

"None." The single word spoken in Rolf's voice was immediate and final. "If you think to raise alarm, never return here. I will cut you down myself."

"Dad," Gorman cautioned in a low voice.

Silence lingered for a moment.

"I meant no disrespect, Rolf. I only thought perhaps some of the servants—"

"There is no need to speak of it further," Gorman intervened. "The plan is set. Only send word to the tavern if something goes amiss. Ah, Sir Lucan."

Lucan had walked into the midst of them casually, not wishing to stymie the conversation, but he knew the group was wary of him already. Combined with Effie's opinion that Lucan was interrogating her, Lucan couldn't risk an accusation of eavesdropping.

"Forgive my interruption," he said. "Effie's given orders that I should care for Agrios." Everyone watched him as if waiting for him to continue. "My only other visit to this domicile occurred when I was largely unconscious, so I fear I wasn't as attentive as I would normally be when one takes command of my mount."

Rolf looked confused. "Lord?"

"I've no idea where the horses are kept."

The group seemed to give a collective, silent sigh of relief.

"I think Rolf has things sorted—I'll take you," Gorman said. He walked past his father with a clap on the shoulder and Rolf slowed his son's progress by only a moment in reaching up and grasping Gorman's forearm firmly. They shared a solemn meeting of the eyes, and then Gorman joined Lucan in striding back down the throat of the cave.

"What did you mean by Rolf preserving his reputation and position by staying behind?" Lucan asked straight away. "Certainly not that Padraig Boyd might be loath to employ him at Darlyrede House in the future."

"Why not?" Gorman suggested. "If the king and Caris Hargrave have their way, Thomas Annesley will be executed. I don't think it likely that Padraig will thank us for that."

"He knows Rolf has nothing to do with this," Lucan said with an uneasy frown. "If he cast guilt upon everyone under the king's directive—"

"*You too, my child*?" Gorman interjected with a grin.

Gorman had read his thoughts, and the comment surprised him. Who was this man, presumed dead for so many years, quoting Greek from a betrayed emperor? A man whose own father had long held a position of power in one of the wealthiest holds in all of England. A man who had the love of Effie Annesley?

Gorman indicated with a hand near Lucan's arm toward a long, slender shadow in the corridor wall. "This way."

It was another passage, curving and sloping to the left, the uppermost parts of the ceiling hairy with roots. A trickling stream with thin shards of ice at its edges crossed the path to crawl along the wall into the darkness, and the far side was still wet with hoof and boot prints.

"I walked right past it," Lucan couldn't help comment.

"It's well-suited for our needs," Gorman agreed. "There is a hidden paddock just beyond the ridge for grazing in the good weather. We keep few animals though, so they can be cared for in secret if we are unable to leave the Warren for any reason."

"The—gallery, is it? It's the only entrance?"

Gorman grinned at him. "What think you?"

"I think not."

The grin widened. "It is certainly the most convenient entrance."

They reached an open chamber where a rather tidy scene of wooden stalls and troughs comprised the stone stable, the smell one of dung and torch and well-dried sweet grass and minerally water. A pair of children not much older than George Thomas was tending the animals—the horses from their journey, several goats. The children rose from their tasks to stare at Lucan, their brushes stilled.

"Good evening," Lucan greeted them.

They only continued to watch him closely.

"This is Sir Lucan," Gorman supplied. "He's come to care for his horse—that great, black beast, there. What's he called, Sir Lucan?"

Lucan knew that Gorman Littlebrook was well aware of his horse's name. "Agrios. His name means 'wild' in Greek. I named him thusly because he was trapped as a colt from the wild."

The children continued to stare at him, motionless.

Gorman spoke again. "Sir Lucan won't harm you. Carry on."

The children dropped back to their work at once, as if Lucan had ceased to exist.

"Don't be offended if they aren't interested in idle chatter," Gorman murmured as he showed Lucan where all the supplies were located. "They're careful of strangers. Especially men."

"Are their parents here?" Lucan asked.

"Ben's mother is. Have you everything you need?"

Lucan knew he was missing very large pieces of information, but he didn't wish to push Gorman too quickly. If Lucan made an enemy here, he was even more likely to have a dangerous journey north on the morrow.

"It's seems that way. My thanks, Gorman."

"I'll see you in the cathedral, then." He turned to go.

The clattering of brushes falling into buckets drew Lucan's attention and he turned to see the two children linking hands before scurrying up the narrow corridor after Effie Annesley's lover. The girl dared glance over her shoulder at Lucan with narrowed, suspicious eyes as the boy pulled her along by her hand. The thumb of her other hand was in her mouth.

They weren't wary of him—they were terrified.

Lucan stood for a long time staring up the black passageway where only the sound of cold trickling water could be heard beneath the peaceful and tired sighs of the animals.

A picture was forming. And Lucan didn't like the outline of it at all.

Chapter 10

They rode northwest out of Northumberland. By unspoken agreement, they avoided the section of road that ran before the ruins of Darlyrede House—or perhaps Gorman had predetermined it away from her hearing. Either way, Effie was thankful—she had no desire to gaze upon that place of nightmare and suffering while en route to retrieve Thomas Annesley.

The first known survivor...

Effie shook herself and rode on through the lightening gray mist of the wood.

They should cross over into Scotland before sunset, and pass the night at the safest place in the world outside of the Warren. There they would gather whatever supplies were lacking, and wait for word from Rolf.

The White Swan hadn't yet existed when Tommy escaped Darlyrede, she mused to herself. It had been naught but borderland scrub, dark and cold, the same time of year that the party of the Warren now set off. Thomas Annesley had been alone, wounded—so young. And no one had believed he hadn't committed the terrible crime that chased him.

No one had believed him.

Effie glanced at Gorman on her left as the party slowed and bottle-necked at a stream crossing.

There had been no one to help Tommy, unlike the others who'd come after him. And even now, Effie would not help him. She would lead him at last to the slaughter.

Effie turned her attention back to the road and led the way over the bridge, thundering up the looming hill of pale green winter grass.

Only George mattered now. And nothing nor no one would change her mind—not Thomas Annesley, not the king, and certainly not Lucan Montague.

* * * *

The White Swan looked no different to Lucan than the occasion of his only other visit, at least a pair of years ago. He'd only stayed for a single night, but he remembered the smiling couple that had welcomed him and the clean, bright interior. It was an inn, true, but one oddly unsoiled and cheerful as a setting for ale and food and socializing and travelers seeking other climes. It had been…wholesome, in a strange way that wasn't typically attributed to inns.

There wasn't even a woman to be bought.

The wide windows were not shuttered even in the depths of winter, only covered over with thicknesses of pale skins to keep out the chill and wet, so that the whitewashed interior gave the illusion of perpetual spring inside the thick, daubed walls. Two hearths on opposite ends of the common room blazed, and the air was scented with the perfume of hops and dried lavender and rosemary. Lucan couldn't help but sigh in pleasure as the group entered the common room, the setting sun turning the white window squares as rosy as the stained-glass panes of a cathedral.

The wifely half of the owners called out to them at once, and Lucan remembered her cheerful disposition right away. "Good evenin' to ye." Her eyes were wide as they swept the group, ending at Lucan, and then went at once to Effie. Her red hair was piled high beneath her kerchief, and her matronly bosom swung as she wiped at the wooden surface. "Have ye come for a *meal*?"

Effie's mouth curved in a smile, showing Lucan a glimpse of those creases at the corners of her eyes again, which he found oddly fascinating. "It is well, Mari—he's with us."

The woman tossed the rag to the countertop at once and came around the bar, calling behind her as she went, "Gale! *Gale!* 'Tis the family!" She reached Effie and embraced her, kissing her cheek loudly, and then proceeded to do the same with each member of the party, locking into an extra-long embrace with the Asian-looking Kit Katey. "My little snow drop," Lucan thought he heard the proprietress whisper.

At last she came to Lucan. "Yer new," she said with narrowed eyes that were glistening, perhaps with unshed tears. "And yet, I've seen ye here before, have I nae?"

"Madam," he said with an awkward bow. "I can indeed claim the pleasure of staying in your fine establishment."

"Aye, I remember you. It's been a bit, though," Mari said, working through her memory. "'Twas nearly summer—the strawberries were in. But not last. You stayed one night, and had a great, black beast with you."

Lucan was surprised. "Indeed."

She eyed him up and down. "A little thicker then, were ye nae? Have ye been ill?"

Effie laughed. "Mari, this is Sir Lucan Montague, a knight of King Henry. He's accompanying us on a journey north."

"A knight, are ye?" the woman said with widened eyes. She gave a flinch of a curtsey. "How do?" She looked over her shoulder then and bellowed, "*Gale*!" so that Lucan fancied his hair fluttered.

"Come in, come in," Mari continued in more dulcet tones, gathering the group toward the cluster of tables in the floor as a mother hen gathers chicks under her wings. "I'll bring out the ale and—och! There you are, your buggery old goat."

Effie had been about to sit, but rose once more to be enveloped in the disproportionately bulging arms of the middle aged man who came through the back doorway, a long white apron covering his front.

"Effie, lass," he said warmly. He clasped forearms with Gorman and Chumley, while giving a hearty, "Lads," toward the remainder of the group. He touched Kit Katey's cheek gently. "Dearest."

"This is Sir Lucan Montague, Gale," Mari said pointedly, glancing at him. "He's an *English knight*."

"That so?" Gale said and approached Lucan with his hand out. Lucan took it and gritted his teeth at the man's massive grip. "Eh now, wait a bloomin' moment—I know you."

Lucan opened his mouth, but Mari beat him to it. "He's stayed here before."

Lucan opened his mouth again.

"Last summer," Mari offered.

"That so?" Gale said. "Well, sit down, all! I've a fine, warm stew all but ready." Everyone sat, save the dark-haired woman, who seemed wont to hover near Mari.

"Lamb?" Gorman asked the proprietor.

Gale shook his head, thick with black hair that flowed back from his lined forehead. "Nary a one, Gorman. Nae for weeks."

Lucan's intuition prickled—this wasn't a query about the contents of the stew Gale had made, Lucan was certain. But it was yet the dead of winter—why would Gorman Littlebrook be asking after a lamb?

Gorman nodded and pulled his chair forward a bit by grasping the seat between his thighs. The rest of the group seemed to relax.

"You might not see any more for a while," Effie said.

Mari crossed herself, prompting Gilboe to do the same. "Pray God, never. What have you come for?" she asked, and Lucan noticed she kept glancing at him suspiciously.

"We're on our way north, to find my father," Effie said. Mari and Gale looked at each other, but said nothing as Effie continued. "We thought we'd stop here for supplies before continuing on."

"Well, then. That's verra fine," Gale declared. "Come along, Brother Gil—you can aid me in dipping out the pitchers."

"You bless me," Gilboe said with a grin as he rose, winking at Chumley.

"Don't drink it all," the man muttered. "I know you religious types."

The monk departed the common room at Gale's side, and Lucan noticed the black-haired woman had gone ahead of them toward the back of the inn.

"We've nae seen her in so long," Mari said in happy breath. "She looks well. Is she well?"

Effie nodded. "She's very well."

Lucan felt awkward again. It was very clear that the people gathered at the White Swan this evening had a history together, but Lucan couldn't for the life of him figure out what it could possibly be. Neither Mari nor Gale seemed to be the sort to be taken for criminals, and the very nature of the group meant that there were no easy parallels to be drawn between any of the members. Lucan was the odd one out, but he thought it madness—they all should have been odd ones out, to each other. None of them were alike, in the least.

What commonality could they possibly share?

His twisting thoughts were interrupted by the return of Gilboe and the others, bearing trays of cups and tankards and many pitchers. As the group passed them about the table, Gale returned, this time with a dozen wooden bowls emitting thick, delicious-smelling steam. As the windows darkened fully, the talk turned to stories and jokes and Lucan was drawn into the fringes of the group, so that he forgot his earlier suspicions.

The bread was crusty and fresh, dense and seeded, and Lucan couldn't help the hum of appreciation as he chewed the chunk he'd dipped in the rich stew.

"Good, innit?" Bob the Butcher's Boy said on Lucan's left. "Gale's the best cook in all of England."

Lucan swallowed the food. "Then why is he in Scotland?"

"Taking over, I'd say," Bob assured him an exaggerated wink.

Lucan chuckled and the good food had started to relax him somewhat as he addressed the party at large. "What mysterious supplies do we seek that we might find only in the village beyond this good guesthouse?"

Several groans rose from around the table. James Rose rolled his eyes. "Here we go," he muttered.

"What?" Lucan demanded.

"What supplies?" James Rose mocked. "From where shall we—ahem—*prrrocure* them? Whom shall pay for them, and for how much?" He paused and eyed Gale suspiciously then demanded, "Sir, why is this ale wet?"

Everyone chuckled and Effie answered. "Sir Lucan has a fondness for inquiry. His desire to know things is insatiable."

Lucan took the ribbing graciously. "I just assumed it would save time to gain our provisions nearer the village of Darlyrede. If your intention is to travel quickly…" he let the sentence trail off and waited.

The party shared glances.

It was Gorman who answered. "We don't often make our presence obvious in the village."

At the risk of posing yet another query, Lucan asked, "How do you get your supplies then?"

James Rose waggled his eyebrows. "We steal them." He popped a piece of bread into his mouth and chewed, grinning all the while.

Lucan looked to Effie and saw that she was watching him with an expression akin to challenge on her face. All of them were, actually. And no one refuted James Rose's statement. Lucan then looked to Chumley, rumored to have at one time been a sheriff of famous repute, who surely might give some indication about these illicit activities. But Chumley only wore an indulgent look on his face, as if Lucan was that same naïve boy he'd been the night Castle Dare had burned.

"Well," Lucan said in a careful fashion. "I suppose I should be glad that we've come to market."

Everyone laughed again, and the potential tenseness of the moment was dissipated. Lucan realized that it would do him no good to rail at the criminal activities of criminals while forced to travel in their midst. His only hope was to survive the journey without incurring any further charges himself. He again tried to ignore the niggling question in his own head:

Why did they no longer seem as much like criminals to Lucan?

* * * *

Effie sat in the common room with the others until all who were left were Gorman, Chumley, and Gale. She had unburdened herself to Mari about George Thomas, and been heartened at the woman's encouragement and wise words. Effie would get her son back, of that Mari had no doubt. After the kindly woman had bid them all good-night, Effie soon followed, taking up one of the little chimney rooms on the second floor in which she and Gorman had shared many nights.

She lay in bed staring at the underside of the roof, trying not to dwell on the idea that Lucan Montague might be just beyond the wall at the foot of the bed.

She knew what she—what the Family—must look like from the outside. Criminals. Freaks. Thieves. Tricksters. For the first time since she'd come to live at the Warren, she had found herself embarrassed by James's flippant answer to Lucan Montague: *We steal them.*

Would she have been better off having stayed at Darlyrede? What if she had played the game of the nobility as Lucan Montague had? She could have turned a blind eye until she was older, perhaps, wealthy in her own right. Then…

Then nothing, she told herself. They would have turned you; married you off to some scabby, rich old lecher. You would have never been free. You wouldn't have had George—and think of the fate of all the family. Padraig Boyd would have had no chance of claiming Darlyrede while fighting against Vaughn Hargrave and whomever you married.

Perhaps Vaughn would have married you to Lucan.

Her breath caught in her chest at the idea. It wasn't impossible. Lucan had been beholden to the Hargraves, and wanted his lands returned to him. Vaughn Hargrave wanted control—of everyone and everything, always. What better way to do that than link his granddaughter and his little noble puppet in marriage?

Effie rolled onto her side, dragging the scratchy wool coverlet under her chin and bringing her knees up to curl into a ball while she watched the thin strip of faint, flickering light beneath the door. She had done the right thing then. She was doing the right thing now.

Wasn't she?

It didn't matter. Everything was already in motion—had been in motion for years. It was just now speeding up, as she'd known it always must. She only had to hold tight to what and who she knew was right, and see it through to the end. The first part of that would hopefully be completed with the dawn, and then she could consider what steps would have to come next: Find Thomas Annesley.

Thomas Annesley will soon be dead because of you. Your own father.

Your brothers will lose everything.

The family will be arrested.

You will be arrested.

What would happen to George? The king would not simply hand over the heir of Darlyrede House to his common father.

Effie squeezed her eyes shut and hummed the song she always sang to George when he was tucked into his bed to try to drown out her own raving internal voice that hinted at the unthinkable.

* * * *

Gorman was not beside her when she woke up, but he was in the small, low-ceilinged chamber, washing his face.

"Is it late?" she asked, raising up on one elbow.

"Early," he said before drying his face and beard with a snowy white cloth. "I could no longer lie still and I didn't wish to wake you."

Effie pushed the thin, hard pillow double and laid the side of her face against it. "Everything will be fine, Gorman."

"I know." He wrapped his belt about his waist. "I'll just feel better when we have word. Distracting our friend Lucan should do much to occupy my time today."

Effie could see that he was anxious—perhaps she was the only one in the family who could have seen it. But she let it go, allowing him to change the subject. "You're taking him with you?"

"I doubt he'll be left behind, nosy as he is." Gorman smiled.

Effie smiled back. "True. Besides, I don't know if he should be left alone here in case the message should come while we're out."

Gorman seemed surprised. "Do you think he'd raise the hue and cry?"

"Don't you? It would be his duty to the king."

Gorman seemed to think about it. "I don't know that he would. Perhaps we've not given Sir Lucan enough credit."

"Oh, his head is plenty big."

"No, I don't mean praise." Gorman came and sat on the side of the bed, and Effie instinctively tucked her feet beneath his hip. "He's been on the trail of Thomas Annesley for years, Effie. If Lucan's only concern had been the king's pleasure, he could have dropped everything and chased him down. Instead, he kept on with alerting all the sons, and even petitioned the king on Padraig's behalf."

"What he wants is Castle Dare returned to him," Effie reasoned.

"Of course he does. And why shouldn't he? The man's been without home for a score of years."

"With Vaughn Hargrave for a patron all the while. I'm surprised that you of all people should accept his striving."

"I'm surprised you of all people should condemn him for it," Gorman said gently. "None of us under God's heaven had any say at all about the manners of our births. If I could claim a hold, secure a future for George, I would do it for you both."

Effie felt ashamed. "I'm sorry."

He leaned forward and kissed her temple. "Naught to be sorry for. Let's go have some of Mari's sweet porridge—I've missed it."

* * * *

Lucan left the White Swan on the heels of the group only at their insistent urging. Only Chumley was staying behind, still abed as usual. Lucan knew either they wanted to keep an eye on him in the village, or there was something at the anomalous inn they didn't want him to see.

Probably both.

But he had to admit that he was curious as to their intentions, and so he trailed about the paths and stalls, enjoying the sunshine and the noise of the crowd. It was market day, fortune of fortunes, and Lucan did not remember the little cluster of dwellings beyond the White Swan being so prosperous.

All manner of things were for sale, despite the late winter season. Hardy storage foods such as squash and roots and cabbages; game meats from the woods; dried fish; grains and flours. There were woven arts and cloth, pots and utensils and implements for the household and farm. One little girl had a reedy basket of kittens who wrestled and tumbled so within that they overturned their cell many times over.

Dana was inspecting between large hands lengths of beautiful, vivid scarves from a stall, causing Lucan's brows to raise in relief—a womanly purchase if ever there was one. But then Dana picked up an old, dented helm, admiring it at length before passing payment to the merchant.

Dammit.

The neighboring stall to the one Dana departed offered a variety of miscellaneous items, from jewelry to single shoes to rolls of scraped, reused parchment. Lucan hung back at the corner of a stall across the path and watched as the red-headed Bob approached the merchant, seeming to peruse the wares. Lucan waited for the moment when Bob would slip this or that into his palm and away, but to his surprise, when the owner of the stall drew near, Bob opened his pouch and held forth some unknown object for the man's inspection.

Lucan wandered closer for a better look as the merchant picked up first one then another of what appeared to be jeweled hairpins from Bob's palm, holding them this way and that in the bright sunlight. He nodded and then handed over a coin to the red-headed man before they shook hands and parted ways. The merchant at once laid the hairpins on the oiled piece of leather covering the bench of his stall, arranging them precisely for sale.

Not stealing—selling. Stolen items themselves, likely.

Kit Katey and Winnie caught his eye next, further down the path, as the beautiful Asian woman stooped next to the basket of kittens. Kit's face and hair were covered by a veil, and Lucan wondered if she was wary of being recognized or simply didn't wish to be stared at for her striking features. She tilted her face up toward Winnie, and the gray-haired woman made a series of signs. The little girl minding the basket unhooked the latch and reached inside to withdraw one of the balls of fluff, holding it out to Kit Katey, draped over her palm like a limp rag. The innocence of the scene struck Lucan and a strange feeling came over him as he watched the young woman nestle the tiny creature to her face.

Winnie raised her eyes then and her gaze went directly to Lucan's across the way, as if she'd known he'd been there all the while. She touched Kit's shoulder and nodded in Lucan's direction before walking toward him.

"Good day, Winnie," he said.

She signaled with one fist and arm, waited expectantly, then pointed to him.

"Is that good day?" he asked.

Winnie smiled.

"Well, then"—Lucan imitated the motion—"again."

She seemed pleased, and tucked her hand into Lucan's elbow, drawing him deeper into the market. They were passing Kit Katey again, and now Gorman was there, handing the little mistress of the basket a coin while the Asian woman still knelt in the dirt in rapturous adoration of the animal that was now apparently hers.

"It will be difficult to travel with a kitten," Lucan remarked to Winnie as they moved on down through the market.

Winnie shook her head. A slash of hand, two forked fingers astride the side of her palm. She pointed toward the White Swan, the hanging sign just visible above the crowds' heads.

"Ah, I think I understand."

She pulled him to a stop before a stall boasting every manner of dried vegetation imaginable to Lucan. Her gaze roved over the baskets and bundles, reaching out occasionally to lift a stem or broken-off piece to her nose. She nodded to herself and then poked Lucan in the ribs before tapping a pair of bundles then pressing on the boot of his wounded foot lightly with her own toes.

"I need this?"

Winnie nodded, her lips set. She made a signal with her hand, but Lucan didn't know what it meant.

He looked up at the stall keeper with a grin. "I'll take those, I suppose." He handed over a coin and Winnie selected her purchases, tucking them into her sleeve.

He glanced back down the path and saw Gorman and Kit Katey again standing close to each other, each admiring the woman's new purchase, stroking its tiny head.

A sharp, two-note whistle raced over their heads, and Winnie's arm tensed beneath Lucan's. Gorman and Kit immediately raised their heads, Dana suddenly towering over them; Bob and Effie materialized out of the oblivious crowd—all their faces turned toward the White Swan.

Gorman left Kit to join Effie in the street, their hands reaching out and clasping together as they made their way toward Lucan and Winnie.

"It's Chumley," Effie advised Lucan, and her eyes were serious when her gaze met his.

Lucan turned with the old woman and joined the party as they weaved their way against the current of the market day crowd back toward the inn. He spied James and Gilboe ahead of them.

Here, Lucan thought, he would at last find out what the group had been actually waiting in the village for.

What he had been waiting for.

But when he ducked into the White Swan's bright exterior, he was disappointed and somewhat puzzled at the sight that greeted him.

"Rolf?"

Darlyrede's steward paid Lucan no mind, his eyes fixed on Gorman who had come to a solid halt just inside the door. Gorman's chest heaved as he stared across the space separating him from his father.

"Is it done?" Gorman rasped.

Rolf nodded, his familiar face strangely frozen inside his beard, a pained, intense expression flickering in his eyes.

"Gone." Rolf's usually melodic voice was hoarse. "It's over, son."

Gorman dropped Effie's hand and met his father in the middle of the common room floor in a colliding embrace. A muffled sob came from Gorman where his face was hidden in his shorter father's neck.

"Aye, aye," Rolf rasped. "It's alright. It's alright, now. You'll never see it again."

Lucan's stomach turned at the tender scene between the two men he'd come to think of as stern and stalwart, but it was from concern and alarm rather than disgust.

Kit Katey joined father and son, tentatively laying her slender hand on Gorman's wide back and allowing Rolf to take her up in a one-armed embrace.

Winnie slid her arm around James Rose's slender waist. Chumley laid a hand on Bob's shoulder. Gilboe crossed himself, his eyes closed and his head lowered, Dana mimicking his pose.

Lucan felt someone take hold of his hand. He looked down and Effie was pulling him back toward the door.

"Come on," she said quietly.

Back in the street, Effie led him away from the market center and toward the sloping dirt road that curved toward the river.

"You're wondering what that was about, I suppose."

"I am," Lucan said. "Rolf was to stay be—"

"Gorman told me just this morning that I was not giving you enough credit," Effie interrupted. "So I will tell you. But I'm warning you now." She came to stop at a crossroads where a narrower, dirt track intersected the main pike. The wind blew the tendrils of her hair loose from her plait and the late, low afternoon sunlight burnished her skin with a cold glow.

"If I should tell anyone, you'll kill me?" Lucan grinned.

Effie did not answer his attempt at lightheartedness. Her face was solemn, without trace of anger or outrage.

"Elsmire Tower burned last night."

Lucan stilled, unable to even blink as her gray gaze bored into his eyes. She continued.

"Rolf led those left behind at the Warren in burning it to the ground after he knew we would have had plenty of time to reach the White Swan."

"Why?" Lucan asked at last.

"You know the story of Rolf's son, supposedly run away or dead many years ago after being accused of theft."

Lucan nodded.

"Gorman hadn't run away. He was taken. To Elsmire Tower. Adolphus Paget kept him prisoner for more than five years."

Confusion seized Lucan's brains. The frown seemed to freeze the flesh of his face. "What? That's absur—" Lucan stopped mid-sentence. That day in the wood where the family had ambushed him and Padraig Boyd, the day Effie Annesley had shot him in the foot, the day Adolphus Paget had been killed, blooming once more to fuzzy life in his mind.

Gorman had looked down upon the man as he lay dying. "Were I you, I'd be cautious throwing my lot in with the likes of this innocent." He'd nudged Adolphus Paget's shoulder roughly with the toe of his boot. "His riches are made from the sale of slaves. Young slaves. Girls, stolen away. Lads, as well. Isn't that so, Adolphus?" He'd crouched down suddenly so as to look into the nobleman's anguished expression, upside-down to him.

Effie continued over Lucan's pain-filled recollections. "Paget used Gorman as bait on his travels, to lure other victims into his clutches, to blackmail uncooperative nobles into keeping their mouths shut. He threatened Gorman by telling him that if he tried to escape or send word to his father, he would have Vaughn Hargrave kill Rolf."

Lucan's mind was reeling. "How *did* Gorman escape, then?"

"Gale," Effie said. "He was the cook at Elsmire years ago. He grew suspicious at the activities of Paget and Vaughn Hargrave and although he had no power to do anything to stop them, he refused to turn a blind eye to the suffering. He and Mari took Gorman and a few other children that night, straight after their supper, from beneath Paget's very nose."

"Paget didn't sound the alarm?"

"How could he have?" Effie asked. "All of the children Gale and Mari took with them had been abducted by Paget or his deviant followers. As far as anyone outside the hold knew, Elsmire had only lost a pair of servants. They crossed into Scotland for safety, and Gale built the White Swan."

"Gorman eventually told them about his father, Rolf, at Darlyrede," Lucan guessed.

"Yes. It took months of planning to get a message to Rolf to come when next Hargrave went on one of his many trips. They didn't dare write who it was from, or the reason behind the trip. It's a miracle Rolf came at all. Perhaps somewhere in his heart, he suspected that his son was still alive."

"But why didn't Rolf then expose both Hargrave and Paget?" Lucan asked.

"You still don't get it, Lucan," Effie said, her voice strained. "Tell me, who would have believed him?"

Lucan stared at Effie for a long moment, trying to come up with an argument in his head. But a hard knot formed in his stomach as Lucan realized Effie was right—no one would have believed such an outrageous accusation about two of the richest, most powerful noblemen in the north of England. Rolf would have lost any means to secure another position. No livelihood, probably deemed a liar or an extortionist. He likely would have spent the rest of his poor, miserable life with a price on his head, while affairs carried on at Elsmire Tower and Darlyrede.

Effie turned back toward the inn, and Lucan followed her. He could do nothing else, rendered completely powerless by the tale she was telling him.

"It wasn't you who killed Adolphus Paget in the wood," Lucan realized. "It was Gorman. Padraig said to me that day that it was as if you had been lying in wait for us. And you were. You had tracked us."

"We watched you and laid the trap, yes. Of course. Rolf told us Paget had chosen to ride in your hunting party," Effie explained. "It was the best chance we would ever have—no guards, on our own territory."

"The woods are Darlyrede lands, though."

"My father's territory then," Effie shot back coolly.

Lucan let it go. "What about the others? How did you all come to live in the caves?"

They were nearly back at the White Swan now. "Perhaps another time," she said briskly. "Gorman needs me." She pulled ahead of him and walked toward the door.

"Effie," Lucan called to her.

She paused, turned sideways to regard him.

"I won't betray Gorman."

"What on earth has Gorman done that you might betray?" she asked simply, and turned back to enter the White Swan.

Lucan stood thinking for several moments and realized his predicament—Lucan hadn't seen Gorman kill Adolphus Paget, and Effie had never affirmed that it had been him who'd fired the fatal arrow. Lucan had been with Gorman all the while on the journey into Scotland, while Elsmire was being destroyed. And any criminal activities thus far carried out while on the road had been done, if not exactly with Lucan's participation, certainly without his interference. He was as guilty as any of them on this journey.

Clever, clever Effie Annesley.

Chapter 11

They left the White Swan the next morning, the party leaving Rolf holding Kit Katey's kitten in the dooryard, Mari and Gale waving and calling them down the road with good wishes.

Lucan met Rolf's eyes, and Lucan saw a strength there he'd not recognized before. The steward, that necessary cog in the machinery of wicked Darlyrede House for as long as Lucan could recall, and all the while harboring the grief of the loss of his son, and then, later, the rage at Vaughn Hargrave's role in his ruin. Day in and day out, Rolf had managed Darlyrede with unquestionable integrity, and yet it had been that very man, the man Lucan had trusted above any other in the hold, who had directed the bandits of the wood to Lucan and Padraig's hunting party that day, knowing that any of them could have been killed right alongside of Adolphus Paget. There had been no apologies.

Rolf had done that thing for his son. Had burned to the ground the castle where his son had been held prisoner. And now that son was doing what he must to save his own boy, George Thomas.

Lucan gave Rolf a single nod.

Rolf answered with the same.

The party headed west on the village road.

Lucan's left boot felt tight around his foot, packed, as it was, by Winnie that morn with the bruised herbs wrapped in tallowed cloths. He didn't feel any difference except perhaps a tingling sensation in his toes, but he rather thought that was due to loss of circulation.

No matter—it had caused the old woman to smile at him and pat his leg encouragingly, and so Lucan had decided to indulge her.

James Rose cantered along at his side in the middle of the party. Despite the gay morning sun behind them, the sullen young man presented his typical smirking expression.

"Glasgow, prepare thyself," he muttered darkly.

"Have you ever been?" Lucan asked.

"Nay," the young man admitted. "The White Swan is the northern extent of my travels. I can only hope my arse doesn't freeze immediately upon our arrival."

Lucan chuckled. "I too wish for spring to make a hasty arrival, if we are to persevere beyond Glasgow and into the Highlands once more."

"You've been there many times," James assumed.

"More times than I cared to," Lucan said. "Glasgow is a fair reprieve though, compared to the islands of the coast, or worse, the north where Caedmaray lies. I feel no shame in admitting dread at fording the North Sea again in pursuit of Thomas Annesley."

"You're hoping you'll simply happen upon him again, then. Just take him back with us? 'Ho, there, found you?'"

Lucan looked sideways at the youth's scathing tone. "Have you a better idea?"

James Rose shrugged. "Effie gives the orders; I follow them."

Lucan nodded with a sage expression. Leave it to a young man to find fault with a plan and yet offer no other solution. So he was surprised when James spoke again.

"I do find it unlikely that the bloke will simply be waiting on you to apprehend him in the same manner you did last time—in some village or on a fishing skiff. He's no idiot; he knows what's at stake for him should he step foot onto English soil again."

"Waiting on us, perhaps not," Lucan allowed. "But he's on his own. No resources, no compatriots."

"Much like the first time he escaped."

Lucan nodded. "True."

The youth was silent for a moment. "We'll be wasting our time in Glasgow," he muttered. And then James Rose kicked at his horse's sides and pulled ahead of Lucan, leaving him in the sparkling, cold light of dawn.

Lucan shook his head. The hotheadedness of youth. He remembered it well. A young man seeking always action, often at the expense of planning. That had been Lucan once, long ago. Had he not been in faraway France with Iris to look after, there was no telling how he could have ruined his own chances at recovering Castle Dare. Thomas Annesley was no longer an impetuous young man.

Lucan frowned. This current thread of thought was somehow now unsettling to him, like a tiny sliver just under his skin that he could feel snagging at his touch but unable to make out with his eyes to remove. But he had no time to worry at it as Kit Katey's ambling mount filled the spot recently vacated by the sullen James Rose.

"Good morning," Lucan said.

She smiled shyly at him and ducked her head in way of greeting. It was the most interaction Lucan had had with the girl, and he had to admit that he was more than a bit curious as to the exotic beauty's secrets.

"We've not been properly introduced," Lucan tried.

"I know who you are," Kit Katey replied right away in her lilting accent. "Sir Lucan Montague, of the Most Noble Order of the Garter of King Henry. You are English. You have a sister. You own a land that you cannot claim, and a hold that is no more."

A surprised smile spread across Lucan's face. "Ah, you have proved me wrong. And so now I find myself at a disadvantage."

"How so?"

"I only know you as Kit Katey," he explained. "Is that because of your affection for small felines?"

"My name was Qi QiangTing," she said.

"Was?"

"When I was rescued. But it is difficult for English to pronounce." She paused. "I do like kittens, though."

Lucan took a bold tact. "Who rescued you?"

"Effie is correct—you ask many questions."

"You needn't answer them if you don't wish."

"I know that." Her eyes flashed at him, and Lucan realized that the girl wasn't shy—she was sly. She was careful. His mind went at once to the children in the cave stables.

"Gorman rescued me," she continued. "I was Adolphus Paget's… companion for many years."

"But you're just a child," Lucan blurted.

"I am a score and two."

Lucan was shocked—he thought the girl no more than ten and three.

"My village was in the path of an attack from enemies in the north against the emperor. I was taken hostage and sold to a band of Mongol traders. They brought me to Constantinople where an English merchant bought me for trade in London."

Lucan knew he was staring at the girl—woman, he corrected himself—but he couldn't help it. The way she spoke of her captivity was so matter-of-fact and Lucan—no innocent, himself—felt heat creep up his neck.

"You knew Gorman at Elsmire Tower," he stammered.

Kit shook her head. "No. Gorman had been gone for some time. He saw me from the forest one day, when I was permitted to walk in the sun. He saw my chains."

Lucan didn't know what to say, and so he let the silence grow between them until Kit Katey spoke again.

"He came back, day after day, for weeks, until he had made a plan. He took me to the White Swan, to Mari and Gale."

"Didn't you wish to return to your village?"

"There is no village to return to," she answered quietly. "I could not stay in Scotland—those who live in the town of the White Swan thought me a devil. The Warren is my home now. Gorman and Effie and the others are my family."

"And so, what? You'll simply live in a cave forever?" Lucan couldn't help but ask.

"You say that as if I were still a prisoner. Gorman did not simply rescue me from Adolphus Paget—he freed me. I go where they go. I help when they need." She watched him closely for a moment. "You wonder why I have come on this journey."

"Frankly, yes," Lucan admitted.

Her smile was small, yet the intensity of it nearly took Lucan's breath.

"There was a reason I was taken from my village alive, English knight. If I told you, you would not believe me. But perhaps before our journey is ended, you will see." She looked ahead at the road rising beyond the party of bandits, her smooth face serene, and despite everything she had told Lucan her deepest secrets remained locked behind those mysterious dark eyes.

Lucan stewed. It seemed that the longer he was with this motley group of criminals and refugees, the more he learned, the less he knew. Not only about them, but about the very people who populated his own land. He was not so naïve as to misunderstand what Kit Katey's true role to Adolphus Paget had been. And to think that this atrocity had been perpetuating long before Lucan had been exiled to France. Perhaps even before his parents had died.

Had they known?

His heart skipped a beat. No. No, not his father—honorable and fair. Not his mother, kind and generous.

Then why had they not brought attention to what everyone else in the land had seemed to already know? Why hadn't they helped Thomas Annesley?

Why had they died?

He thought of the niggling splinter James Rose had left him with. Tommy wouldn't dare venture among strangers for refuge—no one could be trusted. And those who would have helped him were perhaps dead or already royal guests in London. But still… *We're wasting our time…*

He thought of Kit Katey's proclamation—that Gorman had not only saved her, he'd freed her.

If word did somehow reach Tommy that Euphemia Hargrave, his child with his beloved Cordelia, was alive, how would he ever hope to find her in the vastness of Britain, without exposing himself to those seeking to apprehend him for bounty? He had no one to turn to, just as he'd had no one to turn to that night he'd escaped Darlyrede House with barely his life. If it hadn't been for—

Oh, my God.

Lucan pulled up hard on Agrios's reins, bringing the mount to a prancing halt on the road.

Gilboe, riding behind him, let out a rather unchaste string of curses.

"We're going the wrong way," Lucan announced loudly. He looked around the band, half turned to him, their horses stomping, their breaths clouding the morning air. His eyes met Effie Annesley's, wide and pale in the bright sunlight, and it was to her that he spoke.

"I know where Thomas Annesley is."

* * * *

Effie kept her distance from Lucan Montague while the band made camp in the rapidly descending night, and while they sat around the fire preparing the meal. She kept her distance, and yet she kept him in sight, closely watching his solemn, slender face, his quick, efficient movements as he ordered his own possessions.

If what he had said on the road that morning was true, it was possible that Effie would at last meet her father in only a matter of days.

A bowl of food was pressed into her hands and then Gorman was lowering to a seat at her side. "Just go talk to him, Effie."

"I've no need to." She picked up a piece of meat between her forefinger and thumb and blew on it. "We've decided."

"But you're not yet convinced."

She turned to look at Gorman. "Are you?"

Gorman took his time chewing the mouthful of food, staring at the fire. He nodded, then swallowed. "Aye. It makes sense."

"Nothing makes sense," Effie grumbled.

"Nothing makes sense to you because you're scared." Gorman reached down and wrapped his warm, strong fingers around her thigh, squeezing briefly then rubbing the spot. "You're afraid that if you let it make sense, and then you're wrong, something bad might happen to George and it will somehow be your fault."

"Lucan Montague doesn't care about our son, Gorman."

"Eff," he said softly. "Effie, look at me. It is so easy for us—all of us here"—he glanced around the fire—"to assume that everyone is evil. That they're all out to harm us and each other; to steal from us, or hurt us. But we know that's not true. And we can't live the rest of our lives suspecting everyone we meet as having wicked intentions for us the first time we let down our guard. I don't want George Thomas to think of the world that way."

Effie looked away from him—she didn't want to see the truth in his eyes, because Gorman was right: it was too frightening.

He squeezed her thigh again and then released her to attend once more to his dinner. "Go talk to him. Or argue with him. You won't get any peace until you do."

Effie sighed and then stood up. Kit Katey was walking toward the pot over the fire and so Effie handed her bowl to her friend. "Here, take mine." She wiped her hands on her trousers and then walked purposefully around the blaze to the colder shadows where Lucan Montague sat with his skin of drink and a hunk of Mari's bread.

"How sure are you?" she demanded.

Lucan raised his eyes slowly, one eyebrow cocked. "Good evening. I'm quite well, thank you. Would you care to join me?"

Effie rolled her eyes and sat down on the log he'd pulled to the fringes of the group. "You can stop with the forced chivalry."

"I've practiced long enough, I should hope it's not forced now."

"How sure are you?" she pressed again.

"I'm sure."

"That tells me nothing."

"No one can tell you anything, Effie, because you already have all the answers."

Anger rose in her chest, covering over her anxiety, her worry, her uncertainty, and she embraced it. "If I didn't want to know, I wouldn't have asked."

"You wanted to come over here to argue with me after Gorman wouldn't take the bait," he replied easily. "He likely sent you to be rid of you so that he could eat his dinner in peace, with more amiable companions." He gestured across the fire to where Gorman and Kit Katey and Dana were laughing over some bit of conversation.

The anger flashed to humiliation, but before she had a chance to lose her temper, Lucan continued.

"I'm *sure*. Harriet Payne—pardon me, Cameron—Tavish Cameron's mother, saved Tommy's life the night he escaped from Darlyrede. She hid him, she nursed him—and he always intended for her to have a home at Roscraig. Your brothers are all in London, and Tommy surely must know that Padraig is making a bid for Darlyrede. He'll be waiting with Harriet for Tavish to return, to hear what has happened. He's safe there, and he knows it."

Effie stared into the flames to avoid his eyes. "No matter what the king decides for Padraig, Thomas Annesley never has to go back to England."

"I'm certain he realizes that."

"But he doesn't know about me." She turned toward him again.

Lucan shook his head. "No. No one knew about you." The way he said it, the way his eyes stopped when they met hers, caused her breath to catch in her throat. "Not even me."

Effie swallowed, and thankfully it was Lucan who looked away this time while she spoke. "It will be worse somehow, if you're right. If he's there. He's finally provided for his sons, and is safe. But once we arrive, he'll have no choice."

Lucan looked at her again with those icy eyes now rimmed with firelight. "Meaning you won't give him one?"

Effie felt her eyebrows draw together. "But…George Thomas…"

"If I've learned anything about Thomas Annesley in these many years of study of his family, it is that once he lays eyes upon you, he'll"—Lucan broke off, his expression seeming to tentatively caress her skin as he looked at her. "He'll be completely at your mercy. Family means everything to him. Perhaps that's where you got it from."

Gooseflesh raced over Effie's arms. She felt strangely weak in her legs now and was glad she was sitting. She forced herself to speak. "You mean you…I…*we* won't force him back to London, as the king wishes."

"I did that once," Lucan allowed. "I was wrong. But, no, I don't think either of us will need force him to do anything."

"Are you worried about my son at all, Lucan?"

"George will be safe with Henry, Effie. He'll be safe with his uncles." He paused. "I wouldn't have left him otherwise."

She knew her eyes widened with surprise, because Lucan grinned and it made her heart flutter.

What was wrong with her tonight?

"We'll be there soon. You'll see. I know you don't trust me—"

"Gorman does," Effie interrupted.

"And I trust Gorman," Lucan finished. "So perhaps there is hope for the two of us yet."

The way he'd lumped the pair of them together as 'two of us' caused Effie's heart to flutter again.

"Perhaps there is," she allowed.

"If you don't shoot me again."

Effie smiled, despite the tumultuous feelings swirling like a cyclone inside her. She leaned a bit closer and caught the warm masculine scent of him.

"Don't tempt me."

She stood and walked away from him, feeling his gaze on her back the whole of the way.

And still her heart raced.

Chapter 12

Lucan couldn't stop watching her now.

He knew he was a fool for it, but since the night three days past when Effie Annesley had sat with him around the fire, Lucan seemed to have developed a sixth sense about her proximity to him. He knew what her hair smelled like now, the way the skin on her forehead creased when she worried, the elegant fan of lines at the corners of her eyes when she smiled, the flush of her cheeks when she laughed. He couldn't recall noticing any of those things on their journeys to and from London, but now, it was as if she'd cast a spell over him.

Or perhaps it was Winnie who'd cast the spell, with those blasted, smelly herbs.

Regardless, Lucan was beginning to wonder if being so long on the road in such dreadful weather was starting to affect his sanity—he now felt a flare of jealousy whenever Gorman touched Effie's arm, or when Effie leaned in close to Gorman to speak something low in his ear. At night, while the band slept around the dying fire, Lucan couldn't seem to close his eyes even when it wasn't his turn to keep watch; he lay there thinking of the years of memories Effie shared with Gorman, how they had made a child and were raising him. How they had gathered such a group about them as to be closer than any family Lucan had ever known, now traipsing across the countryside on a potentially deadly mission and giving little care for the laws of the land. The family had their own laws.

And Lucan wasn't part of them, not really.

He couldn't help his mind from going to the After. After they had found Tommy; after they had returned to London. After whatever judgement was handed down. If Lucan was free, who would surround him? Who would be his family? Iris, his closest blood relative, was married now. He had no other—no cousins, aunts, uncles—with whom he could claim a familiar relationship. Even his friend Ulric would be busy with his duties to the king, and they'd never had that sort of close acquaintance any matter. Perhaps he should return to France and seek out his extended relation. If Henry kept Castle Dare from him, it may be his only option.

Start over. Alone.

He'd been so consumed all his life with finding the truth that would lead to his revenge, he'd never stopped to think what his life might look like in the case of success. Who would he rebuild Castle Dare for? What would be left of Northumberland when the dust settled?

He grew more maudlin as the afternoon wore on, and his rocking rear in the saddle caused his lower back to tighten. Clouds gathered overhead, and Lucan thought there would be rain later that night. He would be glad to reach the small village and pass the night there—hopefully in his own chamber where he wouldn't be forced to watch or hear Effie and Gorman as they carried on with their easy interactions. Edinburgh and then the Firth of Forth lay just beyond the fresh breeze that teased them. Two more days, at most, and Tower Roscraig would be in sight.

A caravan approached them on the road—a wide, tall-sided wagon bracketed by a retinue of rough-looking characters. They took up the whole of the track and so the band divided and eased their mounts off into the rough on either side while they passed. Eight riders—no, ten perhaps. Lucan only paid them passing heed until he realized the rest of his party was watching the travelers with much closer attention.

Lucan glanced at the wagon, draped to cover whatever cargo was contained within. A corner flapped, a flash of pale around a board, a glint in the shadows. The wagon rolled past, and Lucan looked more closely at the men riding behind. They were dirty and mean of face, and made no pretense of acknowledging the courtesy the band had shown them. One man glared openly at Lucan, holding his gaze as they passed, even turning his head to do so as if in challenge.

Lucan turned his gaze toward Effie, stopped only a few feet from him, but she was looking at Gorman through the swirling dust over the road.

Gorman nodded at her as if in answer to an unasked question, and then called out, "Kit Katey, James; with me to the fore." Gorman kicked his mount and the three sped away up the rough into the trees, in the direction in which the strange, dark caravan had now disappeared.

"Gilboe and Winnie," Effie commanded, "wait for us here with Sir Lucan."

The remainder of the band—Bob, Dana, and Chumley—at once turned their horses' heads back the way they had come.

"What are you doing?"

Effie only glanced at him. "Business. If we're not back in an hour, follow."

"I'll follow now, thank you," he said, urging Agrios after the blonde.

"Lucan," she snipped. "You don't want any part of this."

"Another robbery, you mean."

"I don't have time to explain it to you."

"I'm a quick study—I'm certain I already have it figured out."

"Stay out of the way, or a wounded foot will be the least of your troubles," she tossed over her shoulder with a glare. "Hah!"

In moments they were back in the woods, and Lucan could hear shouting ahead even over the pounding hooves. The caravan was stopped, and the riders to the rear were dismounting in a hurry. The next events seemed to happen in half-time, and yet everything at once. Lucan caught sight of Effie reaching over her shoulder into her quiver, her horse still galloping toward the group. Her bow raised—

Effie, no, Lucan wanted to say.

She fired.

The rider who had glared at Lucan fell to the road with a scream even as Effie reached for another arrow.

Bob swung his leg over his saddle and crouched, his reins in his hands. He neared one of the dark clad riders and leapt from his horse, flattening the man to the ground. A blade flashed, a gurgling scream was cut short.

Dana singled out the only rider still mounted, and the pair raced toward each other astride. The rider's swinging flail was easily evaded, and Dana pulled the man from his saddle by the front of his tunic and dashed him to the road before leaping down upon him beyond the wagon, out of Lucan's sight.

Chumley rode straight toward the wagon, so fast that Lucan thought the man was going to collide with it, but Chumley, too, leapt from his saddle onto the wooden structure, his boots turning under him like mill wheels as he scaled the side and reached the pinnacle. The driver appeared over the crest and Chumley delivered two swift blows to the man's face before picking him up and throwing him from the wagon. The driver landed on his head with a sickening crunch and crumpled to a stop. He did not move again.

Lucan swerved around the wagon where Gorman, Kit Katey, and James were surrounded in the road by the other four riders, swords drawn. The trio stood in the center, their backs to one another's; James and Gorman wielded long swords, Kit a pair of short blades decorated with streaming red ribbons at the handles. Two men already lay dead at the side of the road.

An arrow whizzed through the air and one of the riders staggered, the projectile finding purchase in his upper arm like the spindly branch of a winter tree. The injured man staggered and folded in half, but in the next instant swung his sword wide, ready to swipe at Effie as she thundered toward him, too late in re-knocking her next arrow. She would be upon him before she could fire.

Lucan swerved around, drawing his own short sword and guiding Agrios with his knees. A swift thrust at the back of the man's neck and he fell dead beneath Agrios's hooves, the well-trained mount leaping and kicking his way free from the body. Lucan pulled around and halted the beast in time to see the trio in the center of the road spring into action.

They spread out from each other, each having located their own target, and now they stalked them, testing the distance. Gorman was first to act, rushing forward, meeting steel with steel. Two clanging, ringing thrusts, and his opponent fell.

James Rose was not quite as straightforward, dancing around the rider's flank, swirling the tip of his sword before the man's face with his own typical smirk. "Watch out," he taunted. He flicked the earflap of the man's leather skull cap, and the severed piece went flying away. "Next is your *ear*," he warned in an excited whisper, wiggling his eyebrows.

The rider turned and began to run into the woods.

James dropped his sword down by his leg for a moment, dejected. "Oh, come now; must we run?" He sighed and then sprinted after the fleeing man, his sword held above his head. "Fine! But you're it next round!"

Only Kit Katey still faced her foe, and none of the others seemed inclined to come to her rescue as the beautiful woman circled her challenger, her slippers rising and falling in a graceful creep, her short swords crossing each other, weaving in the air, their streamers dancing in elegant patterns. The man charged like a rabid dog. A blur of red, like exotic birds' feathers, swirled in the air before him and Kit Katey stepped back, the swords held juxtaposed before her face, the blades running red.

The man rocked to a halt, his sword fell to the dirt. Red lines, faint at first, bloomed into stripes, then ribbons, and then the man's jerkin was awash in the color. He lowered his face as if to look down at his front, but then his head fell from his shoulders and thudded to the road in the instant before his body collapsed at Kit Katey's feet.

Kit Katey made a low bow over the fallen man as birdsong spontaneously returned to the forest.

James came stomping up onto the packed track. "He was a fast one," the young man gasped, swiping at his eyes with his forearm. "Shit ran me a quarter mile."

Gorman and Kit Katey were already cutting purses and gathering weapons.

Lucan sat atop Agrios and let his gaze rove over the carnage that lay in the road as reality slowly dawned on him: he'd done this. He'd participated in this slaughter of strangers, no matter that his contribution had been made in order to save Effie Annesley's life. Lucan Montague, Knight of the Royal Order of the Garter, enamored fool, had just set upon a band of travelers, and now there were nearly a dozen men dead in the dirt.

Dead, and being robbed.

Lucan's stomach turned.

He looked around for Effie and saw her atop the wagon with Chumley and Dana, pulling back the filthy canvas covering the cargo. A woman's scream shot through the air, but it didn't come from either Effie or Kit Katey—and definitely not from Dana. Lucan urged Agrios closer toward the wagon.

His heart stopped. Through the slats, he saw what must have been a dozen women and girls, in various modes of dress—and lack thereof. It seemed that all of them were weeping.

The oldest looking of the women—strawberry blonde and perhaps a score—held her bound, dirty palms up toward where Chumley and Effie were looking down at them.

"Please," she begged. "Please don't hurt us."

"Ah, we're not going to hurt you, love," Chumley soothed. He held his hand out toward the woman. "Come on out now."

But Effie was already climbing down into the melee of bodies, and Lucan could only see slices of her through the wooden slats as she drew her short blade and began cutting bonds, one after another as she made her way from the front of the wagon to the rear.

"There you are," she said quietly. "Up you go—out of this thing. Careful. Turn 'round. Is this your mum? Tell me true. Go on, then, and stay close to her. That must smart—we shall have it looked at in a moment."

Lucan felt as though he were frozen into place on his saddle as the forest around them grew darker with approaching evening and the clouds seemed to lower to the treetops. Around him, Bob and James and Gorman were dragging the bodies of the caravan riders from the road into the deep underbrush. Chumley and Dana were helping the women and girls to the road, where Kit Katey waited to receive them—herding them together with a gentle touch or slow, graceful gesture.

Finally, Effie climbed from the cage of the wagon to the top and stood a moment, looking about the road. She seemed to pause to perhaps count the women gathered with Kit Katey and Dana, then her gaze suddenly swung to Lucan, with the twilight forest behind her.

"It's no longer safe to stop in the village," she said to him. "We must put as much distance as we can between these woods and ourselves before these monsters are discovered. God willing, most of the women are from Edinburgh." She paused, her gaze never leaving his. "Your aim was true."

She made the sign Lucan had seen Winnie perform a hundred times now. *Thank you.*

He nodded at her, still unable to speak.

"Let's gather the horses," Gorman called out, disrupting the brief moment. "Bob, you drive the wagon. We'll put the lasses astride and lead them. Look lively, now—let's clear out before anyone comes across us."

Lucan swung down from Agrios at once and set to, waving the spooked, hungry-looking beasts back toward the road where Gorman and James caught them. He couldn't help but liken them to the frightened women and girls Kit Katey had gathered and calmed with her touch and quiet words. They finished quickly and managed to turn the wagon around in the road, seating the mother and child next to Bob. Everyone else was mounted, some of the women wearing borrowed cloaks, some riding two astride, and they set out for where Winnie and Gilboe waited in the road ahead.

It would be a long night, Lucan realized to himself as he fell into the pack behind Effie and Gorman, the stars now hidden by the thick blanket of clouds. He felt a cold drop of rain on his cheek. But he reckoned it would have been a much longer night for the women now under their care had they not passed on the road when they did.

Too long of a night. Too long of a life, likely.

Ahead of him, Lucan saw Gorman reach out his hand toward Effie. She took it and they were joined for a brief moment before their fingertips slid apart. Lucan's heart clenched in his chest as the rain began to fall in earnest.

Stupid, foolish Lucan Montague.

Chapter 13

They used the canvases as shelter for camp that night when they finally stopped. The rain fell steadily through the bare trees—large, cold drops that cracked on the dripping covering and then ran together in rivulets and ribbons and then streams into the cold mud around the raised fire. No one opted to take shelter in the filthy, shit-smelling wagon, and beneath the canvases was smoky and windy and wet despite their best efforts. Their party now nearly tripled, they had not quite enough food, but Effie was at peace as she looked around at the faces huddled together for warmth, chattering in relieved tones as they were ministered to by Winnie and Kit Katey.

Effie used to lie awake at night and worry over how many were lost forever. How many passing so close to the Warren, smuggled into and out of and through Northumberland that they had missed, and would never know about. But that fate was not for these girls.

Fourteen lives, saved.

Fifteen, if she counted her own life, saved by Lucan Montague.

He was sitting beyond the fire across from her—he always seemed to place himself at the extreme distance from Effie, but still in sight, like the North Star. Effie could tell that Winnie was attempting to coax his boot from his foot, but Lucan seemed to be putting her off in his stilted, polite manner.

She smiled to herself. Foolish man.

Effie made her way around the fire, pushing up on the overlapping, sagging edges of canvas to slough the water off as she went, until she stood before the victim and his perpetrator.

"You might as well just go ahead and take the boot off, Sir Lucan."

He looked up at her as if hoping for aid. "It will be fine until we reach Roscraig. Good Winnie need not trouble herself this wet night. She should rest."

Winnie looked up from her crouch at Effie with an exasperated expression, and her hands flew in the firelight.

"Ah, I see," Effie mused, and then looked back to Lucan with a smirk. "Winnie wants to know if your foot feels warm."

"Actually, yes," Lucan said with a triumphant look that he turned toward the old woman as he addressed her. "Yes, it's quite warm, despite the chill."

"If the dressing's not changed," Effie continued the explanation, "the herbs will burn a hole in your scar and reopen your wound."

Lucan was still for a moment and then bent toward his boot ties. Effie took a seat at his side, partly to make him uncomfortable, partly to watch Winnie work.

And partly to be near him? a little voice inside her head queried.

"You really should just listen to her," Effie said in a loud whisper, taunting him in an effort to distract herself from her traitorous thoughts.

The boot came off and Winnie placed Lucan's wrapped foot in her lap.

Lucan lifted an eyebrow. "*Listen* to her, should I?"

"You know what I mean," she said, buffeting his shoulder with her own reflexively, as was her habit with Gorman and the others. It caused his eyes to flash at her though and so she looked back to his foot as her cheeks heated.

Lucan broke the awkward moment. "Have you always been mute, Winnie?"

Winnie shook her gray head and made some swift signs.

Effie chuckled. "She used to speak a fair better English than you. With nicer manners, as well."

Lucan stiffened, which only caused Effie's chuckle to grow and Winnie to smile serenely.

"Oh, don't be offended, Sir Lucan," she said. "Winnie is the smartest one of us in the Warren. Smartest in all the north of England, I'd wager. May I, Winnie? You know if I don't, he'll only assault you with questions all the night."

Winnie signed.

"Well, yes, it's true that it will likely happen any matter."

The old woman tossed Effie a look and then another pair of signs. *I like to hear him speak—don't you?*

Effie ignored her, choosing instead to fill in Lucan while their clothes steamed together in the humid air under the canvas.

"Winnie is a physician."

"What?"

The old woman tried to contain her smile as she busied herself, but Effie could see that she was enjoying this part—she always did.

"It's true," Effie continued. "She trained at the university in Bologna, under Maestra Dorotea Bucca. She was quite famous."

Winnie paused to let her hands talk.

"She actually knows *four* languages," Effie translated. "And she has performed many operations on many important people."

"What happened?"

Effie paused for a moment. "She came back to England," she said quietly. "The men in the guilds wouldn't admit her because she wasn't married to a physician, although her father had been famous in Italy for his skill. So for her to practice—no matter that she was better trained and more capable than any floundering idiot turned out in London or Oxford or the odd monastery—was illegal. Although they were happy enough to keep her about to solve their problems for them and make them look competent."

Lucan continued to look at Effie patiently.

Go on, Winnie encouraged. *It's fine.*

"They were called to a home where a little boy was ill," Effie said. "The physician in charge called for a remedy, with which Winnie strongly disagreed."

A common illness, Winnie signed, almost to herself. *So simple.*

"He didn't listen to her," Lucan guessed.

Effie shook her head. "The boy died. Winnie accused the physician of malpractice before the boy's parents *and* the university *and* the guild. It was taken up by the court. The physician was fined and left London in disgrace, but not before he and some of the guild had their revenge."

Here, Winnie looked up at Lucan and opened her mouth, showing the scarred stub where her tongue used to be. Effie felt Lucan tense at her side. Winnie looked to Effie and made another short sign.

Tell him.

"They cut out her tongue," Effie said. "And they raped her. And although it was no secret what had been done to her, everyone that could have helped her by bringing the men to justice ignored it. They didn't want the same—or worse—happening to them."

Winnie tucked in the end of the fresh, dry wrapping around Lucan's foot. *I do better work with the family now,* she signed. *Sir Lucan may put on the boot.*

"She's finished," Effie said.

Winnie gained her feet and Lucan reached out for her hand before she could move away. Winne paused as Lucan brought the bony, spotted back of her palm to his lips.

"*Grazie mille, maestra*," he said against her skin. "*Sono grato.*"

Winnie bent down and kissed each of Lucan Montague's cheeks before squeezing his hand and walking away.

After a long, quiet moment, the murmur of the band in the background, Lucan said in a low voice, "When did the world go mad? And why did I never see it?"

"No one wants to see the victims, Lucan," she answered in an equally low tone while she studied his profile in the firelight—all angles and planes and so beautiful in the flickering glow. So much like the boy he'd been the night Castle Dare had burned, and yet so different. "The poor. The immigrant. Their tormentors—not the ones on the road today, but the ones who employ them—they are rich. Powerful. No one dares go against them."

He looked to her. "You do."

"Not just me," Effie whispered. "You too, now. I hope."

She didn't know what had changed—was it the rescue or the rain or the very air?—but she suddenly wanted Lucan Montague to kiss her, more than she had ever wished to be kissed by anyone in all her life. But she could feel the weight of eyes on them, as if everyone around the fire had suddenly become interested in their conversation. And still, she felt the physical pull of him as if slowly leveraging herself over the edge of a cliff, and she so desperately wanted to let go.

"I have to go," Effie whispered suddenly.

His nod was barely perceptible. "I know."

"It's just…why is it different now? Is it only me, or—?"

"No," he interrupted, his gaze holding hers. "No. It's not only you. I noticed it—"

"Today," she finished for him. "It's odd, isn't it? When we so dislike each other?"

"Very," he agreed.

Effie forced herself to stand up and walk directly away from Lucan Montague. She found a seat on the other side of the fire, made for her when Kit Katey and Gorman moved apart. She sat as if landing in a safe haven, where the pull of Lucan could no longer threaten.

Still, she felt him watching her through the fire.

And she held that feeling close to her well into the long, cold night.

* * * *

The party skirted Edinburgh the next day, breaking on the fringe of the city while the handful of girls who resided there were returned to their homes. The cheerful sunlight seemed to mock Lucan though, as the band were forced to carry on to the bridge over the Firth west of the city with the majority of their charges—some had been sold to the traders, either by their employers or their families, so that if they returned, circumstances would likely only worsen for them. Some had come into Scotland through the harbor at Leith from foreign lands. Some of the girls couldn't remember ever having any family at all.

Lucan's dark mood improved somewhat when it was decided that he should lead the caravan from this point forward with Chumley at his side. He knew this area, knew their destination. And he would no longer have to catch glimpses of Effie and Gorman through the riders. It helped that Chumley had returned from the city with a jug in each hand, and he passed one up to Lucan before mounting.

"Thirsty, love?" he asked easily.

"I am indeed, Chumley," Lucan acknowledged darkly, urging Agrios forward.

"I thought as much." He adjusted his seat and then caught up with Lucan's horse in a double trot. "'Tis not an easy road we travel." He whistled over his shoulder and James Rose appeared on the other side of Lucan, escorting him up the road ahead of the caravan. He realized what they were doing—making Lucan out to be a man of import, travelling with his household. The only attention they would attract now would be admiration—a man so wealthy that all his servants rode astride.

They passed over the bridge easily, the keeper clearing the way for them as foot passengers and those of lesser means now stepped to the rough to let them through. Lucan heard jingling just behind him and glanced over his shoulder to see Gilboe and Dana tossing out coins. So many people with raised hands. So many poor, their ragged and dirty garments blending into the drab winter landscape. They seemed to be part of the bridge, part of the road, springing from seemingly nowhere and vanishing at once when they turned from his sight. Fifty… no, a hundred.

Surely there had not been such crowds when last Lucan was here.

No one wants to see the victims, Lucan…

"God bless ye, lord," a stooped man called up to Lucan, holding the coin in his clasped fists. He kissed it. "God bless ye and yer house, forever."

Lucan felt a pinch of shame—he'd done naught for these people to receive such exalting. The coin wasn't even his. It was all a lie. He was already half drunk in the saddle and wished to be anywhere but there in the moment.

They rode on past the bridge and the cluster of merchants and beggars on the far side of the Firth, the band now able to spread out a bit on the road. Chumley and James dropped back behind Lucan, and he was glad to not have to pretend at conversation.

The twisting road narrowed after a pair of hours, and Lucan began to recall his last visit to Tower Roscraig, when he had accompanied Tavish Cameron to its door for the first time as its laird. But the village they now entered was nothing like the first time Lucan had seen it—there were no shredded flags or faded marks on the trees warning of sickness. The fallow fields lay empty, true, but they also lay clear and dark and expectant, butting up cleanly to the village that now appeared occupied to the bursting and as busy as if it were midsummer.

The narrow, single file bridge over the deep dry ditch surrounding the keep was little changed, but now colorful banners rippled on the stone walls of Roscraig beneath its battlemented twin towers. The villagers milling about their business in the tidy tracks between the dwellings looked at them curiously, but none seemed overly alarmed at their presence. Lucan halted at the end of the bridge.

"Wait here," he said, rather more gruffly than he'd intended.

Silence met his command, but those riders nearest him sidled away until there was a clear path between Agrios and Effie Annesley astride. Their gazes met.

"Will you go on with me?" Lucan asked, and although the meaning behind his words was innocent, the phrasing of it startled him and he worried that the party would hear an alternative plea behind the efficient query.

"I'll wait," she answered with her chin lifted, her expression one of impatient irritation. "Perhaps he's not even here."

She's frightened, Lucan realized. And then thought that perhaps he was, too.

He turned about and urged on Agrios, who didn't hesitate at the narrow bridge, now improved to have sturdy railings on both sides. He dismounted before the thick wooden door, remembering the scars and gouges it had previously bore. Now the wood was smooth and dark and oiled and looked to be in fine condition. Lucan raised his fist to bang on the planks.

But before the first blow could fall, the door was yanked open with a whoosh of air and Harriet Payne stood in the doorway in her familiar kerchief and double-bodiced apron, her eyes wide and sparkling. There was a flush to her cheeks now, and the hem peeking out from beneath her apron skirt was embroidered and fine. Little polished gems hung from her earlobes and there was a hammered bracelet around her wrist. She looked ten years younger from when Lucan had seen her last—well cared for and happy.

And in that moment Lucan knew that he'd been right.

"Sir Lucan, for heaven's sake," she gasped. "Is it Tav? Glenna? What's happened?"

"Mistress Payne," Lucan said with a bow. "Forgive me for any worry my appearance might have caused you. On my honor, the laird and his lady were quite well in London when I saw them there as a guest of the king." He paused. "How wonderful it is to see you again."

Harriet clasped a hand to her bosom with a sigh. "Thanks be to God! I thought"—she broke off with a flap of her hand and Lucan saw her eyes glancing nervously toward the party on the road. "Doona mind my foolishness. 'Tis glad I am to see you, as well, Sir Lucan, sure. But if you know that Tavish weren't here, why've you come?"

"We've come to see Thomas, Harriet," Lucan said quietly.

Harriet Payne went stone still. "I don't ken what you mean, Sir Lucan. Thomas who?"

"I think you do ken. Thomas Annesley."

"Thomas Annesley!" Harriet hooted a nervous laugh. "You're having me on. Why on earth would you think Thomas Annesley would be here, of all places? And why would you be needing to find him?"

Lucan remained very calm, very slow in his reply. "I know he's here, Harriet. I've brought someone for him to meet."

Harriet was already shaking her head, little nervous movements. "'Tis sorry I am that you've come all this way, Sir Lucan. But you're mistaken. Who told you he was here, any matter, the daft bugger?"

"You did," Lucan said. "When you opened the door looking like a lass in love."

Harriet's eyes widened and she pressed her fingertips to her cheeks. "Like a lass? I…whatever do…such nonsense."

"May I and my party come in?" Lucan asked. "We've come a very long way. Northumberland, in fact," he clarified. "Darlyrede House is no more. Vaughn Hargrave is dead."

At this, Harriet stilled again and some of the color drained from her face. "Oh, mercy. Oh…mercy." She suddenly braced her arm against the stone jamb and pulled the door a little closer to her. "Nay. I'm sorry but…oh, you've gave me a shock, is all. But I canna"—she broke off her nonsensical ramblings and looked up into Lucan's eyes. "Dead, you say?"

Lucan nodded.

Harriet glanced behind her as if seeking assistance. "I'm nae prepared for visitors, I fear. You...perhaps you could stay in the village. Aye. I'm certain there is—"

"Harriet," Lucan said softly. "He'll want to meet her."

The older woman looked up again, her eyes worried. "Her?"

Lucan nodded and then he looked over his shoulder, down the length of the bridge, where Effie Annesley had dismounted and now stood at the side of her horse, the reins in her hand hanging down by her side. She looked young and wary and beautiful in her braid and her trousers and her quiver. Lucan waved her on.

She hesitated. Then she turned and handed the reins to Gorman, paused to say something Lucan couldn't make out. Gorman shook his head and nodded toward the keep. Effie wiped her palms on her trousers and then stepped on to the bridge, crossing to Lucan on her own, each fall of her boots ringing out hollowly in the dry moat below the wooden bridge.

She locked eyes with Harriet and the two women held one another's gazes until Effie arrived at Lucan's side.

"Harriet," Lucan said, "this is Effie Annesley, Cordelia Hargrave's daughter. She's come to see her father."

Chapter 14

"Effie," Lucan said, "this is Harriet Payne."

The old woman stared at Effie for a long moment after Lucan's proclamation, and Effie took the opportunity to stare back. She was a handsome woman, the hair beneath her kerchief streaked white within the dark, and Effie recognized the resemblance between her and the man called Tavish Cameron, whom she had seen at Henry's court.

Her brother, with whom she had never spoken.

This was the woman to whom her father had fled the night her mother had been murdered. The night Effie had been cut from her mother's body.

"Cordelia Hargrave?" The old woman looked up at Lucan with confusion and perhaps a bit of suspicion, clear on her lined face.

"It's true," Effie answered, drawing Harriet's attention once more. "Thomas Annesley is my father. Is he here or not?"

"But…how is that possible?" Harriet Payne seemed lost as she looked back and forth between Effie and Lucan, and then her eyes went to the crowd beyond the bridge. "And who are they?"

"Harriet," Lucan said quietly. "Perhaps it would be best if we explained everything to you both at once." He held her gaze, not unkindly, but pointedly.

"Please don't take him away again, Sir Lucan," Harriet choked in a whisper. "I couldna bear it. I've waited so long…"

Effie's heart stuttered. He *was* here.

Lucan reached out and took the old woman's hand between his own. "On my honor, mistress. I shall not force Thomas to do anything he doesn't wish to do. Shall I send our friends around to the postern gate for the time being? For you can be sure that they *are* friends."

Effie glanced up at Lucan. He considered the group from the Warren his friends now?

"Aye," Harriet said distractedly. "I'll send a maid with food and drink for them."

Lucan turned as if he would go to them, but Effie laid a hand on his arm—she would never have admitted it aloud, but she couldn't bear the thought of him leaving her in that moment.

"Where is the gate?" she asked. "I'll tell them."

Lucan pointed to the eastern side of the hold. "Just there. The back of Roscraig is a point over the bay.

Effie nodded and quickly relayed the information to the group through sign. She then looked back to Harriet.

"I'm ready."

The older woman stepped back from the door and Effie preceded Lucan into a long central corridor connecting the two towers, a tall, arched opening at the far end with the portcullis raised and the view of the gray firth beyond the long finger of structures beckoned like a peaceful dream. Harriet closed the door behind Lucan and then at once crossed the stones to the stairs curving up the right wall into the East tower.

Effie's guts felt atremble as she climbed behind the old woman, but Lucan Montague's presence at her back encouraged her onward. Her lips, nose, fingertips, toes, felt frozen, but her neck was hot. She shivered.

They came to a wide landing that boasted a doorway on the right, the stair picking up once more at the far end of the floor and disappearing up into the darkness of the tower. Harriet Payne passed through the doorway, and Effie followed.

The hall was beautiful. Tall ceilinged, with a long, dark trestle in the center, ringed with carved chairs and topped with a trio of ornate candelabra. Colorful tapestries adorned the walls on either side, leading like sentinels to a pair of soaring windows that flanked a massive hearth which hosted a crackling fire. Above the mantle, a wide portrait featuring three figures watched Effie's approach.

But it was beneath that portrait, one hand on the mantelpiece, his head turned away to watch the goings-on through the left-hand window, that the only occupant of the hall stood. A man with graying hair beneath a pushed-back fisherman's bonnet, his trousers thick and sturdy looking, his practical blade on his belt below his billowing, long tunic.

"Tommy," Harriet called out in a thin, cracking voice.

The man turned his head, his gaze bouncing off of Effie to go to the man behind her. He straightened, his brushy eyebrows raising.

"Lucan?" he asked quietly, and then his gaze came back to Effie and the entire universe seemed to slow its spinning to a halt as Effie came to the end of the trestle and stood not ten feet from Thomas Annesley.

Baron Annesley, Lord of Darlyrede.

Murderer and fugitive.

Fisherman.

Widower.

He looked at her, his brows now knit together, his head cocking slightly. His face was weather-worn and tanned, almost stained. And she remembered that he had lived a hard life for the past twenty-five years—a life on the sea. His long arms jutted out from his sleeves, the wrists and finger joints knobby and swollen. His clothing was still that of a common laborer, and yet it all appeared new and of fine quality.

Effie swallowed and raised her chin. "Are you Thomas Annesley?"

His head cocked a bit further, his eyes narrowed. "Doona take me as unkind, child, but I'd ken who is doing the asking of that question before I answer it. There are many who are out for Thomas Annesley's hide. Your fair face is somehow familiar to me, but…nay, your hair is light. I canna think where we've met. Nae Caedmaray."

"No, not Caedmaray," Effie allowed. "We've never met. I was given the name Euphemia Hargrave the night I first drew breath at Darlyrede House, some thirty years ago," Effie said. "But I now go by Effie. Effie Annesley."

Tommy's head straightened, then his back. His face paled beneath his bronzed skin, as if he suddenly recognized Effie's face. "Cordelia?" he rasped.

Effie nodded and forced herself to swallow before she could speak. "I am your daughter."

Eternity seemed to pass before Tommy took one halting step, then another. "Cordelia," he whispered again, his complexion reddening. And then with a staggering advance, he came to his knees before Effie, wrapping his arms about her.

"I thought they had taken you both," he sobbed. He gained his feet and took her into his arms roughly, still weeping.

Effie's arms hung limp at her sides as emotion swirled around her in a fury, shocking her into stillness. Was this really happening?

"Father?" she whispered.

"Aye, my girl," Tommy said, squeezing her tighter. "I'm here. I'm here."

And then Effie's arms went around his waist, felt the solidness of him. Her fingertips clutched at his woolen tunic.

Her father. Her parent. Her blood. Her family. Here, now.

"Father," she breathed, tears of a long-forgotten little girl at last releasing in a flood break, years of loneliness and isolation, fear that she would never find him, never know, at last able to find release in this Scottish castle, in the arms of an old man she had never met, but who her heart had recognized at once. She clung even more fiercely.

They pulled apart from one another after several moments and Effie at last looked into his eyes.

"My God," he breathed. "You are the image of her. Of your mother." He led her by the hand to the chair at the head of the trestle and pulled it out for her. "Sit down."

Effie glanced around the grand space and saw that Lucan and Harriet had quietly quit the room. She screeched the chair closer to the table, just as Tommy did to the one he dragged near.

"There were no portraits of her at Darlyrede," Effie said.

"There used to be," Tommy said. "The last was your mother and I in the costumes we were to wear at our wedding."

Effie shook her head. "I've never seen it."

"My God. My God. *Effie*." Tommy looked down at the table top briefly. "How did you…how did you know? What do you know?"

Then Effie told him of the years of doubt while in that plush prison Caris Hargrave had made for her; of circumstances and people and timelines that did not add up. The family she was to have come from that was never spoken of, never alluded to—Effie had never even been told from where they supposedly hailed. She spoke of the talks she'd had with Father Kettering, stories and rumors she'd heard from the village. Slowly the people who'd known the tales had vanished or died, and somehow this man, Thomas Annesley, was being blamed.

"I knew it wasn't true," Effie said to him. "What they were saying. I could see it with my own eyes. People who came to Darlyrede were there one day and gone the next. And Vaughn Hargrave only became richer and more powerful." She paused. "I knew how old I was. And I'd heard…I'd heard dreadful stories of Vaughn Hargrave's personal attendants. And then the night that word reached Darlyrede that Castle Dare was afire, I hoped what they said was true—that it was you who had done it. I prayed it was you. And I went to find you."

"It wasna me, lass," Tommy said sadly. "I didna start the fire that took Sir Lucan's parents and home from him. I was, by then, a long time at Caedmaray."

Effie nodded, trying to block the images of the burning hold, the devastated rage of young Lucan Montague from her mind—now was not the time to dwell on her own pain from that night. "I know."

"But you didna return to Darlyrede House," he guessed.

"I couldn't. I knew my…my grandparents were evil. They'd lied to me, and although I couldn't accuse them outright, I knew they'd had a hand in the disappearances in Northumberland. And I suspected one of them had killed Cordelia. I know now that I was right."

Harriet and Lucan reentered the hall then, each of them bearing a tray. Harriet poured the drinks. "Lucan?" the handsome old woman prompted. "You must tell him."

"Darlyrede is gone, Thomas," Lucan said, his handsome face grave. "It burned. There is nothing left. Vaughn Hargrave was killed in the blaze."

Tommy paled beneath his perpetual tan. "Padraig?"

"Padraig is well. And he was a hero that night," Effie said, leaning forward. "He saved many who were gathered there for a feast. Including Iris Montague, Sir Lucan's sister. They married the day after the fire."

"My Padraig is wed?" Tommy's lined eyes widened. "Harriet, did you hear?"

Harriet Payne tucked her chin with a please smile. "Oh, that *is* grand."

Effie's father stood and held his hand toward Lucan. "We're practically family now, you and I."

Lucan grasped the old man's hand with his own. "Congratulations, Thomas. You seem to be amassing quite a number of daughters-in-law of late."

Tommy nodded vigorously and sat down with a sigh. "Glad I am of it. *Hoo*." He rubbed his trembling, callused palms over his face and then dropped his hands to his knees before looking once more at Effie, and she saw that his eyes were redder than they had been. "Vaughn Hargrave is dead."

Effie nodded. "Caris survived. And she is why I have sought you." She paused to take a long drink of the wine Harriet had set before her. "At first we thought she, too, had perished in the blaze. But she somehow managed to escape the ruin. Once she had, she abducted my son and stole away to London to seek King Henry's protection."

Tommy leaned forward slightly. "Your son? My grandchild?"

Effie nodded again and gave into the small smile that pulled at her lips. "George Thomas. He is six."

"Harriet," Thomas said to the old woman in voice full of amazement. "George Thomas." He looked back to Effie. "And your husband—where is he?"

Effie pressed her lips together and drew a steady breath through her nose. "George's father and I did not marry. He has come on this journey with us, however."

Tommy was solemn, but he only nodded. "Go on, lass."

"Caris Hargrave admitted privately to Sir Lucan's sister—now Padraig's wife—that it was she who killed Cordelia, and cut me from her body," Effie said. "But she is still publicly blaming not only you, but me and the people I have resided with for the past fifteen years, for the atrocities committed across Northumberland. She has accused us both before the king, and Henry has taken guardianship of George."

"That mad bitch," Tommy muttered.

Effie couldn't go on just then. She had never imagined that speaking aloud to a veritable stranger the words that meant George's safety would be difficult, but now it was as if each dreadful revelation leading to the next was a herculean feat. She couldn't help but look toward the tall man in black to have mercy on her.

He did not fail her. "The king still wants you, Thomas," Lucan said. "And he plans to place Effie on trial as well before he decides what is to be done with your grandson."

"Holding him against our return, is he?" Tommy said in a low voice.

Effie nodded and opened her mouth to explain, but Thomas gave her no chance.

"I'll go," he said.

"Tommy, nay!" Harriet gasped.

"Aye. I will," he insisted. "I'll nae have Caris Hargrave within arm's reach of my blood and kin. Had I known that Effie...all those years." He paused a moment as if to collect himself. "I'd have pulled down Darlyrede with me bare hands. So I'll nae stand by now and allow it," he insisted, shaking his head and muttering a dark stream of Gaelic.

"Oh, my God, my God," Harriet moaned into her hands and then slapped her palm on the trestle table, her face flying around to regard Lucan. "You promised, Lucan! You promised me! *They'll hang him*!"

"Mistress Payne," Effie interjected, half rising and placing a hand on the old woman's forearm. "Do not lose hope." The woman whipped her head around to Effie, but rather than retreat, Effie took hold of Harriet's hand in both her own. "That satchel, just there on Lucan's hip—it's full of evidence, Harriet. Six months of evidence Iris Montague compiled while posing as Caris Hargrave's personal maid. It will damn half the nobility in Northumberland for the atrocities they've committed."

Harriet's face was still pulled tight with angry fear. "Is this true, Sir Lucan?" she demanded.

He nodded, reaching into the satchel at once and withdrawing Iris's leather portfolio. He set it on the tabletop and then pushed it toward Tommy. "The king won't be easily able to ignore it."

Effie's father undid the leather thong and withdrew the thick stack of sheaves carefully, almost delicately. He flipped through the uppermost pages, his forehead creasing into a frown.

"My God." He looked up at Effie. "What have they accused you of?"

"Murder," Effie answered straight away. "And robbery."

"Lies?" Tommy asked calmly.

"I consider what I've done neither murder nor robbery. Simply that I've spent the years since escaping Darlyrede building a community of those who've been wronged. And together, we have tried to take back for the people some of what has been stolen from them." She paused, letting Tommy sit with his surprise, her throat tightening. "I waited a long time for Padraig. For you."

"Oh, my lass," Tommy murmured and left his seat to embrace her again.

"The notorious band of criminals that populate the forest around Darlyrede," Lucan inserted himself into the conversation, and Effie was glad of it. She turned her face against her father's shoulder while he continued. "They've been Effie's family for fifteen years. Some of them have accompanied us to Roscraig."

Tommy nodded. "That's fine, then. That's just fine. They are welcome." He looked down at Effie and stroked her hair. "But you see that portrait there over the hearth?"

Effie looked again at the trio of solemn faces presiding over the hall, a noble looking man and woman, with a young boy between them.

"Me young self. And Myra and Tenred Annesley. Your other grandparents. Tower Roscraig first belonged to them, and then to me, and now to your brother Tavish. But it is also your home. And so tonight, your family shall be welcomed as my own kin, for that is what we are. Tonight, we will *celebrate*."

Effie embraced her father again and felt for the first time that perhaps—just perhaps—their wild plan might actually work.

Her eyes met Lucan's over Tommy's shoulder, and his handsome face was softened, his blue gaze intense as he watched her openly.

Not only might their plan work—they could *win*.

* * * *

They feasted that night, although the women they'd rescued from the road chose to take their meal with the servants in the kitchen. Harriet, in her typically kind fashion that Lucan so admired, had seen promise in a handful of the young women liberated from the slavers, and offered them employment at Roscraig. The others would journey on with the family to Gale and Mari at the White Swan to be set into new lives.

Thomas seemed to take an instant liking to Gorman Littlebrook when he was introduced as the father of his grandson, and Lucan felt a surge of jealousy as the two men talked and exchanged stories throughout the meal. Each time Thomas laughed at Gorman's down-to-earth humor, each time the bearded man spoke Effie's name with a smile in the telling of a tale, each time he spoke of his son, Lucan's guts twisted a little tighter, his spine got a little stiffer. He could barely smile at Bob's juggling, managed only to clap politely at Gilboe and Dana's pairing in a sweet ballad. Even the copious amount of wine Lucan put down did little to loosen the strain. He was one of the first to bid the company good-night, and venture through the main entryway to the West tower and the guest chamber Harriet had called to be prepared especially for him.

Lucan closed the door and leaned back against it for a moment with a sigh. He realized this was the same chamber into which Glenna Douglas had interred Harriet and Tavish and himself that first night at Roscraig, although the atmosphere inside was wildly changed. The fire crackled merrily, burnishing the tasteful fixtures in a warm, quiet glow. He wouldn't have recognized it.

Lucan's own life was unrecognizable now.

He pushed away from the door and drew the satchel strap over his head, setting the burden on the table as he walked toward the chamber's single, tall window. He ducked beneath the heavy drape covering the shutter and then pushed the barrier open to look out over the village.

He drew a deep breath of the cold air. Lights from several cottages twinkled in the night, a pair of doors stood open across the main track from one another—a sign of prosperity, if ever there was one in a village, that a dwelling was so well provided for in winter that the interior became too warm. Lucan took in the scene as his eyes adjusted to the night, noting the smooth village paths and tidy homes. The occasional contented bleat of an animal over the distant hush of the Firth was like gentle music flowing around the stones of Roscraig, and Lucan recognized that Tavish Cameron had created a place of peace and success for himself and his wife here. A safe place. A place they would raise up a family to prosper for generations.

What would Lucan's future hold? All he could possibly lay claim to was a stretch of grazing land at the moment, and that was under conditions from the king. Besides Agrios, Lucan had nothing.

A dark shadow of movement on the main road caught Lucan's eye, and he saw a man on horseback between the dry moat and the village, a hood raised against the chill wind blowing in from the Firth behind the hold. The man slowed his mount near the end of the bridge and seemed to look up at the tower, keeping the posture for several moments before turning the horse's head away and disappearing into the village.

Turning away for home, happy and satisfied, Lucan fantasized. His day's duties, whatever they may have been, complete.

Lucan realized he was becoming more maudlin by the moment and put it down to the wine he had overconsumed. He fastened the shutter tight and pushed through the drapes to re-enter the chamber, which now appeared too bright and cheery to his night-eyes.

He removed his belt and gambeson, unlaced then pulled off his boots, then crawled into the comfortable bed, but sleep was yet far away. On the morrow, they would depart for London where Lucan would once more relinquish Thomas Annesley to the king.

His thoughts turned back to the weary man on the Tower road, returning so late to the village. And Lucan envied him his honest trade, fearing that his own duty would fall far short of the mark of his conscience.

* * * *

The morning came too soon after a night of fitful slumber. Thomas was in the great hall with Harriet Payne when Lucan entered, their hands clasped together on the tabletop, their faces leaned close.

Harriet was first to notice him and pull away. "Good morrow to you, Sir Lucan. Everyone is gathered in the courtyard."

"Already?" He felt foolish at having blurted the question.

Thomas nodded. "Effie thought it best that we were off at once. For wee George's sake. You had already retired when it was decided."

"I've packed you a fair meal to break your fast on the road," Harriet offered, and the compassion on her face was almost too much for Lucan to bear.

"Of course." Lucan was nonplussed, but tried to cover it. "I thank you, Mistress." He stood for a moment longer before he realized that the older couple was likely saying their goodbyes here in a bid for privacy. He quickly gave a stiff bow. "I do hope we see each other again."

"Oh, now," Harriet scoffed, leaving Thomas and striding over to Lucan in her efficient manner. She took both his hands and leaned up on her toes to kiss his cheek. "You take care of my Tommy now, you ken?" she whispered near his ear before she pulled away. "And yourself, as well."

"On my honor, I shall do all in my power to see that no harm comes to him."

"I know you will," she said with a smile. "Send my Tav and Glenna home to me soon."

"Fare thee well, Mistress Harriet," Lucan said. He looked past the woman. "I'll meet you in the courtyard, Thomas."

Tommy only raised his hand in acknowledgement as Harriet hurried back to him.

Lucan felt the stares of Myra and Tenred Annesley from the portrait as he quit the hall. Neighbors to Castle Dare; friends of his parents.

It sent Lucan's thoughts tumbling.

Iain Douglas, longtime keeper of the Tower for his friend, Thomas—

—Archibald Blair. Murdoch Carson. Jessie Boyd. Adolphus Paget. Vaughn Hargrave.

All of them now dead. It seemed a trail of the dead followed him wherever he went.

Or perhaps it was a trail of the dead he was following.

He skimmed down the curving staircase, made his way across the stones of the entry hall toward the rear archway of the towers and emerged into the sunshine of the courtyard.

A group of Roscraig servants along with the party from the Warren gathered within the low stone walls of the courtyard. Gorman noticed Lucan's approach and hailed him.

"I've had Agrios brought out and packed for you."

"My thanks, Gorman." Lucan at last let his gaze go directly to Effie. "Good morning."

"Good morning," she replied, but her eyes did not meet his.

"Here he is," Chumley called out gruffly. "Mount up."

Lucan at first thought that Chumley was speaking of himself, but a glance over his shoulder showed him Thomas Annesley striding into the courtyard on his rolling gait, wearing his fisherman's bonnet and his sturdy costume, a small bag across his back. He kept his gaze straight on as he approached his horse, his whiskery jaw set.

Lucan again felt that this was a private moment on which he was intruding, so he turned back to Agrios and pulled himself into the saddle.

Without waiting for word, Lucan urged Agrios toward the postern gate and left the courtyard.

A village man was just making his way past the bridge on the tower road, his belts lashed tight across him, his deep hood drawn up, and Lucan felt a tingle of recognition as the man rode past without looking in Lucan's direction. The villager urged his mount into a trot and disappeared over the rise.

Recognition turned to suspicion: Could it be the same man he'd seen last night?

How would you ever know? Lucan asked himself. A man dressed for winter travel, nothing specific to recommend his place in society. Likely he was nothing more than an alderman, off to do the council's business while the lord was away. He knew well that Tavish Cameron only surrounded himself with the most capable of men. Lucan put himself down to a superstitious fool, touched by too little sleep and a foul humor.

The sound of riders approaching swelled behind him. Lucan glanced over his shoulder and saw Tommy giving him a wave. He spurred Agrios forward on the road, their first destination west to the bridge over the Firth and then to Edinburgh; then south east to the White Swan; then ever south, through the wasteland that had been the Northumberland of his birth and onward to London.

To his fate.

Chapter 15

"It has taken less than half the time to travel so far," Gorman said at Effie's side, the noon sun high and bright above, as if it was in a hurry to expend all its heat before the thick line of clouds creeping across the sky from the western horizon reached them. "At this pace, we shall reach the White Swan day after tomorrow."

"Leaving the wagon at Roscraig was a good decision." Her head was still spinning with the events of the past day, and she was glad to have Gorman's easy conversation to anchor her, as usual.

"If I've learned anything about our knightly friend," Thomas Annesley spoke from her right, "'tis that he is most efficient."

Gorman laughed in response.

Effie couldn't help but let her gaze fall upon the man riding before them in pair with Chumley. Lucan Montague was tall and dark in the saddle with his black horse, his black garb, his black hair. She could see the white clouds of his breath billowing up before him, dissipating in the sunshine. He had not spared her so much as a glance since they'd crossed over the Firth.

"Do you care to press on through the village, Lord Thomas?" Gorman asked.

Tommy chuckled. "I canna in good conscience answer to that title, me lad."

"It's the truth," Gorman said easily.

"What say you, daughter?"

A warm emotion blossomed in Effie's chest. *Daughter.* "If the clouds chasing us hold rain, I say we stop. We must be mindful of Winnie, and we have coin to spare now from the traders. The journey from London was filled with enough rain and ice to last me the remainder of my life."

"Sir Lucan," Tommy called out, and the dark-clad man looked over his shoulder, slowing his mount somewhat.

"Yes?"

"Would that you keep Effie company for a time," her father said in his quaint, acquired brogue, adopted after so many decades on Caedmaray. "I'd have a word with Master Littlebrook."

Effie frowned but maneuvered her horse between Lucan and Chumley's. Well, next to Lucan, for Chumley swung his own mount away.

Two to the front, two covering, she remembered crossly.

They rode along in silence for several moments, their horses' clopping falls on the dirt road muffling any bits of conversation she might have overheard.

"Why do you hate me?" Lucan asked abruptly, his tone one of curious puzzlement.

She knew her eyes were wide when she turned to him, and she was so completely surprised by his question that she didn't take time to formulate a careful response.

"Because you represent everything that is wrong with Northumberland."

"How?" he insisted. "I've not made that place my home in fifteen years. Unlike *you*."

"It's in your blood," Effie insisted. "You can't help it."

"You're of noble blood as well," Lucan said. "What makes yours hallowed over mine?"

Effie frowned. "I'm actually doing something to take back our land."

His tone was incredulous. "And I'm not?"

"Your aid is incidental. No doubt if you hadn't been forced on this journey, you wouldn't raise a finger to help us. It's different."

"It's bullshit," he stated in a rather vulgar fashion, completely out of his stiff, proper character. "You hold some specific injury against me, and I'd like to know what it is. You owe me that much, at least."

"I beg your pardon?"

"It was I who realized where your father would be hiding, saving us a wild goose hunt all through Scotland. And even if you *had* ended up at Roscraig eventually, you would have never gotten past Mistress Harriet without me."

Effie scoffed. "I think you're forgetting what we've persevered the past fifteen years," she said. "An old merchant's wife guarding the door would have proven no obstacle."

"I think *you* underestimate Harriet Cameron. The woman took beatings placing her at death's door in order to protect Thomas Annesley upon his escape from Darlyrede, and then for years afterward to protect her son from his stepfather. You would have had to kill her, and I do doubt that would have placed you in a very good light with Thomas."

Effie frowned.

"And," he continued in his smug, superior tone, "*I* carry the very information that could exonerate your father and return Darlyrede to your family."

"It's not *your* information," she pointed out. "It's your sister's. You *lost* yours in the fire at Darlyrede. Rather irresponsible, actually."

"I located your brothers," Lucan continued, unfazed. "Three of them, in fact. Without me, you would still be an orphan, without family."

"Let me touch the hem of thy garment, master," Effie gushed and rolled her eyes. "I was never an orphan. I simply didn't know where my family was."

"But rather than seek them, you chose to align yourself with a misfit band of lawbreakers and while away the years honing your criminal expertise."

Effie was stunned into silence for a moment. But only one moment.

"*Criminal expertise*? I was a fifteen-year-old girl when I escaped Darlyrede, Lucan." She made a sound of disgust in her throat. "And it's still so difficult for you to understand why I hate you? Really?"

"Yes," he answered at once. "I've never done anything to harm you. Quite to the contrary, as I've already pointed out. I didn't have to accompany you to London in the first place," he added gruffly. "Especially after you *shot me*."

"You simply can't stand it when someone isn't in awe of you," she accused.

"That's not it at all."

"It certainly is." They were riding a little faster now, likely a response to the growing heat of their conversation. But Effie could tell that the rest of the party wasn't hurrying to match their pace. "You think everyone should fall at your feet for your position with the king, your title, your education, your oh-so-diligent determination to uphold the assumed honor of your sainted name. Your prissy decorum that announces to everyone how much better you are than them."

"My education was my own doing," he informed her. "Vaughn Hargrave sent Iris and me to France to get us out of the way of him claiming Castle Dare lands."

"Yes, he did want you out of the way," Effie agreed. "But you're not as smart as you'd like to think; it wasn't only to have an easier time to try to steal away your inheritance and add it to his own coffers."

"What was it then, O wise one?"

"It was because you were the last person outside the Warren to see me alive the night I ran away, and he wanted to make sure you couldn't speak of it once it was discovered I was missing," she snapped, regretting it immediately, wishing she could take it—and all the other words that poured from her mouth—back even as her accusations built. "I came to you at Castle Dare the night of the fire."

"No, you didn't," Lucan argued.

"I found you—you and Iris were near your nurse. But it was you I spoke with. Don't pretend you don't remember."

"You didn't," Lucan insisted. "The only people who came to us that night besides Hargrave were servants of the hold."

"Perhaps you could ask your old nurse," Effie suggested.

"I can't," Lucan scoffed. "She died later that same night, overcome with smoke while trying to retrieve some of our personal possessions. I felt dreadfully guilty for it."

"Is that what Hargrave told you? God, you'd think by now you'd have gone over in your mind everything he'd ever said to you and realized it was all a lie." Effie let silence hang between them for a moment, letting his words hover in relief against the backdrop of the information she was telling him.

"You *weren't there*," he insisted through clenched teeth.

"I begged you to take your sister and go to the king with me that night. Do you remember your response to my plea that we should seek aid from the crown?" Effie demanded in a lower voice.

Lucan turned his head toward her then, slowly. His face was ashen. "That wasn't you."

"You struck me," Effie said. "You accused me of trying to rob you, and ordered me from your sight or you said you would kill me yourself."

"It wasn't you," he repeated.

"You called me a wretch, not worthy to labor in the house of Montague." She paused, and dealt the final blow. "You were holding your mother's burned slipper in your hand. And you struck me with it. As if driving away a stray dog."

He turned his face forward once more toward the advancing road, but Effie didn't think he was actually seeing anything.

"I was wearing—"

"A white gown," Lucan said dazedly.

"Actually, it was pale blue." She paused. "But it likely looked white in the night."

"You had no cloak," he accused. "I assumed you were of Castle Dare because you had no cloak. And"—he broke off.

Effie didn't want to tell him where her cloak had gone. He likely wouldn't believe her, and it didn't matter now, anyway. It had been the foolish gesture of a wealthy young girl who'd had no idea how close she would come to freezing to death that night.

"The Hargraves had been to Castle Dare that evening," he said. "They'd dined with my parents. A special occasion my father had planned."

"God damn it, Lucan—*I know*," Effie said. "That the Hargraves were both away was what allowed me to escape. It was their rule that one of them should always be in residence, and they almost never broke it."

"What happened to you?" Lucan asked after some time. "After the fire—where did you go?"

"The wood," she answered easily. "I had nowhere else to go, so I ran blindly. I stumbled into a snare and was trapped. I would have frozen to death by morning if Old Robin hadn't found me."

"Are you at last to tell me who Old Robin is?"

"The old lord of Locktrey."

"Locktrey?" Lucan frowned. "That tiny place was abandoned decades ago. There wasn't even a village. Only an old Saxon ruin. What little land it claimed was—"

"Absorbed into Darlyrede lands," Effie finished for him. "There wasn't a village, true. Just the ancient wooden keep, and the spring. Old Robin and his few servants. Adolphus Paget wanted the water. Hargrave gave it to him as a *gift* in return for the specimens Paget supplied." She paused a moment, remembering the gruff old hermit. How kindly he had grown toward her, how instrumental in her life.

"He died ten years ago, this spring," Effie said at last. "He was wary of me at first, having come from Darlyrede, but once he realized I was never going back there, he taught me to shoot, and to track. How to rob a man on horseback without ever spilling blood, although there was plenty of blood spilled. By the time he died, we had started building up the family in the Warren—refining our purpose. Clarifying our mission. Rescuing those who needed it, taking in those who had managed to escape. Gorman was one of the last ones to arrive before Old Robin died. I'm glad they knew each other."

"And so you truly are the leader of the band," Lucan said.

Effie nodded. "Robin left them in my care."

"Because you'd proven yourself?"

"Not really," Effie admitted. "I was capable, certainly. He saw to that. But it was because I was born to a noble family. Old Robin never gave up hope that, one day, I would be able to win back Northumberland for good."

"So, let me see if I understand," Lucan said contemplatively. "You loathe me for things I did and said to a person largely a stranger to me, on what was arguably the worst night of my life?"

"You could have stopped it."

"I was ten and six, Effie," he barked. "I'd just lost my father *and* mother, *and* my home. I suddenly had a little girl to look after. I'll not apologize for having a wonderful home with loving parents prior to the fire. I'm not responsible for your bad childhood. And between the two of us, you're the only one with Hargrave blood running in your veins. So perhaps you might consider that all your good deeds are done either out of guilt or to stave off the tendencies of your own kin."

Effie felt as though Lucan had reached out and slapped her again, and so this time she wanted to strike back. "Perhaps you might consider then that your family was killed in a fire on the very night both Vaughn and Caris dined at Castle Dare, at your parents' request, I might add. That fire wasn't an accident, Lucan, and you might also ask why it is that Vaughn Hargrave wanted your father dead."

"That's impossible to prove. I've already tried," he said through tight lips, as if the idea pained him. "I don't know why. Perhaps he wanted the land."

"For what?" Effie demanded. "Darlyrede lands border the same river. The keep is gone. Sheep graze on the land to keep it from running to woodland."

"What are you suggesting, then?"

"I'm not *suggesting* anything," Effie snapped. "You've spent so many years investigating everything and everyone with any connection at all to Darlyrede and yet you claim to have no idea the evil that's gone on under your very nose—likely because you don't want to see it!"

She jerked her horse's head around too swiftly, she knew, but she couldn't stand to be with him another moment. All those old memories, which had largely drifted down, down into the depths of the ocean of her past, had risen with a furious, bubbling vividness, and hearing him speak of his sainted parents and her own dirty bloodline had made her feel angry and ashamed and more than a little uncertain that her own emotions toward him were valid.

Of course they were valid, she told herself as she rode past her father and Gorman, not caring that their heads whipped around to watch her as she retreated to the back of the caravan. She hadn't been able to build the family and sustain the Warren because she was a naïve fool.

Effie turned her mount at the rear of the party and pulled forward on the outside of Gilboe. She looked straight ahead. "You're up, Dana."

She knew Dana and Gilboe exchanged wide-eyed glances, but Effie ignored it as Dana rode ahead in an increased cloud of dust.

Two to the front, two covering.

Gilboe cleared his throat gently. "Do you wish to—"

"I do not."

"All right." The monk was silent again for a moment, but then began chanting aloud in Latin in his quite lovely *guttoris* register, honoring the patron saint of Finland, of all places.

Winnie, riding just before Effie, twisted around in her saddle.

Are you well?

Yes.

Are you lying?

Yes.

Winnie faced forward in her saddle once more, but then Kit Katey, who rode next to her, looked over her shoulder to peer at Effie. It was only since Adolphus Paget had been killed that Kit Katey had been able to venture out regularly with the family—as his favorite, she had been actively sought after she'd escaped. Effie valued her friendship—and her skills with the blades—more than almost anyone else's in the family. This woman knew loss of home and pain and longing, perhaps in different circumstances than Effie, but with the same sorrowful depth.

The young woman's straight, black hair twisted down her back in a single, long plait, and her snood emphasized her dark, exotic eyes and warm complexion. There was pity there, but not the sort that made Effie bristle. Perhaps not pity then, but empathy and recognition. She nodded once at Effie, and Effie returned the gesture with a curt one of her own.

There didn't need to be words between them, there never had been since the night Gorman had rescued her and carried her into the Warren in his arms.

Then Kit Katey, too, faced forward once more as Gilboe broke into another chant, praying the family down the road now with *Sacris solemniis*.

Effie glanced over her shoulder; nothing behind them save a lone rider wearing a deep hood with a small pack across his saddle. He was too far away to be an immediate concern, and seemed to be falling further behind—likely being unwilling to pass such a large party alone, lest they be a band of thieves.

This thought made Effie give a dark huff of laughter. Whatever happened next, it was clear that no amount of physical attraction would allow her and Lucan Montague any chance of a friendship. Besides, she only wanted George, and her father, safe. Lucan assisting in both those ends would give Effie as much peace with the man as was likely possible.

If they never saw one another again after London, that would be the best outcome for everyone.

After all, what other choice was there?

Chapter 16

Lucan chose a seat at the far end of the table on the opposite side of where Effie Annesley sat between Thomas and Gorman. The rain fell in a hushed roar just barely audible over the sounds of dining and drinking and conversation in the little common room of the inn where they'd stopped for the night. He'd thought to put distance between them after their clash on the road, but his unfortunate vantage point gave him the perfect view of her perfect profile, and every move she made beckoned to him from his peripheral vision.

Lucan sat next to Gilboe; Dana, across from the monk. The oddly matched pair were engaged in a game of dice between their trenchers, to which the winner of each round was entitled to the next tankard. Lucan tried to distract himself from the woman sitting down the length of the trestle by covertly examining Dana.

Adam's apple—unquestionable…ish.

Hair—silky, blonde, curling.

Lips—pink, plump.

Breasts—perhaps…?

Wrists—as thick and bony as Lucan's own ankle. *And* fringed with coarse black hair peeking from beneath a delicate sleeve.

"Dana," Lucan said abruptly, not considering that he'd likely already had too much to drink to engage in any respectable discourse. "How is it that you've never been married?"

Lucan felt more than saw Gilboe's round, strangely hairless face turn to regard him.

Dana, however, only continued to look at the tabletop with pursed lips and fluttering eyelashes. "Why, Sir Lucan, what a personal inquiry."

"Are you offended?" he asked.

"Not if you're proposing. I suppose that is a wonderful excuse to find my way to your nice warm chamber tonight."

Gilboe threw back his head and laughed like a donkey.

Lucan couldn't help his grin. He didn't allow himself to dwell on the thought that, had Dana answered him in such a fashion weeks ago, he would have bristled and sputtered and ranted denials. "That doesn't answer my initial question."

Dana gave a little wiggle on the bench. "Well, I suppose the only truthful answer I can give is yes. I was married at one time. Long ago, mind you. *Ages*. I was little more than a child."

Lucan waited, but Dana wasn't forthcoming. "What happened? Were you widowed?" *Just say 'my husband' or 'my wife'...*

"Oh, nothing so convenient as that, I'm afraid. I was jilted, if you must know and can believe it."

"No," Lucan denied gravely.

"Yes." Dana looked smug, but only pressed pink lips together. "At least there were no children to contend with. Your roll, Gilboe."

Lucan sighed. From down the table a roar of laughter rose, and Lucan couldn't help but glance that way again as he brought his tankard to his mouth. Effie had covered her face with both her palms as if in embarrassment, but her shoulders were shaking with laughter.

Suddenly Thomas gained his feet and raised his tankard, waving it around at the otherwise empty common room. "Me own daughter, ladies and gents. Doona trifle with her."

Gorman drew Effie to his side in a one-armed embrace.

Lucan felt wetness dribbling over his knuckles and he looked down to see ale spilling onto the table through the crack in his tankard beneath his crushing grip.

"*And then*!" Bob the Butcher's Boy announced loudly before rising and, not content with merely standing as Thomas had, he stepped onto the bench, towering over the party. "The poor bastard was made to walk the whole way to Sheffield with his cock still in the—well, you know. No trousers at all! Only boots!"

"Served him right!" Thomas crowed happily.

Lucan wanted to know. He wanted to know the whole of the story they'd just told, he wanted to be included in the history, in the knowledge of their adventures and escapades. He wanted to know all the people they'd saved, all the criminals they'd outed or stolen from or sent to Sheffield with their cocks out.

But Lucan was still an outsider. An outsider who had hurt Effie Annesley today, he knew. He'd hurt her because she had hurt him first, suggesting he had simply overlooked that his parents were somehow of the same ilk as the Hargraves. Everyone in the group regarded him as privileged and oblivious to their cause. A man out for himself, who would only do the right thing when forced.

That wasn't true. Was it?

Perhaps not, but he knew that he'd been wrong in the things that he'd said to her. Dead wrong.

He allowed himself to be drawn into three rounds of dice with Dana and Gilboe, deftly shifting his seat when Dana's foot began rubbing up the inside of his calf. He lost each time, but bought the tankards with a smile and bit of a sense of reparation. These were good people. Strange people, true. But good. He recalled the faces of the women and girls in the slave traders' wagon when they'd been rescued—their expressions as though they were experiencing a miracle. Lucan was starting to recognize a difference now between the law simple, and what was right and good, and it was the family from the Warren who was teaching him.

It was Effie Annesley teaching him. Effie and her brothers. And her father, Thomas. Thomas Annesley, where the story began and where it would soon draw to an unknown conclusion that Lucan would not likely be part of.

"I'm done in," Lucan said, no longer able to sit happy beneath the weight of his guilt and self-recriminations and the unknown future. The band didn't seem wont to bring the drinking and merriment to a halt anytime soon, and in truth, Lucan wasn't surprised; this wasn't his first journey with them, after all. He stood from the bench and tossed a coin to the tabletop. "No match for the pair of you. Enjoy with my compliments."

"What a gentleman," Dana tittered.

"A valiant effort, Sir Lucan," Gilboe praised sagely as he raked the coin into his hand. "No shame in a fair loss."

Lucan shuffled from behind the table and walked toward the rear of the common room and the narrow door that hid the stairs to the short upper floor. The majority of the band were sleeping in the stable loft, but Lucan and Effie and Winnie would each share the two rooms upstairs. Thomas had refused the offer to share Lucan's chamber, saying he was unused to such luxury and would rather bed down with Gorman and the others. Lucan had wanted to comment that he'd seemed quite comfortable in Roscraig's fine hold, but he'd held his tongue. Let the man have his choice—he'd done without such a thing for long enough.

Lucan traversed the undulating steps to the constricted walkway above and pushed into his chamber. The bolt on the door was missing its sleeve, but there was a tiny, ancient brazier glowing in the center of the floor, and the room was cozy beneath the eaves—Lucan reminded himself to stoop as he staggered to the pot in the corner.

No Bannockburn Protocol for him tonight, thank you very much.

Relieved of his physical necessity, he ducked from beneath his satchel strap and looped it over the post at the end of the bed, then crawled beneath the wool blanket onto the thin ticking, which although didn't afford much in the way of plushness, was filled with down and insulated from the cold in a magnificent fashion as he stretched himself out with a sigh. The pillow, too, was of the same construct, and Lucan was able to punch it precisely to cradle his neck and head. He stared toward the invisible ceiling through drooping eyelids, hearing the laughter—and now wildly pitching song—waft up through the floorboards.

Effie and her family. Lucan alone.

Always alone…

He must have fallen asleep right away, because the next thing he realized was that he was riding Agrios across the fields of Castle Dare, Effie Annesley before him on the saddle, her trousered legs over to one side as she leaned back against him. His arm was laid across her slim midriff, her head just beneath his chin, and he could smell the heady fragrance of her hair. It was spring, the bees buzzed frantically around Agrios's hooves, the trees budding and blooming and the first tiny, white and purple wildflowers springing up tall and spindly in the grass. Below them, the river ran full and wild, and the wood spread out as far as Lucan could see.

"It's good to be home," Effie said in the dream.

Lucan brought his hand up from her abdomen to cup her breast and she turned her face up to his. Lucan lowered his mouth to those sweet, irresistible lips, anxiously anticipating the taste of them…

Something cold and firm rubbed up the length of his calf, causing Lucan's eyes to snap open—it was a foot. There was someone in his room—someone in his bed.

Damned Dana.

His right arm shot around in a blink, instinct taking over even while he was still snared in the dregs of sleep, and his hand clasped around a slender throat.

Slender, and smooth, and definitely no Adam's apple.

His face was inches away from the intruder's.

"Sorry, sorry," Effie Annesley slurred. "I think I'm in the wrong bed."

* * * *

Effie knew she was drunk. So drunk that she had stumbled into Lucan Montague's room and crawled into bed with him, thinking it was Winnie who took up the other side of the ticking.

But it was definitely Lucan—she could smell him in the darkness, feel the warmth of his breath just above her flushed cheeks. It wasn't Winnie's hand now loosening around her throat.

"Effie?" Lucan whispered.

"Sorry," she said again. "I didn't remember which was ours. I guessed." He was leaning over her, his hand still lightly on the skin of her neck, the side if his hand resting on her collarbone. She brought her hands up to either side of his ribs. "I want to say that I'm sorry," she muttered. "Anyway. This afternoon. I didn't mean to—"

"Shh," he whispered, and his thumb stroked the side of her throat, just beneath her ear. "I'm sorry, too. We seem to bring out the worst in each other, do we not?"

She nodded, but wondered in her drunkenness if he would understand. "I don't want that," she confessed.

She didn't think she was imagining that his face was nearing hers. She could feel the draw of his well-shaped lips just above hers in the dark. Her hands slid further around his back, and she raised her head, just a scant inch, and there he was.

Lucan's mouth slanted over hers at once, their kiss deep and deliberate. A jolt slammed through Effie's body, and she was glad that she'd drank so much, alcohol blunting the power of the physical meeting with Lucan Montague. Immediately, the depths of her body yearned for him. The kiss grew even more firm, hungry; Lucan's hand wrapped around the back of her neck as Effie forced her right knee up between Lucan and the mattress beneath her, drawing his body into the cradle of her legs and then arched her back to press her pelvis into his hard manhood.

He groaned against her mouth and pulled his face away only an inch.

"Are you naked?"

"Shh." Her hands slid down to grasp his hips as she arched up again, pulling him tight against her. "I want you, Lucan."

"But Gorman…"

"I'm not married to Gorman."

"You're drunk."

"So are you." She ran her right hand down the front of his trousers, cupped him, her expectations of Lucan inside her now driving her to a frenzy. "Let's just do it. We both want to. Please. Please, please, please." She punctuated the pleas with kisses.

He groaned again, and his hands went to his waistband, loosening his ties. Effie let her knees open wide now and kissed the crest of his cheekbone, cradling his head. She felt the hot, wide tip of him press, rub up and down her cleft, and then he seated himself at the entrance of her and pushed inside.

Effie cried out, clutching him to her. Lucan shushed her then covered her mouth with his own as he began to ride her. She raised her knees, gripping his ribs with her thighs, digging her nails into his back. The old wooden bed beneath them creaked and squeaked and even the sound of it was sensual, her breath was like a bellows in her nose. Over and over, he rocked her deeper into the mattress. She turned her head away to gasp for life-giving air and another cry escaped her.

Lucan covered her mouth with his hand, driving into her harder now, faster. "Shh," he warned darkly. "They'll hear us. They'll know."

She peaked then, her entire body seizing, expanding. Lucan kept his hand over her mouth as his thrusts came quicker, and then he too reached his climax, and Effie felt him pulsing. She cried out rhythmically to the throbbing of her womb, the sound still muffled by Lucan's palm. It seemed that her climax had done little to sate her want of him though, for she was arching against his length again, yelping against his hand.

"What is it?" he whispered against her ear. "Are you afraid it's over?"

She raised up to kiss him madly and savored the feel of his tongue thrusting deep in her mouth.

He pulled away, Effie sucking his tongue as he went. "I've got you in my bed now," he murmured darkly. "I'm going to keep you here all night."

And, to Effie's delight, he did.

Chapter 17

The chamber above the inn didn't get much lighter with the dawn, but Lucan sensed the new day had come just the same.

He didn't wish to open his eyes. He knew he would feel the copious amounts of drink he'd consumed the night before, and he didn't feel at all rested—his dreams had been too vivid, too real, too wonderful to have allowed him the dark nothingness of drunken oblivion. He had no desire to return to the mundane world of road travel and kingly decrees and benevolent bandits. He had made love to Effie Annesley all the night, and it had been so real, so passionate and consuming. He could still smell her skin, her most intimate parts…

He opened his eyes at last to regard the black beams and time-darkened thatching of the underside of the roof. Naught but a drunken dream. His head was splitting already.

He rolled over to his side to prepare to stand, and his back and thighs twinged as if he had walked a score of miles in his sleep. He slid his legs over the side of the bed and sat up with a groan.

I'm not married to Gorman, he heard in his mind.

Please, please, please...

His breathing stopped, and he slowly looked over his shoulder. The bed was empty, of course, but then his gaze stuttered over a little dark string and he wondered at its origin. He took it between his fingers and realized it was a leather thong, which one might use to tie up a parchment, or a small packet of fire starter, or…Effie Annesley's braid.

He drew his fingers through her hair, tangling in the plait, slid the leather tie from its end as she rode him...

It all came flooding back to him then, every touch, every stroke, every sigh. He'd made love to Effie Annesley in this very bed, for hours—she'd fallen asleep in his arms.

In that moment, his heart leapt. It was real. She'd wanted him as much as he'd wanted her, until at last it had been impossible for either of them to resist. What did it mean for their future? Lucan's heart was still beating too fast for the early hour and so he took a breath and found his way to the pot, his naked skin prickling in the frigid air of the chamber—the brazier had gone out long ago, but the heat he and Effie Annesley had generated in the bed they'd shared had rendered it useless, any matter.

His immediate physical needs attended to, Lucan's next priority was dressing so as to stop his chattering teeth. He found his trousers and undershirt, stockings and garters strewn about the shadows of the floor, his gambeson where he'd left it, and pulled them on as quickly as their stubborn fastenings would allow. He sat back down on the edge of the ticking and donned his boots in deference to his frozen toes, and then gave an irritated sigh.

Should he woo her now? Were they to couple?

Ridiculous.

He was no starry-eyed virgin. Yes, he and Effie had shared a night of phenomenal physical release, but he didn't know if it would have any outcome whatsoever on their official relationship.

Regardless, he must make his way below. The band needed to be on the road as early as possible in order to reach the White Swan that evening, and Lucan was starving. He would take his cue from Effie Annesley and behave accordingly. Likely, it was no matter to her. A bit of sport. A release of pent-up passion as a result of the tumultuous few weeks she'd experienced and the strain she was under.

But Lucan's heart beat faster once more at the idea of seeing her.

Lucan gave another sigh and stood up. There was no use delaying it—he'd faced worse in his life. He turned, reached to the bedpost for the strap of his satchel and froze.

He stepped quickly and looked to the other post—nothing. A frantic glance at the headboard revealed no worn bag, heavy with the square outline of the portfolio inside.

Blasted Effie Annesley.

Anger flared for a moment and Lucan struggled to remain calm. She'd taken it when she'd left his room. For what reason, he knew not, but there was no other explanation.

She was so drunk, she didn't even know into whose bed she'd crawled, he chastised himself. *So drunk that she stayed with you all the night.*

He shook his pounding head free of those troublesome ideas. Effie had the bag. Lucan just didn't know why she'd taken it.

He threw open the door and skimmed down the treacherous steps.

Thief.

Manipulative, thieving woman.

The door at the bottom of the stair was closed, and he flung it open, sending it crashing into the wall behind. All eyes in the common room raised to him upon his entrance—the whole of the party, breaking their fasts in morning silence at the trestles.

Only Effie Annesley kept her eyes on her bowl. Lucan's heart stuttered at the sight of her despite his fury. She looked like a figure from a da Panicale painting, the light finding the side of her face and giving it a glow like polished ivory. Her hair was plaited and knotted at her nape, and Lucan knew it was because she had been unable to locate her leather tie—which he still hid in his gripped fist.

The toadish, aproned matron of the inn tossed him a glare. "Mind the *door*! What is it with you lot?"

"Good morrow to you, Sir Lucan," Thomas Annesley called out. "Plenty of porridge left."

Lucan strode across the floor and stepped over the bench to the empty spot at the trestle at Thomas's side, directly across from Effie. He sat. Still, she did not raise her face.

But Winnie, seated to the right of her did. She stared directly at Lucan with a serene if serious expression.

Kit Katey was on Effie's left, and she gave Lucan a small smile before lowering her eyes to her breakfast once more.

A steaming bowl of gray mush was set before him, but Lucan ignored it, keeping his gaze pinned on the blonde across from him, even as he picked up his spoon.

Lucan looked at the slight frame of Effie Annesley—no strap crossed her chest. Everyone else at in the hall had their personal possession near them at table.

She finally glanced up. "What?"

"The satchel?" Lucan quietly suggested.

Effie blinked. "What about it?" She didn't seem at all bothered by his distress.

"You have it?"

She frowned. "No? Why would I have it?"

"You didn't take it?"

"What do you mean? Why one earth would I"—she broke off. "Where's the bag, Lucan?"

"Something amiss, Sir Lucan?" Gorman called out from down the table.

Lucan's heart creaked to a halt, his blood continuing to rush in his ears. "It was gone from my room when I woke."

In a flash Effie was up from her seat and had the old matron gripped from behind, her tray crashing to the floor, a knife pressing against the largest of the woman's bloated chins. "Where is the bag?"

"What bag, mistress?"

"Don't trifle with me," Effie warned. "I will cut your throat in an instant. The bag that was in that man's room last night. Just tell me where it is, and I shall let you go. We can forget it ever happened."

"I don't know anything about a bag!" the old woman sobbed and shook. "I never went in the chamber after setting the brazier—I swear!"

"Your servant, then," Effie hissed.

"Nay, mistress! Nay!" The woman squealed. "Were only me last night. I sent the rest home to save the wages!"

Thomas got up from the table and strode to where his daughter held the woman captive, reaching out to gently take hold of Effie's wrist and pull the blade from her hand.

"Easy, lass," he said. "Let her go—she speaks true. She followed us out of the common room last night and made her pallet in the kitchen."

The old woman spun out of Effie's embrace as soon as she could and rushed from the common room with a hitching sob, leaving the mess of the tray on the floor.

If Effie's skin had looked like polished ivory before, now it had lost all semblance of living color, like the frigid snow that had covered the land, blinding, blue-white, cold. Even her lips were drained of warm hue.

Lucan looked around at those gathered to either side of the trestle. "Did any of you see…?"

"No," Gorman answered right away. "Winnie went up before her, but Effie retired when the rest of us did. The innskeep locked the door behind us."

"Besides," James Rose scoffed, "why would any of us care to take charge of the damned thing in such secret? We've no need of it."

Some members of the band were murmuring to each other, but Lucan noticed that Winnie herself had again fixed him with a solemn stare.

She knows, Lucan realized. *She knows Effie spent the night with me.*

Effie was still standing over the mess in the floor, her father's arm laid across her shoulders. "Are you certain you had it with you in the chamber last night?"

Lucan glared at her. "Of course, I'm sure—that satchel is priceless. I hung it on the post before I went to bed, and when I woke, it was gone."

"The front door was open." Chumley spoke from the end of the table, where he cradled a mug of warmed wine in his hands—he didn't look up from the contents of his cup. All eyes turned to him, including Lucan's. "I thought it was the innskeep sweeping the dooryard or fetching wood or some such bollocks and she'd not pushed it to afterward. But when she came through from the kitchen with the tray, she gave me a nasty look before walking over and slamming it shut. She'd thought it was me, I suppose."

"It could have been anyone, then," Bob offered glumly. "Gone before we woke, to who knows where."

In Lucan's peripheral vision, Gilboe crossed himself.

"Come," Thomas was saying gently to Effie as he led her back to her spot at the table. "Let's just think about this a moment. Nae need to get all a-fluster."

"There is a need, Tommy," Effie insisted loudly. "That satchel is the only thing saving you from the gallows. The only thing!" She placed her forehead in her hands. "Without it, you daren't return to London."

"Well, now," Thomas began, easing back down into his own seat.

"She's right," Lucan said, needing to squeeze the words through his constricted throat. All Iris's work, the risk she'd taken with her very life… gone. All gone, while under Lucan's protection. "Going back now guarantees your death."

Gorman shot to his feet. "Are you suggesting we simply abandon George?"

Thomas looked up at Gorman. "Nae one is suggesting any such thing."

"You'll get your son back," Lucan said. "I swear it."

"You shouldn't promise such things," Effie said in a low voice across from Lucan, her head still in her hands. "You have no power to sway Henry—it's Caris Hargrave's, Vivienne Paget's, word against yours. And mine." She raked her fingers back through her hair as she looked up at him. "Me, you, Tommy—all three of us are damned."

"How could you not know someone crept into your chamber last night?" James demanded. "No one can so much as shit without your nose up his backside."

Lucan tried to stay calm, but he felt his ears heat. "I don't know," he said hesitantly. Winnie hadn't taken her eyes from him the entirety of the time, and Lucan's skin was crawling. "I noticed the bolt on my door was missing the sleeve, but…I don't know," he repeated. "I was…"

"Drunk?" Chumley offered mildly.

"Yes," Lucan murmured.

"Oh-ho!" James Rose barked. "It seems the saintly knight of the realm has executed a…how do you say?... faux pas!"

Dana frowned disapprovingly. "Stop. That is unnecessary, James. I'm quite certain Sir Lucan feels badly enough about losing the only evidence that could exonerate Thomas and free little George."

"I didn't *lose* it," Lucan insisted. "It was stolen."

"Iris warned us not to travel with it," Effie whispered. Her eyes were on the tabletop, but she seemed to be looking through it.

Lucan scrubbed his hands over his face with a growl of frustration. "We can't leave now."

"What, you're hoping whoever stole it will bring it back?" Gorman scoffed. "There's nothing of value in it to anyone else. Any common thief would realize at once that it was only paper and toss it in the river or burn it."

"No," Lucan insisted. "It wasn't a common thief. It couldn't have been. Nothing else in my chamber was touched—my sword, my boots, my own bag. Easy plunder." He broke off as the answer occurred to him. "We've been followed. This whole time."

"No, we haven't," James Rose said with a roll of his eyes.

"We have," Lucan stood up, unable to sit still with the realization. "I saw him on the Tower Road—I thought he was a villager or the sheriff late returning. But then I saw him set out before us the next day. He rode a sumpter, with a black tail."

"A man in a deep hood," Effie said. "With a pack across the back of his saddle. His sleeves were fur."

Lucan's gaze went to her, his blood chilling at the confirmation. "Yes."

She looked across the room at him. "He was following us on the road yesterday. I saw him after our row, although he dropped back when I turned to watch him. It could have been the same man we encountered at the inn."

"*God damn it*!" Gorman shouted, and he too stood up to stomp about the room.

Gilboe winced and crossed himself.

"That's it, then," Thomas said quietly. "He'll have destroyed the packet for Caris Hargrave."

"No," Lucan mused, his mind racing. "No, I don't think so, Thomas."

"Neither do I," Effie added. Everyone turned to her. "If he indeed was hired to steal the information, Caris wouldn't trust him to dispose of it. She'd want it in her hands, first."

"*Yes*," Lucan said, low and emphatically. "She would want to see the charges that could be leveled against her, even in unsupported testimony, and come up with explanations for them all."

"*Then* she will destroy the evidence," Effie added.

Lucan nodded. Clever Effie Annesley. "I concur. Absolutely."

"So, what you're saying." Bob leaned his elbows on the tabletop and held his palms apart, as if showcasing the ideas he was speaking aloud. "Some bloke hired by Caris has stolen the satchel to take it all the way back to London, where it's actually the most dangerous to her? She's mad to snoop through it all and then burn it or what have you?"

"Of course, we can't really know until we return. But it's precisely what she would do," Effie said. "It's why she was mad to know if I was truly dead. She wasn't grieving for me all those years with her ridiculous farce of mourning, she wanted to be certain I would never talk about the things I knew. She's not afraid of being caught. She never has been. She's always been able to create some wild explanation that can't be disproved. It's as if she has a charm upon her."

"What if you're wrong?" Gorman interjected quietly. His question was spoken to the group, in a hypothetical tone, but Lucan noticed that he was looking directly at Lucan.

"I don't accept that," Lucan said with a shrug. "I'm not wrong."

Dana spoke up meekly then. "But what if you are?"

"This is bollocks." James Rose propped his boot heels up on the tabletop and leaned his shoulders back against the wall behind him. "What's done is done. I say we leave Tommy at the Swan safely over the border and make a plan to rescue George. To hell with the rest of it. Let them all devour each other."

"We'd never be able to breach Westminster unnoticed," Lucan muttered crossly.

"Oh, I'm sorry," James gushed. "I should have been more clear; by *we*, I didn't mean *you*."

"Henry will never let us be, James," Chumley argued. "He'd burn all the forest down to find us. The Warren would never again be safe."

James shrugged. "So we move."

"Move?" Gilboe's nonexistent eyebrows rose.

"Why not?" Bob asked. "I think James's plan is a good one. There's plenty of work to be done near the Swan. More friends. More resources."

"But it's not our home," Effie argued.

Kit Katey said the first words she'd spoken that morning, in her quiet, musical voice. "You mean it is not Northumberland."

Silence filled the common room until Winnie rapped on the tabletop with her knuckles and then moved her hands in a swift stream of signs, pointing to Effie, then to Lucan in the midst of the silent monologue. Everyone then turned their gazed to Lucan. His stomach fell into his boots.

"What did she say?"

Effie met his gaze. "She asked what would happen to you if we rescued George and then escaped."

"Who cares?" James muttered under his breath.

"I care," Dana objected with a frown.

Lucan looked around at the band watching him. "Well, I'd lose my position and rank, obviously. I could never step foot in London again. My family lands would be forfeit." He paused. "I suppose I would return to France." He rallied his ire. "James's plan still doesn't account for Effie's brothers—Thomas's sons. Tavish and Lachlan would likely be returned to Scotland, although reluctantly, I'm sure. But Padraig..."

"Padraig," Thomas echoed quietly, and Lucan could hear the fondness in the very name. "Padraig would have naught."

"Nor Iris," Lucan reminded them all.

"And Caris Hargrave would win," Effie said darkly.

The room was silent again for a moment.

"We go back to London," Thomas said, breaking the heavy silence. "We stick with the original plan. I surrender to the king. We try to find the satchel before the trial. If we canna," he paused and then looked around at all gathered. "You take George and run like the devil."

"Tommy," Effie whispered. "Henry will hang you."

But Thomas was looking directly at Lucan now. "If I canna get close enough to her before I'm done in, you kill Caris Hargrave, d'ye hear?" Thomas's gaze never left Lucan's face. "You make sure that bitch is dead. I've spent me whole life running from Hargraves. Being frightened of me own shadow. I'm done runnin'. I trust in God that he will at the last hour preserve me, and if He do nae?" Tommy gave a half shrug and a shake of his head. "I'm done runnin'."

"Thomas," Lucan began.

"Nay. I'll nae be swayed. And I'll have nae more talk of it." He stood and picked up his pack. "Let's go chase a hooded man."

Effie was stone still for a moment, staring at her father, and in that pose, Lucan could see Thomas's profile in his daughter's jawline. Her eyes were glossy with unshed tears.

Effie stood from the bench. "Mount up."

Gorman clapped his hands once loudly. "You heard him—let's go chase a hooded man!"

The common room expanded with shuffling sounds then. All the members of the band left a coin on the trestle for the poor innskeep before walking out the front door. Lucan leaned over to place his coin and saw that James Rose was now staring at him, with the same intensity as Winnie had done. The young man said nothing though, merely shrugged his pack higher on his shoulder and preceded Lucan into the overcast morning.

And Lucan realized Tommy was no longer the only member of the band with a price on his head.

Chapter 18

Effie kept as much space as was reasonably possible between herself and Lucan Montague without attracting undue attention. Sitting at her bowl of porridge earlier that morning, waiting with bated breath for him to appear, her stomach had been in knots. Her worst fear was that he would make a scene about the night they'd spent together.

Or that he would act no differently at all.

How foolish, how shallow she had been, to think of either of those things as the worst that could happen.

She could see him now, riding vanguard next to her father, as Effie rode at Winnie's side behind the group of women they would leave at the Swan. Lucan looked no different from any other time she'd watched him from the saddle, and yet she knew now what lay beneath that fine, black, quilted gambeson. She knew that the thickness of his thighs were so much more than revealed by the trousers he wore. She knew the intimate curve of his buttocks behind his hips, the carved muscles in his chest, the way his neck tasted beneath his hair. She knew the very length and power of him.

Her mounted seat was uncomfortable as they rode south east, but each twinge only reminded her of the reckless passion they'd shared. One flesh together, and despite her self-loathing, it had been so sweet.

Effie could feel Winnie's eyes on her still, and so she gathered her courage and glanced to the right. "Are you well?"

The old woman nodded mildly, her gaze keen, inquisitive.

Are you?

"I've been better." Effie turned her eyes ahead, but heard the whispery snap of Winnie's fingers. The old woman kept her signs low and hidden from the riders behind them.

You came to bed late last night. You were with him.

Effie didn't respond. How could she? Anything she said at this point was moot.

It's not like you.

Effie couldn't speak aloud her next query. *Does Gorman know?*

If he doesn't, he will soon. Seeing the two of you together made me want to weep. You can hide it not.

Effie felt her chin flinch, her breath catch in her chest. "Are you angry with me?" she asked aloud, her voice husky with shame and also with resentment.

Winnie's sparse, gray eyebrows rose. *Why angry? I want you to be happy.*

Effie was surprised by the answer. "Then why did you say you wanted to weep?"

Things will change, she signed. *The old days are gone. The Family will never be the same.*

"We don't know that," Effie argued.

I know that. And so do you.

Rather than making her feel better, Winnie's matter-of-fact statement only increased the guilt Effie felt. Winnie was probably right—even if the best possible outcome was reached in London: Caris Hargrave was charged and found guilty of her crimes, and Effie and her father were exonerated, they couldn't very well continue to live unnoticed at the Warren. The wrongdoings would be exposed, everyone in Northumberland on alert to Effie and the band's presence and mission. Should they remain in the wood, those in power wouldn't stop until every last one of them was dead.

And where would Thomas Annesley's place be? Darlyrede was destroyed, and Effie knew that if her father felt the same as she about that house of hell, he never wanted to dwell upon that tainted ground again, any matter. Would he return to Scotland with one of the two strangers who were her half-brothers?

What of Padraig? Iris?

What of George Thomas, and Gorman?

What of Lucan?

"It's my turn to take rearguard," she said as an excuse for escape and turned her horse out of the caravan to circle behind Bob. He took the cue at once and moved into the spot next to Winnie while Effie pulled ahead next to James Rose.

"Anything?" she asked him.

He shook his head.

They rode along in stilted silence for several moments, and a feeling of dread began to form in Effie's stomach. Winnie was right—they knew. They all knew, and she didn't know how.

"James," she began.

"Don't," he said.

Effie was taken aback. "Don't what?"

"Don't speak to me."

"I beg your pardon?"

"How could you do that to Gorman?" he demanded between his teeth, keeping his voice low. "How could you do that to all of us?"

"What are you talking about?"

"Don't insult me. Everyone save Tommy and Gorman saw it plainly as soon as Montague came bursting into the common room. It would never cross Gorman's mind that you'd do such a thing, and Tommy doesn't know you well enough, obviously. Still enamored with the idea of having a daughter, I suppose."

Effie went quiet for a moment. She couldn't really deny it, but she had to know. "What did you think you saw?"

"You *looked* at him," James said, biting off the words. "Before, it was a glare of contempt or irritation. But this morning, you *saw* him. You looked *to him*. And the way the pair of you were feeding off each other, crafting your little theory and you hare-brained ideas." His voice grew in turns comically shrill and then deep and proper. "Don't you agree? Oh, I say, indubitably. Certainly, Sir Lucan is right. No, no! It's Effie who is right, without doubt." He made a sound of disgust. "It was sickening. Likely whoever it was that stole the satchel stood around for the show without the pair of you even knowing. I'm sure you made it worth his while, the way you're sitting your saddle."

They rode along in silence for a quarter mile before Effie was in better control of herself to speak. "I'm going to pretend that you didn't speak to me that way," she said calmly. "Regardless of what you think, James, I'm still your—"

But the young man cut her off, adjusting in his saddle. "My turn for point." He urged his mount out of the convoy and into a trot to the front of the party.

She didn't expect to see Lucan Montague riding back toward her.

"What are you doing?" she demanded, James Rose's attack putting her on the defensive and causing her to want to lash out. "Point falls back to second."

"Forgive me," he said crisply. "I'm new."

Effie rolled her eyes. "What do you want?"

He lowered his voice. "Did you…tell anyone about…?"

She hoped the look on her face conveyed her horror. "Are you mad? That's the last thing I'd want to brag about."

"You didn't seem quite so appalled last night. In fact, I distinctly remember you beg—"

"Just shut up, Lucan," she snapped. "No, I didn't tell anyone anything. But apparently, everyone save Gorman and my father has already figured it out."

"How?"

"I have no bloody idea." She sighed. "I'm sure Winnie put two and two together when I didn't come to bed until dawn."

"You could have been with Gorman," he argued.

"In the stables with everyone else? Or out in the rain?"

"You could have been just…talking. Late."

"Naked?" she insisted. "I'd put my shirt on inside out before I left your chamber. She had to point it out to me before we went below."

"I see," he allowed. "But she didn't tell the others? Or signal to them. You know what I mean."

"Apparently you and I were *speaking* to each other differently in the common room this morning," she said stiffly.

"Were we?"

She shrugged. "I don't think so."

"Neither do I."

"Well, any matter, it was noticed." She looked over at him. "Has anyone said anything to you?"

"No," he said. "They're all…looking at me, though."

Effie nodded and pressed her lips together. "Well, they're not only looking at me. James Rose is ready to place me in the stocks as a fallen woman."

"He's a shit."

"He can be," Effie agreed. "When someone he loves is being hurt."

"Will he tell Gorman, then?"

"No," she answered right away. "As prickly as he is over it, he wouldn't interfere in that way. Gorman's like a father to him. I thought I was like a mother."

They rode on for a bit in silence before Lucan spoke again. "Will you tell him?"

"I hadn't planned on it, originally," she admitted. "Since it will never happen again."

"Won't it?"

She whipped her head around to look at him, and his handsome face genuinely seemed confused.

"No," she scoffed, her cheeks tingling. "Of course not." She faced forward again, ignoring the tumbling in her stomach. "But since everyone else suspects it, it's only a matter of time. I'd prefer to wait until we have recovered George—Gorman has enough on his mind right now."

Lucan said nothing, and after several minutes her curiosity got the better of her and she glanced at him. "What is it?"

"Hmm?" he said, as if she disturbed him from his thoughts. "Oh, yes. Certainly. You should wait."

Effie felt her brows knit together. "Oh." She bit her tongue, pressed her lips together. But in the end couldn't seem to stop herself from turning toward him again. "Did you think that we would—?"

"No, not really. Of course not."

"Good." She faced the road again, noticing that they had fallen a bit behind the caravan. "It was stupid."

"Stupid," he agreed.

They looked over at each other in the same instant and then quickly looked away again.

"If you do choose to get blazing drunk again, however," he said suddenly.

"Stop," she warned. She couldn't help but looked over at him and caught his gaze taking in her legs. "Stop, Lucan. You're not making things easier. God help me, I sincerely hate you." Effie faced forward once more, her heart racing, her breaths coming fast and shallow.

"I know. You shot me. It can't be debated." He paused. "I'd still risk it."

And, just like that, she wanted him again.

* * * *

The winter sun had long since set by the time they reached The White Swan, but no one had wanted to camp in the cold and dark. Lucan was glad of it, longing once more for the bright, clean inn and the kind proprietors' care. He needed a place to catch his breath, strengthen his mind. He needed to *think.*

Effie had moved through the caravan to avoid him after their conversation, putting as much distance between them as possible. He never managed to be paired with James Rose, and that was just as well—Lucan had grown quite tired of the young man's rudeness, and he didn't think it would do him any favors with the family to teach the lad a lesson on the road.

Besides James, the rest of the band seemed to treat Lucan much the same, save for a bit of awkward stiltedness at each changing of positions. He felt Dana's genuine sympathy though, and it touched him. Kit Katey actually smiled and spoke with him at length, and Lucan was surprised and pleased at the beautiful young woman's sudden loquaciousness. It took his mind from the troubles plaguing him in the dark. He learned that her name in her language—Qi QiangTing—meant 'Wondrous, sustaining red rose,' and he had to agree that Kit Katey was indeed both wondrous and sustaining for all that she had endured at the hands of the English.

Lucan was honored to ride into the White Swan's dooryard at her side.

As if she had been watching for them, Mari threw open the door of the tidy building and gave a cry of welcome, moving at once into the midst of the horses, specifically to the women who were strangers to her, and taking charge of them as a mother hen would her chicks. The group was noisy chaos in the dark until Gale arrived with a brace of torches, and everyone sorted their mounts and their possessions and saw them tended to before jostling each other into the common room, which was so clean and inviting that Lucan wanted to weep like a child.

He could only imagine the relief felt by the lost souls finding refuge here for the first time.

Thomas Annesley was greeted warmly, as was Lucan himself, but rather than buoy his spirits, it caused Lucan's guilt and his loneliness to increase. Gorman taking the seat on the bench next to him was the final straw—he quickly ate the hearty, delicious food Gale served him, his head down. As soon as he had swallowed the last mouthful, he rose.

"My gratitude for the superb meal," he said to his hosts. "If you will excuse me."

Gorman looked up with a half frown, still chewing. "Alright, there, Lucan?"

"Just tired," Lucan said. "Goodnight."

He thought he heard James Rose mutter something nasty to the group, but Lucan didn't pause to force the issue. In truth, he just wanted to escape.

Stupid. Cowardly. Failure.

He pushed inside the small, whitewashed room, becoming reacquainted at once with the narrow chamber. The bolt on the solid door slid easily and true. The quarters were only a fraction of the size of the rooms at most inns of his experience, but none had ever felt so clean, so comfortable, so safe.

The bed was narrow, but it did not sag, and even in the remainder of that dreary winter, the fresh smell of the clean linens scented the small space perfectly. There was a tiny stand with a little wooden bowl and pitcher, a slice of soap and a single piece of toweling. Typically, beds were wider, and often shared between travelers unless they had significant coin, and Lucan recalled his first solitary stay there and the way he had marveled at the inn's strange—but very pleasant—appointments. Because of the size of the chamber, the upper floor could house perhaps ten guests, whereas most inns might boast five larger chambers of shared lodgings, and now Lucan understood the purpose.

No questionable goings-on at the White Swan. Shelter for those poorly used. Shelter and safety and peace.

Peace.

Lucan thought of how he'd failed in losing the portfolio—and he accepted now that he had lost it. He'd no longer allow himself to hide behind the semantics of "stolen." Unless they could find the man who'd taken it, either on the road or in London, there was little chance that Thomas Annesley would ever again be free. Little chance of finding out the truth of what had happened to Lucan's parents, even if Henry did return Castle Dare lands to him.

And who would really care? he thought to himself. Iris, who had her own worries about her husband—who just happened to be Thomas Annesley's heir? No. His dead parents? No. Roul and Amée Montague weren't coming back. Lucan knew the fire that had killed them was no accident, and he was certain that Vaughn Hargrave—who was also already dead—had his hand in it. What more could he gain by trying the issue of posthumously accusing the man of killing his parents in Henry's court?

A soft rap sounded on his door and Lucan's heart stuttered. He wondered if it could be Effie and found himself unable to move.

"Sir Lucan?" Mari's voice called out quietly from the corridor.

He unbolted the door to find the short, round woman stepped back across the corridor, holding a flat, circular object covered with a towel in one hand and a mug in the other.

If ever there had been a less threatening sight, Lucan couldn't imagine it.

"I've brought you a bit of pudding and some warm cider," she said with a gentle smile. "Gale's is the best, you'll see. You've had a long, cold ride today, and I reckoned you wanted it. A hard day, as well, from what I gather." Her eyes were knowing.

Lucan's throat tightened. "Thank you," he rasped as he took the offerings, looking at them as if they were containers of gold—no one had ever cared for him in such a way without being duty bound or paid handsomely for it.

"Thank *you*," Mari objected. "Gorman says that if not for ye, the poor doves might not have been saved. Effie could have been badly hurt, or even killed. He's been singin' your praises since you left."

Guilt squeezed him again. Damned Gorman. Virtuous bastard.

Lucan stood in the doorway feeling the heel, his hands full of gracious food from a thoughtful woman. His eyes prickled and he was terrified he might start blubbering at such kindness that he didn't deserve.

"You sleep well, now," Mari whispered and reached out to squeeze his forearm and gave him a wink. "Say your prayers. And don't mind James."

Lucan turned back inside the room and set the bowl down on the ticking before closing and bolting the door. He carried his cider back with him and balanced it on the meager corner of the stand while he took off his boots and belt and loosened his gambeson. He turned back the coverlet and then retrieved his cider, crawling beneath the thin wool. He rested the mug against his hip before lifting the worn cloth, and the spicy-sweet fragrance of the pudding touched a physical place in him.

He'd ruined the most important mission of his life. Since the day Effie Annesley had shot him in the Darlyrede wood, he felt as if his orderly existence had spun out of control. Nothing that had happened since then had been within his command, within the orderly realm he'd kept for himself for the past fifteen years. He'd failed in his undertaking, betrayed Gorman, and fallen in love with Effie Annesley. And yet, Mari had thought enough of him to bring him a bowl of warm pudding and a cider.

He realized then that everything he'd ever been working for was naught but a lie. A meaningless farce. Mari didn't care if he was a knight with a claim to a Northumberland estate. She didn't care where the women they'd rescued came from, who they were, or what they'd done. She didn't care that Gorman and Effie had never married, or if Dana was in fact a woman or a man. She didn't care that Chumley was a drunk—he had cause enough, didn't he? Mari loved them all, just because they were under her roof.

And Lucan suddenly understood the meaning of the word 'good.'

Say your prayers, she'd reminded him.

How long had it been since Lucan Montague had prayed? How long since he'd done more than allow his mind to wander in some chapel while a disinterested priest droned? How long had it been since he'd believed his prayers were heard by anyone or anything, or that they even mattered?

Since the night his parents had died, he realized.

He ate the pudding and finished the cider slowly, savoring each bite and sip, trying to squeeze the caring out of each tang of spice and flavor. He leaned over and set the vessels on the floor, and with the taste of Gale's good bread pudding in his mouth, he lay down on his side and faced the guttering candle.

By the time Lucan Montague had finished his prayers, the chamber was dark, and the candle wax was cold.

Chapter 19

They stayed at the White Swan for two days, resting, gathering supplies, getting the women settled. And Effie was glad of the refilling of her spirit and her resolve, even if the tension of trying to avoid Lucan Montague caused her shoulders to ache.

Avoiding him while he was never far from her mind.

Gorman was Gorman. They didn't share a room at the Swan—they seldom had, for years now—but they still ate together and worked together and shared their little jokes.

James Rose barely looked in her direction, his young face—by all evidence now a man's—bearing the tell-tale wounded expression of betrayal, so much like the night he'd been freed from Elsmire Tower. Effie had seen that look many times, on many faces; it wrenched at her heart to think that she was the cause of his pain.

Kit Katey sat next to her at meals, their shoulders just touching, as if she could somehow take a little corner of Effie's burden onto her own narrow frame.

And no one at all spoke of her sin.

Tommy got on at once with both Gale and Mari, of course, and under his direction the band made sure the Swan had plenty of firewood, the well was kept free of ice, and the animal pens tidied with fresh bedding over the thick, decaying layer of the stalls, which kept the structures humid and warm.

Effie wore one of Mari's old skirts while her trousers dried by the fire, and for once she wasn't annoyed at the way her prickly legs touched at her calves above her boots. She was not ready for battle tonight—there was a big enough fight ahead of them all and she held on to this last bit of peace in the empty common room greedily. Her bag was packed once more, ready to depart on the morrow. Ready to reach the Warren and leave most of their party to the safety of the caves before charging on to London and to George Thomas.

George. How she missed his small face. His clever speech. His little ways at play or at his lessons. She could see him so clearly in her mind when she closed her eyes. How Tommy would rejoice in him, she knew—their spirits were so similar.

"All ready to go?" Gale's voice pulled her from her reverie, and she raised her cheek from her fist to look up at him as he entered the common room in his long white apron, carrying a tray of bread rounds that would be used in the supper.

She nodded as he slid the tray onto the end of the trestle and then slid himself onto the bench at her side. She leaned at once into his shoulder.

"Your da's a good sort," Gale said quietly.

Effie nodded. "I think so."

"I'm proud to have stood in his place until now."

She looked up at him. "Whatever are you talking about, Gale?"

He shrugged his big shoulders, a gentle giant if ever there was one. "The two of you are nae well acquainted yet. When you have gotten to know one another better, he'll be your da, in truth."

"That doesn't mean you and I will change."

"Of course nae. You'll always be mine and Mari's lass. If we'd have had wee ones of our'n, we'd have wanted them all just like you—fiery and full of heart." He reached across himself to squeeze Effie's hand on his arm. "But then I suppose that's what the Lord had in mind for us—to have nae one or three bairns, but a hundred."

"A thousand," Effie said through a smile.

"And so, as your honorary da," Gale said with a mock-solemn look, "it's me duty to tell you that you're making a mistake."

Effie froze. "A mistake?"

"With our proper knight friend."

Her cheeks heated. "I know."

"You canna keep pushing him away like that."

Effie looked up at him again. "What?"

"We all knew this day would come, gel. Even you, I suspect. I'm not saying it shallna be hard nor painful, but it's necessary."

"I still don't know what you're talking about, Gale."

"Aye, you do," he said gently. "But that's nae matter. You'll work it out on your own. Only don't wait too long, ken? You'd nae disrespect either man by pretending that they doona matter enough to you to face it head-on. You've always met your battles squarely. That shouldna change, even if everything else will."

Effie pulled away slightly and sat up straight, as his echoing of Winnie's prediction faded into the shadows of the quiet common room. "Nothing will change. People make mistakes, is all. Sir Lucan has his own agenda and his own future planned. Gorman is George Thomas's father."

"Aye," Gale said even more gently if it was possible. "But Gorman's nae *only* George Thomas's father."

Effie turned a confused frown up to him. "I must be tired. I'm not following you very well."

"You will if you think upon it." Gale gave her a pair of firm pats between her shoulder blades and slid out from the bench. "Come now—let's set out the bread."

* * * *

Lucan Montague didn't show his face at dinner, and no one mentioned it at all amidst the happy chatter over the meal—not even Gorman. And although Effie gratefully allowed herself to be drawn into the familiar meal pattern of the White Swan, she couldn't help her darting eyes that kept fitful watch of the doorways.

Where was he?

She knew the fact that no one had asked where the dark knight was was even more telling than his absence. It was a rule in the group that no one—*no one*—went anywhere alone beyond the Warren, not even at the Swan.

And after George Thomas, not even once they were returned to the Warren, she suspected.

Soon dinner was over, and the drinking began. Drinking and dice and draughts—a last night of pleasure before the hard road that lay ahead. Dana took charge of Gale's little lute and sang lovely old ballads in a breathy voice. Effie picked up the last tray and walked back to the kitchen in Mari's old, swishing skirt where several of the rescued girls were doing the washing up with the proprietress, smiling, joking, amidst the clattering of knives and cups.

"Thank you, my dear," Mari called over their heads with a smile. She was in her element now, Effie knew.

She stepped back toward the door. "I'm for the pit," she said, neither loudly, nor in a whisper. No one answered her, no one looked her way. She backed against the plank slowly and pushed it open just enough to slide through, and then she eased it closed.

The yard was dark, and the wind cut through the space like little whipping ropes, slashing at her thin blouse and molding the skirt to her legs. The only lights ahead of her in the dark night came as little sparkles through the timbers of the horse stable. She wrapped her arms about her and set off at a trot.

Effie pulled open one half of the double door and slipped inside, feeling her shoulders relax at once as the warm, humid smells enveloped her in a welcoming embrace. Four torches lit the space over the stone thresholds at either end. Lucan's head popped up over a half wall at the very last stall as the door creaked shut.

"It's only me," she called out.

"Oh." He stepped from the stall into the aisle, a saddle bag dangling from one hand. "Is everything alright?"

"You weren't at dinner."

"Mari brought me a round."

"What are you doing out here?"

He gestured with the bag. "Preparing Agrios."

"Oh. I thought perhaps you were avoiding me"

"I was," he admitted. "I thought it best if everyone could relax this last night."

She began walking down the aisle toward him, not really even noticing it was happening, but unable to stop herself. "Is he well? Agrios?"

"He's well nearly anywhere he has fresh oats and a dry bed."

She was halfway to him now. He'd discarded his black gambeson and stood in the aisle in his white shirt and black trousers, like a charcoal sketch if only his eyes hadn't glittered so pale blue in the torchlight.

"Why are *you* here, Effie?"

She stopped then. "I was worried about you."

He arched one black brow. "I do doubt that."

"We have a rule," she continued inanely.

"I know the bloody rule," he said. "That's not why you've come. So why don't you just come out with it?"

"I..." Effie stopped, swallowed. For some ridiculous reason, she felt as if she could burst into sobs at any moment. *Vulnerable*, a voice whispered in her ear. *That's what you are. Afraid.*

"I just needed to know where you were," she confessed at last. "I don't know why."

He turned his head away and muttered something that sounded like a curse.

"I do know why," he said to her, and his eyes glittered. "But we both know we shouldn't. Especially not now. Especially not tonight." He tossed the bag in his hand into Agrios's stall and then took a step toward her. "It's too complicated."

Effie, too, stepped forward, hesitated. "I know."

"It will only make it harder for you." Another pace.

Her breath caught in her throat. God, help her—what had come over her? "*I know,*" she whispered. "But…but I don't think I care anymore."

Lucan held his arms from his sides, his palms out. "Neither do I."

Effie lurched forward, closing the space between them in a rush, flying into Lucan's open arms and raising her face for the kiss that he granted her at once. His arms wrapped around her back, spanning her, lifting her against him, turning to carry her into an empty stall.

"I need you, Lucan," she said against his skin. "I can't explain it. I just want you again so much. Everything is—"

"Shh," he said against her neck as he backed her up against the wall of the stall. "I've got you." His fingers gathered up the sides of the skirt little by little, letting the cool air caress Effie's bare legs. "Help me," he commanded, pressing his hips into her stomach.

Effie's hands jerked at the laces at his waist until he was freed to her clutching hands, her skin delighting in the feel of him. He dropped his mouth back to hers with a groan. His hands wrapped around the underside of her buttocks and lifted her above him. He stepped forward, wedging her against the rough wall and then let her slide down, slowly, slowly, until she was fully seated on him.

Effie let her head lay back against the boards and her eyes close, her breath coming in and out of her nose in the quiet stable air. Her hands rested on Lucan's shoulders as he buried his face in her breasts, hooking his hands beneath her knees and pulling up. She ran her fingers through his hair, laying her cheek against his temple as she gasped open-mouthed, her eyes squeezed shut.

Seconds became minutes, stretching out into an eternity made up of nothing but the scratching of fabric on wood, wet whispers of flesh, ragged breaths in the quiet space. The shadow of the empty stall hid their wickedness, sheltered them, encouraged them, until their passions were spent.

Effie felt dizzy, hot, weak. He slipped out of her and let her down upon her feet, but kept her constrained against the wall as he kissed her again, without an ounce less desire than the first time. He caressed her breast, squeezed it gently.

"Better?" he murmured against her lips.

She nodded guiltily and he kissed her again.

"Go inside to your rest," he advised. "You'll be missed soon, and if you stay much longer, I'm going to turn you 'round."

"Come to me tonight." She clutched at him, begging for another kiss until he granted it. "No one will know."

"Go," he said, stepping away.

"Come to me tonight," she insisted.

His smoldering gaze caused her stomach to clench.

"You know I will."

She turned and walked from the stable toward the back door of the inn on unsteady legs, her head held high in an effort to mask her shame.

Effie knew she couldn't bear to slip into the midst of the group again so soon after leaving Lucan Montague's arms. She took a candle stand from the kitchen bench unnoticed and went directly upstairs and to her chamber, bolting the door behind her. After lighting the wick from a straw thrust in the brazier, she curled into a ball on the bed.

God, she could still feel his hands on her. She could taste him, feel him inside her. Her entire body seemed to vibrate from his lovemaking and, try as she might, she could not even bring to mind the image of Gorman Littlebrook's face, and it frightened her.

A tear escaped from the corner of her eye and vanished into the pillow ticking, causing Effie to swipe at her face angrily.

Lucan Montague did not love her—he could never love her. They hated each other. She'd shot him, for God's sake!

Why do you hate him? a little voice in her head asked.

Because he hated me first. He hated Northumberland. He left them—abandoned us all.

He was sent to France. He was but a boy—he had no choice.

He was Vaughn Hargrave's lapdog.

Vaughn Hargrave held hostage his very life—his lands, his coin.

He aided him.

He agreed to aid the king. And now he is aiding you. You don't hate him. You want to. But you don't hate him at all...

You love him. Madly.

A soft rap sounded on her door, and Effie froze. She pushed up onto her hip and swiped at her eyes.

"Who is it?"

"Only me." Gorman.

Effie took a deep breath and scrambled from the narrow bed, smoothing down her hair as she crossed to the door. She slid the bolt free and cracked open the door.

"What's wrong?" she said.

"Nothing," Gorman answered. "I was worried about you."

Effie's guilt intensified hearing the same words she'd spoken to Lucan only an hour ago.

"I thought I'd get an early night."

He watched her closely and stepped forward, pushing the door open and looking about the room, cocking his head to peer under the bed, glancing behind the door—she knew it wasn't lovers he was looking for; unfortunately Gorman knew the games too well.

"You're alright?"

Effie nodded. "Yes."

Then, to her dread, he reached out and caressed her hair, taking another half step into the room. "Want some company?"

She tried not to flinch away from his touch. "I've got a terrible headache," she said.

"I see," he said, and it was likely her imagination, but Gorman's rich voice seemed to have cooled. "Do you want me to stay with you, any matter?"

"No," she said, waving away his concerns. "Don't deprive yourself of the last night of comfort we're sure to see in weeks on my account."

"Kit has agreed to sing," he cajoled with a smile. "For Mari and Gale, I think, but we shall all benefit."

And now she could return her own smile genuinely. "That *is* a treat. I know you love her songs." She placed a hand on his chest, over his good, strong heart. "Go. Enjoy. And don't worry about me."

Gorman stepped forward and took her lightly into his arms, kissed her forehead. "Sleep well."

Her hand slid from him as he backed into the corridor, and Effie closed the door after him. She rested her forehead against the wood, listening to his footsteps stomping down the stairs.

* * * *

Lucan entered the common room, his personal satchel on his shoulder. A quick glance told him that Effie was absent, and he turned toward the stairs.

"Oh, Sir Lucan!" Dana called out. "You're back—how lovely. Not running off again just when the festivities are high, I hope? Kit is to sing for us."

Lucan's pause spanned only the blink of an eye, but in that time he weighed his options. Effie was upstairs, and he had every intention of joining her later that night. He could barely stand the thought of being so close to her and not in her bed, now that he knew her desire of him matched his own need of her. But he was to wait until the others were abed any matter, and then he would spend this night doing what she wanted him to do, what it seemed neither of them could now do without, until the dawn.

"Of course not." Lucan held up his satchel. He turned and walked up the stairs, hearing voices before he was halfway ascended. His head appeared above the second floor, and he saw Gorman standing in a doorway, a swish of skirt beyond his boots.

Skirts he'd just held up while taking Effie Annesley in the stable.

Gorman stepped further into the room, and he saw his arms go about Effie, his head descend.

Lucan walked up the remainder of the steps silently and slipped into his room, closing the door. He flung his satchel across the small cell.

He wanted to go back into the corridor. He wanted to go to her room and tear Gorman Littlebrook to pieces.

Gorman, his friend.

Blasted Effie Annesley. What game was she playing?

* * * *

Effie waited until what must have been well past midnight for Lucan to come. The White Swan had been silent for hours. She tossed restlessly in her bed and then at last crept across her floor and opened her door the slightest crack to listen.

Not a sound.

Should she go to him? She wanted to—she verily ached with the want of it.

She closed the door and went back to her mattress. She was pathetic—like a bitch in heat. It wasn't like her. Nothing was the same as it was, and she didn't even recognize, nor could she predict her own actions. She was frightened, unsure, desperate—a terrible combination of feelings for one who was to soon storm the stronghold of the English monarchy in order to rescue her son and her father.

She'd never felt this way with Gorman. And that she loved Gorman was indisputable.

Pull yourself together, she told herself. Get some sleep. Twelve hours in the winter saddle tomorrow will cure you of your wanton restlessness.

She rolled over, pulled the coverlet tight around her shoulders and squeezed her eyes shut.

A whispering voice bid her goodnight with, *It's just as well; he could never love you.*

Chapter 20

It was harder leaving the White Swan this time for everyone, Lucan observed—himself included. He knew it would be the last place for a very long while—if ever—that he could relax without looking over his shoulder. Perhaps the last place he would claim ownership of Effie Annesley's body.

He certainly didn't hold any of her heart.

The party was greatly reduced after leaving the rescued women behind in the care of Mari and Gale, and so there was no point or rear, and everyone naturally paired off on the ride: Tommy and Effie, Dana and Gilboe, Kit Katey and Gorman, Bob and James Rose; leaving Lucan to ride alongside Winnie. It suited him—she was a quiet companion and her nonjudgmental demeanor soothed him as he caught glimpses of Effie Annesley through the riders as the unseasonably warm, sweet air shimmered around them, hinting at spring.

So close to him, her body so familiar, and yet still completely out of his reach.

She's only used you, he scolded himself. *You fool. Perhaps she and her band have done good for the people, but it was likely only to make up for the sins of her own blood. She is a Hargrave after all, no matter what name she calls herself. Her manipulation skills are at least equal to her dark lineage. She sought you, both times, and was not coy about admitting it. After all, she had to keep you engaged, enslaved—using the only thing she had that you could not freely gain on your own. Tempting you with the idea that she could be yours, that she could love you, and you could be her rescuer and redeemer.*

Clever Effie Annesley. She had certainly fooled him while he was making love to her. And even now, he could hardly string two sentences together without the memory of her body invading and distracting his thoughts. And while it should have made Lucan angry or vengeful, he only felt humiliated.

They reached the Warren just as the sun was setting, and all who had remained behind in the caves were joyously surprised at the party's unexpectedly swift return. Rolf Littlebrook and Thomas Annesley made a hearty introduction and soon everyone was sitting about the fire in the cathedral eating supper and talking. Effie and Thomas and Gorman were inseparable, and as far as Lucan could tell, she didn't once glance his way. He'd had enough. He was still a free man this night, and he would not voluntarily torture himself while so close to his own birthright.

Agrios had rested a bit and eaten, and so Lucan quietly removed him from the underground stables, purposefully ignoring the pale, moonfaced children who watched him warily. This time they didn't flee. Lucan walked Agrios out to the point, where the animal trails picked up, before mounting and riding on, splashing across the little tributary that would eventually spill into the river.

The night was still balmy, the moon ripening like a pale apple. Even Agrios seemed to relax as they swished out of the water up the bank of quietly greening grass onto Castle Dare lands. They crossed slowly to the small copse of twisted trees that had at one time stood just beyond the wall. Some of Darlyrede's now thin sheep, no one left knowing enough of the numbers to gather them all up after the fire, were huddled there in the night gloom, and for the first time, Lucan wondered if those sheep weren't descended from Castle Dare stock.

They could be Lucan's sheep.

He dismounted, leaving Agrios among the drowsy ewes and walked toward the jagged knoll, where grass had grown around and in some places over the stone ruins of his family home. Once there, he stepped onto a large, cut block. The footprint of the hold looked so much smaller than he had remembered. Barely larger than a couple of cottages pressed together, even though the keep had risen three levels. He stooped to pick up a handful of the broken stone. Two centuries old, Castle Dare had been built by his French ancestors with funds gained as reward for aiding the rebellion against Henry III in favor of the French king, Louis. Eventually though, they'd all become English, like their neighbors. Like the Annesleys. Like Lord Hood. Like the Hargraves.

Lucan had been born here, both he and Iris. To loving parents.

The fire licked up to the night sky; Iris, in her nightgown, clung to Lucan while her bare feet stood ankle deep in cold mud, sobbing, screaming...

The small, pale hand grasping at his sleeve. You must come away with me at once, with your sister. Hurry, before he comes for us all. Come now!

Now, Northumberland was a wasteland. Scorched. Entire families gone, destroyed. What might the future have held for them all if Lucan had recognized Euphemia Hargrave that night, and heeded her?

Lucan frowned and shook the memory away with a toss of his head.

The crack of a stick sounded like a shot in the stillness behind him and he spun about, his hand going to the hilt of his sword. Gilboe stood to the side of the copse, his face glowing in the moonlight.

"I thought it best if I announced my arrival," he said with a smile and then hefted up a large jug in his left hand. "Tot?"

Lucan had thought he'd come to this place to be alone, and so he was surprised at the relief he felt at seeing the strange monk. He tossed down the stones he'd been holding and began walking back to the copse.

"What are you doing out here, Gilboe?"

The monk eased himself down on a rock with a sigh. "Effie sent me," he said, twisting at the cork. "We have a—"

"A rule," Lucan finished for him, sitting down at Gilboe's side. "I know." He took the jug from the man and turned it up to his mouth.

"She said you'd be here." Gilboe withdrew two cups from the folds of his robe and held them up. "Sir Lucan, for shame. What poor manners you've acquired. Let us be civilized."

Lucan swallowed behind his grin and swiped at his mouth with his sleeve before pouring full the cups Gilboe held. "Are you to look after me while I brood?" He replaced the cork and set the jug in the chilled grass and took one of the cups from the monk.

"Not at all." Gilboe held the cup up in a salute. "To your health."

"And to yours."

After swallowing with another sigh, Gilboe continued. "She only wanted to make sure you were well."

"She wanted to make sure I wasn't abandoning the cause."

"That too, perhaps," he acquiesced. "I'll leave you to your peace once we've had our talk."

Lucan looked sideways at the man.

"Oh, come now, Sir Lucan," Gilboe chided. "Am I not trained to be a counselor?"

"I'm not certain you're trained to be anything, to be quite honest, Gilboe."

"Fair enough," he said. "And we shall get to that, too, if you like. Later."

Lucan sighed, bringing the cup to his lips. "Go on, then."

"Very well." Gilboe paused for a moment. "Let her be."

Lucan stared at the man, trying to craft a bored expression on his face. "Let who be, Gilboe?"

"You know damned well who." He didn't raise his voice in ire, as was maybe his right, Lucan admitted to himself. "You're confusing her. Distracting her. Preying on her weakness, even if you don't mean to."

Now Lucan did take offense. "*I'm* confusing *her*?"

"Yes," Gilboe answered firmly. "It's causing friction in the family. If Gorman finds out before you've returned to Westminster and seen this thing through to its end, I'm afraid people will choose sides."

"Mine or Gorman's?"

"Don't flatter yourself; Gorman's or Effie's."

It was a blow to his pride, but one Lucan realized he likely deserved. The monk continued.

"The first thing that must be done is to get little George Thomas back. And then, somehow strive to see that Tommy is exonerated of his crimes. What happens after that, only God knows. But if you muddy the mission by bringing outside emotion into it..."

"Wait, why is this only my responsibility?"

"Well, she's not fucking herself, is she?"

Lucan's eyebrows rose at the atypical vulgarity.

Gilboe looked back expectantly, blinked, likely because he had no eyebrows.

Lucan looked away. "Go on."

"Let her have her own crises, is what I'm saying. And besides, it *is* adultery. And adultery is a sin."

Lucan huffed a laugh. "You must be joking. After what has gone on around here?"

"I do not joke about sin, my son."

"You and I are likely the same age, Gilboe."

"But we are all children of God. *Son*." He reached for the jug and uncorked it, pouring them both another generous serving. "Besides, if you push the issue with Gorman, he will likely reach up your arse and, with one firm shake, turn you inside out. So perhaps you will think about it." He held up his cup again. "To your health." He lifted the vessel to his lips.

"To my insides staying inside," Lucan muttered.

Gilboe nearly choked on his drink, but then carried on as merrily as if they'd not just been discussing Effie Annesley. "So, now you wish to know: am I really a monk?"

Lucan swallowed. "I do indeed."

"Well, I am, in fact," he said proudly. "I was given to the abbey when I was seven years old, and I grew up there. Loved it so. Even the beatings."

"Beatings?"

"I was rather incorrigible."

"Not much has changed."

"No," Gilboe said happily. "It was only as I grew older and ascended through my vows, with more responsibility to the church, that I began to see the wicked things afoot in Christ's very house."

"This sounds bad." Lucan lifted the jug and obliged them both in anticipation.

"*Money*," Gilboe sneered.

"Oh, that's a relief. Usually—"

"Everything was about money," Gilboe pressed on, as if Lucan hadn't spoken. "The taxes on the church were hellish—and I do mean that literally, understand. And do you know where that money went, good Sir Lucan?"

"I can't begin to guess."

"*Rome*," Gilboe spat the word, in a way he'd never heard him intone even the worst vulgarity. "The Pope. Not to the orphans. Not to the poor. Not to the small village churches that had too many mouths to feed. All. The way. To Rome." He slapped his thigh with each phrase. "Gah. I *hate* Rome." He downed the wine in his cup.

"So how did you end up here? At the Warren?"

"We had just squeezed all the parishioners for their last coin, and I saw it piled up in a big golden chest, waiting for the guards to come and take it away. A golden chest, even! And something in me broke. I ran for my life, with the Cathedral tax chest."

Lucan burst out in laughter. "You actually ran?"

"Down the road. Carrying that bloody heavy thing. I couldn't figure out a way to get mounted with it." Gilboe chuckled. "Fool. Good thing Old Robin came out of the wood and tried to rob me."

Lucan's tipsy laughter shot into the night on a foggy bark. "What did you do?"

"I told him that the bastards *I'd* stolen it from were right behind me, and if neither of us wanted to be drawn and quartered, not to mention *excommunicated*, we would do well to find a place to hide it." Gilboe's turn to pour. "I've been here ever since. The spiritual guiding light for all souls." He toasted himself this time and drank the cup to its dregs.

"What will you do after?" Lucan asked suddenly. "If no one can return to the Warren. Go back to the Swan?"

Gilboe shrugged. "I don't know. Perhaps for a while. I hope to eventually find my way to Bohemia. There was a man there, Hus, whose teachings I greatly admired. He's dead now, but I've a feeling his ideas are only just the beginning of something great. Perhaps one day they will even reach England."

Gilboe stood and took up the empty jug and the cups. "Make sure you kiss Winnie goodbye before you depart. She's fond of you."

"She's not going?"

Gilboe shook his head. "Nor I, nor Dana. London is not safe for any of us three to so tempt a second visit, especially when there is a near guarantee of trouble."

His words sobered Lucan. "I might not see you again."

"You might not." He transferred the cups to beneath his other arm and held his hand toward Lucan, who rose and took it firmly. "*Dominus vobiscum*, Sir Lucan."

"*Et cum spiritu tuo*, Gilboe."

The monk turned and began walking back into the shadows.

"Gilboe!" Lucan called out.

The rotund man turned. "Yes, Sir Lucan?"

"Forgive me, but whatever happened to your eyebrows?"

"Oh, that," Gilboe scoffed. "Dana plucked them all out. An experiment of sorts that didn't exactly turn out as we'd hoped. I let that lunatic get away with too much. No matter, I rather like it now. Good luck, Sir Lucan." With a wave of the cups held together like a cross, the monk vanished into the night.

Lucan sat in tipsy contemplation for hours before bedding down to sleep under the tree with what might have been his own sheep, Agrios keeping drowsy watch. He understood that this might be the last time he would ever touch Castle Dare lands, and Lucan left his fears, his wishes, and his prayers deep in the soil before he closed his eyes to a dreamless, cold slumber.

Chapter 21

Only six of the Warren family departed for London—Effie and Gorman, Chumley, James, Bob, and Kit Katey. Lucan Montague and Thomas Annesley made the party eight, which made Effie's heart ache in a foreign manner. The even number of the group should have meant that each rider had a partner, but Sir Lucan seemed unobliged to participate.

Once more, he was the man she'd first known—solitary, stiff, proper. He held himself apart from the band despite Tommy and Gorman and Kit Katey's best efforts to draw him back in on the journey south. Effie hadn't realized how much a part of the group he'd become until he was no longer there.

Why had he become so cold toward her? Since the night at the Swan when he'd failed to visit her room, his demeanor had only grown more detached. He wouldn't so much as look at her now, and that, combined with her anxiousness to see George Thomas again, caused the burgeoning spring warmth, the bright sunshine, to be somehow dimmed and still tainted with winter's frost. The week's journey seemed to last an eternity.

The morning they at last came upon the outskirts of London, a trio of riders passed them on the road just a mile from the city walls, single file; two men, with a woman riding in the center. Chumley tossed his head at them as they passed, and Effie looked closely. The woman's face was bruised, and beneath the edges of her cloak, draped in an effort to hide it, her hands were bound to the saddle.

Effie swung her horse round at once and saw the trio nearing where Lucan Montague—hanging far to the rear, as usual—had already brought Agrios to a halt in the center of the road, effectively blocking the way.

Chumley and Bob thundered past Effie on her left, Gorman and James on her right; Kit Katey came alongside Effie.

The black destrier, Agrios, raised his head in an alert fashion giving the trio a wary sideways posture.

"Give way," the front rider shouted at Lucan. "Give way, I say! I'll run you through."

Lucan Montague looked back at the man with a bored expression on his face. He didn't reply.

"Oy!" The man riding behind gave a yelp as the four from the band surrounded him.

Effie and Kit Katey spurred their mounts, splitting to ride around either side of the group of men to flank the imprisoned woman.

"You are safe now," Kit said, reaching out with her blade and severing the ropes with two quick, careful upward slices.

The woman was wild-eyed as she scrambled to grab up the reins with hands that were purple-striped from the bindings and cold. "Hah!" She shouted, buffeting Effie's mare to the side and bursting through the party, turning her horse back south and riding as if all the demons from hell were on her tail.

The rider in the front, realizing their prey was escaped, slouched down and attempted to charge where Lucan Montague sat atop Agrios, as still and perfect as a marble statue. The man drew his sword, holding it tucked in like a lance, his intent clear if Lucan failed to move, but likely more than a threat than an actual challenge—Effie well-knew the type that traded in human lives. All the same, Effie held her breath as the horse gained speed.

In the last possible moment, his movements a blur, Lucan drew his short sword, deflecting the attack with a sliding crash of steel while piercing the man's unguarded flank. The challenger flipped backward over his horse's rear, Lucan's blade sliding free, and the horse galloped up the road, riderless. The man lay bleeding in the road, unmoving.

Lucan took out a black kerchief and wiped his blade before letting the piece of fabric float to the trampled dirt and sending his blade home in his hilt. He looked up and met Effie's gaze, but his expression never changed. He began riding toward her, and Effie's heart caught in her throat.

"Let's have your purse," Bob was saying to the second villain, still hemmed in by the band.

"We paid good coin for that bit!" the man argued shrilly, his fear just beneath the surface of his words.

"I'm sure you must have a little something left, love," Chumley cajoled. "I'm a sheriff, you see, and that one there, who so neatly dispatched your mate? He's one of the king's own. So, you can give over what you have and escape London with your life, or you can take your chances with us and hope to live long enough to see the gallows."

"Here! Here!" the man stuttered. "Have it then!"

"I rather fancy that cloak," Bob said admiringly.

The man struggled to free himself of it.

"Off you go then!" James Rose called gaily. He leaned over and slapped the horse's rump. "*Au revoir*!" The pair raced up the road, swerving around the body of his fallen comrade.

Lucan drew near now, but his gaze turned forward. "Thomas, if you'll accompany me. I've a feeling we shouldn't all enter the city at once. There are some tasks I'd see to at the house so that you are prepared for the morrow."

"Aye, Sir Lucan. You take care now, lass," Effie's father said to her. If Thomas Annesley was beset by nerves, he was hiding it well.

Lucan looked to Gorman now. "Meet at the Strand." He spurred Agrios into a trot, he and Tommy leaving the rest of them clustered together on the road.

No one said anything for a pair of awkward moments, and for some reason, Effie felt as if everyone was looking at her. Thankfully, Bob broke the tense silence.

"Are we to do anything with that one?" he said, motioning with his head toward the body in the dirt. "We're fearful close to the gates. Someone could come along at any moment."

"I don't clean up after Lucan Montague," James said stiffly. "I say we leave him there. If questioned, we tell them that a man dressed in black dispatched him in defense of a mounted attack."

"Aye," Chumley said at once.

Gorman nodded. "Agreed. Keep it simple. Effie?"

"Fine." She turned her horse's head southward once more.

She tried not to let her thoughts dwell on the idea that the last time Lucan Montague had ridden into London with her father, it had led to a sentence of death. He could even now take Tommy straight to the king and put end to the whole thing, gain his reward and be gone before any of the band even realized what had happened.

No, Effie told herself, remembering the way Lucan had dispatched the slave trader on the road. If he didn't care at all, he would have simply let the man pass and not risked his life to make sure the villain never harmed another soul again.

Trust him, a voice said. *Even if he cannot love you, he is always true to his word. And he knows Tommy is innocent.*

Something brushed her arm and Effie looked over to see that it was Kit Katey who had touched her.

"It will be all right, Effie," she said with a gentle smile. "He is bad now. But he is still good. And very soon, you shall see George."

Effie faced forward with a frown, not understanding what her friend meant. But one thing she said was true: on the morrow, she would have her son back, no matter who or what it cost.

* * * *

They were not stopped at the gates of the city, but Lucan hadn't expected they would be, which is why he'd insisted on taking Thomas ahead. It pleased him that no one paid him and Thomas Annesley much heed as they traversed the crowded, narrow streets toward Lady Margaret's home, other than to call out their wares and attempt a sale.

Thomas didn't say much, and Lucan suspected it was from worry. His breeding certainly showed through—not many men could be expected to carry on for a second time toward a meeting that almost certainly meant his death. He allowed Thomas his silent reverie out of respect, and also because, in truth, Lucan felt he himself had never been so troubled of spirit.

He was relieved when the tall façade of the Strand House at last came into sight. The stable boys took hold of the mounts at once, and Lucan was a bit surprised when Stephen didn't appear.

"A moment, lord," he said to Thomas. "While I announce us."

The English noble-turned-Scots-fisherman only nodded and struck up a cordial conversation with the lads while Lucan mounted the steps to the ornate door. Two raps with the knocker had yet to entreat a response, and so Lucan looked back down to where Thomas and the stable boys still congregated.

"Anyone about the house?" he called out to the lads.

"Aye, lord," the older one said with an enthusiastic nod. "Fair ta burstin' about the house of late."

Lucan frowned and raised his hand to grasp the iron knocker again when the door at last opened and the solemn face of Stephen appeared in the opening.

"Ah," he said coolly. "Sir Lucan, what a surprise to see you again. Good evening."

"Good evening, Stephen," he said, preparing to step forward in the moment the steward moved from the opening.

But Stephen did not move. "How can I be of assistance?"

Lucan hesitated. "Am I no longer welcome at the Strand?"

"Of course you are welcome, Sir Lucan," Stephen replied. "On Lady Margaret's express orders."

"Good. I've a smaller party with me this day that will be arriving momentarily, if you would alert the staff."

"I'm very sorry, Sir," Stephen said. "But that won't be possible. We've not room with Lady Margaret's other guests."

"Other guests? Has Lady Margaret returned from Greece?"

"Indeed she has, Sir."

"I'd speak to her, please, Stephen."

"I'm afraid she is rather occupied at the moment, Sir Lucan," Stephen said calmly. "Perhaps you could call on her on the morrow." He glanced toward Thomas. "May I tell her with whom you've arrived?"

Lucan opened his mouth, but paused as a figure walked briskly across the entry hall behind Stephen, glancing toward the door as he went. Perhaps it was only his imagination, but the man had the same coloring, the same hawkish features as the spy at the inn.

Perhaps the same man that had followed them to the Swan.

Perhaps the same man who had stolen the satchel.

"Who was that?" Lucan demanded.

"I beg your pardon, Sir?"

"Behind you, just now," Lucan clarified, leaning to attempt to see around the steward. "That man."

Stephen pulled the door slightly tighter about him. "I'm sure I don't know, sir. Lady Margaret has many guests at the moment. And who have you arrived with, again?" he pressed.

Lucan's instinct tingled. He hadn't trusted Stephen at the very last of their stay at the house on the Strand, and now the man's prying and refusal of entrance shouted danger to Lucan.

"No one," Lucan said. "Only a servant." He stepped back from the door. "You'll tell Lady Margaret I called?"

"Certainly," Stephen assured him. "May I tell her where you can be found while you await your audience with the king?"

Now Lucan *knew* something was afoot. He took another step back. "No. No, that won't be necessary, Stephen."

"Very well. Good day to you, Sir Lucan." The steward closed the door.

Lucan trotted down the steps and took Agrios's reins from the stable boy. "Come on," he muttered to Thomas. "Quickly. Keep your head down, and don't look toward the house."

"What is it?" Thomas took charge of his mount and they both gained the saddle, Thomas following Lucan away from the house.

"Something is amiss," he said as they trotted down the street, retracing the path on which they'd just arrived. "The house is no longer safe for us."

"Why isn't it safe?"

"I don't yet know," Lucan said. "But Margaret has never turned me away before. And I swear I saw a man within that looked like the one that tried to waylay us on our journey north."

"Could it be him that took the satchel?"

"I don't know, Thomas," Lucan said. "I just don't know."

They only waited perhaps a quarter hour before Lucan spotted James Rose's tall, lean frame in the saddle, weaving toward them. Lucan could tell that, despite the young man's animosity toward him, James was alarmed at Lucan's and Thomas's presence at the head of the alley. He turned aside and spoke words that did not reach Lucan's ears, and a moment later, Effie came riding through the group, concern on her pale face.

"What is it?" she demanded.

Lucan briefly told the group what had transpired at the house, his refusal at the door, and his suspicions. Chumley cursed quietly.

"Where do we stay, then?" Gorman asked. "If Lady Margaret is somehow in league with our enemies?"

Lucan looked about at all of them. "We could try our luck at one of the inns," he said. "I'm not at all certain we won't be followed."

"Why would they follow us now, though?" Bob asked. "They already have the satchel."

"To kill us," Effie answered at once. "Or at least myself or my father. Perhaps Sir Lucan, as well."

Lucan nodded. "If Caris Hargrave has the evidence in her possession, all that is needed to guarantee her victory is for the witnesses against her to be dead."

"But what about your sister?" Gorman asked. "She's in the very lion's den."

Lucan nodded, the dark realization coming to him as his gaze automatically went to Effie's. "Indeed, she is."

Effie looked away, her expression crestfallen.

James Rose sighed. "Would you care to share with the rest of us what is apparently so obvious?"

"We've got to go on to Westminster, at once," Lucan said.

"Now?" Gorman clarified with a frown. "Tonight, unprepared?"

"It's the safest place for us," Lucan said. "At least, safer than any in the city will likely be, if indeed Lady Margaret is against us."

"You led us into a trap," James Rose accused. "That bloody fancy house was never safe. We shouldn't have gone there in the first bloody place."

Lucan didn't argue with the man, for he could in fact be correct.

"Must we all go?" Kit Katey asked. "The king knows not of us."

"And it's right to keep it that way," Chumley said.

"There is an inn on the west side of the city, not far from the Strand," Lucan said. "The Red Hart. It's expensive, but safe. Gorman and Kit Katey, you two arrive together; Chumley, you arrive after with James and Bob. Perhaps...you could insinuate you were a sheriff surrendering a criminal to the crown."

Chumley grinned. "Why, Sir Lucan, are you suggesting we tell an untruth?"

Lucan gave him a half grin.

"No," Gorman interjected. "I'm coming, too. It's my boy's life on the line here. I'll fight to the death so that he comes out of Westminster at my side."

"We can't go in swinging sword, Gorman," Effie said. "This isn't Darlyrede. Give us a chance to—"

"To what?" Gorman demanded, and it was perhaps the first flare of temper Lucan had ever seen the man display toward Effie. "As soon as they see Tommy, he'll be locked in a cell. They'll not let you leave, Effie. And Sir Lucan will surely be followed if he tries to send word."

"Ulric, my captain, is trustworthy," Lucan said. "I can send him with any news."

Chumley cursed under his breath again. "No. No more goddam outsiders. Would that Gilboe had come. He can at least come and go largely undetected in his monk's garb."

But Gorman was shaking his head. "The three of you are most at risk and so it stands to reason they'll not let you out of their sights. Regardless of Sir Lucan's confidence in his captain, Chumley's right. And I can't sit back and wait for word that may not come or come too late. That's not me. Effie, you know that's not—"

"I know," Effie insisted calmly. After a brief pause, she looked to Lucan. "Perhaps a knight's apprentice is called for?"

He caught her intent at once. "Indeed, I do think it's time I took on an assistant." Lucan looked toward the tall, resentful young man glaring at them all. He nodded. "James."

He rolled his eyes. "They'll never take me for it."

"Why not?" Lucan pressed.

James met his eyes and glared at him. "You don't know what you're asking of me."

"*I do*," Effie responded.

"You don't have to do it, James," Gorman interrupted. "I'll go myself. As George's father, it's my responsibility."

"Gorman," Kit Katey said quietly, reaching over to touch his thigh. "It is a good plan. They can succeed."

"James will be free to come and go as is needed," Lucan said. "He can be the messenger, without being tracked. I wouldn't suggest it if I didn't think he was more than capable. And if there is trouble, I'd have no other's ready sword at my side."

"Just so," Chumley agreed. "None better than James."

James Rose's expression was unfathomable as he looked at Lucan. But he seemed neither flattered nor impressed.

Lucan turned to the group. "What say you all?"

A moment later, Lucan was forced to look away as Effie maneuvered her horse near Gorman's and clasped his hand firmly before leaning to meet him in a brief kiss.

The four of them rode on toward Westminster.

"I've never had an apprentice before," Lucan mused, seeking to dispel the tension. "How are you at shining boots, James?"

"Fuck you, Montague," James muttered.

Effie and Thomas both laughed aloud.

And in that moment, Lucan understood that they were, at least for this night, still bound together. And it gave him courage.

Chapter 22

They were taken at once through the maze of Westminster to a large antechamber, where the king's own secretary was entertaining. The man, blond, with a high forehead and slim beard seemed annoyed at the guard's interruption as he leaned down to speak low near his ear. The secretary was on his feet at once, setting aside his wine goblet and striding toward them.

"You allowed him to walk freely through the place?" he was growling as the guard hurried at his heels. "Restrain him," he spoke to the other two guards standing just behind the group while he flicked his fingers at Effie's father. "Take him to a cell at once."

Effie opened her mouth to protest, but felt the touch of Lucan's hand on her own. His frown and the slight shake of his head stayed her.

"I'll be alright, lass," Tommy said as the two burly guards bustled him between them. He looked old then, frail, flanked by the stern-looking guards, their chests plated with armor. "I've been the king's guest before, eh, lads?"

"Take him; go," the secretary commanded. He looked to Lucan. "Montague. So you've proved true. Who's that with you?"

"My apprentice," Lucan said at once. "Hello, Hatteclyffe; good to know the king still lives, despite your care."

The man ignored Lucan's sarcastic greeting. "You had no apprentice before."

"He stayed in the city," Lucan explained. "I'd no reason to believe we'd be detained, so I had no need of him."

"But now you do?" the secretary asked with a smirk. And then he looked to James. "Does this apprentice have a name?"

"James Montrose, lord," he said with a slight bow. "From York."

The secretary's pale brows rose. "The Belgians? Ambitious."

Effie could feel Lucan's curiosity, but he said nothing.

"I'm certain the king will see you on the morrow," the secretary said, still to Lucan. "You'll have a chamber for you and your boy for the night. Certainly, you'll wish to see your captain."

"If he is not otherwise occupied," Lucan acquiesced.

"Giles will locate him, if he's not already gotten wind of your arrival. As for you," he said, turning at last to Effie, "I'll put you in with the rest of your lot. Giles?" The guard standing to the rear of the secretary stepped to the side to face his superior. "Take her up to the north wing with the other Scots rubbish."

Effie felt her face heat, but she said nothing as the guard approached her, his hand out, as if he would take her arm.

She pulled out of his reach. "I'm not a prisoner, am I?"

The secretary gave her an oily smile. "Certainly not yet."

"I want to see my son."

He looked at her with a touch of confused amusement. "Do you?"

"I'd speak to the Scots before I retire, Hatteclyffe, if you don't mind. They were part of my duties, after all, and I'd see that they've been cooperative."

"Not cooperative in the least," the secretary said. "But His Grace well expected it."

"*My son*," Effie insisted. "Where is he?"

Hatteclyffe turned an exasperated face toward her. "You don't have a son until the king says you have a son. You really shouldn't wear trousers, mistress," Hatteclyffe advised in a mock confidential tone. "They make you forward. Unbecoming." He glanced back to Lucan. "Very well," the secretary said dismissively. "Giles will wait for you to show you to your room, lest any ideas of subterfuge come to mind."

"Perish the thought," Lucan said. "I'll send Montrose for more suitable clothing for the lady before he retires."

"Wise, wise." Hatteclyffe said with a nasty smirk, and then turned away even as he spoke. "Good evening, Montague."

"This way, sir," the guard said, leading them from the antechamber and through dark, echoing corridors.

No one spoke further as the frigid air within the compound wrapped about the group like a shroud—so much colder than out of doors as they walked briskly through the twisting passages that Effie's skin broke out in gooseflesh beneath her sleeves. She tried to still the panic that wanted to rise within her, saving her questions for Lucan when they were afforded some sense of privacy.

Was she being taken to a cell, after all? Hatteclyffe had not struck her as a man whose words could be trusted.

But they ascended rather than descended staircases, and at last came to a set of double doors in the center of a wide corridor, flanked by two more guards.

"I'll wait for you here, sir," the guard advised Lucan.

"Thank you, Giles," Lucan said and then reached for the handle and charged through the door just as easily as if he was entering his own home. Effie and James followed.

The space was long and tall like the corridor they'd just left, but a hearth presided over the far, narrow end, and the center of the floor was occupied with a long trestle and benches. To either side of the hall were four doors, all at various stages of openness, and interspersed with short couches and chairs. Muffled chatter seemed to filter out into the smoky central chamber.

A man stood at the hearth staring into the flames, his back to the door. Dark, curling hair, wide of shoulder. He looked 'round as the door opened.

"Lucan," he said with relief.

"Tavish." The two men met to the side of the trestle, first in a handshake and then an embrace.

"'Tis good to see your face again," he said, pulling away and smiling. "Have you seen Mam?"

"I have. She is well, as is Roscraig. You've done a miracle there, Tavish."

"Thanks be to God. I'm fair to going mad here, keeping them all from burning the place down." His eyes flicked to Effie.

Lucan turned. "Tavish Cameron, Effie Annesley and James *Montrose*." He paused and looked to James, making obvious the use of the young man's true surname. "Yes?"

"Oh, why not?" James said with an eye roll. "It's out now, I suppose."

Tavish stepped forward and held out his hand to Effie. "At last."

Effie gave a curt nod and placed her hand into his. "You're Harriet's son."

"I am." Tavish then extended his hand to James. "Montrose? Your family from York?"

James shook hands. "Yes."

"Burghers."

"Yes."

Tavish gave a squint. "Mercenary bastards."

"Undoubtedly."

Tavish laughed heartily. "Welcome to you."

"Mama?"

Effie's heart seized in her chest, and she spun to the first doorway on the left where the call had come from. And there he was, his little red head a blur as he ran at her.

"George Thomas!" She went to her knees to catch him, and then unfolded into a seat on the floor, holding his slender body, cradling the back of his silky hair in her palm. "Oh, George, I've missed you so!"

"And so I have you!" He pulled back and gave her a sound kiss in the vicinity of her eye, so that Effie laughed. Then he looked up.

"James!"

"Hello, twig." He caught the boy up under his arms and swung him high in the air before placing him on his feet once more.

"I must tell them all at once!" George gasped with wide eyes and then ran back toward the doors, hanging in the frames, shouting, "My mama is here! My mama has come back! I knew she would come back! Hurry, everyone! My mama!"

He ran back to her giggling and Effie scooped him up in her arms again, seating him on her hip.

"I'm not a baby anymore, Mama," George advised. "You needn't carry me. I'm ever so grown."

"How grown you are," Effie said, marveling in the change of his speech. "But it has been so long since I've seen you, won't you indulge your old mother?"

George giggled gamely and threw his arms about her neck.

One by one, the doorways filled with figures. Iris, with her mahogany hair flying behind her, dashed from a chamber to embrace Lucan, while the others—two women and two men—emerged warily into the central chamber.

"Where's Da?" Padraig she recognized at once, and he looked mostly the same, if somewhat thinner, with more worry crowding about his young eyes. "Is he well?"

"He's here," Effie replied. "They've taken him into the king's custody, but he is well."

The red-haired woman at Padraig's side took in Effie's costume with one obvious glance and a mischievous glint came into her eyes.

"Well," she said slyly. "What have we here? A lass in trousers?" She looked to the long-haired man who emerged from the doorway before her. "I didna know that was an option for the king's court."

"It's not," Lucan interjected. "Hello, Finley. Thrown anyone from a bridge lately?"

The red-haired woman gave a scrunch-nosed frown. "Nay." She walked boldly toward Effie. "I reckon you're Lachlan's sister."

Effie couldn't help her unsure glance at Lucan.

He came to her rescue. "Let's get this out of the way, shall we?" He touched Effie's elbow so lightly and briefly that she shouldn't have noticed it, but her skin tingled all the same. "Effie Annesley, allow me to present Finley Carson, her husband there, Lachlan. Tavish you've met; his wife, Lady Glenna. Roscraig is their home."

A cool-looking blonde with a regal bearing nodded toward her. "How do you do?"

The largest man in their midst, the tawny haired Lachlan Blair, moved through the central chamber stealthily, his gaze pinning Effie as if he would read her very thoughts.

"Effie," he said.

She raised her chin. "Lachlan."

"Braw George Thomas there tell us all that you live in a cave, and rob wealthy nobles."

Effie blinked. "That's not all I do."

His mouth curved down and he nodded approvingly. He looked to James. "Lachlan Blair."

"James Montrose." He shook hands with the men in turn, and nodded deferentially to the ladies. "Ma'am. How do you do?"

George's arms tightened suddenly around Effie's neck. "Oh, Mama, I'm ever so glad we've come to London. It's been the most wondrous of days."

A beat of silence passed, and then laughter broke out in the central hall, startling Effie for a moment before she joined in.

"Come," Tavish Cameron said, sweeping his arm toward the table. "Let us become better acquainted as guests of Henry before we get down to the business of tomorrow."

* * * *

Lucan took a seat at the table, and noticed that James at first sought to claim the spot between him and Effie, but Effie thwarted him by swinging George Thomas's feet to the bench first and then sitting down next to her son, forcing James to sit on the opposite side of her. The shuffle was a relief to Lucan, who dreaded breaking the news to Thomas's children—and his own sister—that the satchel containing the evidence against the Hargraves had been stolen.

"Drink?" Tavish called out over their heads, and everyone in the group answered to the affirmative, either with their voices or a raising of their hands. Iris assisted him in serving the group, while George Thomas apprised his mother of the many activities he'd been engaged in during her absence.

"I can tell my numbers to a *hundred*," he said, leaning his face so close to hers that their noses brushed together as he still stood on the bench. "*And* I can write my first names. Tutor won't allow me to write my surname, as he says it's not co-firmed."

"It is confirmed," Effie advised him with just the hint of a troubled frown. "Your surname is Annesley, just as is mine, and as is your grandfather's."

George gave an excited squeal and a wiggle. "Is he here? Can I meet him, too?"

Lucan could see the shadow of sadness in Effie's smile. "He is here, my love. And I do hope you will meet him soon."

"George Thomas has been taking his lessons with the king's son," Tavish advised as he stepped over the bench, a goblet in his hand. "He's doing quite well."

"Edward is my friend," George assured Effie. "He's only a tiny bit older than me, but ever so jolly. He wishes to be a soldier when he's grown, and fight for his father, because he's not well, you see."

"Is that so?" Effie remarked with a smile. "And have you been keeping your company elsewhere?"

"I have seen Grandmama two times," George said, holding up his stubby thumb and forefinger. "Once with my lord and another occasion with Auntie Iris."

Lucan's gaze followed Effie's to his sister.

"He's been closely looked after," Iris commented quietly, and Lucan's love for his sister grew even more.

His guilt, also, expanded.

"But that's no matter now," George Thomas piped up. "For on the morrow, you will meet with my lord again and then we might all go home to the Warren. Isn't that right, Mama?" He placed his little hand against Effie's cheek to gain her full attention. "Is father here, as well? To carry us home to Northumberland?"

Effie turned her face haltingly toward Lucan, George's palm still splayed across her skin.

Lucan drew a deep breath. "The king's secretary told me just now that Henry will most likely hear us on the morrow. But, there is a problem." He raised his face to look at each of the company in turn—he owed them that much. "The satchel containing Iris's portfolio was stolen on our return to London."

No one around the table said anything for several moments, and Lucan's announcement hung in the air like a noxious stench.

At last, Iris spoke. "How?"

And then he told them all he could—the journey, their suspicions, the cold reception they'd received at the house on the Strand.

"Lady Margaret Stanhope?" Padraig interjected.

"Yes," Lucan said.

Padraig looked around the table with a frown. "She's been to see the king," he said. "Yesterday, in fact."

"What did she say?" Lucan asked.

Padraig shook his head. "I don't know. Whatever it was caused a stir, though. She swept from the hall as if all the hounds of hell were after her."

"I don't understand it," Lucan said, reluctantly. He hated the unsure feeling knotting his stomach. "Margaret was already gone when I returned to London. What could she possibly have to do with any of this? She couldn't bear me any grudge."

"Perhaps she was bought by Caris Hargrave," Lachlan suggested. "It wouldna be the first time Darlyrede's money has been ill-used."

Lucan shook his head. "Margaret is beyond wealthy. Caris Hargrave could have nothing she wants."

Then James spoke up. "Perhaps it's not something she wants, but something she's seeking to keep hidden."

The table stilled and Lucan could feel the weight of the anxious stares upon him.

"No," he said quietly. And then, louder, "No. Margaret wouldn't have anything to do with the likes of the Hargraves or the Pagets."

"Her husband, then," Effie suggested.

Lucan shook his head again. "No. *No,* I don't believe it. He was too well respected."

"That's regardless. Just because you are fond of someone," Iris said gently, "doesn't mean you know their true nature. I nearly found that out too late."

"But she's been in Greece, Iris!" Lucan exclaimed. "She left right after Tommy was sentenced. Completely removed from all of this!" He rubbed his brow.

"Did she know why you surrendered Thomas the first time?" Glenna Douglas asked calmly.

Lucan's gaze went to her. "I don't know," he said in irritation and then thought. "Yes, she did. Yes."

"And shortly after Tommy escaped his execution," Lachlan said, "Margaret Stanhope fled England for Greece—or wherever it was she actually went, if she even went anywhere at all. She knew something she wasn't telling you, Lucan."

Lucan's head ached. "She wouldn't betray me," he said. "She couldn't have. At that point, my only duty was to alert you all to Thomas Annesley's existence."

"What *did* you tell her, exactly?" Effie asked him, and her voice held none of the previous animosity, although he could hear the tension in her words and he wondered stupidly if she was imagining bedtime secrets shared between lovers; if she was jealous.

"Little more than what everyone in England already knew," he answered. "She'd likely heard more rumor than I, being in London." Everyone was still staring at him, and so he sighed and relented. "I told her about Thomas and Cordelia. About the Hargraves, and their supposed grievances against him. That's it." Lucan held up his hands. "That's all I knew myself, at the time."

"The steward then," James offered.

"Stephen?" Lucan mused a moment. "Perhaps. I don't know how. I can't imagine what he would gain."

"Coin," Finley answered right away. "A debt owed by a noble."

"It doesn't matter." Tavish sighed. "We may or may not find out on the morrow if Caris Hargrave has gained the evidence against her. The only thing we know for certain is that we no longer have it in our possession."

"Which means all our proof is gone," Iris murmured, and each word was like a blade to Lucan's heart.

"You must simply write it all down again," Glenna Douglas said, her voice cool and matter of fact, rising above the humid emotion that hovered over the table. "Whatever you can recall—each of you."

Lucan nodded. "Yes. You're right. Even if it's only testimony, perhaps gathering it altogether in hand will have some sway."

"All of us must commit to posterity all that has happened to us," Tavish said. "Our childhoods, our struggles against the Hargraves. Iris, your employment under Lady Caris; Padraig, your skirmishes once arrived at Darlyrede; Lucan, everything that has happened since your arrival in London. Perhaps if they are all fit together..."

"What about us?" James said, and all eyes turned to him. "Effie and me. Our friends. Should Effie put the whole of what's happened to her in writing, none of us will leave London."

"He's right," Effie said. "Although our actions were more than justified, the Crown will likely only hear the crimes of it. Adolphus Paget is dead, and someone must be blamed for it, despite the accusations against him."

"If you don't tell the truth," Padraig said, "Da will die."

Effie clutched George Thomas to her. "I'll not risk my son being taken from me."

Lachlan slapped his hand on the tabletop. "I'll not allow Thomas Annesley to be killed for crimes he didn't commit."

"I'll not be executed just so that you might skip back to Scotland as you jolly well please," James sniped.

Lachlan rose from the bench, and James followed suit.

"Stop," Padraig said. "We're all here for the same purpose."

"No, we're not, Padraig," Effie said quietly. "You and Tavish and Lachlan have homes to return to in Scotland, out of Henry's reach. Lucan and I"—Lucan's stomach clenched at her casual pairing of their names—"are fighting not only for our lives, but for our future. If we tell publicly everything we know and the king still rules for Caris Hargrave, there is no place in England either one of us will be safe."

She turned to look at Lucan directly. "We must get George out of Westminster, perhaps out of London altogether. Tonight. I'll not bear false witness against my father, nor will I admit to the things I've done in the name of justice and mercy as crimes."

Lucan understood now that Effie was prepared to see the entire thing to its end. He looked to James but didn't even have chance to speak before the younger man was nodding.

"I'll take him. Now."

George clutched at Effie with a little yelp. "Mama, no! I want to stay with you!"

Effie stroked the boy's hair. "Shh. James will take you to Father, George. I'll see you soon."

"No," he insisted, squeezing her more tightly and closing his eyes, perhaps against the reality of his immediate future. "You come with us."

"I cannot, my love," she soothed. "Your grandfather and your uncles need me. But your father has missed you so very much. And he is staying at an inn! It will be such an adventure. And you can tell him all your numbers."

"You will come for me before bedtime," he pressed.

Effie paused. "I will do my best. It might not be quite that soon."

"I want to see my grandfather. He is the only one I have. Edward doesn't have a grandfather, but I do."

"Perhaps soon," Effie said. She pulled away from him and kissed both his cheeks. "Go with James. Give your father my love."

Lucan's heart clenched in jealousy and self-loathing.

"Come along, twig," James commanded, standing from the bench and untying his cloak. "A horse-back it shall be."

George seemed to find new life then, and giggled as he stepped upon the tabletop to swing himself around James's shoulders. The cloak was reattached, the hood draped to disguise the thin lump that was the lad across his back.

James turned to Lucan. "I'll be back."

Lucan nodded. "I know."

"Not for you," the young man clarified. "For Effie."

"I know," he assured him with a grin.

Iris took Effie into her arms as James smuggled George from the chamber. Lucan spoke to Giles briefly, and then returned to the room, sitting once more at Effie's side. He pulled his rolled packet out of his gambeson and began undoing the ties.

"I do hope you have more parchment and ink," he said gruffly.

They crowded back around the tabletop, and together opened the door to the past.

Chapter 23

They were shown to the same hall in which Effie had first met the king on her previous audience, but this time the space was filled with spectators standing on the stone floor, their chatter soaring up and through the wooden buttresses like swallows.

Every nerve in Effie's body seemed alive beneath her borrowed gown as the group was led through the crowd. She hadn't seen Lucan since he'd left the apartment in the early hours of the morning, and although she had laid down on the bed in the chamber she'd been given, she hadn't slept at all. James had at first insisted on staying with her, but Lucan had warned against it, if they were to keep up the charade of apprentice. And so, refusing a promise to not kill Lucan in his sleep, the last member of Effie's Warren family had slipped through her fingers and was swallowed up into the dark interior of Westminster, leaving her in the company of a family that were so many strangers.

Lucan was here now, though, standing at the far end of the aisle before the dais. He looked fresh and crisp and, as usual, completely removed from the spectacle taking place around him.

The atmosphere in the hall was festive, and Effie suspected—hoped—that, because of the suddenness of the court, those gathered were little more than perpetual hangers-on and gossips who thrived on court intrigue. Their stares were weighty things upon her skin, and they made no pretense of their gawking as she passed through their midst toward the man sitting in his ornate chair. The group paid their homage and then Effie and Thomas Annesley's other children and their wives were shown to a set of benches on the floor, opposite the aisle where Caris Hargrave already sat at Vivienne Paget's side, a host of other nobility behind her. Effie recognized some of the faces, including Lord Hood, and the reality of what was to come hit her suddenly, and the room swam for a brief moment.

"Alright?" Finley Carson whispered.

Effie nodded, her eyes going to her father—his whiskered chin was lifted, his gaze going over the heads of the crowd. If he could bear it, sitting in a lone chair to the side of the dais opposite where Lucan stood, so could she.

She looked up at the king again, and for the first time, caught sight of a worn leather satchel on a low table at the king's side. Effie's heart skipped a beat and she sought Lucan's face through the crowd.

He was watching her. She glanced pointedly toward the satchel, but he only gave a disinterested blink and looked away as the intendant came to the center of the aisle to announce the commencement of the king's court.

"Sir Lucan Montague," Henry called.

Lucan gave a deep bow. "Your Grace."

"You have, for the second time, brought the fugitive Thomas Annesley into custody. England thanks you for your service. You are dismissed."

A low gasp came from the benches around Effie.

"But, my liege," Lucan began, "I would speak testimony to the issue of—"

"The return of your property will be addressed, I assure you," Henry interrupted. "But not until I have this more pressing matter out of my way. As Annesley has already been sentenced, your services are not needed at court at this time. You are dismissed," he insisted. "*To observe*."

Lucan bowed again and then turned crisply on his heel to walk past the end of the bench near where Effie perched. She looked up at him as he strode by, but he paid her no heed.

"Thomas Annesley," the intendant said.

Effie's father stood.

The man then read out a long list of crimes going back thirty years, as well as the addition of several more misdeeds including escape of the Crown.

"How do you answer?" the intendant demanded.

"Not guilty, Your Grace."

Henry looked at Thomas thoughtfully. "So you have said. Have you further proof of your innocence?"

"My child by Cordelia Hargrave is present, Your Grace."

The crowd in the hall gasped and twittered.

"And do you know how she came to survive your betrothed's murder, Annesley?"

"Caris Hargrave claimed her as a distant relation, my liege. She was brought up at Darlyrede as their niece."

"What is this person's name, Annesley?"

"She was given the name Euphemia Hargrave at her birth."

"You were not there to directly witness these events?"

"Nay, Your Grace. I was by then in Scotland. I had no idea our child had survived until I met her when she came for me."

"In Scotland," Henry clarified with a scowl.

"Aye, Your Grace." Thomas cleared his throat self-consciously.

Henry's shrewd gaze went directly to Effie, and he nodded to the intendant.

"The king calls Euphemia Hargrave."

Effie gained her feet at the announcement of that hated moniker, and made her way slowly down the aisle, where she again paid homage to the king's presence. She could feel the stares like fleas beneath her gown. Henry nodded at the intendant again.

"The king calls Lady Caris Hargrave."

Caris made a great show of feebleness as Vivienne Paget helped her to stand and shuffle forward toward the king. She was perhaps only four feet from Effie's side, and it caused Effie's stomach to turn.

"Your Grace," Caris croaked. "Forgive my poor health."

"Fetch the lady's chair," the king called out. Once she was again seated, this time in the aisle, the king continued. "Lady Hargrave, is the woman to your right the one known to you as Euphemia Hargrave?"

Caris turned her gaze toward Effie, and although the woman's feigned expression was one of weariness and perhaps even a touch of fear, Effie clearly recognized the sparkle of anger that hid there.

"She is, Your Grace."

"The same one you claimed was your niece, who went missing from Darlyrede house some ten and five years past?"

Caris looked back to the king. "I confess that is true."

"Is she, in fact, your granddaughter, born of Cordelia Hargrave?"

Effie could hear the tension in the air as everyone gathered strained their ears, waiting for the answer Caris Hargrave would give.

"She is, Your Grace."

The crowd broke out in murmurs.

"Miss Hargrave," Henry said, raising his voice to be heard above the commotion. "Why did you abscond from your home at Darlyrede House?"

A million things rushed through Effie's mind at once. She knew she could put herself and her family at the Warren in grave danger with how she chose to answer the king. She thought of George Thomas, and Gorman, and of Mari and Gale. She looked at her father.

The truth would be heard.

"Because I knew that Caris Hargrave had killed my mother, and that Vaughn Hargrave was a monster who was, along with several others in positions of power, responsible for the abduction and torture of hundreds—perhaps thousands—of innocent people in Northumberland and beyond."

There was no gasp of surprise this time, the shock of the crowd so sudden and deep that the only sound recognizable to Effie was the thudding of her own heart.

"That is a serious accusation, Miss Hargrave," the king warned. "Have you any proof?"

"Caris Hargrave admitted as much to Iris Montague, while she was in her employ."

"Montague?" the king repeated. He nodded to the intendant.

"The king calls Iris Montague."

A moment later, the woman stood at Effie's side.

"You are now married to Padraig Boyd, I understand. How exactly are you related to Sir Lucan Montague?" the king pressed although it was impossible Henry didn't already know.

"Lucan Montague is my brother, Your Grace," Iris said.

"How did you manage to come into the service of Lady Hargrave?"

"I escaped the convent where my brother and I had been interred since our parents were killed in the fire at Castle Dare. I intended to find out the truth about why they were killed."

"You didn't feel it was an accident."

"No, Your Grace."

The king turned his attention to Caris once more. "Did you know the girl's history when she came to you?"

"I did not recognize her as the child of our dear friends," Caris whispered, her tone full of false shame. "Iris Montague had taken the name and station of a housemaid."

The king looked back to Iris. "You kept your true identity hidden."

"To protect myself and my brother," Iris admitted.

"Just when did Lady Hargrave admit to the claims made by Miss Hargrave?"

"While we were trapped in the dungeon of Darlyrede House. She had poisoned me and taken me there to kill me after she discovered who I really was."

"That's a lie," Caris Hargrave interjected. "We were indeed trapped by the flames. But Iris was only there because the dungeon was our one hope to spare both of our lives from the fire." She paused and shook her head ruefully. "I had grown much attached to her—loved her, in fact. I had no idea she had come to Darlyrede with the intent to destroy me utterly."

"And so, Lady Hargrave, you deny that you confessed such atrocities to the girl?" the king pressed. "Whom you were under the impression was another person altogether?"

Caris lifted her chin. "I do. This is nothing but a gang of thieves set out to rob and destroy Darlyrede House, as well as sully the name of my dearly departed husband. It's an attack of the common against the nobility, Your Grace."

The king looked back to Iris for a long, thoughtful moment. "You are dismissed, madam."

Iris hesitated.

The intendant frowned at her. "Take your seat."

"Where have you been these past fifteen years, Miss Hargrave?"

Effie swallowed. "In Northumberland, Your Grace."

Henry raised his eyebrows and waited.

"I've made my home among friends."

"These friends wouldn't also happen to be the same band that has terrorized the roads around Darlyrede House, would they?"

"I cannot say, Your Grace."

"Why didn't you come to me with these concerns, these suspicious?" the king pressed. "As a young girl?"

"You wouldn't have believed me," Effie said.

"You're right," Henry agreed. "It's absurd. A respected noble, the richest house in Northumberland?" His gaze roved over the group of Thomas Annesley's children still seated on the benches. "There is no proof beyond hearsay. And of course, we also have the accusation from Lady Vivienne Paget. Lady Paget? Your charge?"

"That woman," she sinewy, dark woman sneered, "ambushed and killed my husband during a hunt in the wood around Darlyrede House. She killed him dead—shot him from his horse with an arrow while she cowered in the trees in the midst of her fellow criminals."

"Were you present at the time your husband was killed, Lady Paget?"

"No, thank God," Vivienne Paget gasped. "But there is another here who was, and will testify. Lord Edwin Hood."

The kindly lord was called and came to the center of the aisle.

"Lord Hood, do you confirm the accusations of Lady Paget?"

"I was present that day, Your Grace, yes," the lord said. "And I did witness the death of Adolphus Paget, as did Lucan Montague and Padraig Boyd, who sought to save Lord Paget's life."

"Who fired the fatal shot, Lord Hood?"

"I cannot say, Your Grace. Most of the band wore masks."

"But Miss Hargrave was part of that company?"

Lord Hood glanced sorrowfully at Effie. "Yes, my liege."

"Was she bearing a weapon?"

"Yes, my liege."

"Did you see her fire it at any time?"

"Yes, my liege. She shot Sir Lucan Montague in the foot."

The crowd gasped again.

"You are dismissed, Lord Hood."

The king looked back to Caris Hargrave. "You deny having anything to do with your daughter's death?"

"I certainly do, Your Grace," Caris gasped. "I found her body after Thomas Annesley had ravaged her. My husband, a skilled surgeon during the wars, managed to save Cordelia's child's life. That I hid her true identity out of a desire to protect her from the terrible truth, I must confess, is true."

"Why would Thomas Annesley kill the woman who was carrying his child, and whom he was to marry the following day?"

Caris shook her head. "I don't know, Your Grace. Perhaps he was mad. Or, perhaps..." she paused slyly. "He suspected that the child Cordelia carried was not his. She was very...well-loved among the villagers."

"You're disgusting," Effie hissed. "I know the truth about what you did to those poor girls, and so did my mother and my father."

Caris looked directly at Effie now, with a wash of thick, false pity on her lined, gray face. "I still love you, child. And I hope you and your little boy will return home with me. It matters not to me that he is the bastard child of a commoner."

Effie's stomach lurched as if she were again ten years old and looking helplessly into those lying eyes.

The king thankfully broke the spell. "Miss Hargrave, have you any evidence to prove any of your accusations against the late Lord Hargrave?"

"Besides my written testimony, and that of my relation, Your Grace?"

"I have read your supposed testimonies, and remain unconvinced. Although filled with quite the tales, any nitwit could ascribe to paper that Christ shall come into London on a unicorn, Miss Hargrave. It doesn't make it true."

"Then, no, Your Grace. I do not."

Henry beckoned to his intendant and spoke quietly to him for a moment. The intendant straightened.

"The king will enjoin a short recess."

Those seated rose while Henry made his way from the dais and away into the doorway in the rear wall.

Effie's breath rushed out of her, and she stumbled back to sit on the bench while her half-brothers crowded around her.

"This isn't good," Tavish remarked darkly.

"I'll kill her," Effie whispered, staring through the bodies standing about her, seeking a glimpse of Caris Hargrave. "I'll kill her rather than let her get away with this. Before the king returns, if I must. Someone, give me a blade."

"Stop it, immediately," Glenna Douglas commanded. "Get hold of yourself."

Her sanity was spiraling away from her, Effie knew. She felt a hand on her back and turned to see Lucan.

"You must tell him about the Warren. We should bring them in. James could go—"

"Are you mad?" Effie demanded.

"Henry won't ignore them. Chumley, and Gorman, as Rolf's son—Caris can't deny her own steward. And Gorman and Kit Katey can testify to the nightmare of Elsmire Tower."

"You'll have us all hunted, Montague," James accused in a harsh whisper. "You've no idea what you're saying."

"The king will rule justly—"

"The king will rule in favor of those who have filled his coffers," Tavish interjected. "James Montrose is right, Lucan. You've always had the protection of your title. You don't understand what it's like for a common man. We've no guarantee of justice because we cannot afford it."

"I'll tell him myself," Lucan volunteered. "I've nothing to lose."

His words sliced Effie's heart.

"No," Padraig said quietly. "He suspects you've been taken in by Tommy now. He won't believe you. All you'll succeed in doing is forfeiting Castle Dare."

Effie held up her hands. "Am I the only one who has noticed that the satchel is on the dais? Where did it come from?"

"Everything we've said—and more—is confirmed in that portfolio," Iris said. "If Henry's seen it, he can't deny it."

Finley frowned. "Perhaps it's empty. Or had things removed."

Effie looked up at where her father sat, still guarded by the two men. He was handing a goblet back to a guard with a smile of thanks. His attention turned back to Effie, and he saw her watching him. He nodded, his smile remaining.

"If you don't tell him, Effie, Thomas will hang." Lucan's insistence cut through her attention on her father.

"Come off it, Montague," James scoffed. "He'll hang anyway. You knew that when you agreed to drag him back here the second time. You're not fucking all of us."

Lucan lurched toward James, but Lachlan and Padraig intervened, pulling the pair away.

The short trill of a horn announced that the recess was over, and everyone gained their feet once more as Henry made his way back to his chair. He spoke briefly with his intendant before sending the man to the front of the dais.

"Hear ye, hear ye, His Grace will now give his ruling. Thomas Annesley, remain standing." The intendant waited patiently while Thomas gained his feet once more; he stood straight and tall, his chin still lifted.

"On seven counts of murder of one of rank, you are guilty." The crowd gasped, but the intendant continued, only raising his voice. "On thirty-two counts of murder of common folk—both named and unnamed—you are guilty. On two counts of arson, you are guilty. On thirteen counts of robbery, you are guilty. On two counts of larceny, you are guilty. On three counts of treason, you are guilty."

Effie's vision grayed and she must have wobbled, for Padraig and Finley were at once at either side of her, bolstering her with their hands.

"Your sentence shall be announced at forenoon on the morrow, with the punishment carried out immediately on New Palace Yard. Alleged heirs and issue of the guilty, please come forward." The intendant stepped back deferentially to the king's side.

"Tavish Cameron and Lachlan Blair," the king said. "You will take your households and depart back to Scotland at noon on the morrow. If you are found in England again, I will have you arrested and tried in abetting this farce."

"Your Grace," Tavish began.

"*Do not return,*" Henry nearly shouted. He looked to the youngest of the sons. "Padraig Boyd, you shall remain at Westminster while evidence against you is reviewed. Infiltrating the king's army while taking part in a coup against a noble house is punishable by death. And as for your new bride," here, Henry looked to Iris, "because of your brother's faithful service, you shall be lucky if I only have your marriage annulled for your own good. Perhaps France is the place for you, after all."

"I'd stay with my husband, my liege," Iris replied.

"You don't have a choice, madam," Henry answered with a squint. He looked to Effie. "Euphemia Hargrave, you have committed grave misdeeds against the family that, from all appearances, was only trying to better your station in life and shield you from the awful truth of your parentage. The personal accusations against you are severe. I order that you are stripped of the name given you at birth and you are under no circumstances to return to Northumberland. As for your son, because Lady Hargrave is in no condition to care for, and indeed, has yet no suitable place to raise a child of such a young age, the boy known as George Thomas shall be remanded into the care of the Crown until he is of such an age of majority as to be entered into service."

Henry looked at Caris Hargrave. "You will be granted a loan from the Crown to rebuild your home, Lady Hargrave. Although I regret to tell you what you already likely know—that it shall be too long in the construction for it to ever be completed in your lifetime."

Caris Hargrave hid her face in her kerchief.

The king looked back to Effie. "Where is your son?"

Effie's lips felt numb, her hearing was muffled. She wasn't sure she understood the question at all, although surely it wasn't so complicated. "I...I don't know, Your Grace. I've not yet seen him today."

Henry nodded, as if this was a perfectly acceptable answer. "Seek him tonight for your good-byes." He looked to the intendant pointedly.

"All rise," the man called.

Henry left the dais through the little door in the rear wall, his scribe snatching up the satchel and following.

Thomas Annesley was led away by the two guards.

And Effie fainted onto the stone floor.

* * * *

Lucan and James helped Effie through the crowd while Thomas Annesley's sons and daughters-in-law did their best to shield the woman from gawking eyes. Effie was mostly on her own power by the time they reached the apartments, and she went directly to her chamber and closed the door behind her, leaving James Montrose bracing himself on either side of the doorframe, his head hanging down.

Finley and Lachlan, too, went to their chamber. No one spoke. Lucan sat down at the long central table, the air in the common room stale and cold and heavy. Padraig sat across from Lucan, his forehead lowered onto his clenched fists while Iris sat at his side, her hand stroking his back. Tavish Cameron and his wife took places at the end of the table, joined together by one hand each.

"That's it," Padraig said hoarsely, his voice sounding loudly flat against the tabletop. "It's over."

No one refuted him.

"I'm gone," James Montrose announced, pushing himself away from the doorframe.

"Where are you going?" Tavish asked with a frown.

"I've got to warn the others to get out of the city," he said as he walked toward the door. "Once they discover George is missing, they'll alert the guards, and they'll never get through the gate."

"James, wait," Lucan called. "You'll be followed—"

The young man spun around and for moment, Lucan thought James would swing. But he only stabbed a finger at him.

"Shut. Up," he said through clenched teeth. "Shut up." He left the common room and slammed the door behind him.

Iris was watching Lucan with pity in her eyes.

He'd failed. He'd failed Thomas Annesley. He'd failed his sister, and their parents. He'd failed Tavish and Lachlan and Padraig. He'd failed James and the family of the Warren.

He'd failed Effie. And George Thomas.

He'd failed Northumberland.

All their lives were in ruins because of Lucan. Because he'd said nothing when he'd had the chance, pridefully assuming that the king thought so highly of him, that surely Henry would ask his opinion on the situation. An opinion Lucan had stayed up the remainder of the night crafting for just that moment when he would be given the floor to speak before the court.

Dashed.

It was Lucan's fault.

Perhaps tomorrow Henry would return Castle Dare lands. Tomorrow, after Thomas Annesley was hanged and dead and Effie was exiled, and all the sons were scattered.

It wouldn't matter then.

And so, in that moment, he realized what he must do.

He pushed back from the table and stood up, looking down at Iris. "If I'm not back before tonight, seek out the protection of Lord Edwin Hood. He was a good friend to our parents, and will see that you are cared for, whatever the king decides."

"What are you doing?" she asked.

"What I should have done when I first brought Thomas Annesley into London," he said, and then followed the path James had taken from the room.

Chapter 24

The room was cold and dark when Effie closed the door behind her, shutting James—shutting everyone—out, but it suited her. She *felt* cold and dark.

"Didn't you bring in a light?" a male voice asked in the gloom, causing her to jump.

"Gorman?" Effie whispered.

A little flame flared brightly, and she saw the outline of his bearded face as he bent over the candle, touching the straw to the wick.

"*Gorman*!" Effie rushed across the room and into his arms on a sob. "Guilty," she rasped. "The king said—"

"Shh," Gorman hushed, stroking the back of her head and steering her to the side of the bed where they both sat. "I know. I heard."

Effie pulled away. "You were there?"

He nodded. "I couldn't bear not knowing. I bribed a guard to find out where the apartment was."

"Where's George?"

"At the inn with Kit Katey. For now. But we must go, as soon as I leave here."

"I know. Where? Not the Warren."

"No. Mari and Gale's, I suppose. He'll not be safe in England now." He paused. "Are you coming?"

Effie swallowed and lowered her gaze to the floor as pain pierced her heart. "I can't. I owe my father that I should see it through to the end. He's giving up his life for our son, Gorman."

"Aw, Eff, I know that. I meant, are you *ever* coming back to us?" Something in his tone made her look up at him. "*Us*, Effie. The family. *Me*."

She stilled. "Where else would I go?"

"France?" he suggested pointedly. He stared into her eyes, his own gaze still so kind, so wise, and in the next moment, the last shred of the life Effie had known was incinerated.

"You know."

"I've known since the Swan. I'm not stupid."

Her flesh went ice-cold, but her face burned. "Why didn't you say anything?"

"What should I have said?" he challenged. "It's been obvious since the two of you met in the woods the day you shot him that there was something deeper between you and Lucan Montague. You have a shared heritage, a shared past. I knew that day, I think, that you weren't done with each other." His voice lowered a bit, and Effie could hear the sadness in his words, which broke her heart wide open. "I only didn't know that it would lead to you falling in love with him."

"Gorman, no—you don't understand. I've been so confused! It didn't mean anything!"

"Don't say that it didn't mean anything," he warned in a low voice.

"Why?"

"Because I know it's not true. You aren't the sort of woman who gives herself lightly. If you were, I wouldn't love you."

"That's just it," she rushed, and she slid from the side of the bed to her knees before him. "If you loved me, you would have married me years ago. I never would have been in this position."

"Now, that I do take offense to," he said. "Nothing I did or didn't do drove you to Lucan Montague's bed."

She was ruining this—destroying it with each stuttering word, it seemed. "You're right. I'm sorry. But it's not too late," she whispered. "If you can forgive me..."

"Don't you see? There is nothing to forgive." He cupped her face in his hands. "Ah, Effie. I will never, ever love another woman in exactly the way I love you. You gave me my son. You were there for me in my darkest days after escaping Elsmire. *I...adore...you.*" He placed a gentle kiss on her forehead and Effie closed her eyes, releasing a hot, double stream of tears.

"I want the best for you, always. Which is why I *didn't* marry you. No matter what the king said in his court today, you are poised for greatness, and you will take our son along with you. Being shackled to me would only bring shame to us both—you for giving up the place where you could do the most good, and me for allowing it."

"Then why, after all I have been through this day, are you punishing me?"

His expression was alarmed, intense. "Oh, my love—I'm not punishing you. I'm *freeing* you. For so many years, it's been the two of us, Eff. We didn't just make do with the lot we were cast, we *burned*. And it was glorious and right and true." Now his hands went to her shoulders, bracing her. "That time, for both of us, has passed. Perhaps it has been passed for a long while."

"But I still love you, Gorman," Effie said, through her tears. "So much. I don't think I can go on without you."

"Oh, now," he said with his familiar smile within his beard. "I know that's not true. Any matter, you will never be without me. Not really."

"No one can ever take your place," she swore. "Not in George's life, and not in mine."

He pulled her up from the floor and onto his lap and held her in his arms as she, too, embraced him, relishing the familiar feel of his stocky body, the scent of him, the gentleness covering the strength. He would never hold her like this again, she knew.

"I wouldn't let you go if I didn't think you would be safe," he said as he stroked her hair. "If I didn't think he would love you as well as I do."

"He doesn't though," she choked.

"How many other men whom you've shot have ended up in your bed?" he said in a teasing voice. "I don't think I'm wrong about this, Eff," he insisted quietly. "But we shall soon see, I suspect."

She pulled away and wiped her eyes. "What do you mean?"

* * * *

Lucan argued with the guard for a full five minutes before the man agreed to interrupt Hatteclyffe's meeting. And then he argued with the secretary for another quarter of an hour before the pompous man assented to sending the king a note. Lucan paced in the corridor for what felt like hours, waiting for the door to reopen.

Hatteclyffe looked grim. "This is not going to go well for you, Sir Lucan."

Lucan waited.

The secretary sighed and opened the door wider. "You've two moments. And I'll have you know that I've just had my backside gnawed upon by a very disgruntled monarch."

"I owe you, Hatteclyffe," Lucan said as he passed.

"I beg you, don't even let on that we're acquainted after today."

Lucan walked quickly down the narrow, dark-paneled passage that led to the king's private solar. Henry was seated in a chair, a tray of food on the square table at his side, while several servants filed out through a doorway on the opposite side of the chamber. Next to the tray of food, the leather satchel rested.

The king looked up as Lucan entered, his eyebrows raised. "I am losing patience, Sir Lucan."

Lucan went to one knee at the edge of the table. "I beg your pardon, my liege. Truly."

"What do you want?"

"Thomas Annesley is not guilty, Your Grace. Caris Hargrave—"

"Stop," the king said, holding up one slender hand. "Stop there. Unless you have a shred of evidence as to the Hargraves' guilt, say no more. If you slander her further—"

"This is the evidence!" Lucan said slapping the leather bag on the table. "Everything inside, put down by my sister's own hand! Iris entrusted it to me when I last departed your court, and it was stolen on the journey to return Thomas Annesley to you!"

Henry raised one eyebrow, and his expression was neither amused nor intrigued.

"How did…who gave it to you, my liege?" Lucan stuttered, seeming to have lost all ability of proper speech.

"Well, it wasn't you, was it?" the king quipped. "Although you had ample opportunity to do so. You didn't trust me then, and you don't trust me now."

"Because if you've read what's inside that portfolio," Lucan said, "you know that everything Caris Hargrave said in your court today was a lie."

"And as I told Miss Hargrave," Henry warned, "any nitwit can write down a tale that pleases them. It does not make it true."

Lucan stared for a moment, the bottom falling out of his stomach. "Are you saying that none of the testimony matters?"

"Between titled nobility and common criminals?" Henry clarified, his eyes widened. "Parliament would have my head. At the very least, I would lose every shred of support from any landowner worth more than two shillings."

"You're just going to let them get away with it," Lucan said. "You're going to hang an innocent man tomorrow, to protect your coffers."

Henry's face darkened. "Take care how you speak to me, Sir Lucan." Then the king sighed wearily. "You must look at it from my position. I had to make the *legal* decision. And the *facts* as you claim them are nothing more than rumor! Hearsay! Every titled person in the court today spoke *against* Miss Hargrave. No one of any standing whatsoever can vouch for her—her contemporaries are all lawbreakers! What was I to do? Had I given her an inch, every prisoner awaiting the gallows would concoct such outrageous tales of their innocence, I'd never have any peace!"

"*I am titled.* My sister is of a noble family. That testimony was put down in her own hand," Lucan insisted. "Vaughn Hargrave caused the fire that destroyed Castle Dare and killed my parents the very night Euphemia Hargrave escaped Darlyrede House. I know it."

Henry's gaze bore into Lucan's. "Where. Is. Your. Proof?"

Lucan threw up his hands and collapsed back into a chair.

The king smirked. "By all means, do sit down." He sighed again. "Lucan, listen to me. If there was a single witness of repute to a dastardly character—not simply distasteful, mind you—or to any of the crimes that have been levied against the Hargraves, I could perhaps entertain a broadening inquiry. But even though Lady Towsey thought this bag—"

"*Lady Margaret* gave the satchel to you?"

The king pressed his lips together a moment, realizing his misstep. "She's not a stupid woman, Lucan."

"This is unjust," he said. "I took you for a king of the people."

"Careful," Henry warned. "You go too far."

"No," Lucan argued. "I didn't go far enough when I had the opportunity." He paused. "Only one more thing before I go."

"Oh, what is it? Castle Dare, I suppose."

"No," he said. "Give me leave to take Effie Annesley as my wife."

Henry's eyes widened—Lucan had at last been able to surprise the king. "Come again? You wish to marry the daughter of Thomas Annesley?"

Lucan nodded. "And take her son as my ward."

Henry rubbed his chin. "Surely you realize that would only cause conflict with Caris Hargrave. I've already exiled Euphemia from Northumberland."

"Which is why I will willingly forfeit my father's lands and ask your permission to take them both to my extended family in France. I will resign my rank in the Order."

"You would give up your entire birthright for *France*?"

"Not for France," Lucan clarified pointedly.

Henry was still for a moment, his long face held in his chin as he contemplated. "But what of your sister? Do you also ask for her leave?"

"I beg Your Grace to show Iris mercy by allowing her to return to Caedmaray with her husband," Lucan said. "Or wherever he chooses to go. Padraig Boyd never meant to deceive you, my liege. His greatest wish was to become a soldier under your command. Let them go. Let us all go and try to build something of a life." Lucan felt his throat tightening and had to stop and swallow and take a breath. "Try to build a life after losing Thomas."

"Gah. *France.* What a waste. An utter *waste,*" Henry muttered with a frown. The king sighed and Lucan thought he saw a shadow of great sadness flit across the king's already solemn face. "Very well."

Lucan stilled. "Your Grace?"

Henry nodded. "I consent. But let us keep it between the two of us until after tomorrow's necessity is done. You are taking Caris Hargrave's blood kin, after all, and I will no doubt suffer the repercussions of that. So I only ask that it be accomplished with discretion."

Lucan nodded. "I swear it." He stood. "May Thomas's children see him?"

"What?" Henry frowned. "Oh, yes. Yes, of course. He's been moved to one of the more comfortable cells. It was all I could do. Tell Hatteclyffe to have food sent down. Stay as long as you like. He deserves that much, I suppose," Henry murmured, and the realization of the king's obviously troubled conscience about the matter somehow made the ruling all the more painful.

Lucan bowed. "Thank you, my liege."

Henry waved a hand at Lucan and then turned his attention to his wine goblet, not looking at Lucan again while he made his way to the door and exited the chamber.

Lucan paused around a turn in the paneled corridor, out of the sight of the guards. He leaned his forehead against the cold, hard wood while painful tears swelled in his eyes.

It wasn't enough, he knew. It wasn't nearly enough. But it was the best he could offer her.

Lucan pressed the inner corners of his eyes with his thumb and forefinger and took a bracing breath.

Now, he had to face Thomas Annesley. And Lucan knew that this man's permission would mean far more to him than that of any king.

* * * *

The hoarse, muffled sobs that filled the small stone chamber when Padraig embraced Tommy caused Effie's insides to clench. The raw pain and fear shown by a man Effie already knew to be so courageous in the face of insurmountable odds terrified her to her soul.

And yet she could not help her bitterness. Padraig had known Thomas Annesley as a father—a true father—all his life. All Effie could claim was a fortnight of road travel, and the guilt of delivering the man to an unjust death.

Lucan Montague was already present when Effie and her brothers and their wives had been led down to the cell. Their eyes met at once, but slid away awkwardly.

Gorman had been at least partly right—Lucan had been about something to Effie's benefit, arranging this last night for Tommy and his children. He wouldn't be there to tell though, when she returned, as he had planned to sneak out of Effie's chamber and Westminster on his own after the sons of Scotland had quit the apartments.

Padraig pulled himself together and they all sat down at the makeshift meal, an old table and splintery, wobbly stools squeezed into the cold cell. The kitchen had served this last meal well, and there was both wine and ale. Everyone tried their best to lighten the atmosphere—Tavish had brought down draughts from the apartment, Effie had dice in her pouch. Tournaments ensued and eventually the sound of laughter rang against the stones as each one took on their share of the herculean task of making Thomas Annesley's last night on earth one filled with family and love.

Effie sat at Lucan's side, his presence screaming at her despite her best efforts to ignore him.

"I spoke to the king," he murmured.

"Obviously," she replied. "Thank you."

"I spoke to him about you," he clarified. "You and George Thomas."

She looked at him then, into those icy blue eyes that she'd thought cold for so long. Now she realized the color wasn't from coolness, but like the dazzling light at the source of a blaze—glittering and blinding and containing all the warmth of creation.

"George Thomas is likely even now on his way to Scotland." She looked back down at the cup in her hands. "I will join them after everything is over tomorrow."

"Henry has given his leave that I might take you both to France."

Her head turned quickly again. "What?" she whispered harshly.

"I think he believes much of what was said in court—maybe much of what was contained in the portfolio. But you were right—he's afraid to stand against the nobles."

It was a hollow victory, and Effie let his comments go unanswered. "What about Castle Dare?"

He gave a shrug. "I can't go back now. Not after this. To know so much that has been gotten away with, and to have my hands tied. We could marry. Start over in France."

"You're asking me to marry you?"

"It's the best solution," he said, his brows knit together. "You and George will be under the protection of my family name. It's the least I can do."

Effie's heart ached. He wasn't acting out of love, he was acting out of guilt and duty to her father.

"So I'll just leave the rest of *my* family to whatever fate befalls them next then, shall I?" she challenged quietly. "Take George away from his father to be surrounded by foreign strangers? Gain protection by taking a titled husband and forgetting everything I've fought for, for fifteen years?"

"What are your other options?" Lucan demanded in an equally harsh whisper. "Penniless in Scotland, like Thomas? Living at the Swan on Mari and Gale's charity? What prospects will George have there?"

"I can't leave them," she said, shaking her head. "Not to save my own skin. It would be the ultimate betrayal."

"Thomas agrees with me," Lucan said pointedly.

"*You asked him*?" Effie hissed even as she glanced toward her father, who was laughing and clapping Lachlan on the shoulder as his middle son bested Tavish at dice. Lucan continued while she watched the trio.

"He knows just as well, if not better, than you how hard life can be for those who've been made commodities by the rich. He wants better for you and for his grandson, and he knows I can provide that."

"Then we shall let him think that is what will occur," Effie said quietly.

"What is *wrong* with you?" Lucan demanded.

"I've been loved outside of marriage by a man whose fidelity I never doubted," Effie said, each word slicing into her heart. "I'll not be trapped inside a marriage to a martyr, and I won't subject my son to it, either." She stood up and left his side before he could reply, taking a seat next to Thomas as he challenged Lachlan at the dice.

Tommy glanced over at her, a sparkle in his faded blue eyes. "Lass, you'll bring me luck, for certain." He rolled and gave a triumphant chuckle before pushing the dice across the table to his son. He looked at her again. "Have you spoken with Lucan?"

"I have," she said. "He's told me you gave your permission."

"Aye," Tommy agreed with a nod. "Och, that's too bad, laddie! Let me show you how it's done." He rolled again. "What did I tell ye? Who's next to challenge the old man?"

He turned his smile to Effie, and it nearly broke her heart. "I've nae worries about you nor my grandson with Lucan. When he makes his pledge, he holds it unto death."

Effie put her arm around his narrow shoulders and laid her temple against his rough shirt as Padraig took Lachlan's place.

Tommy grabbed up the dice. "I love ye, gel," he said as he shook them in his hand and then threw them. "Oh, ho! What a beginning, laddie! You'll nae be besting me now!"

"I love you, too, Dad," Effie whispered into his shoulder.

Chapter 25

It was a perfect spring morning when Lucan and the others gathered on the New Palace Yard just beyond Westminster. The sun shone like a million candles, causing the warm breeze to nearly sparkle and the emerging green of the grass and trees to glitter with new life. Indeed, the very atmosphere was one of high frivolity and it seemed to Lucan that all of London had turned out to see Thomas Annesley hanged, crowding into the public area of the grounds on a beautiful day.

Jugglers performed while vendors walked through the crowd selling their meats and sweet buns. Several ale carts were bustling with customers. Families were spread out on blankets, children tumbling over the yard.

Lucan and the others were seated on a row of benches before the hastily erected gallows. All of them were ashen and drawn of face, Effie most of all, perhaps, even as she sat in her old woodland garb—a wordless rebellion, perhaps, against the king and his court. Her sentiment, at least, was obvious—she cared nothing for London or its inhabitants, she had no respect for its ruler, and she didn't care what any of them thought of her. All color seemed to be gone from her skin and even her hair, so that she appeared to be a sketch left out in the rain—faded and blurry, and likely to tear at the slightest touch.

She didn't want Lucan or the protection he'd offered her. And why should she? He had failed her. He had failed himself.

A trumpet sounded and the king and his entourage took their seats within the covered box to the left of the gallows. Caris Hargrave and Vivienne Paget made their way into the row behind the king, their sick triumph earning them a favored seat. None of Thomas's children looked toward the box, but Lucan did. He wanted to be sure that Henry saw him, saw the condemnation in his eyes. This was no ordinary man who would die today.

Thomas Annesley was a survivor. A hero.

The hooded hangman mounted the platform first, followed by Thomas, escorted by a chaplain and then two guards. Effie's father was wearing a clean, loose shirt and his own old trousers and boots. His gray hair was damp, combed back neatly from his forehead, and the drying furrows of it lifted stiffly in the breeze.

His hands were bound behind him.

When Thomas looked down at the benches and smiled at them all, Lucan thought for a moment he might vomit. This was wrong, so wrong—nothing in the world could ever be right again.

And you delivered him to it—twice.

The intendant stepped forward with a wide scroll, and as he spread it, the crowd quieted, straining to hear as the man recounted the charges against Thomas Annesley.

"For these crimes," the intendant announced so loudly that his voice barked, "you are sentenced to be hung by the neck until dead." The intendant lowered the scroll and turned his head to give the hangman a crisp, single nod.

The hangman stepped toward Thomas and placed the thick, pale noose around his neck, adjusting the coil and the knot, seeming to take great care that it rested comfortably where his neck and shoulder met. The hangman stepped away and picked up a dark square of material, neatly folded on the platform.

The intendant looked to Thomas. "Have you any last words?"

Thomas nodded. "My life has been worth it, if only for those people come to see me off today," he said, then pressed his lips together tightly as he met the gaze of each person seated before the gallows ending with Tavish. "Tell yer mam I do love her."

Then Thomas turned to address the king's box. "Your Grace, I swear by God Almighty, whom I do hope to be seeing shortly, that I've never taken a life in all my years and during all my troubles." He paused. "My only regret is that I didna know enough to have killed Vaughan Hargrave and his wretched wife with me own hands."

The crowd gasped at the proclamation, but Thomas only turned back to look one final time at his children. "God bless you." He gave a teary wink and then raised his eyes over the crowd, as if to the horizon, or perhaps to heaven.

The hangman stepped forward with the cloth between his hands, and slipped the hood over Thomas Annesley's head.

Lucan heard a muffled sob—he thought it might have been Finley, but it could have very well come from his own mouth.

Somewhere behind the gallows, a drum rattled as the hangman moved to the lever that would drop the platform away beneath Thomas Annesley's feet.

Lucan watched Thomas's shoulders rise and fall deeply—his last full breath.

No. No. He couldn't allow it. Even if it meant his own death—he couldn't think of a future without Effie, any matter.

Lucan gained his feet in a rush and opened his mouth.

"Stop!" The faint scream was little louder than the breeze over the drum trill, but it called again, only slightly louder. "Stop, I say! *Stop*!"

The hangman froze in place; the intendant turned a quarter of the way 'round to face the king's box. The crowd murmured, many turning to look backward toward where the shouts—and now hoof beats—challenged the drumming. Lucan, too, turned.

"Stop at once!" It was a woman's voice, and she came careening across the yard, her mount swerving through the crowd, the hood of her silk cape thrown back against her shoulders as she galloped toward the king's box, and her auburn hair—Lucan knew it was graying at the temples—streamed out behind her.

Margaret Stanhope.

The guards before the king's box raised their arms and stepped before the sovereign and the drumbeats rattled into silence as Lady Margaret reined in her dancing mount. She turned around to look over her shoulder toward the bench and her eyes found Lucan, still standing as if in a dream.

"Lady Margaret," Henry said, his admonishing tone unable to hide his surprise. "What is the meaning of this? It is cruel to prolong this family's torture."

"She's here, Your Grace." Margaret gasped and then gave a bow from the saddle. She spread her arm long, indicating the yard and gate behind her, just as a brace of trumpets filled the air with their melodious shouts.

Pennants appeared over the crowd—red and gold and white—snapping in the breeze from the tops of their impossibly tall poles. The crowd's murmuring grew.

"Lucan," Effie said, drawing his attention as she grabbed his arm. "What is she doing?"

"I've no idea," he said to her. He stepped onto the bench for a better view and held his hand out to Effie, who joined him.

"Your Grace," Lady Margaret said again as the pennant-bearers penetrated the fringe of the crowd and revealed a golden litter being carried by eight men. "Allow me to present Countess Elpis of Mystras."

* * * *

Effie didn't know what was happening, beyond that the hangman had just removed the hood covering her father's head as everyone on the green looked to the sparkling, glittering, curtained litter. When the mounted woman made her proclamation, Effie saw Caris Hargrave slowly stand from her seat behind the king.

The litter was placed on the ground and two guards stepped to the fore to open a half door and pull back the curtain. A moment later, a slender form, in layers of flowing black lace from head to foot, moved forward, one hand bracing heavily on a golden cane.

"King Henry," the woman said in a crisp accented voice, inclining her head. "I do hope you will forgive my interruption. Any messenger I sent would have arrived with me, as my ship only came up the river in this very hour."

"What is the meaning of this, Countess?" Henry demanded. "Mystras's ambassadors are not scheduled to be my guests for another year."

"This is true," the countess allowed, "but when I heard from Lady Margaret about the scandalous trial that has captured the tongues of every noble far and wide—when I heard the names of those involved—I knew I must come myself, and at once." She glanced back over her shoulder through her veil toward the gallows. "As it is, I see that I was almost too late."

Effie saw Caris Hargrave scramble for the box door.

"I have come to deliver a writ of arrest for Vaughn Hargrave and his whore, known to us on Mystras only as Caris."

A guard halted Caris Hargrave's escape, and she reluctantly turned around to face the lace-clad woman.

"Countess, we are in the middle of an execution," Henry advised. "I'm not at all certain your claims of—"

"Again, forgive my interruption, Henry—I mean no disrespect to your court. But in the interest of the peace and good relations between England and Greece, I respectfully request that any punishment decided as a result of this *woman's* testimony be postponed." The woman raised her arm and handed a roll of parchment to the nearest guard. Elpis flicked her finger toward the box. "The warrant."

Henry's guard took the parchment and handed it up to the king, who unfurled it at once. After a moment, he raised his surprised countenance to once more face the Greek woman, more splendidly outfitted than his own queen.

"My father," Elpis announced, "was a surgeon in Constantinople when I was born. He had taken into his employ a sly army deserter who showed remarkable aptitude for learning the intricacies of the operations he practiced on the wounded. That young Englishman was a commoner, given to the army in payment of his father's debts. His name was Vaughn Hargrave."

"No!" Caris gasped from behind the king. "That is a lie! My husband never knew your family!"

"Oh, but he did," Elpis assured the box. "He lived in my father's home with my mother and my sister and myself. You knew them too, did you not, *Lady* Caris? Quite elevated in station now, since your time behind the taverns on Mystras."

"I demand you cut this woman down at once!" Caris screeched. She gasped, her thin chest heaving. "For slandering my name and that of my late husband! A baron! Am I not your loyal subject, Your Grace?"

"You are not!" Elpis cried out stridently, her accented voice cutting through the warm spring air like the sharpest battle sword. "The king holds the proof in his own hand! I never dreamed I would have my revenge, and now that it is before me, I will have it to the fullest measure!"

The very budding leaves seemed to tremble with the royal woman's rage and some foreign emotion in Effie's stomach stirred.

"Vaughn Hargrave was not content with his role of apprentice," Elpis continued. "And his depravity and hunger for cruelty knew no bounds. My father was a pious man, and when he discovered Hargrave using his pet, Caris, to bring him subjects from the village—foreigners, soldiers who would never be missed—so that he could perform his experiments in secret, he turned him out into the street and told him to follow the returning English company, led by Lord Tenred Annesley, back to England for his just punishment for desertion."

Effie's gaze flew at once to her father. Tenred Annesley was her grandfather!

"But Vaughn Hargrave couldn't accept that, having grown so used to his new position in society," Elpis said. "And neither could Caris. She was infuriated that her benefactor was being sent away, and so the night the company left, she stole into our home and took my sister, Chordileia, who was not yet four years old."

"Cordelia?" Thomas called out from the gallows. "My Cordelia?"

Elpis turned and, for the first time, addressed Thomas. "Yes, Lord Annesley, I believe they are one and the same. Caris was a whore on Mystras, popular for being unable to conceive regardless of how many men she knew—she couldn't carry a child of her own. I am both astounded and thankful that Caris was so brazen—or so stupid—to have not bothered to change my sister's name after she abducted her. As if any of us would have ever stopped searching for word of her whereabouts."

Elpis looked back to the king. "The paper you now hold charges Vaughn Hargrave and the common Greek subject, Caris, with kidnapping of a royal member and mutilation adverse to Christian doctrine. They've been wanted in Greece for more than two score years, Your Grace. If you will allow me to return her for her judgement, the prizes on their heads belong to the English Crown."

"The letter said my father and Vaughn Hargrave fought together," Thomas called out, interrupting the countess's speech with his desperate words. "That they were in Constantinople, and that he saved my father's life. That he was made an officer."

"They were in Constantinople," Elpis allowed. "But your father wouldn't have sat at a table with Vaughn Hargrave. Tenred Annesley was a respected lord, and the last thing he would have done was entrusted his most treasured possessions—you, Thomas, and his beloved Darlyrede—to a depraved villain such as Hargrave. The letter granting him your guardianship as well as your father's estate was a forgery, I'm quite certain. It's likely that it was he who caused your parents' deaths, my dear."

The king looked very grave. "I expect I still retain the decree," Henry said.

Then, for the first time, Effie allowed the little ray of hope pecking at her heart to squeeze through.

There was a scuffle behind the king, and a guard seized hold of Caris Hargrave while another held aloft a blade. "She would have harmed herself, lord."

The king disregarded the weak and helpless woman, now in the grips of two of his own guards. "If this writ is genuine," Henry advised Elpis with a frown, "and all you say is true, Countess, then Darlyrede House never left the possession of Thomas Annesley in the first."

"And Cordelia Hargrave, as she was known," Elpis advised, "was never an English subject. She was Greek nobility." She looked past the king to where Caris hung limp, her dark eyes glaring, her chest still heaving. "Caris is my prisoner, and I would return her to my country to receive her just punishment."

Effie looked now to Lucan, and found that he was already watching her.

"She's nothing to me," Effie whispered, her lips numb. "Caris. Vaughn Hargrave. They are nothing to me. Evil strangers. Their blood runs not in my veins."

"Not a drop," Lucan confirmed as he took her into his arms, and she needed that strength, that firm embrace to ground her while her mind whirled with the possibility of a new reality. But then he braced his hands on her shoulders and held her away from him.

"Get down," he commanded.

"What?"

"Hurry." He helped her from the bench and then strode past the gallows, pulling Effie by the hand. "Undo that man at once," he commanded the hangman as he marched toward the golden litter and the woman clad in black lace.

Effie looked up just in time to see the hangman lift the corner of his mask, and James Montrose gave her a cheeky wink. "As you wish, lord."

There was no time for shock, as Elpis's guards were immediately alert to their approach, but the king waved a hand.

"Let him pass," Henry said. "If I know Sir Lucan, he has something urgent to say. I can suppose already the matter it entails."

Lucan came to a halt some ten paces from the countess and, after first paying homage to Henry, he gave Elpis a deep bow. He looked at Effie and tugged on her hand as if prompting her, but Effie would not bow—not yet. She pulled her hand free and took two steps toward the woman.

Is this what her mother would have looked like had she lived?

"Countess," Effie said. "My name if Effie Annesley. I am Cordelia's daughter."

The two women stared at each other a long moment, and then Countess Elpis extended a pale hand draped in black lace toward Effie. Effie took it.

"You are not only Chordileia's daughter," Elpis said.

"Your Grace," Lucan said, interrupting the woman's enigmatic statement. "I posit to you now that the judgment handed down cannot stand. Thomas Annesley is not simply innocent of the charges against him from this vile creature, he is in position to bring his own case against the Crown itself."

"Barrister now, are you, Sir Lucan?" Henry smirked. "I suppose you'll be wanting your lands back, after all."

Effie turned to find Lucan. He had given up Castle Dare for her and George Thomas?

"Caris Hargrave must face judgement in England, Countess," Henry continued. "If what you say is true, she is culpable in the deaths of English nobility, and scores, at least, of false accusations against a peer."

"Greece's charges are older, and take precedence," Elpis argued.

"She is in England, *now*," Henry said with a frown. "I will not have her stolen from under my nose if she has made a farce of my court."

"I beg your pardon, Henry," Elpis said coolly, "But your inability to detect a mercenary liar is not Greece's concern. You've had more than enough time to bring this woman to justice. I would not have had to come all this way to see it served myself."

"Elpis," Lady Margaret warned quietly as the occupants of the royal box bristled and murmured. "You are not in Greece."

Effie took a moment to recognize the handsome beauty of the woman whose home had given the family shelter. The woman who had sought to aid them, strangers. The woman who ruled her own domain. Effie wondered if she and Margaret Stanhope were actually very much alike, even down to the fact that each woman had been Lucan Montague's lover.

"But very well," Elpis said suddenly. "As I have only just landed, I shall be content to remain in London while you carry out the formalities. As long as it is understood that, ultimately, Caris Hargrave belongs to me."

Henry gave a single nod. "I find those terms agreeable. The trial shall commence on the morrow. With"—Henry produced the old leather satchel—"the evidence to be heard fully in defense of Lord Thomas Annesley. Lord Annesley, you are freed to go where you would pending the hearing—I have no doubt of your eager attendance. Guards, take Lady Hargrave and Lady Paget into custody." The king stood and departed at once with his entourage.

Around the New Palace Yard, the crowd erupted in shouts and rowdy murmurings—they'd been denied their execution, at least for that day.

Elpis's fingers, still wrapped around Effie's, squeezed as Thomas appeared at Lucan's side, in the midst of Effie's brothers. He embraced Lucan with tears in his eyes, and then pulled away to give the countess a bow.

Effie noticed that James, in his hangman's hood, was nowhere to be seen.

"M'lady," Thomas said. "I thank you for your timely intervention."

"Thomas Annesley," Elpis mused. "At last, we meet."

Lady Margaret sighed. "For the love of all that is holy, might we *please* continue the introductions at my home? I've never had a more trying year in all my life, and it's only March! My steward has threatened to resign!"

The group laughed.

"What a marvelous idea, Margaret," the countess said. "I have long anticipated seeing your London house."

"To the Strand, then?" Lucan asked those gathered.

"To the Strand," Thomas agreed. "Perhaps this time, they'll let me in."

Everyone laughed again, and Elpis took Thomas's offered arm. "Won't you ride with me, Lord Annesley?" she asked as she steered him toward the litter. "I would hear about the young woman my sister grew up to be."

"Gladly, m'lady," Thomas said with his cheeky Scot's smile. "There's nae been a day passed that Cordelia's nae been with me. It would be my honor to share her with her kin." He looked back at Effie and gave her a wink. "I'll see you at the house, lass."

Effie turned and watched the litter depart, surrounded by her brothers and sisters-in-law, Lucan at her side.

Tavish spoke first. "I suppose he always did have a way with the ladies."

His cool, blond wife sniffed. "For the countess's sake, perhaps we shouldn't tell Harriet."

"Let's get our things from the apartment," Lachlan suggested. "I've had all the king's royal hospitality I can bear."

The all turned away, but Effie held back, tugging on Lucan's hand, trying to ignore the awkwardness that had suddenly grown up between them.

"What is it?" he asked.

Effie looked up at him for a long moment. "You were going to give up Castle Dare for me."

"I wasn't going to," Lucan said. "I did."

"Why?"

He frowned. "Why? Because I love you, Effie."

"You never told me."

"I didn't think it mattered. I know you love Gorman. I only wanted—"

She cut him off by throwing her arms around his neck and kissing his mouth. Lucan's arms were around her at once.

Effie pulled away from him only enough to look up into his face. "I thought you'd changed your mind about me when you didn't come to me at the Swan."

He blinked. "I did come to you at the Swan. But I saw Gorman in your room. I thought—"

"I turned him away, Lucan," Effie said. "I didn't know you had seen him. But I turned him away. Gorman knows about us. He knows, and he's given his blessing."

"Then why did you refuse to marry me?" Lucan demanded.

"I didn't want you to marry me out of duty," she said. "That's no way to start a life together, even if it would have made it easier for me."

"What about now?" Lucan pressed. "Not France. Northumberland. It will still be a difficult life, even with Caris gone. Perhaps for a very long while. Henry will let Caris Hargrave return to Greece—he'll not charge her here—mark my words."

Effie felt her eyes widen as the realization dawned on her. "The king won't be forced to charge any of the nobility if he lets her go."

Lucan shook his head. "His coffers will be spared."

"But the nobility will be not," Effie promised him. "Not with us there to watch over them. Northumberland will be protected, to Edinburgh," Effie mused.

"And further. Edinburgh, the Highlands, and beyond," Lucan agreed.

They met in another kiss, heedless of the passersby that grinned at the black knight and the woman dressed in trousers.

She pulled away again. "Did you know it was James? Is that why you were going to try to stop it?"

Lucan gave her a puzzled frown. "Did I know who was James?"

Effie grinned and shook her head. "Never mind. I'll tell you later."

Chapter 26

Caris Hargrave felt no differently than she ever had as she was led away from the green by the king's guards. She felt no guilt, no fear—perhaps a slight irritation with the day's events, but that was all. Her body, as it had been for as many years as she could call to memory, was numb.

Just numb.

Behind her, Vivienne Paget was apparently not numb, as she shrieked and screamed and squawked and struggled against the king's men who led them deep into the bowels of Westminster. Lady Paget's cries became more shrill the further they descended, the cool air wrapping around them like a wet shroud. Obviously, Lady Paget had little experience with such a place, but fortunately for Caris, the atmosphere was sweetly familiar.

"Oh, do shut up, Vivienne," she demanded, and the strict admonition must have shocked the woman, for the narrow, twisting stone stairwell was blessedly silent for a time.

Until they came to the cell, that is. And then Lady Paget once more began protesting in earnest, her panic causing her voice to shake and crack, her too-thin body to bow and flail within the grips of the guardsmen as they dragged her to the opening through which Caris had walked calmly. Eventually they pitched the old woman in and slammed the barred door shut, the key squealing in the lock. The guards walked away, leaving the two women in semi darkness, the faint light from the only torch down the corridor coming in through the bars striped and sinister.

"Oh, my God," Vivienne moaned. "Oh, my God." She squatted down on her haunches against the stone wall, her hands up around her ears, rocking her gristly form back and forth. She was still dressed splendidly in her velvet gown with chain and jeweled blade, while Caris had stupidly lost hers to the guards in the king's box.

Caris watched the woman with high interest. She'd never seen Vivienne Paget in such a state, in all their years of supposed friendship. Of course, Caris didn't actually hold Lady Paget as her friend—Caris had never had any friends at all. Not even Vaughn, really. But whereas before she might have pretended sympathy for the woman—she was very good at knowing how to feign the expected response—she knew it was no longer necessary, and she chose to simply observe Vivienne Paget's terror.

Perhaps she might break altogether, Caris realized with renewed life. Especially if she was helped along.

"Vivienne," she called out. "Vivienne?"

Lady Paget raised her eyes with a whimper, her head still grasped between her hands.

"Elsmire Tower is gone," Caris said lightly. "It burned. There's nothing left."

Lady Paget shook her head.

"They sent word not long after Euphemia first appeared before the king. You know it was her, don't you? Her and her little band. Some of whom must have been your...*guests*."

Lady Paget's head shook more quickly. "No. It's my home. I will go there when this is over."

"You have no home now," Caris advised, cocking her head while she watched the woman unravel—it had been so long since she'd seen someone give up their sanity. She walked toward her, slowly, her slippers gliding on the filth of the floor. "But it's no matter. When the king hears what's gone on inside the hold, you'll be hanged."

"No," Lady Paget moaned.

"Everyone will know," Caris mused.

Vivienne stilled and her face slowly raised again as Caris stood over her. "You," she whispered. "This is your fault. You...you *commoner*. You're not even noble. You never were. You're a whore."

"But I'll die a baroness," Caris said. "Henry will never try me. Never strip me of my title. I promise you that. You, however, will be forever remembered as a monster."

"It wasn't me," Vivienne sobbed. "It was *you*. You and Vaughn and Adolphus. *It wasn't me*!"

Caris crouched down and reached her arms around the woman's waist. "Here now, sit down a bit. It will be alright. You're overcome." As she withdrew her arms, she took hold of Vivienne's jeweled dagger and slid it from the sheath. "Here, show me your palms—let me see them."

The crazed woman held up her palms obediently, at the terminus of her vulnerable wrists. In two quick slices, Caris had laid open the pale flesh and then backed away while the woman struggled to understand what had just happened to her.

"No," Vivienne gasped as the red welled over her skin and to the invisible black of the floor. "Help me. Help me!" she screamed, and then began walking toward Caris on her knees. "Help me!"

Caris lifted her slippered foot and kicked the woman over, where she lay jittering on the stones. As the movement slowed, Caris drew nearer, crouching next to the woman whose life was flowing out of her. Caris watched her eagerly.

"It's fine," Caris said, almost soothingly. "It will be over in a moment, and then nothing. Peace. Blackness. Sleep. You'll soon see."

Vivienne Paget's lips moved, and so Caris leaned closer.

"God, forgive me," she breathed.

Caris frowned and straightened. She looked down at the blade still in her hand and then in the next instant, drew it down both her own forearms. She fumbled with the slick, sticky weapon to place it in Vivienne Paget's still, cold grasp, closing the limp fingers around it, and then Caris retreated to the far corner of the cell and sank to her bottom to wait for the blackness, for the sleep.

She'd won. She won, over Greece. Over the king. Over the English peasantry. She'd won, over ungrateful Chordileia. Over Thomas Annesley and Euphemia and the Pagets and even over her beloved, cruel Vaughn, himself. There would be no triumph for Elpis or for Henry. Caris Hargrave, who had once lured drunken soldiers from the taverns of Mystras to the villa to be butchered, was dying in a palace, as a noblewoman. And then it would be over.

And for Caris, there would at last be peace.

She was still numb, although she tried to sense the slipping away of herself. It was no use—she'd been numb her entire life and that last coveted sensation, the one she'd witnessed so many times in the young women she'd shown such mercy as their lives slipped away, was denied her. She chuckled at the irony.

But even in the blackness of the cell, figures began to appear; people and faces she recognized, and others that were strange, and only claimed the suggestion of humanity. Caris strained to see their blurred features in her dimming gaze. She blinked slowly—it was as if they were shaking their heads so quickly their features were smeared as they approached the corner where Caris slumped.

How? she tried to whisper, but there was not breath enough left in her already stiff lungs for the solitary query. Some of these people… they were dead. Had been dead for decades. Caris knew, because she'd watched them die.

Her heart was slowing, slowing…

And at its final, sluggish beat, as the pale hands laid hold of her, Caris realized that although there would indeed be blackness, it was far from over. There would be no sleep, no peace for her in the hands of her victims.

For the rest of eternity.

And the numbness, at last, left her.

Epilogue

"Well, let's just say he's going to have a dreadful headache when he wakes," James said with a grin for everyone seated around Lady Margaret's grand table.

"One would think a professional hangman would be more aware of his surroundings," Tavish mused.

James shrugged. "I left him a ha'penny in his shoe."

"I couldn't be at all certain that we'd arrive in time," Lady Margaret interjected. "When Stephen recognized Mister Montrose attempting to breach my house, their quick thinking saved the day. How my steward laid hands to an appropriate costume—"

"What would you have done if you'd had to pull the lever?" Padraig interrupted.

"Lucan was going to stop him," Effie quipped and the warmth in her gaze was worth more than all the king's fortune.

"Fat lot of good that would have done." James snorted. "Delayed it, perhaps. But I'd already cut the noose." James grinned, so obviously—and rightly—pleased with himself. "Tommy might have broken a leg, but I was hoping he'd be stunned enough by surviving being hung that he would lie still beneath the platform till I came for him. I daresay I couldn't have done it without my new mate, though."

Lucan raised his goblet as he sought out the blushing steward standing to the rear of Lady Margaret's seat. "To Stephen, and to James!"

Stephen inclined his head graciously toward Lucan. "I do hope all is forgiven now, Sir Lucan."

"If only we had trusted each other, eh?" Lucan suggested.

The steward's only response was a mild grin.

"Pass the pitcher if you would, Sir Lucan," Bob asked, seated to Lucan's left.

He reached across and accommodated the young man as the conversation about them rose and mingled. "I know everyone's tale but yours, Bob. Chumley and James; Rose and Kit. Something at least of Dana. Gilboe, Winnie. But you've never told me how you came to be in the band. Why you're known as Bob the Butcher's Boy."

He shook his head and looked down, his pale, round face a mask of sorrow beneath his orange hair. "It's a bad tale, I'm afraid." He pinched off a piece and bread, popped it into his mouth and chewed before glancing up at Lucan. "I'm not proud of it. Don't know that I should tell you, lest you think poorly of me."

"I can take it," Lucan assured him kindly, and he could feel the gazes of everyone at the table on them now—especially Effie's. Always Effie's. "If it's something you wish to share. You're not obligated, of course."

Bob nodded thoughtfully. "Most of 'em know already, I suppose. Well, you see…it's all because of me dad, of course."

Lucan felt his brows draw together and he braced himself. "Yes?"

"He's…a butcher."

Lucan blinked. "You mean he's killed people."

"Naw, mate—I mean he cuts up venison and lamb and the like for folks. He and mum live just over in Newcastle."

Lucan felt his head draw back. "But how did you end up…?"

"Ah," Bob shook his head again with a grimace. "I didn't want to be a butcher. We'd no money for a commission as one of the king's men. I knew Gilboe from the abbey, and Effie agreed to let me stay. So I battle evil and eat stew. And I've *very little* to do with entrails." He leaned forward to half whisper conspiratorially. "A mite squeamish, you see. Keep that bit to yourself, if you would."

Lucan took a moment to process his surprise and then gave a huff of laughter that grew into a sincere guffaw, his ears reddening with how he'd been bracing for the worst.

To think, after all this, Bob the Butcher's Boy was likely the most normal of them all.

"Mama, is Grandfather coming home with us?" George Thomas piped up in the midst of the laughter, from his location on Thomas's lap. One spindly arm had been hooked around the old man's neck since their first meeting, and already the child was mimicking every move his grandfather made.

Effie turned her head to look at Lucan.

The room quieted, and Lucan remembered that the band was still getting used to the idea of Effie without Gorman, even though George Thomas's father had made no pretense about his suddenly obvious interest in the exotic Kit Katey, seated at his side at the far end of the table.

The Countess Elpis spoke up loudly. "Of course, my niece will return to Mystras with me. She and her son. They will wish to take their places in the family."

Effie looked at once to the regal old woman. "Mystras?"

"Certainly," Elpis said. "Your testimony shall be imperative in the trial of Caris Hargrave."

Lucan saw Effie's forehead crease, and he wanted to take away her uncertainty, but he knew he couldn't. It was her right to choose to start over in a land where her own name guaranteed her freedom and power and wealth, where George Thomas's future would be bright. Lucan couldn't stop her—he wouldn't stop her.

"Och," Thomas lamented gruffly. "She canna go so very far. Not with so much of her family already here." He reached up and stroked the little boy's red hair and his whiskered chin flinched. "And me own grandson."

Lucan felt everyone's attention turn to Effie. She dabbed at her mouth with her napkin, and Lucan saw her take a deep breath, her mouth set.

Just like Thomas's, Lucan realized.

* * * *

Effie's heart beat heavy in her chest as the weight of her decision hung over the table. The presence of Lucan Montague at her side gave her strength—the fact that he had not at once denied the countess's request made her love him all the more.

"Countess Elpis," she said at last, looking at the woman directly and for a fleeting moment, again wondering if she was looking into a face like her mother's. "I thank you for your offer. I do wish to know you more, and to come to know my mother's family. But..." she paused, looking around the grand dining hall of the Strand house. At Gorman and Kit Katey; at the sons of Scotland, her brothers; at George, and Tommy; at the rest of her family of the Warren. And finally at Lucan.

"While perhaps it was brought about by the tragedy of my mother being stolen away to England so many years ago, I know that I am already surrounded by my family and people, for whom, like my father was willing to do, I would lay down my life. It is my duty to return to Northumberland

and try to somehow help heal the barony, by starting to right the thousands of crimes committed by the Hargraves."

Lucan reached for her hand when she continued. "I know that, together with Padraig and Iris, we can defend Northumberland."

Lucan spoke then. "We cannot do it without Gorman. My friend. The only one of the Warren who didn't want to kill me at first sight."

Gorman chuckled. "Perhaps I should have."

Everyone laughed good naturedly, as Kit Katey beamed a proud smile at him.

"This is unacceptable," Elpis said suddenly. "While I understand your desire to stay in the land you have given up so much for, I do feel that I cannot abandon you here with no prospects. I must have something to show for my journey, to corroborate the adventure I have known." She frowned, her jowls like a bulldog, and then her gaze softened as she too, looked upon Gorman and Kit Katey.

"Ah, that is just it. I shall have the father of my great nephew," she said in a pleased voice.

Gorman's eyes widened.

"Yes, of course," the countess continued. "Your own father holds a position of honor in a noble home, does he not?"

Gorman nodded. "He did. He was the longtime steward of Darlyrede House, my lady."

"That decides it," Elpis said. "You will be given similar status in my own household. You may return within the year with Mystras's ambassador to visit, or to stay in England if the position does not suit. And it will be a wonderful excuse for your son to visit the palace. Greece does not keep the same rules as does England in regard to marriage—in our eyes, you shall be equal to my niece." She looked to Kit Katey. "Perhaps you might bring a companion with you? Mystras is home to many of our friends from the East."

Gorman looked back to Effie, and she could see the uncertainty, as well as the excitement, in his eyes. Here was his chance to overcome his past in England, to fully become the man he deserved to be.

"But what of you and George? Where will you be?"

"Roscraig, of course," Tavish said. When everyone looked toward him, he continued. "It's not so very far that the overseeing of the construction will be a problem. We have plenty of room and our village thrives. Padraig as well, or at least Iris, while her husband seeks to confirm his place with the king."

"Bah," Lachlan said. "Young Padraig would rather spend his days in the shadow of Ben Nevis, on the sea."

Padraig grinned. "That does sound fine, although I would make a living for my wife and child while Darlyrede is rebuilt."

There was a beat of silence while everyone realized Padraig's meaning, and then Margaret called for more wine to be brought to toast the announcement of Iris's pregnancy.

After the well-wishes were all spent, Tavish continued. "Da, I'm assuming you'll be joining us at Roscraig?"

"I'd be nowhere else." Tommy smiled. "If your mam will still have me."

Gorman turned to Kit Katey. "What say you, Qi QiangTing? Will you journey east with me?" Her shy smile and nod made Effie's heart surprisingly light.

"It's settled then," Effie said, and turned back to Lucan. "We'll spend our time between Roscraig and the Warren."

"The Warren?" Lucan repeated.

Effie nodded. "Right after you marry me."

"Look out, Sir Lucan," Gorman interjected in a jolly voice. "She's been harping on that for years. Relentless."

Everyone laughed, even Lucan, while he leaned forward and kissed her lips gently. "Blasted Effie Annesley, I'll marry you tomorrow, on the green, before the king."

"I'll say yes," she answered in a whisper. "I love you, Lucan."

"I'm to have two fathers?" George Thomas exclaimed suddenly.

The countess Elpis laughed. "Isn't it grand, young man?"

George Thomas's eyes were round. "Ever so grand!"

Tommy handed Effie's son gently over to Gorman where he was snuggled at once between his father and Kit Katey, and her heart ached now with the fullness of her joy.

Her father stood from his chair and slowly raised his cup.

"To Cordelia," Thomas Annesley said, his voice catching on the emotion in his words. "And to Scotland."

The men all stood.

"To Cordelia, and to Scotland," echoed the room, and the words were like a prayer.

Printed in the United States
by Baker & Taylor Publisher Services